Praise for the novels of Sharon Page!

BLACK SILK

S0-BRT-372

"Wonderful, well-written Regency with emotion, blindingly hot sex . . . and a surprise ending. The hero is to die for." —*Romantic Times* on BLACK SILK, a Top Pick! (4 ½ star review)

"Superb erotic Regency romance . . . delightful page-turner. Sharon Page heats up the era."—Harriet Klausner

"Steamy and adventurous . . . enticing and enjoyable. . ." —*Romance Reviews Today*

BLOOD RED

"A blazing path into forbidden dreams . . ."—*Romantic Times*

"Ms. Page weaves an erotic and suspenseful tale. If you're a lover of vampire romance, curl up on a cold winter night with **Blood Red** to warm your heart!"—*Just Erotic Romance Reviews* (Gold Star Award)

"An erotically charged tale . . . a wonderful action-packed story that combines suspense, intrigue, horror, bondage and yes, a whole lot of sex."—*Coffee Time Romance*

BLOOD ROSE

"Page's **Blood Rose** has scorching love scenes to make you sweat and an intriguing plot to hold it all together."—*New York Times* best-selling author Hannah Howell

"**Blood Rose** is an action-packed, sexy paranormal overflowing with suspense, horror and romance. Sharon Page is a master of the menage—prepare to be seduced!"—Kathryn Smith, *USA Today* best-selling author

"The female protagonist is completely believable, and the two vampire-slaying heroes . . . are simply hot! This is a thoroughly entertaining read."—*Romantic Times*

"Buffy the Vampire Slayer meets Regency England! Two sexy, to-die-for heroes, a courageous heroine, and a luscious ménage make **Blood Rose** a sinful treat."—Jennifer Ashley, *USA Today* best-selling author

SIN

2006 National Readers' Choice Award Winner for Erotic Romance/Romantica

"How do you have an orgasm without sex? Read *Sin* by Sharon Page! . . . Thoroughly wicked, totally wild, utterly wanton and very witty in its execution, *Sin* is the ultimate indulgence."—*Just Erotic Romance Reviews* (Gold Star Award)

"Strong, character-driven romance . . . extremely sensual and erotic."—*Romantic Times*

"Sinfully delicious. Sharon Page is a pure pleasure to read." —Sunny, *New York Times* best-selling author of *Over the Moon* (anthology) and *Mona Lisa Awakening*

"Sharon Page blends history, emotion, and hot, hot, hot sex within an amazing love story. Blazing erotica!"—Kathryn Smith, *USA Today* best-selling author

"Wonderful characterisations . . . and sultry, sexy love scenes will have you begging for more! Five Angels!"—*Fallen Angels Reviews*

"*Sin* is a perfect example of exquisitely rendered erotic romance . . . this book caught my attention with the opening lines and never let go . . ."—Kate Douglas, best-selling author of the *Wolf Tales* series

Hot Silk

Sharon Page

APHRODISIA
KENSINGTON BOOKS
http://kensingtonbooks.com

APHRODISIA BOOKS are published by

Kensington Publishing Corp.
850 Third Avenue
New York, NY 10022

Row
Page

All Kensington titles, imprints, and distributed lines are available at special quantity discounts for bulk purchases for sales promotions, premiums, fund-raising, and educational or institutional use.

Special book excerpts or customized printings can also be created to fit specific needs. For details, write or phone the office of the Kensington Special Sales Manager: Kensington Publishing Corp., 850 Third Avenue, New York, NY 10022. Attn: Special Sales Department. Phone: 1-800-221-2647.

Aphrodisia and the A logo Reg. U.S. Pat & TM Off.

ISBN-13: 978-0-7582-1491-1
ISBN-10: 0-7582-1491-X

First Kensington Trade Paperback Printing: October 2008

10 9 8 7 6 5 4 3 2 1

Printed in the United States of America

For my parents

1

"The choice is yours, my love. I want you—you know that. Meet me tonight, in the gallery. Don't wear your gown. Wear something easy to remove . . ."

Grace Hamilton knew she should be scandalized by Lord Wesley's proposition. She should refuse. But she had been trying to stay strong and good and proper for a week and she could not resist any longer.

"I do not know, my lord," she whispered. He stood behind her, away from the hot, sparkling chandeliers and the swirling crowd, in the shadows of the ballroom at Collingsworth, ancestral home of the Marquis of Rydermere. Lord Wesley's home and a place she had no right to be.

Grace stood by dark gallery doors, wearing a borrowed gown, terrified everyone would see her for the fraud she was.

His lordship rested his hands gently on her waist, his long fingers splayed to meet across her middle—she hadn't expected him to touch her yet and the contact stole her breath. "I will be waiting," he murmured, his voice a possessive growl. "If you aren't there at midnight, I will have to assuage my broken heart elsewhere."

How many other ladies here would accept his proposition? A wave of his hand and any number of women would beg to be kissed by him, would eagerly agree to meet him for sin. Dozens of women here wanted to marry him; their calculating eyes fixed on the prize—to become Marchioness of Rydermere.

This house teemed with lovely ladies of good birth, but Lord Wesley had singled her out, had pursued *her* ever since her arrival. From the first moment he had bent over her hand and let his lips play magic on her fingers through the thin muslin of her glove, she had been entranced. And each look he cast her way, each hot and intense glance, had assured her he felt the magic every bit as much as she.

Or was she wrong? What, after all, did she know about men in love?

"Midnight. By midnight," she teased, feigning a confidence she didn't feel, "you will know if I am coming or not."

His breath tickled her neck, a hot caress. "Wicked wench. I'll be there." He moved closer to her, leaving the shadows to press his body against hers. She both stiffened and melted as a hard ridge snuggled against her silk-clad bottom.

"I can't wait to grasp hold of this lush, fashionable arse—" With a groan, he ground his erection against her curves, setting her heart racing. "That, my golden nymph, is for you."

And then he was gone.

Grace snapped open her fan and beat it so feverishly the thin silk tore from the spokes. She'd never had a man do this to her before. Be so bold. Be so gruff and direct and lusty—

"What was my rascal of a brother saying to you? Oh, Grace, you aren't going to faint, are you? Your face is aflame."

Grace started guiltily as Lady Prudence joined her in the private corner. Her friend's closed fan rested against her lips, half hiding their firm line. "Did you let him coax you here?"

"No . . . I needed a rest," Grace lied.

Lying had never been her talent and she doubted Lady Prudence was fooled. Her friend gave a tip to her head so the candlelight caught the tiny diamonds and sapphires threaded through her dark hair. Lady Prudence was so lovely. It was astonishing to Grace that she had such a friend.

"Don't believe a word he says," Lady Prudence warned, her gray-blue eyes very solemn. She bent close to be heard clearly over the graceful melody of the waltz. "My brother is a scoundrel."

Couples twirled past, elegant and glittering beneath the glow of a thousand candles. Gentlemen's hands rested lightly on slender backs; ladies' gloved hands entwined with those of their partners. Skirts swirled around graceful ankles and coattails fluttered to give glimpses of muscular male bottoms.

Grace sighed. "Aren't most of the men we encounter scoundrels at heart? That is what makes them so interesting. But no gentleman would ever really behave as a scoundrel with me."

"For which you should be profoundly grateful." They were the same age, both eighteen, but Lady Prudence suddenly looked wise and mature. "You are so exceptionally beautiful, Grace, you will make a devastatingly successful marriage."

"Will I?" She was running out of time. Within a week or two, the fashionable world would all be in London. Her eldest sister Venetia was already in London, in a rented townhouse, drawing erotic art to save their family, and their mother was sick with worry.

And Grace could save them all. All she had to do was marry.

She ground the toe of her slipper into the gleaming parquet floor and gripped her fan until the splintered spokes bit through her gloves. All she had to do was capture a titled man and she could keep her family from the workhouse. She could return her mother to the world that had cast her out.

Since Grace had turned thirteen, her plan had been direct and simple. She would marry a title. She would make things right. Everyone had told her she was lovely, that she would grow to be a great beauty. She had overheard the secret conversations, when matrons had told her mother how valuable her beauty would be.

"Grace, I am serious." Lady Prudence gripped her shoulders and gave her a gentle shake. The silk of Grace's gown—one of Lady Prudence's that she had bought but later decided she did not like—shimmered around her legs. "Do not believe a word my brother says," Lady Prudence warned. "There is not a young woman on this estate that he has not . . . had intimacies with."

"I know." And Grace did. She knew she was a fool to imagine that Lord Wesley, a wealthy heir, a devastatingly handsome man, would want to marry a nobody like her. But she knew, even after only a week, that she could not bear to settle for anything less. It was not his title she wanted—it was him. The man.

Grace tapped her lips with her torn fan. She wanted it all. Could she not only marry well, but also marry a man she loved and desired? Or was she simply hoping for too much, when her family's security was at stake?

Prudence had adopted a motherly air. "There are many gentlemen who are already besotted with you, Grace. Lord Ornsbrook, who is a viscount, and a wealthy one, is a thoroughly respectable catch. Pelworth hangs on your every word, and he is an earl!"

Grace swallowed hard. Either man should be perfect: young, reasonably attractive, and tongue-tied around her, which should be a good sign.

Prudence pointed with her fan at a lanky blond man laughing his way through the dance set. "Even Sir Randolph Thomas, over there. He possesses a fortune! Yes, he's an atrocious dancer, but, really, a woman never dances with her husband."

"Prudence, no—"

"Or Lord Wynsome. Such a suitable name. He melts every woman's heart. And he's heir to the Earl of Warren. He's delicious, isn't he? I'm certain he would take one look at you and—"

"Stop!" Grace cried. The Earl of Warren was her grandfather—her mother's father. He had thrown her mother out and barred all of them from his house. Lady Prudence, of course, knew not of that. Like everyone else, Prudence believed the lies Grace had carefully cultivated—the lie learned by her and her sisters. Her mother was respectably married, her father, a sea captain who was away, far across the world, hoping to make his fortune. But that father was her mother's fictitious creation.

She would never dare tell anyone that she was Lord Warren's illegitimate granddaughter and that her father was really Rodesson, the famous and scandalous artist of erotica. Or that her eldest and talented sister was the one now painting the erotic works that bore Rodesson's name.

Lord Wynsome had no idea she was, in fact, a cousin to him. There was no way he would guess, but it was still her greatest fear that he somehow would, that he would expose the truth to Lady Prudence.

Prudence was her entry to the ton, to the world of rich and titled and delicious gentlemen—

She couldn't dare risk Prudence's friendship. And, in truth, she dearly loved her friend.

"But, still, there are more," Prudence said cheerfully. "Over there—" She stopped abruptly. "Oh good heavens, what is he doing here?"

Grace never heard that tone of voice from Prudence. Low, serious . . . fearful. Surprised, she strained to look.

A gentleman stood at the entrance to the ballroom—he towered head and shoulders above the crowd. He must have been over six and a half feet in height. And his hair—it was a wild mane of dark blond that streamed past his shoulders, unruly and wild. She knew, by instinct, that it suited the man.

He gave an enormous grin, which revealed deep dimples framing his handsome mouth and brilliant white teeth. Several servants were trying to push him out. With his arms crossed over his huge chest, he appeared to be an immovable wall.

The butler hastened up to the fray, but the mysterious guest merely amiably punched the servant in the shoulder.

Laughing, openly amused, the gentleman refused to budge. To Grace's shock, she saw his head turn and his gaze slide over the crowd. Toward her. She was staring, but so was everyone else. There was no reason he should feel her curious gaze out of the hundreds of others.

Polite decorum decreed she should look away, but she could not stop watching him. His skin was golden bronze, close in color to his luxurious hair. He was obviously a man who exposed his body to the sun. Even bathed in the light of a chandelier, he stood too far away to reveal the color of those penetrating eyes, but she guessed they would be blue.

A silly fancy. She forced her gaze to move demurely away. But she was still aware of him; it was as though the music had stopped and the dancers had whirled away into the night, and there was no one in the ballroom but the handsome stranger and her.

The strangest sensation gripped her, along with a heat that threatened to set her skin on fire.

She'd desired Lord Wesley, but she'd felt nothing like this—

Every forbidden erotic picture, every one of her father Rodesson's erotic drawings—those she'd secretly looked at— spilled through her heated mind.

She wanted this man, this powerful, compelling stranger. She wanted to know what it would be like to lie underneath him and part her legs and take him inside her. She wanted to know how his skin would taste to her lips and her tongue. To know if he would be rigid and big and if he would fill her completely and make her scream in pleasure. She wanted to see him naked, taste him naked, and make love to him until they were both sweaty and senseless—

He was staring at her.

Grace felt it. Felt an answering fire rush over her skin.

Preposterous! How could he even see her? But she glanced up, enthralled by the moment, knowing their gazes would lock—

Or was he looking at Prudence? Wouldn't that make more sense?

He was not looking at either of them. Abruptly he turned on his heel and strode out through the gilt and ivory doors.

Her fan was in tatters beneath her fingers and her heart felt two sizes too big for her chest. Her throat was tight and dry. Her drawers were indecently wet.

She had to know. It was like a sudden addiction. "Who was that?" she cried.

"My half brother." Prudence's voice shook with . . . anger? Fear? An emotion Grace could not quite define.

"You have a half brother?"

"He's a bastard," Prudence continued, her voice contemptuous, using a word she should not. "My father's by-blow. His first-born child, in fact, and my father is stupidly fond of him."

Grace shook at the revulsion on her friend's face. She was a bastard. Would Prudence feel the same way about her if she knew the truth?

Suddenly Grace felt as though she stood on a tightrope, balancing over a pit of wolves. No, this was the ton. Not wolves—mocking jackals with slavering jaws.

"He should be hung," Prudence spat. "He's a highwayman. Can you believe he is so bold as to come to this house? He's probably robbed half the people here! And he was a pirate. Why the British Navy did not kill him, I cannot imagine. He's a murderer, a scoundrel, and . . ." Prudence took a shaky breath.

Grace moved forward, startled by tears in her friend's eyes.

"And our father loves him best!" Prudence cried and stamped her foot.

Grace hugged her friend. "Of course not!"

Prudence pulled out of the hug, shaking. "He does. His mother was a love affair, ours a duty marriage. Of course, he loves dashing Devlin Sharpe. But I *hate* him."

"Why? Because of what he is?" Grace could hardly believe she wanted to press this. Why should she want to hear about the horrors of being recognized as a bastard?

"He murdered the man I loved. If I wouldn't hang for it, I'd grab one of my father's pistols right now and shoot him where he stands."

Grace blinked. "How could he murder a man and escape punishment?"

Prudence balled her hands into fists, and Grace heard her fan snap. "I cannot tell you what happened. Not even you, my dear friend."

She reached out and stroked Prudence's arm as her friend turned red-rimmed eyes to her and asked, "Do I look awful? I have to dance with Lord Wynsome next."

"You look fine." But a chill washed over Grace as she watched Prudence stroll away. Prudence's movements were controlled, precise, and lovely, belying her emotional outburst. If her illegitimate half brother had murdered the man she loved, how could he have dared walk into the house?

And even after hearing what a beast he was, she still ached between her legs. She was still flushed and anxious with desire.

She was supposed to meet Lord Wesley at midnight . . . After feeling all that mad, delirious passion and hunger and need.

She couldn't bear to stand in this crowded, overheated ballroom one moment longer. She needed to escape.

* * *

"You weren't planning to meet me after all, were you?"

Grace jerked away from the study windows and slowly turned around.

Lord Wesley stood in the doorway, the door closed behind him. There had been a key in the lock before and now it was gone.

His cravat was undone, the snowy-white cloth trailing over his black tailcoat.

He'd guessed the truth. She had not planned to meet him. She knew she couldn't—for two reasons. Both that mad moment of lust for a stranger and the fact that she could not have intimate relations with any man until she wore his ring. So, she had slipped into the study and poured herself some brandy to take away the frustration of knowing she couldn't meet him. But she tried to tease, "It is only the hour of eleven. You cannot possibly know that."

"I can guess, Grace." His lordship prowled toward her, his hip brushing a gilt table and setting the crystal glasses tinkling upon it. She saw from his unsteady gait that he'd been drinking. But then, so had she.

"I know you are afraid," he said. "I know what you want." He brushed back the now unruly locks of his white-blond hair.

"You do?" Brandy was hot in her blood. She leaned back against the arm of the settee. "I don't even know what I want."

"Yes, you do. But you deny it."

"I liked you much better when you were direct. What do I deny, my lord?"

His dark eyes—a stunning blend of violet and blue—held hers. He was breathtakingly beautiful. Much more so than that coarse and bold highwayman who was his half brother. "You deny that you want passion. Heat. Fire. You want lusty, sweaty, passionate sexual pleasure. You want to strip away the gowns, the corsets, and the bloody propriety. You want to fuck, sweetheart. And you want to fuck me."

She was shocked into breathlessness. The most confident, audacious grin turned up the edges of Lord Wesley's sensual mouth.

"You are drunk." She set down the glass, her heart like a live bird trapped in her chest. He was right. Of course. His very words had set her on fire. "And your sister warned me—"

"That I've bedded a lot of women. So have most of the other men here who act like eunuchs around you. The men who try to treat you like you are sweet and untouchable. Can you imagine a life wedded to one of them?"

"No." It was simply the truth.

"You don't want marriage, Grace. You want sex. You have to take marriage to get it."

She laughed at that, thrown off balance by the entire conversation. Had she already waded in too deep? She could hardly swoon or race from the room now. She had shown him the woman she really was. But she liked speaking this way. Bluntly. Truthfully. It was exhilarating. "And you don't," she challenged. "What would ever tempt you to embark on marriage, my lord?"

"Love. Obsession."

"The desire to possess something precious?"

"Perhaps that."

"I saw a man tonight. Pru—Lady Prudence told me that he is your half brother. That he murdered—"

"Shh." He pressed his fingers to her lips. "That is something that I intend to make right. I intend to spill his blood."

Lord Wesley left her side and he raced over to the desk. She stood, stunned, watching as he wrenched open a drawer. He lifted out a brass box that gleamed in the firelight, laid it on the blotter, and opened it. When he lifted his hands, he held a six-inch dagger poised between the tips of both his index fingers, one pressed to the end of the handle, one pressed to the point of the blade.

Watching her all the while, he dropped the knife to the

desk. It landed on its side with a thud. He stripped off his coat and threw it to the nearest chair—a leather club chair. His cravat and waistcoat followed.

There was only his shirt now. Fine linen between her gaze and his skin. "One day I will exact retribution from my damned half brother. But only if you tell me something that I need to hear."

She stared in confusion as Lord Wesley let his cravat slide off, as he undid the ties of his shirt. As he strode to her he grabbed the knife and he yanked the sides of his shirt apart. He pressed the tip of the blade to his chest, just beneath the plane of his pectorals, on the flesh that covered his heart.

Her heart was in her throat. "What . . . what are you doing?"

"Marry me, Grace. Be my bride. Fuck me tonight and marry me afterward. I cannot wait another moment to have you."

"Or you will stab yourself to the heart?" She was eighteen. She was not a schoolgirl—well, since they hadn't been able to afford schooling, she never really had been, but—

He wasn't really in love with her that much.

Was he?

"I want you."

"Why me?" she asked. "Of all the others? Of all the rich beauties, of all the dukes' daughters, of all the girls who try to move heaven and earth to attract you? No pretty words—the real words."

"Because you are like me."

That mystified her. And then he pushed the blade in and she was stunned to see a trickle of blood race down his body. It would ruin his shirt. "This is madness."

He bent forward, the knife still cutting into his skin, and he skimmed his lips along her throat. She stood, passively, letting the remarkable sensation wash over her. Soft lips—like velvet, like silk. No . . . more than that. Like the touch of a flame. Or the brush of an angel's hand.

"Saying no is madness," he rasped.

His tongue stroked the length of her neck. Her body became fluid. She was wet—indecently, wonderfully wet between her thighs. The stubble on his jaw teasingly scratched her skin. Her pulse seemed to beat everywhere at once—in her head, her lips, her fingertips, her . . . her sex.

"You are beautiful."

How many men had said that? But it mattered, from him.

"Touch me."

"Only if you take the blade from your heart."

"I will plunge it in if you leave me now. If you do not touch me. I cannot live without your touch. I could go to another woman. I know you are thinking that. I could bury my heavy, aching cock into her and fuck until my brain explodes and all the while I would be in pain because I wanted you. Do you have any idea what bloody torture that is?"

"I think I know."

"I want to marry you, Grace. All I need is a yes. One simple word."

"Yes." And there was no turning back. She hungered to touch him, and, once she did, she had to go forward.

If she touched him, she had to agree to do everything a husband and wife were intended to do.

Slowly, she pulled off her glove—a white, virginal, and utterly irritating scrap of satin. She reached out, touching her fingertips to his chest, his skin hot and damp beneath her touch.

"Take the knife away," she breathed. He was drunk and his hand cupped her bottom—a place a man's hand had never been—but she was afraid he would crush her to him and stab himself by accident.

He was young. Spoiled. Passionate. Wild.

Hers. With one simple word.

"Yes," she said again, to ensure there was no mistake, and she released a sigh of relief as he tossed the blade back to the desk. But in the next instant, he slid her skirts, petticoats and all, up her thighs. He pulled her drawers down before she could squeak, held her as she stepped out of them.

"You smell of lust, Grace. You stink of it and I love your smell. I want to cover my hands in it, my cock in it."

His earthy words made her more wet, more creamy and slick, and she could smell herself, flushing as she did so.

"Now, hold up your skirts for me and let me explore."

She obeyed and his hands slid around her naked inner thighs. His palms were strong, a little rough, and as he squeezed her skin she feared she'd fall to the floor.

"Stand up, Grace," he commanded in a growl and his hands skimmed higher, up and up to the juncture of her thighs, to her hot and sticky quim. "Part your legs for me a little more."

She did, aware of the wetness leaking down her inner thighs.

"Ah, yes, good girl," he murmured, and his look of fierce hunger softened with his heartbreaking smile. "Lovely, soft curls."

His fingers combed through them and she squirmed. Her quim felt tight and achy and hot and she was wriggling to ease the tension.

"Is your clit hard now? Would it like to feel my fingers stroking it? Would you like me to rub hard?"

She had no idea. A strangled, confused groan slipped from her lips. His bold erotic talk was what she wanted but not entirely what she'd expected. She was to be his wife—she'd thought he would be sweet. It would be sensuous and they would not speak—

Like a statue, she stood unable to move, and his long, strong fingers slid into her cleft. It felt so good, it felt—

His fingers sawed across her sensitive nub and she screamed. Her cry rang throughout the large room and his lordship laughed in response. "I knew you would scream," he purred, and he suckled her neck, making her cry out again. His lips, his tongue, his teeth—all teased the tingling skin of her throat and turned her body to molten heat.

He fiddled with the buttons of her gown, muttering curses, and she knew then why he had wanted her in something easy to remove. A few gave way, her bodice sagged, and at once his hands were there, lifting her breasts over the ruffled neckline.

She saw the pale curves lift, felt the strain against the silk, then felt her breasts spill out. "God yes," he groaned. "These tits. These enormous, plump, glorious breasts. I've been hungering to get my hands on these for a week."

His head dropped to her right breast and she moaned at the whisper of his silvery-blond hair brushing her flesh. At once, his firm mouth closed over her puckering nipple and he suckled so hard she dropped her skirts and grasped the back of the nearest chair.

Yes, she had played with her own nipples before, but not like this. He sucked greedily, lavishly, then rolled her free nipple between thumb and forefinger. It was so much—too much! She shut her eyes tight, swamped by sensation. Stars sparkled behind her lids. Something hard stroked her nipple—his teeth, she realized. She was astonished. Shocked. A little scared.

But he was a master, skillfully using the hard pressure of his teeth to send her soaring. She drank in his masculine scent and it wrapped around her like a magic spell. Letting her lids flicker open, she saw him suck first her left breast, then her right, leaving a trail of saliva between the two. Her nipples were wet, and harder and longer than she'd ever seen.

Lord Wesley glanced up, fair hair dusting his vivid eyes, and her heart gave a pang. His smile was gloriously wicked. "Enough play, love. Let us move on to the main event."

Grace wanted it to be slow and seductive, but he was far too aroused, she supposed. Tugging at his trouser buttons, he roaned,

groaned, "I'm too damned hard to get these things off, blast it."

She giggled at his loud moan of relief as the buttons gave and his placket opened. He shoved his trousers down just past his hips and she saw it—him—for the first time.

Darker blond hair dusted his abdomen, then made a curly thicket around the length of him jutting out. Before her mesmerized eyes, he wrapped his hand around its girth and gave a stroke that made his eyes roll back in his head.

He dropped to the floor and stretched out on his back on the rug. One arm pillowed his head and he held his . . . his hard cock upright. She stood like a ninny, a little nonplussed by his speed.

"Come here and straddle me," he rasped. "I want you on top of me, Grace. You can control how hard you want the strokes. How deep you want my cock to go."

Perched on top of her bodice, her large breasts stuck out, making it difficult to judge where she was as she lowered to the floor. Her breasts were much too big, unfashionably so, but Lord Wesley could not take his eyes off them.

"They're luscious," he promised. "Now sit on my prick, love, then bend forward and smother me with those tits for a while."

She had never thought they would make love for the first time on a carpet in his father's study. Yet the wickedness of it made it exciting. She was his coconspirator and she liked it. This was what she wanted. This was to be her future.

"Hurry, love," he urged as she fought to push aside the heavy silk skirt of her gown and the layers of lace-trimmed petticoats. "Though I love watching your nipples jiggle as you struggle."

Poised over him, she hesitated. Was she allowed to touch him—to hold his staff while she sank down on top of it?

"I'm dying, Grace." One strong hand clasped her hip through her skirts, and she rubbed her quim along the tip of his cock. The head was wet and smelled lush and primitive, just as she did. She was so slick and he was so hot and rigid that he easily slid into her. Gasping, she lowered and bore her weight on her knees. Her position pitched her breasts toward his face, as he'd wanted, and he arched up with his tongue sticking out. His tongue furled around her nipple as she took his cock deeper. Her walls slowly pushed apart, clenching him tight.

You can control how hard you want the strokes . . . He'd promised that but he was thrusting up to her, filling her, invading her. He plunged up and a twinge of pain startled her. Then it vanished and she wriggled on him, glorying in the feel of being completely full. She lifted and lowered, shocked by the wet slurping as she rose and fell, stunned by the pleasure as their hips collided.

"That's it," he growled. "Fuck me hard. Pound on me and make your tits bounce. I want to watch them slap up and down—"

Both his hands were on her hips, guiding her to slam up and down on him. Her hair tumbled free of her coiffure. Her breasts wobbled heavily. She panted for breath, getting hotter and hotter. Her thighs were slick, her breasts and back and forehead moist. If she bent toward him, she teased her . . . her clit with each stroke—

His face contorted. "God!" He pulled her abruptly forward and she sprawled over him, burying his face into her round breasts as he slammed his hips upward. Clamped to him by his strong arm, she dragged in breaths and squirmed on him. She'd felt pleasure but no climax.

She knew of the climax. She'd seen the expressions in her father's paintings. Of women in ecstasy, melting in pleasure all over a man. Their mouths would be open wide in a scream, their eyes shut, their faces flushed. Sometimes they'd be gouging the man with their fingernails, as though they were fighting for their lives, as though fighting to survive the pleasure claiming their souls.

She hadn't quite got *there*. Suddenly his arms lifted, and Lord Wesley relaxed back against the rug, grinning, and looking disheveled and gloriously handsome.

It was on the tip of her tongue to say, "I love you."

But he gave a coarse laugh. "Lord, but you're a good fuck, as I knew you'd be. Now make yourself decent and get out of here. I'm done with you."

2

Grace ran blindly down the hallway. She passed a gentle-man, but tears of humiliation blurred her eyes and she could not see him distinctly.

Oh God, he would recognize her!

She forced herself to stop. To turn. But the gentleman was not watching her in astonishment, as she expected he would be. He had reached the door of the study and she could only see his back. She shivered at the sight of his raven-black hair, even as Lord Wesley jovially greeted him.

"Wynsome! Come to pay tribute to the master?"

The master? As she tried to absorb what that meant, Wynsome answered, with grudging respect and salacious humor laced in his words, "So, you finally had lovely little Grace Hamilton."

Grace shrank back against the papered wall of the hallway, fighting the hot bile that clawed at her throat. He'd shared his horrible plans with Wynsome all along. It had been a joke, a wager, perhaps. And she'd stumbled right into it, a stupid, gullible girl.

He'd made it clear exactly how 'done with her' he was. She'd whispered, "But m—marriage?" and he'd laughed in her face.

How many other *gentlemen* knew? Did they all?

"She's a treat," Lord Wesley said with callous triumph.

"Every bit as good as I'd conjectured, given that she was a virgin. And, as you will note, she makes my twentieth virgin of the year. Your blunt is at risk, Wynsome. I'll have bedded a hundred by Christmas."

She felt pinned to the wall by their appalling cruelty. This was sport to them.

"The rest of the club will be astounded. There's many who wagered more than they could afford, certain you'd never claim one hundred gently bred virgins."

The rest of the *club?* There were others, possibly dozens, of men involved in this? Men who would all talk of her ruination. This would destroy her. Oh God, what had she done?

All of society would know—every gentleman who had treated her as a gently bred young marriage prospect. Wynsome knew—would he tell the Earl of Warren about it? Would the handsome, white-haired earl sneer at her, calling her the horrid names he had used on her mother?

"What have you done, my dear?"

She gave a strangled scream at the deep male voice that repeated the very question she'd asked herself.

Devlin Sharpe had seen many frightened women in his day. Terrified women. Desperate women. He had seen the eyes of women as they stood on the gallows and waited for the platform to drop away.

But he'd never seen such a mix of fear and loathing and anger shooting from such beautiful and determined eyes. Of course, he did not think he'd ever seen such an intriguing woman before—an intoxicating, alluring mix of angelic golden hair, pretty features, and enticingly carnal curves.

He held the lovely blonde's gaze, aware from the way her eyes darted and her lips trembled that she intended to lie to him. "Don't lie," he warned. "Don't give me a weak story and try to run away. I want the truth. I want to know what—or who—has hurt you."

She straightened, moving away from the papered wall, and Devlin knew exactly what had happened. Her small fingers were curled around the crumpled sky-blue silk of her bodice, holding it up over her generous breasts. Beneath the light of the wall sconce, her soft hair was gleaming gold and poured in disheveled curls over her shoulders and down her back. A tear still clung to the lashes of her red-rimmed green eyes. She smelled of sex.

Hearing his half brother's mocking laugh from the study was the final piece of evidence. "Did he rape you? Or just seduce you?"

Furious at his damned brother, he'd let a snarl creep in to his expression and she drew back. "I should go," she whispered.

"Not through the corridors of a crowded house with your dress hanging off you. Come with me."

"Why?" Her golden brows drew together in suspicion. *Now* the woman was cautious.

"I can negotiate this house without anyone seeing us."

Obviously she could not understand why any man would wish to do her a kindness. She took another step away from him. "You . . . you are a highwayman, aren't you?"

"Of course I would never admit to that, Miss . . . what is your name, by the way?"

Since he'd first spotted her startling golden hair in the ballroom and then indulged himself with a good look at the rest of her, he'd wondered who she was. None of his father's servants had obliged him with a name—they'd been more interested in tossing him out on the gravel drive.

Pity they did not know the secret entrances to the house as he did.

"Your name," he repeated.

"If I do not tell you, it will be one less man who knows." Her lips formed a sneer at that, and he knew she meant her anger for herself.

What was it with some women that they absorbed their

anger instead of using it for some good? His mother had been like that—taking every blasted insult and slap his father had bestowed upon her and swallowing it up herself.

"I know my half brother," he stated, determined to place blame where it lay. "What did he promise you?"

She shook her head. "It hardly matters what he promised me. I should have known he did not mean to stand by his words. I, of all people, should know that—" She stopped abruptly. "Did you murder Lady Prudence's lover, or is that something you will also not admit to?"

Murder? Hell, so that was the way the gossipmongers had described it. Since that had been his reason for returning here, it struck him on the raw. "I shot him in a duel," he said brusquely. "It was all damnably honorable—and I lay stress on the word *honorable*. It was also deserved. Not legal, of course, but I doubt that will be the crime I'll ultimately swing for. It was not murder. I am not asking you to follow me for nefarious reasons, love—and I do need a name to call you, or you will have to listen to endearments all the way up the stairs."

She goggled at him, as young women so often did, but from the slight curve of her lips—immediately quelled—he knew she'd followed his quick speech. "Hamilton. My name is Grace Hamilton."

Devlin took a step backward and crooked his finger. "Trust me, Miss Hamilton. You cannot stay out here with your gown half off. And even if I button it for you—"

"I know. I look far too obviously like a harlot."

She'd tried his patience too far. More roughly than he should, he caught hold of her wrist and forced her to follow him down the hallway. She dragged her heels but had no choice. A thump of his fist against the appropriate molding gave a *snick* and he pried up the secret panel. "In there— there's a hidden staircase to the upper floors. I apologize in advance for the cobwebs and the dust."

Plain fear showed in her large, round eyes. *Blast*. "I have no intention of hurting you, Miss Hamilton. But I promise you, if Wesley took your innocence, he'll marry you."

She paused at the foot of the stairs. "You cannot force him to."

Devlin waved his hand to encourage her to get up the stairs. "A man with a knife at his back can be forced to do anything."

She laid a slender bare hand on the rickety balustrade. "I don't want that. I don't want to marry him. I just want to . . . to turn back time."

"Sweeting—"

She stomped her slipper on the worn floor, the thump swallowed up by the stale air. "Don't. My name is Grace. I told you what it was and I want you to use it. Don't call me names like that."

A strand of a spider's web dangled in front of her face, and she flinched as he brushed it away. The way she'd recoiled made him want to rip out Wesley's sorry guts. Gently, he shook his head, wearing what he hoped was a soothing smile. "I cannot call you Grace. That is an intimacy a man like me is not allowed. I can call you 'love' or 'sweetheart' and live up to my audacious nature, or I can call you 'Miss Hamilton', showing you due respect."

He'd hoped to relax her by making her laugh but she threw up her hands, which made her bodice gape. He caught a glimpse of lush ivory curves with a deep shadowed valley between. His throat dried and his blood rushed down to his cock, making it instantly as hard as iron.

"I don't want due respect!" she cried. "Nor do I want to be an anonymous 'love'. I want—Oh, this is ridiculous. What does it matter what you call me? I can imagine what everyone else will call me."

With that, she turned and began to clomp up the stairs.

"A little quieter, Miss Hamilton," he advised, though he hated quenching her spirited anger. It was just what she needed—the best remedy for humiliation. "A little discretion will keep our secret a secret."

"I don't understand," she whispered ahead, to the dark and the cobwebs. "Why would you help me?"

"I might be a highwayman, but there are certain things I do not steal."

"Like a woman's virtue?" Disbelief rang in her voice.

"Like a woman's heart. Now tell me your story. All of it."

When it began with, "I should have known better—", he growled, and she tried again.

"Lord Wesley has pursued me for a week. He's found ways to get me alone, to be suggestive. I knew he desired me, and I . . . I cared for him. I should have known that lust might not mean his heart was engaged, of course!" She turned, as though to ensure he was not laughing at her. He was not. And he never would. His heart hurt for her.

"I would not have let him . . . well, I was not going to meet him after all. I knew I should not. But he found me, and he told me he wanted to marry me. He asked me what my answer was. And I said yes! And then, it seemed so right to . . . well, to . . . I should have known better."

"And waited until he put a ring on your finger to discover he's a piece of shit? Far better you find out now."

She gasped. "It wouldn't have come to that. He never intended to—"

"Stop interrupting my attempt to make the appropriate point, Miss Hamilton. The mistake isn't yours. It's his. Now let us get you to your room and I'll take care of his bloody lordship."

She stopped on the stair and turned again, brow furrowed with worry. "What do you intend to do?"

"I will ensure they do not ruin you. I can ensure this is kept a secret. I promise you that."

"Why would you do that for me? When it's my own fault."

"It isn't your fault. You're human. You believed a black-guard."

She sagged against the banister. "I've ruined everything. I can't marry. I—"

"There are men who aren't so worried about having a virgin. They'd rather have a woman they enjoy spending time with. They'd rather have love. Now, which is your bedroom?"

That startled her, but she dutifully answered. "The green room. It overlooks the west pond."

"It's at the end of this hallway, then." He urged her up to the landing, knowing he should open the door and let her go. But he bent over her hand, pressing his lips to her fingers, just a brush, and then he rose. "You gave your heart. It is and always will be the most precious gift."

"One I gave to the wrong man." She gave a laugh, a soft, wild laugh. "I gave my innocence to the wrong man."

She was vulnerable now. And enticing, even in the faint light glimmering in from the hallway, even when surrounded by creaky wood framing and a few centuries of dust. She was pink and gold, the sort of treasure that tempted men to madness. He'd faced down pistols, but it took all the courage he had to abruptly turn her by her slim shoulders. To not take advantage and press his mouth to those soft pink lips.

"Slip out into the hallway and go to bed, Miss Hamilton. Bathe yourself, slip into your warmed silky sheets—" He almost stumbled over that image. "Close your eyes and sleep, love." He whispered it. "Do not worry about tonight. I will take care of everything."

"It is not so simple as that," she declared, showing a flash of pride that he could have applauded. "I have no idea what to do when I wake up tomorrow."

"Go on about your life, Miss Hamilton." He thought of all the times he had thought he could not bear to see the sunrise, the nights he thought he couldn't stand to live another day. But he had.

"My life is about marriage, Mr. Sharpe," she whispered. "That is the direction of my every day."

He wanted to say that it still could be, but instead he said, "Then perhaps you should find a new direction for your life, Miss Hamilton."

Then he opened the door, checked the hallway, and watched her go.

This was what she got for looking to a man to rescue her.

Grace threw her crumpled satin gloves to the smooth counterpane covering her bed and she stalked to the bellpull to summon one of Lady Prudence's maids. Unlike all the other women here, she could not afford to bring her own.

A rich, earthy, unfamiliar scent touched her nose and she panicked. She released the tasseled rope before she gave the tug that might ring her death knell. She smelled of *him*.

She could not be attended by a maid. Not when her dress was a wrinkled disaster, her hair was a mess, and she wore the undeniable smell of a man. But she could not take off her own gown and corset. And she needed washing water.

Struggling with the buttons, she stalked to the ewer and basin. There was some left, cold, but it might be enough to rid her of this smell. She could sleep in her corset—well, not sleep, just wait for dawn—but there was still the matter of her dress.

As she struggled with the buttons she could reach, then wriggled and jumped and grunted to get the dress off, Grace muttered aloud, "Lord Wesley is a lily-livered rodent who is not worthy of licking my boots. Horse droppings are more noble than he!"

It might have been silly, but it made her feel better. And as she gave a final push and stepped out of her gown, she sighed with relief. She left her dress in a puddle on the floor, hoping that might explain away the wrinkles, then grimaced as she poured the last of the water into the basin.

She supposed it was punishment for being a fool. She dampened the washcloth and shivered.

Marriage was to be her salvation—it was the only way out—and now she'd thrown that away. As penance, she scrubbed herself hard with the cold washcloth.

What was she to do? She had inherited none of her father's talents, unlike Venetia who could paint and her sister Maryanne who was a gifted author. She was not in the least bit artistic, unless one counted a flair for throwing herself into dramatic disasters.

Of all Rodesson's daughters, she had inherited the most from their mother Olivia:—her blond hair, fine and pale but strong enough to curl and wave, and her mother's famed features. Her eyes were green—like those of her infamous father. Gentlemen admired her figure, which she felt was too plump and generous. But the elderly matrons of Maidenswode, the ones who no longer bothered to watch their tongues, insisted that men were attracted to a generous bosom. Her breasts were apparently worth their weight in gold.

Certainly Lord Wesley had admired her breasts. Apparently it was the only thing he wanted about her.

"No." Grace said it aloud, to make it more resolute, as she rinsed the cloth. "I have to move forward. I need to decide what I can do. There is still marriage after all. I could marry an older gentleman. There's any number of older wealthy peers who would like my breasts, I'm sure—"

"Sweetheart, you do not have to sell yourself that way."

Startled by the familiar male growl, she turned to the door, suddenly tense, aware, uncertain—yet liking the thrilling mix of sensations. "I locked that."

Mr. Sharpe shrugged. "Indeed, you did."

"Do you make a habit of breaking into women's—" She paused, aware of the heat in her cheeks, aware she wore only her corset and shift. Of course he broke into women's bedchambers. He was both a pirate and highwayman—two male pursuits that involved stealing women's virtues.

Mr. Sharpe looked annoyingly smug. "It might surprise you to know that I do not. I usually await the inevitable invitation."

He leaned elegantly in the doorway, propped on his arm, legs crossed at his booted ankles, obviously awaiting hers. The blue of his eyes kept her mesmerized—sapphire blue, dark and glinting in the light of her one candle and her low fire. As spectacular a color as she'd imagined and entirely unlike Lord Wesley's, thank heaven.

Why had he come? What did he want? If she had sense she would send him away, but she needed him—if only to undo the knot in her corset ties. "You may come in, because otherwise someone will peek out their door and see you standing there."

She couldn't help but give a triumphant smile as he hastened off her threshold into her room and shut the door behind him.

His masculine scent, different from his brother's—more earthy, more spicy, entirely seductive—filled her senses, filled her room.

He filled her room.

And in that instant, as she drank in his astonishing height and his wide shoulders, she remembered Lady Prudence's stark fear and accusations. She turned away, struck by nerves, wondering at her own sanity, and she crossed her arms over her breasts. He had openly admitted to dueling and she had brought him into her bedroom.

But he'd rescued her. He had made her smile when any sensible, well-bred woman would be crying so hard she would have to wring out her bedspread.

"I spoke to Wesley."

That caught her attention and she spun around. "What—good heavens, your neck is bleeding!"

His lips parted; his teeth flashed in the audacious grin of a man accustomed to taking what he wished. "Not anymore. I used my overpriced and overstarched cravat to soak it up."

"Lord Wesley attacked you? What did you do in return?"

"I took that stupid knife off him, took him over my knee, and spanked him."

"You didn't! You couldn't have possibly done so!"

He calmly peeled off his glove and winked. "I thought my hand might still be red. My palm is still stinging. I felt childish, bullying behavior deserved a child's punishment. I would have used a belt on him, but the coward fled out into the gardens."

She snorted. Then clapped her hands to her mouth in horror. She'd meant to laugh in the demure and melodic way that women should do, but her natural laugh came out. The horrid snort that always sent her sisters into gales of laughter. Inappropriate laughter, theirs might be, but it was feminine at least.

The highwayman in her bedroom grinned broadly. "Good Lord, did that sound come from you?"

"Yes," she declared with defiance, aware that they now stood on either side of her bed, which was neatly turned down for the night.

He raked back his long blond hair. "You are lovely, aren't you?"

Embarrassment struck. "Before you raised your hand—or your belt—to Lord Wesley, did you discuss my . . . my reputation?"

"Why do you think I was flogging his backside, Miss Hamilton? It wasn't for exercise. It was an indication of how seriously I would humiliate him, hurt him, destroy him if he dared to breathe a word of what happened."

She was half-undressed, and had no idea what to think. How could a highwayman be her knight protector? "But he is your brother, and he must know you wouldn't seriously hurt—"

Clenched in a fist, Mr. Sharpe's hand rested against the fluted column of her bed. His dimple deepened. "He knows I would. How do you think I got him to stop lording his legitimacy and his title over me? I kicked his little bottom at school with my booted foot."

Grace realized that for all she was barely dressed Mr. Sharpe's eyes never left her face. It gave her an odd sense of courage and focused all her thoughts on him. "You went to school?"

"Do I appear uneducated? My master of literature was certain I'd never be more than a hulking, semiliterate beast."

"But you do not use your education!" she protested. "You—"

He leaned closer and the spicy hint of sandalwood, the delectable warm smell of his skin, intoxicated her. It spoke of the most intimate things he did—bathe, shave, even sweat.

"Do not doubt that I use every one of my lessons, Miss Hamilton. I've been known to quote Shakespeare while blowing the mast off an English warship."

"You never have!"

He was laughing now, quietly, the sound throaty and deep. "What—the Shakespeare or the warship?"

"The warship," Grace answered, her tone sharpened by his teasing. "Wouldn't you have been hunted down and strung up by now? You are not exactly secretive, are you?"

"Suffice it to say that I performed some duties for his majesty that made amends."

"For destroying ships? What did you do? Capture a continent and stick the flag in the middle of it?"

"Essentially, yes." He laughed. It intrigued Devlin that Miss Grace Hamilton was speaking entirely about him. It was something he was not accustomed to—generally he let women prattle on about their worlds, content to listen to the lilt in their voices as they spread gossip.

He should go. It was his intention to protect her reputation, not destroy it by taking up residence in her bedroom. But as he was about to bow and bid her farewell, he saw the glint of a tear in the corner of her eye and knew her courage was about to fail her.

"And what can I do?" she asked. "Become a governess? Oh, wait—my schooling is almost nonexistent and most ladies want young women of impeccable reputation for their children. Perhaps I'm qualified to scrub the floors—"

"Gently bred women rarely are. I'd never employ one to tend my home."

"Mr. Sharpe, this is serious. I—" Her lashes swept over her eyes and one sparkling diamond of a tear rolled past her slim nose.

"Don't." He was on his feet in an instant and in front of her, his gloves off. With his index finger, he brushed away the tear, his rough fingertip gliding over her soft, glowing skin. His finger shook. Slightly, but he felt it.

Unable to resist, he brushed his wet fingertip across the curve of her cheek to her slightly parted lips.

She arched up on tiptoe and her palm cupped his jaw. Damn, he hadn't bothered to shave today, enjoying appearing at the ballroom with a day's growth of beard, though it itched. He hadn't worn facial hair since he'd sported a neat beard as Captain Devlin Sharpe.

He had been a pirate, but there were treasures that he refused to plunder. A wide-eyed eighteen-year-old was one. "This is not wise, Miss Hamilton." He caught her hand, squeezed gently, and drew her fingers away from his face.

Her moist, full lips parted, leaving him breathless.

"I want this," she whispered. "I want to erase the bad with . . . with—"

"Grace—"

She put her fingers to his lips and he, who had captained a ship, who commanded a gang of unruly thieves, shut his mouth. He wanted too much to hear this and his heart was in his throat as she whispered, "With you."

3

Mr. Sharpe's hands deftly undid the knot in her corset ties, then slid up to loosen the lacing, and Grace made a simple decision. She would not think. She wanted this. Her body was molten, her arousal slick between her thighs.

Earlier she had given her innocence to the wrong man, to an arrogant and vicious man.

Mr. Sharpe was not a vicious man.

She believed it—

No. She'd promised she would not think. She would simply do.

Wriggling out of her loosened corset, she let it fall to the floor. Undressing before a stranger was not something she should feel so comfortable with—

No. *No thinking.*

Grace lifted the hem of her shift but stopped at her upper thighs. Her drawers were gone. Lord Wesley still had her drawers. She had not collected them before she snatched up the key and ran from his mocking laugh. *I wouldn't marry you, love—good Lord, you are an impoverished nobody. But I do like the idea of acquiring a new mistress.* The remembered words hurt. She hoped the fiend had burned her drawers but feared he would hang them at his club, a souvenir of his beastly behavior.

"Don't think."

Mr. Sharpe's deep whisper, the ripple of his warm breath across her neck, sent a shiver of desire down her back. Had she tensed beneath his touch? How had he guessed at her thoughts?

"I won't," she answered, breathless, and she moved from him to whisk off her shift and let it flutter to the carpet. There, she was nude. He could see every inch of her back—the slope of her shoulders, the curves of her very plump bottom,

He made a low sound in his throat, like a growl. "God, you are perfect."

Instead of turning back to him, she walked to the bed. Only three feet, but it felt like eternity. She was aware of the sway of her hips, the jiggle of her derriere, the foolish way she stubbed her toe into the floor due to lack of attention.

She was so aware: of the harshness of his breathing, the warmth of the fire, which allowed her to prance naked with nary a goose bump, even of the sensual textures of her room. Soft velvet hung around the bed, and the counterpane was embroidered silk. A fur throw was flung across a chair's arms and the soft carpet gave way to the smooth, cool floor.

And as she reached the edge of the bed, she also felt an awareness of her own body she'd never known before. It was as though she could feel her skin breathe. Her nipples stood proud, flushed a dark pink. Her quim throbbed, hot and creaming and yearning to be filled. At the bedpost, she turned, and saw him stripping off his clothes with graceful, deliberate motions. His coat and waistcoat were gone, and, as she watched, startled, he lifted his shirt.

White linen skimmed up over bronzed skin.

Grace clutched the bedpost. His rippled abdomen came into view. Soft golden hair curled over the flat plane of muscle. He shifted, revealing a glimpse of his navel.

Suddenly she wanted nothing more than to drop to her knees and kiss his indented navel, rim it with her tongue and taste his skin. She wanted to stroke those hard, cobbled muscles and explore—

She had to fist her shaking hands.

He lifted the hem of his shirt to his shoulders, his motions casual and unconcerned, as though he did not know she ogled his every move and now had her left fist pinned between her teeth.

She was certain he did know—he flexed his hard, sculpted pectoral muscles before her eyes—but his shirt hid his face and the grin she knew would be there. His nipples, she saw, were dark bronze and as hard as hers.

Then he threw the shirt aside, revealing his entire naked torso and the wicked glint in his vivid blue eyes.

Huge and powerful, his was a body that should intimidate. His shoulders were broad and straight, strong enough to carry a cannon, she suspected. She could imagine him climbing the rigging of a ship, risking his life and laughing all the while.

His well-hewn body did not frighten her, but it made her moan with honest need.

What living, breathing woman did not appreciate a handsome chest? But she had never yearned so much to touch a man's body before.

She let go of the bedpost and walked toward him, pleased to see his hands pause on his trouser buttons and his Adam's apple bounce with a swallow. Her breasts swayed as she moved. He looked at them, and his blatant appreciation made her feel bold. "Do you like them?"

He let go of his trousers and bent to the hollow of her throat. His tongue flicked and she squealed at the shock of sensation. Gently his tongue swirled, trailing down, inch by precious inch, toward her breasts. She shivered at the amazing sensitivity of her skin. Her nipples shocked her by standing harder, growing long and pink.

She could not believe she was letting a man she did not know do—

No thinking!

He rose. Met her gaze. "They're beautiful, love."

His golden hair fell about his face and floated over her bare skin. Casually he blew strands away from his lips and even that simple, unconscious, sensual motion ignited her desire.

She could not believe her naked breasts were only an inch away from his hot, bare chest.

"You are beautiful here—" He brushed a kiss to her chin. "And here." Giggling, she shut her eyes as his soft lips neared. His lips touched her lashes, and she marveled at how erotic it was to feel that caress.

Wet heat surrounded her right nipple and she arched, opening her eyes. The tip of his tongue circled around her areola, making it pucker. His lips parted and her blushing nipple disappeared into his mouth. His cheeks hollowed and she cried out as the pleasure seared her.

He stopped suckling and she whimpered.

Hoarse, raw, his voice washed over her. "But it is the sound of your sighs and moans of pleasure that are the most beautiful to me, Grace."

The look in Devlin's narrowed eyes stunned her. It wasn't lust. It was more than that. He looked awed, as though she was truly beautiful. As though she was lovelier than he expected, or he was more struck by it than he'd planned. And, strangely, she liked that.

After all, he was more beautiful than she had expected, and she was far more struck by it than she'd planned.

His mouth claimed her nipple once more, but with such maddening gentleness she thrust her breasts forward and clutched his silken hair. Chuckling against her skin, he obliged her by sucking harder while stripping down his pants.

Nothing came between his hot skin and his trousers.

Daringly, she touched the ridge of his naked hip. Marveling. Of course, the lean line of his hip was hard, the indent above velvety soft, and his stomach . . . it was an entrancing lacing of pure muscle.

He scooped her up. Not as a gentleman would lift a lady

to carry her if she had sprained her ankle. No, he grasped her bottom and drew her up, forcing her to hook her legs around his waist.

"Mr. Sharpe!" Her soaked and sticky quim pressed against the broad head of his hard cock trapped between them.

"Devlin. I would like to hear you call me Devlin, sweetheart." Surprisingly agile with his trousers around his knees, he made his way to the edge of the bed, then fell. She shut her eyes, certain she'd be squashed, but he caught his weight on his powerful arms, laughing.

Pushing up, he straightened and yanked off his boots, but his hot gaze never left her. She lay with one arm over her nipples, one hand covering her blond nether curls, clinging to modesty. Immodestly, she stared at his cock. Now that he wasn't pressed against her, she could see it—curiosity made her look, carnal appreciation kept her staring.

Her father's paintings had mocked male members—exaggerated them. Some were long and thin and scarlet tipped. Others short and thick and oddly purple.

Mr.—Devlin's—cock captured her with its audacious size and pure beauty. Jutting out, his thick cock curved upward toward his navel. She doubted she could encircle it with her hand. Dark gold hair surrounded it and a pair of large ballocks dangled below.

What would it feel like inside her? Would it be too large? Would it hurt? Just staring was making her honey flow and her hand was no longer merely covering her privates. To her shock, she realized she was stroking her creamy lips. In front of him.

His knee pressed into the bed. Glinting honey-gold in the firelight, his hair fell around his face. "I want you on top, Grace. You can—"

"No!"

Frowning at her desperate shout, he paused. She hurried on. "I want you on top. That is the way I want it . . . please?" She spread her legs in welcome and held out her hands, revealing herself to him in the most intimate and vulnerable way.

A bewitching smile curved his lips and he lifted her hand and pressed a kiss to her fingertips. "Anything to please my lady."

He left her and took something from a pocket of his trousers. Grace stared as he rolled a covering over his cock, mesmerized by the casual way he touched himself. She knew of such things from her father's pictures—a sheath, to prevent a pregnancy.

Don't think.

Then the gentleman vanished with a blink of her eye and a rogue took his place. The broad shoulders moved over her, his lean hips nudged between her thighs, and his strong legs spread hers wider. Bravely, she touched him, skimming her hands over his smooth shoulders, letting her fingertips graze down to the crinkly hair on his chest.

She wanted to relish every inch of him. This was to be the memory she would treasure and she would make it perfect.

Sharing a smile with Devlin, astonished by how natural it felt to touch him, to delight in it, Grace reached down. Eager to touch his cock, to explore him, to pleasure him . . .

"Oh God, Grace," Devlin groaned as Grace's long, slim fingers curled around his aching shaft. Her fingers gripped tight, then slid up and down. They traced the veins that pushed against the skin and made a mind-melting journey up to the straining head.

Miss Grace Hamilton was exploring, and he could barely hold on to his control. He ground his back teeth, fighting the urge to ease her hand away and slide inside her. Deliberately, her hand closed around him and began to jerk him with rhythmic motions.

He stopped her, clasping his hand around her small wrist. "I want to make love to you. To be inside you. Do you want that?"

Before she answered, he guided his cock to her wet, steamy lips, stirring her bubbling honey. He slicked his cock along her clit and she gasped, "Oh yes!" Then she gave a desperate moan that made his cock jerk and his balls contract.

He lifted her leg, touching satin-soft skin, aware she wore her stockings and garters. The gossamer white silk against her ivory skin was erotic, but need hit him so hard he wanted to rip the pretty fabric with his teeth.

He'd never tumbled with a woman who wasn't experienced, boisterous, and willing to give as good as she got. He still bore scars from fierce fingernails and tearing teeth and he liked a woman hammering her heels into his arse.

Tensing, he tightened his grip on his cock. *Control, man. She's precious and you have to make this good.*

Miss Grace Hamilton moaned as he slowly thrust into her, his buttocks tight, his legs and arms stiff with the force of restraint. Beneath him, she wrapped her free leg around his hips, snaked her arms around his neck, and rose to him with a fevered cry of pleasure.

God.

Her hips worked, rising and falling to slick her snug cunny along his shaft. Artless, eager, exquisitely beautiful—she was a treasure a man like him did not deserve. Bracketing his arm around her head, he captured her lips as he slowly thrust in and drew out. A soft whimper spilled into his mouth as he sank into her to the hilt. She surprised him by kissing him hungrily, dueling her tongue with his.

"Harder," she whispered against his mouth. "I like this, but I want you deeper. Harder."

His control shattered. Arching forward, he plunged into her, plundering her mouth and pinching her nipple, rolling it to give her pleasure. He surged in and out, riding high. The slap of his chest against her breasts drove him mad. The slick heat of her pussy milking his cock had him on the brink of explosion.

Her fingernails sank into his shoulders.

Make her come. Make her. Do it for her.

Shifting his angle, he worked until she cried out in shock against his mouth. He slipped his hand beneath her, and found her snug anus with his fingertips. Stroking her sensitive place inside her pussy, teasing her nipple, tickling her rump, he hung on until he took Grace to the brink.

"What—?" Her eyes opened wide, searching his, both alight and confused.

Captured by their sparkling green depths, he murmured, "You're going to come. I'm going to make you come."

"It feels like heaven. Like whipped cream and sugar and better than any sin I've ever indulged in." She moaned and her moan was both sweet and fierce.

He'd never felt so connected with a woman while making love. Staring at her beautiful flushed face, he kept pumping, teasing, stroking—

"Oh! Oh God!" Her head lolled back; then her body arched beneath him. Her cunny clutched his cock, hugged it, pulsed around it.

Like a battering wave, his orgasm rose, flooding his brain, and he almost cried out, caught himself on the brink, and sank his teeth into the silky pillow beside her head. Groaning into it, he joined her in ecstasy, pumping his burning semen into her fluttering quim.

God.

"It was glorious," Grace whispered. "Perfect. Amazing. Magnificent."

Devlin, her highwayman, gave a gravelly laugh and snuggled into her side. This was an intimacy she'd never imagined—being cuddled by a powerful naked man while her heart still hammered and her body felt as though she floated on velvet clouds.

Beneath her sweat-slicked body, her sheets were a jumble, reminding her of how wild she'd been. Regret speared her suddenly—she had made a private vow to put aside her impetuous behavior and act like a lady for the sake of her family.

And now she lay, sighing with pleasure, beside a naked highwayman.

Muscular and strong, his arm cradled her protectively, just below her breasts. "What is wrong, love?"

She shook her head, blinking tears. She had started thinking again and now she could not stop. What had she done? Her behavior was scandalous. This was how her wild, bohemian father would behave. Self-indulgent, her mother had called it.

Fighting tears, she whispered, "My family has no money. We will end up in a workhouse. I was going to marry well. I was going to save us all."

Devlin's lips nuzzled her neck but she pulled away.

"I'd marry you, love, but it would scandalize you and destroy your reputation."

I'd marry you.

His words struck her mute. She had never expected he would even consider marriage.

Devlin rolled up onto his side. Tangled and free, his hair rippled to his shoulders. His eyes sparkled. "No doubt I don't have long for this world—someone will run me through or get a noose around my neck. If you were my wife, you would inherit a bloody fortune—but I fear it would put you at too much risk."

Did he feel he *owed* her an offer? Hastily, she said, "I wouldn't want to marry you."

He cupped her bare breast and teased her shoulder with his tongue before murmuring against her ear, "If you're in trouble, Grace, I'd like to help you. How much do you need?"

She jerked away. "Pay me? You want to pay me? As though I'm a mistress? Or a courtesan?"

A voice in her head screamed, *Take it! Take it. Your family is going to starve. You must say yes.*

What was wrong with her? How could she want to say yes to being paid like a prostitute?

What shocked her was not his offer. What shocked her was that she wanted to say yes.

"It's not payment, love. It's a noble use for my ill-gotten gains. I stole this money, sweetheart. From gentlemen who gamble away fortunes, who drink a king's ransom in brandy, who lavishly give diamonds to whores. Giving it to you is the right thing to do. Can you not see that?"

She struggled to sit up and fought to cover herself with a sheet. "Accepting it is not the right thing to do."

"For God's sake. It might be more noble to starve, but it's insanity. You need the money. You deserve the money."

What else would he think of her? She'd gone from one man's bed to another's, within hours! She slid off the edge of the bed, pulling enough white sheet to cover her. "Why are men so blasted . . . cruel after making love?"

In the silence that stretched, while her silver-tongued pirate gaped at her in surprise, she thought of a painting of her father's she had once seen but had not understood. A gentleman, a peer on bended knee, pursuing a lady, kissing the lady's hand while she turned away and tried to resist. And then, after the lovemaking, the undressed and disheveled lady was clinging to the peer while he tugged on his trousers and tried to escape.

Devlin wanted to help her, but he was offering her money because he'd shared her bed.

It wasn't that she'd expected anything. She hadn't. But he'd discounted her just as Lord Wesley had done. Not as cruelly, but it hurt.

Wesley had wanted to insult her and forget about her.

Mr. Sharpe wanted to pay her and forget about her.

He reached for her, but she stepped back, almost tripping over the sheet.

"Grace."

"You can leave with your purse intact, Mr. Sharpe. All I wanted from you was—" What? Excitement? Better memories?

Now, she wasn't certain.

"I only want to help you, Grace. How can that be wrong? How can that hurt you?" He raked his hair back. "Damn it, I don't understand. What bloody crime did I commit?"

This time she could not run away. Not from her own bedroom without a stitch of clothing on.

The mattress creaked as he jumped to the floor. He stalked toward his clothes. "I'll go, Grace, because I won't hurt you or scare you by staying. But this is not over, love. It wasn't my intention to make you angry or hurt you."

She turned away as he flung on his clothes—most of them, at least.

Her heart had been broken again. The hurt she'd hoped to erase burned even stronger within her, a hot ache around her heart.

She had turned to Mr. Sharpe, certain her heart would not be engaged, but the minute she'd tumbled into intimacy with him, she'd let herself fall in love. Well, not exactly love . . . a hope, a need for connection, a want for partnership.

Now she knew—she couldn't make love without involving her heart. It was as simple as that.

The moment her bedroom door shut with a click, she was no longer sure why she'd driven Devlin Sharpe away.

4

"Grace, whatever are you doing?"

Grace started guilty, caught in the act of sneaking away by her best friend. There could obviously be no other reason to be lurking beside a carriage on the front drive immediately after breakfast. Though her cheeks flushed with instant warmth, she prayed her shame was not obvious as she turned to face Lady Prudence. Dressed in a fur-trimmed velvet pelisse of sky blue, Prudence looked both lovely and distinctly hurt as she hurried down the sweeping staircase to the gravel drive. Overhead, the sky, as though sensing Grace's mood, was strewn with dark gray clouds.

Out of breath, Lady Prudence reached her side.

Light drizzle began to fall, cold and reproachful as it struck Grace's cheeks.

"Are you leaving?" Large gray-blue eyes met hers, revealing Prudence's frank astonishment.

Grace plucked at the skirt of her dull gray traveling pelisse. The gray ribbons of her worn hat fluttered across her face in the cool, damp breeze as rain pelted her cheeks. "I think I should, Lady Prudence." How did she even begin to explain?

Her friend's lips turned down. "Why? Why would you leave without telling me?"

Grace took a fortifying breath as two footmen brought her small traveling trunks outside. One servant hastily followed with an umbrella for her ladyship, but, as Grace sought words that would tactfully explain how gloriously she'd ruined herself, Prudence fixed her with a look of horror. "It is true, isn't it? You made a fool of yourself with my brother."

Well, she had, but the censure in her friend's tone surprised her. Aware of the footman holding the open brolly, Grace said, "Errr . . ."

Prudence snatched the umbrella and held it above her head, letting the rain drip off onto Grace. "We will have to walk a bit, to where they cannot overhear."

In those few yards that Grace walked at her friend's side in silence, she made a decision. She'd intended to lie about the offer of marriage, but now she knew she would not. Why protect Lord Wesley? Yes, Prudence had warned her about him, but Grace had never expected a gentleman to make an offer and then retract it.

Lady Prudence stopped at the end of the south wing and arched a brow.

Grace folded her arms across her chest. "Your brother promised me marriage," she said flatly. "He offered marriage and then he wanted to . . ." How was it always so delicately put? "Anticipate the wedding."

"Oh goodness. You truly did it . . ." Prudence abruptly dropped her arm and backed away. She tipped her chin up and looked down her nose. "You truly thought my brother would marry *you?*"

Shock held Grace motionless on the gravel drive. "Of course I did. He made an offer. He asked me to marry him and he asked me to say 'yes.' And I did. I *accepted* before I—"

"Even if he actually had made an offer, you had no right to accept! Of course he did not mean it. You had to know it was only to get under your skirts. Of course it meant nothing to him." Prudence's lip curled. "You, the future Marchioness of Rydermere?"

Grace was held stunned, like a beetle caught in amber.

She'd thought Prudence was hurt she was sneaking away. She felt her lips part uselessly.

Prudence's harsh words were like a knife blade to her heart. "You are nothing but a wanton tart! And my brother never said he *made* an offer."

"I was not a wanton tart or a liar," Grace answered. Anger had blown away shock. She was completely fed up. "I was your brother's lover," she hissed, "and I am no different a person than I was as a virgin! I am not mean or spiteful. I am not suddenly cruel or vicious or without a shred of kindness."

"Wesley wished to have you removed from the house immediately since you are hardly fit to be an acquaintance of mine."

"He needn't worry. I am leaving." Lord Wesley really was a swine. He was a liar, a scoundrel, a thoroughly cold-hearted, evil snake, and *he* wanted *her* ejected from the house? But he was a man and it was quite socially acceptable for him to be a snake. And she was a woman who should be condemned for believing a gentleman's word.

Lady Prudence's angry voice caught her attention. "I thought you would at least have the decency," she was saying, "to beg my forgiveness."

Her friend no longer looked like a friend. Prudence looked every inch the arrogant lady, and Grace bit her tongue. By adhering to her mother's story that her father was respectable and her parents were legally wed, she *had* lied to Prudence. She had used a false story to enter a world in which she didn't belong, lying all the while to a woman who had honestly wished to be her friend.

In her heart, she did not believe that making love without marriage made her an evil woman, but in the eyes of Prudence's world it did.

She wanted to turn and run to her modest carriage, run away without a word, and let the tears come, but she tried to stand as straight as a lady should.

"I would not think of begging for your forgiveness," Grace said firmly, "but I do owe you an apology." For what, though, really? For simply wanting to be a friend? For being a human woman, foolish enough to lose her heart? But she quelled the burning need to defend herself and said, "I am sorry."

Turning abruptly, not meeting her friend's haughty eyes, Grace walked away from Lady Prudence and out into the rain.

Prudence said nothing, and Grace did not turn back. It was humiliating to be striding through the rain. But humiliation was an emotion she would come to know well very soon. This was just a taste and soon she would have it rammed down her throat.

In weeks, Prudence, her former friend, would be in London, Grace thought as she reached the waiting carriage and the carefully impassive servants. Would Prudence join in the gossip that was certain to erupt when Wesley spread his tales?

Mr. Sharpe promised he had Wesley under his control, but Wesley was a peer of the realm. And a damned arrogant one. Why would he obey Mr. Sharpe?

As she stopped at the side of the carriage, she could not resist—she began to turn, to look for Prudence. Her hand trembled. What would happen in London? Would Prudence even admit to being her friend, or would she deny it?

But as she twisted her head, she saw nothing but the empty drive. Without a word, Prudence had gone.

The liveried footman reached Grace with Lord Wesley's message before she stepped up into the simple black carriage.

"From Lord Wesley, Miss," the young servant said.

Had he actually put his gloating to paper? Could it be an apology?

Irritated at the flare of warm hope in her heart, Grace unfolded the simple page. A summons to meet him at the summerhouse—the lovely stone building that sat upon a land-scaped hill overlooking the garden.

Only a fool—or a glutton for punishment—would go.

But she had to know what he was going to say. Her future depended on it.

"Have the carriage wait," she instructed the footman. Lifting the hems of her skirts, she crossed the drive to the narrow path that wound through the famed gardens of Collingsworth and led to the stone steps ascending to the summerhouse.

Perhaps a quarter of an hour had passed, and her heart fluttered in her chest as she reached the marble portico. Where was Wesley? Inside? Or had he not come? Had he made an idiot of her one more time?

"Come in, Miss Hamilton."

The bold, arrogant drawl drifted out of the open doorway. The lazy, sinfully aristocratic voice had once enticed her—now it set her teeth on edge. But she pushed open the door and stepped within.

This was a summerhouse?

With the luxurious padded benches, inviting chairs, and exquisite carvings and paintings, it was more beautiful than Grace's home. Wesley lounged on a chaise, one booted foot braced against the floor, the other marring the taupe silk of the seat. His greatcoat was flung open; his snug-fitting buff trousers and dark waistcoat gave him the immaculate look of a gentleman in the country.

A grin revealed dimples—just like Devlin Sharpe's. His eyes glinted with wickedness. But she read more than lust there. It was power that excited him and it sickened her.

He crooked his fingers, but she ignored the summons.

Pulling off his beaver hat with one hand, he raked back his fair, straight hair with the other. "Ah Grace, I do not want to leave you in trouble. Prudence has hinted that your family is in dire straits."

She crossed her arms beneath her breasts and of course he looked there. "I am perfectly fine, my lord."

"You aren't. And I'm sorry for hurting your feelings, but truly, love, what did you expect?"

Hurting her feelings? He had called her a whore; he had laughed at her! He'd broken her heart for a wager, had threatened her with ruination. How hard it was to be cold with him when hot anger raged! "I did not expect anything of you, my lord. But you did promise marriage."

He swung his other foot to the smooth floor of white marble veined with glittering black. "But you knew I couldn't marry one such as you."

"No." *And thank heaven for me,* she thought.

"But I have a proposition, my saucy lover. A most generous offer."

Absolute confidence shone from his blue eyes, as though he believed she was holding her breath, waiting on his every word.

"I do not wish to hear it." She turned and walked out. The last sound she heard was a startled, 'bloody hell'; then she ran down the wide steps, wearing a grin. Not much of a victory, but something. Lord Wesley was apparently not accustomed to being discounted.

But Wesley caught up to her by a grove of apple trees—she heard the harsh expulsion of his breath before he grasped her by the elbow. His fingers dug in, forcing her to stop.

Gritting her teeth, she swung around. "Let me go."

"You haven't heard my proposition yet, you little fool." He backed her against a tree—branches ripe with early buds surrounded her. One brushed against her cheek, drawing a fine scratch. Lord Wesley leaned his arm above her head, effectively trapping her.

A predatory smile curved his lips. "I want you to become my mistress. I'll keep you in London. I'll rent you a house, buy you pretty clothes to show off those lovely tits, drape your neck in jewels. And I will visit you now and again, my love, and tutor you in erotic arts."

Flabbergasted, Grace could find no rejoinder. And Wesley

bent forward, waiting with his lips mere inches from hers, obviously certain she would cry, "Yes, yes, yes!"

She would like to plant her hands on his chest and shove him back but refused to even touch him for that. She clenched her fists, certain her fingernails were cutting through her cotton gloves. "Why would you make me such an offer? Was I not just one on your list of conquests for a wager?"

"I want you. For your beauty. For your spicy lovemaking."

"I'd starve before I ever accepted an offer from you."

"Now is a very foolish time for pride, Grace."

"Perhaps, but I could not swallow it now without choking on it. Being with you tends to make things want to come up."

He jerked back. "Stupid witch." He spun away and stormed off down the narrow path until he vanished around a bend, and his golden hair, beaver hat, and immaculate greatcoat disappeared.

A familiar protective growl startled her. "What did he say to you, Grace?"

Devlin strode to Grace, who stood with her back to a gnarled apple tree, her hands behind her, her head tipped back against the bark. This had to be a highwayman's fantasy—finding a beautiful, gently bred lady alone in the woods, one who possessed a perfect face worth swinging for and a voluptuous body that was carnal temptation personified.

But for the first time in his life, Devlin felt guilty over focusing on a woman's sexual attributes. He liked Grace Hamilton. "What did he say?" he repeated. "If Wesley insulted you, I will—"

She turned, treating him to the pink flush in her cheeks and the sparks of tempestuous anger in her green eyes. "Spank him again? Perhaps he enjoys it," she muttered.

Feisty, still. But he could not for the life of him understand why she had followed Wesley out here.

"Tell me what he said, Grace."

She would not look at him. Offended or hurt, he couldn't tell.

For a moment, she chewed the thumb of her white cotton glove. Then she groaned, a very unladylike sound, and, like her snorting laughter, this charmed him too.

"Lord Wesley made a very generous offer. A house in London, enough jewels to choke me, and lessons in lovemaking from the master."

"Did you accept?"

Without looking to him, without a word, she began to stalk away.

Blast, what had he done now? He'd asked a simple question; she was in trouble, she might have accepted. "Grace, stop."

Even his dangerous tone had no effect on Grace. She reached the first set of steps cut into the rock of the ridge and was hurrying down, skirts in her hands. The wind that hurtled over the ridge ripped at those skirts and threatened to steal her hat. Bare branches swooped toward her, and the gray clouds seemed to press closer as though drawn by her fire and heat.

Damnation.

She had stood there and listened to the twaddle his bloody titled brother had fed her, but she ran away from him.

He would not stand for it.

All he wanted to do was help her.

Heedless of the wet rock, he took the steps three at a time. She reached the small terraced plateau before he caught her.

Not there. He was not about to have a confrontation in this place—so he scooped her into his arms. She squealed and pushed against his biceps. "Don't struggle, love. If I drop you here, you'll roll down the steps."

God, she was a delicious weight in his arms. Her lush bottom rested against his forearm and his hand splayed over her shapely back. Instead of taking the path down, he took a narrow track away from the edge of the ridge and found his father's folly. Bushes now obscured the path, but the branches were only budding and the white columns and oriental roof peeked through.

Slowly, Grace slid her hands up to his shoulders and held on as she twisted in his arms. "What is this?"

"Where I was conceived," he said with wry humor.

Pushing open the door with his boot, he gave a sigh. The daybed cushions bore stains and mildew, and dirt and dust coated everything. "Apparently my father hasn't been trysting with the same regularity he used to."

"You are not taking me in there. It was bad enough that I went to the summerhouse at his lordship's summons—I will not be carried in against my will."

Her breath brushed his face, warm and sweet.

"Is it against your will, Grace? Is that the truth?"

God, but her scent drove him mad. Rock hard, aroused to the point he could barely think, he refused to press his interests. He was not going to seduce her. He was not going to act like his damned brother.

"You thought I would be willing to become his mistress. After what he did. What he said. You think nothing of me— of course, you don't—"

Putting her on her feet stopped her words. He touched his thumb to her lips in the doorway of the once sumptuous room where a hundred women had fallen in love with his randy father. Even through the leather of his glove, he caught his breath at the softness of her mouth, the sheer velvet perfection of those rose-pink lips. "I was afraid you felt forced to accept, love."

Her breath hitched—he heard it—and she brushed a soft kiss to his black gloved thumb. "I turned down your offer, Mr. Sharpe. I would never accept his."

Grace could not believe she said the words with such a steady voice. Mr. Sharpe's magnetic blue eyes held her with far more power than Lord Wesley's intimating stance. She could not look away—his sapphire blue irises appeared rimmed with a thin circle of violet, unusual and arresting.

They were alone and it would be so very easy to touch him. Everywhere. His chest. His shoulders. If she wished, she could reach down with both hands and greedily explore the hard length of his cock.

Mystified, she looked up into his blue eyes again. They'd shared one night and it felt as though all barriers had dropped away. But then he knew more about her than anyone. He knew she was capable of going to a man's bed with a broken heart, desperately searching for . . . for hope, she realized.

Was that it? Hope that she had not lost everything with one stupid mistake? Hope that she could still be desired for who she was? Confused, she blinked, now aware that she had no idea what she had wanted from making love with Devlin Sharpe, except a few fleeting moments of connection.

But they had a connection now. It was undeniable.

"I want you, Grace."

His voice was molten sin, his lips smiling in conspiracy as though he could read her very thoughts.

Perhaps he could. Perhaps she was that transparent. Lust showed. Desire showed. She'd spent years trying to be proper—to be from her mother's world, not her father's—and she'd thrown it all away in one night.

The instant his knuckles skimmed her cheek with tantalizing pressure, she tipped her head back, shut her eyes, and moaned. Lazily, his fingers stroked back and forth, and suddenly all she could think of was her quim. How hot she suddenly was. How tight and tingly she felt. She swallowed hard and touched him in return.

Cupping her palm, she cradled his strong chin, the sort of chin that promised strength a woman could rely upon. Firm, slightly squared, a slight cleft in the middle. Smoother than it had been. Devlin . . . Mr. Sharpe had shaved this morning.

Where had he slept? In the house, where he was not accepted? He looked far too immaculate and clean and perfect to have slept rough. Where would he find a bed?

A parching tightness claimed her throat. Men who had no bed often seduced their way into a woman's, as a way to have a roof over their heads, a fire to warm them, and a willing companion to entertain.

He was a highwayman—a man who thought himself above the king's laws. Why should it surprise her that he might have spent the rest of the night with another woman? He knew she had been with Wesley before him and he did not care.

Oh God—had he only slept with her because he'd hoped to spend the night in her bed?

Brushing her lips, his fingers unleashed fireworks in her chest. "Don't think, Grace. I can see it in your eyes. You are thinking too much." He pressed a small, quick kiss to the tip of her nose.

"Where did you sleep last night?"

"I've a room at the local inn."

"Alone?" The word spilled out before she could stop it and she jerked back from his caress, ashamed she had shown how vulnerable she was. But she could not stop *thinking*.

"Alone."

"Why?" She could think of so many reasons. *It was too late to find a woman. None took his fancy. All were in other men's beds.*

His broad chest lifted on a deep breath, and he gripped the doorjamb tightly. Was he frustrated by her prying question, frustrated to waste the time on a lie? Did women bother to question him—or was that the point at which the pursuit lost its allure? That was apparently the way it worked for men, or so she had seen. At dances, she had seen the quick, desperate look that mounted in a man's eyes when a woman began to show her possessiveness.

He leaned over her, so tall that she had to tip her head right back to watch his eyes for a glimpse of his true emotions. "I didn't want anyone else, so I lay awake all night and thought about you."

An enigmatic answer that told her nothing. His eyes were far too carefully shuttered to reveal a thing. He'd bluffed the Navy, for heaven's sake, and surely more than a few magistrates. How vain she'd been to think she could see through his words. "What did you think about me?"

"A lot of very naughty thoughts. Would you like to hear them?"

"No!"

"I think you would." His dimple winked, and she saw his chest move as he visibly relaxed. "Why don't you undress me while I tell you?"

It was as though an entirely different man had taken possession of this beautiful, broad body. Even his voice had changed—it had been a gruff growl when he'd admitted to thinking about her. Now it was a deep, sensual purr, as though he'd relaxed into the role of unrepentant rake.

She made no move to obey and strip him. He took a step forward, and his sheer size forced her to take one back. The door had only just clicked shut behind him when he sank to his knees in front of her.

Frank, yet playful, his dancing blue eyes teased. "I thought about this—about lifting your skirts in a public place, a place I should never dare take such a liberty."

"This is not a public place. Not exactly."

"In June, her ladyship used to hold an al fresco luncheon, an annual tradition. Imagine we are there. Imagine that I found you there, and I turned your chair away from the table, much to the shock of all the gentle guests. Without a word I drop to my knees on the soft grass and I lift your skirts to your hips, just like this—"

Winking, he grasped her hems and pushed up the weight of her sturdy wool skirts and the white petticoats beneath.

Cool air brushed her thighs, a sharp and exciting contrast to the heat of her body.

"The whole world is going to know how much I desire you, how damned tempting you are."

"I wouldn't—" She was caught up in imagining, until she thought of all the guests looking as condescending and judgmental and angry as Prudence. "Of course you could do that. You are a highwayman—and a man—so you can get away with anything."

"And with me as your champion so could you, Grace." He bent and touched his mouth to her drawers, letting his tongue touch the fabric and his hot breath slide through. He opened the lace-trimmed slit and buried his face there, and she almost jumped. His tongue slicked all over her quim, bathing her with pleasure, tasting her most intimate flavors.

"I would sit you up on the table like the sweet, sumptuous dessert you are, and eat you this way. And all I would care about is tasting you and pleasing you. And all you would want is to come on my face."

He flicked her clitoris with his tongue and sensation streaked through her. Her legs shook, her muscles straining, and she drove her fingers into his hard, wide shoulders. Wet, hot, so shockingly intimate, his tongue circled, stroking the side; then he twirled its tip against the very top of her clitoris and she screamed, "Mr. Sharpe!"

"Devlin," he murmured against her sticky nether lips. Then his lips played on the swollen, throbbing nub, his teeth grazed it, and she pumped against his mouth and sobbed.

He stopped again and she suddenly found her fists punching his shoulders. "Oh don't . . . don't."

Feasting on her cunny had mussed his hair, and the dark honey-colored locks tumbled over his eyes. Eyes that gleamed with delight at her desperate plea. "I want to learn what delights you, what thrills you, what you fear to try . . . I want to learn how to make you come."

Learn? He spoke as though it took a long time. As though there were lessons. She would be going away today. This was her last time with him . . . her last chance to look into his mesmerizing eyes and share sighs and moans and laughter.

There was nothing to learn about her. She would be gone.

With a low chuckle, he teased her nether lips with his tongue and gently touched his finger to her juicy entrance. She was so wet his fingers filled her. He thrust them in and out and she moaned over and over. Whimpered when he moved his fingers away.

His big hands closed on her derriere and pulled her to his face. He rocked her and she found her rhythm, stroking her clit against his hot, raspy tongue over and over. Stars burst behind her lids and she could barely suck in breath for moaning.

She was grinding on him, but he worked his mouth against her and she gave her body to the tension coiling inside—

He drew back and she surged forward. He wanted to leave her there, on the brink, but she couldn't—

Even as his mouth drew back, her orgasm burst inside. She couldn't stop it. Her body seemed to melt into a puddle of molten cream, and she flowed all over his face, crying his name. Sobbing with thrilling delight. Moaning and moaning until her lungs were empty, her throat was dry, and she was certain that if she spread her arms, she'd fly.

She collapsed but he was there, lowering her into his embrace. Her salty, ripe, erotic taste teased her lips as he kissed her. He kissed her hard and passionately, and she was a boneless, silken, languorous puddle held in his arms.

"Grace, love—" Husky, raw, his voice washed over her.

"I thought," Grace whispered. "I thought I wanted memories that would keep me happy when I went to bed alone—"

Devlin felt Grace change in his arms from a melting, well-pleasured woman to a stiff and awkward lady in an instant.

Brushing back unruly strands of her pure gold hair with a jerky motion of her pretty hand, she gazed up at him.

Rigid, thick, swollen to the limits of its skin, his cock was pulsing, and desire and lust and need nagged in his head, harder to ignore than cannon fire. Her head had dipped and he licked his lips, savoring the taste of her wet, hot, fragrant quim. He doubted his selfish half brother had done that to her.

He bent to capture her lips again. It would be better if they did not speak, but she shook her head. "I want—"

She pulled from his embrace, tugged down her skirts. "Oh, but I was wrong. So very, very wrong. These memories are much worse than those of Wesley! These make me hot and frustrated. They will make me yearn."

He couldn't help the surge of pride. The bloody grin that came to his lips.

She glanced up. "You would smirk, wouldn't you?"

"I like to hear that I pleased you, Grace." Her curls fell about her neck, and he brushed them aside to put his lips to her damp throat. He had not had enough time with Grace.

He wanted days with her. Weeks with her.

With a shudder that went to his soul, he remembered the last time he had been unable to live without a woman. What a bloody mistake that had been.

Grace pulled away, stealing her luscious vanilla-scented skin from his hungry mouth. "You did," she muttered. "How you must know that you did."

"I am your champion, Grace, and my world is about sexual pleasure. Free, unfettered carnal exploration. Anything you desire, any way you wish—no judgment, no pain."

"For you perhaps. It would never be that way for me." She shut her eyes and groaned. "And my coach was waiting to leave! What will they think?"

Skimming his hand up, he pushed up heavy skirts and lace-trimmed petticoats. Grazing his thumb lazily around her quim, he said, "With me as your champion, Grace, you do not have to worry."

"But you cannot be my champion, Mr. Sharpe. I can never see you again."

5

August 1820, Near Brighton

"Wake up, Devlin, darlin', I'm feeling randy."
Devlin grunted, rolled over, and tried to ignore the
pouting female purr and get back to his dream—he had been
at a picnic, laid out on his stomach on a plaid rug, devouring
Grace Hamilton's juicy pussy under her frothy skirts. But
even pulling the pillow over his head did not help. His dream
was gone, so he shoved the pillow aside and cracked open an
eye to be greeted by plump breasts and doe-brown nipples.

Lucy leaned over him, bosom swaying, and gave a wriggle
of frustration. "Hurry up, Dev. I'm about to pop, and then
ye'll miss all the fun."

"If he won't wake up," cried another feminine voice, "we
could tie him up and take advantage of him. With our clever
mouths, he couldn't resist for long."

Lucy twisted on his bed and the morning light cast a gold
sheen along the sloping profile of her breast. "Hush, Bess,
why should he want to resist?"

Beneath his lashes, Devlin saw Bess sashay into his bedchamber. Her dark curls were loose and fell over her bare
breasts, but she quickly pushed back her demure hair and
thrust her lush tits forward. As usual her nipples were rouged
and he wondered which of his men had done that for her.

Bess shrugged. "He's still obsessed with that hoity-toity girl he can't have, of course. But I've got a few lengths of rope with me, and I think we could finally make him forget her."

"I've no need of rope to capture a man's interest."

Lucy's tone was playful, but he heard the winsome note behind it. Devlin knew she no longer went to the beds of the other men—she waited for him. And that was a bloody bad sign.

She yanked down his sheets before he could catch them. She bent her head and he sucked in a harsh breath as her auburn hair cascaded across his naked stomach. Rigid from his dream, his cock bounced up for attention and his moistening juices leaked out into the hair around his navel.

It was physical need, and he'd buried himself in purely physical lust for two years. That and taking a few mad risks that had resulted in bullet wounds to both shoulders. The bullet that almost hit him in the thigh had proved too damned close for comfort, though. A reminder he was a fool to take risks while his thoughts centered on Grace Hamilton.

Lucy's tongue flicked skillfully over the head of his cock, and his juice bubbled out in response. Devlin groaned as his balls clenched tight and arousal shot hot and harsh through his body. His cock wanted to get slick and plunge into a willing woman, but his head and heart didn't want to join in the fun.

Her mouth opened wide, and, before his eyes, his rigid prick vanished between lush pink lips. Lord, her mouth was hot fire, snug and loving around his shaft. Her tongue cradled his cock and dragged a growl from his throat.

"No, lass." Devlin reached for Lucy's bobbing head. Like any man, he loved to fuck a woman's face and loved a woman who let him thrust hard, but right now, despite his raging erection, he was not in the mood for physical oblivion.

Hell, he wasn't even masturbating to take the edge off. He was beginning to enjoy the pain.

Bess began twining black ropes around her large, bouncing breasts and he gritted his teeth. He shot up in the bed. "Not now, ladies. Go find one of the others."

"They're all exhausted," Bess muttered.

Wrapping his sheet around his hips as he swung around, Devlin got to his feet. "Even Nick? He's never sated."

"He was jug shot last night and now he thinks he'll die if he even opens his eyes to the sunlight," Bess complained as she roughly rubbed the rope against her hard nipples. "Now, look at yer prick, Dev. Hard as a tree limb and weeping like a waterfall. Ye need to have a good, hard ride, Captain, and I'd be happy to ride ye until ye burst."

From where he stood, with the sheet jutting out over his rigid cock like a white flag, Devlin could see over the fields leading to his manor house. A lone horseman drove a black gelding hard. The rider's coat flew out behind him like wings.

Horatio. And the way he flowed with the galloping horse over a hedge told Devlin one thing.

Grace was on her way.

Slender arms slid around his naked chest from behind. Lucy's flowery perfume rose to his nose. "What is it, Dev? Why could we not just 'ave some fun, like we've always done?"

"Not today, love. I've a jape to do."

"In daylight?"

"Ye'll get caught, ye stupid bugger!" Bess flopped back onto his tousled bed. Wearing a bold smile, she stroked the frayed end of the rope over her glistening quim.

She was tempting and she knew it.

Lucy darted around to his front, with her arms clasped around him. Her breasts brushed along his side, the hard nipples tracing a line that made the hairs on his nape stand on end and his cock jerk. She faced him and looked him in the eye. Hell, she was a pet. A sweet thing, with unruly red hair, an endearing spray of freckles, and blue eyes that blinked beneath thick gold lashes. Normally those eyes were saucy, and Lucy was on the lookout for her next erotic adventure.

Devlin took a step back, almost stumbling over the sheet.

Lucy looked scared. For him? The fear in her expressive eyes wasn't the kind of fear that meant she was worried she'd lose the roof over her head if he were clapped in Newgate.

She was afraid to lose him.

"Not to worry, ladies," he reassured. "Now I've got to get dressed."

"Let me help." Lucy gave his nipples a naughty tweak.

The bed creaked. He glanced to the side, intending to suggest to Bess, who kneeled on his bed, that she take Lucy off to find one of the other men. There were six, for Hades' sake. Surely one was able to service a pair of lusty women.

But Bess had her arms folded across her chest and eyed him like a governess who'd just caught him with his trousers down in the act of ruining his eyesight. " 'As this got somethin' to do wi' 'er?"

Christ Jesus, who was in charge here? "I've got a coach to rob, ladies, and I need to pull on my trousers and concentrate. So, both of you, hurry your luscious arses out the door."

Bess stomped out the door, trailing her ropes. Lucy hesitated and turned back. "Dev, we've been together a long time now, 'aven't we."

He put on a grin that had melted most women he'd met. "You aren't planning to propose, are you, Lucy?"

She gave a quick shake of her head but the wistful light in her eyes tore at his heart. "Course not, Dev. But I'm worried about ye. Ye've been acting right odd of late. It's not really about some woman ye haven't seen for two years, is it?"

"There comes a time in every man's life when he begins to act like a blooming idiot, and it's my time now, love."

She frowned. "That's not an answer, Captain Devlin Sharpe." Slowly, Lucy let her pretty ivory hand fall from the doorjamb. Her lips turned down and gave a quiver that almost made him take a step toward her. Cursing below his breath, he stood his ground. He had no right to make any promises—even wordless ones—that he could not keep. Waiting, her breasts lifting with a deep, hopeful breath, Lucy finally let her shoulders slump. But then she straightened, and he grinned, knowing she was determined to keep her pride. Radiating that pride, she walked out of his room.

His door shut with a click. A man's lusty laugh sounded through it, and Lucy gave a squeal—a damned convincing one for a girl who had apparently been wounded by his rejection.

He hoped she enjoyed herself.

In this house, women casually trotted about naked. There would likely be an orgy after breakfast.

He'd gambled on playing the highwayman on the well-traveled road leading into Brighton, where the ton retreated in the hot summer months. The climate suited him and the risk was high, throwing him into challenges he enjoyed. He'd been able to have his men watch Grace, who was staying in Brighton with her sister Venetia.

He'd gambled that Grace would be traveling at some point—perhaps returning to London.

Horatio arriving at full gallop was a sign his gamble had paid off.

Was she traveling with just her sisters? One of her powerful brothers-in-law?

His men thought him insane. He probably was.

Lucy gave a loud, theatrical moan of pleasure from the other side of his door. Trying to torture him, he knew. Blood surged to his rigid cock in answer, but he was thinking of making Grace moan like that.

Devlin smashed his fist into the plaster wall as his sheet slid down his hips. Hell, he had a damn good life here. Why was it no longer enough?

My dearest granddaughter . . .

The elegant handwriting jiggled before Grace's eyes as the carriage wheel dropped into a rut. A wave of nausea rose as she focused on the words, clutching the seat to steady herself.

For so many years, I have wanted to write to you, to make myself known to you, but I could not. The earl would not hear of it. I believe it is foolish to keep only anger and resentment against one's heart for comfort, but there are those that believe it far more foolish to embrace forgiveness. Is not forgiveness only for those of great strength? But I have learned, in the decades that have passed, that anger may burn hot but it gives cold comfort.

Silver now graces my hair, and I have long since forgotten what it is to hold a child. It is in these days that I yearn less for the embittering satisfaction of being the one in the right, and more for the joy of seeing my eyes in a young woman's face, my smile in a girl's happiness.

Would you come to me, Grace? I wish to see you, while I am able. If you are willing to grant me this, to reunite, I warn that it cannot be done at my home. I wish to meet you where the past is not of significance, and where the future surrounds us. How tragic it is that a woman cannot meet her granddaughter in her rooms, but that is the madness of my life, and I long since learned to adapt and not battle. On the surface, it seems that I dare not defy the earl, but women do, in subtle ways, and it is so much more pleasant to keep peace.

Come to me for the 15th of August. Lord Avermere has invited me to his lovely house on the Isle of Wight, very near Cowes. I have made him aware of my wishes—and so you will be admitted and you may join me here. Such a dear man, Avermere has readily agreed. Please come, Grace. For I have

*seen you in London, and I have seen in you the
woman I once was, and I wish, so very much, to
know your mind and your heart, and to do so before it is too late.*

Yours,
Sophia Augusta, Countess of Warren
Directions follow below

Grace touched a smudge of ink. Had her grandmother's
tear made that smear of grayish ink? She wiped at her own
cheeks, brushing away the drops there. The pressure of her
thumbs had crinkled the paper and she carefully smoothed
the small creases. This was the letter she had yearned for
since her childhood.

It was worth every lie she had told to slip away from the
house Venetia and Marcus had taken in Brighton. And both
her sisters, Maryanne and Venetia, were so caught up in their
children and the social whirl of the seaside town they really
had not noticed her leave.

They thought she was off to visit Lady Prudence at a house
party close to Worthing. A lie, but they didn't know that Prudence despised her. Anyway, she was with the coachman and
a groom, so her sisters had no reason to worry over her.

Grace lifted the letter and cradled it in her hands.

Why didn't she just tell her sisters the truth?

Now that she was the sister-in-law to two both wealthy
and powerful titled men, she moved in a different world—she
lived in the world of the Countess of Warren. Three times she
had seen her grandmother: at Lady Chatsworth's musicale,
where she had seen how beautiful her grandmother still was,
with her upswept silver hair and patrician profile; then, at the
theatre, where Grace had been certain her grandmother had
turned her opera glasses onto Marcus's box and had searched
out a glimpse of her granddaughters; and once at Lady

Collings' ball, the most significant event of the Season for unmarried girls. For one fleeting moment, Grace had been certain her grandmother had smiled at her across the ballroom.
She'd blinked in surprise, only to find she had lost the moment, and her grandmother had risen and left.

And now the letter.

Each time she read it, a different emotion claimed her.
Hope. Fear. Happiness. Excitement. Sheer, unadulterated terror.

She was a Hamilton woman, and she had to keep up the
family tradition of meeting fear and terror head on.

Except, of course, for the fear of telling her plans to her
sisters.

Grace rapped the ceiling to signal the coachman—one of
Marcus's best—to pick up speed. Delays had plagued her, the
problem with creating a tissue of lies. First, Venetia had way-
laid her with questions; then Maryanne had bluntly asked
why she would be traveling to visit Lady Prudence when they
never appeared to even have a conversation in public.

But then both her sisters had become distracted by their
children. Maryanne's baby, Charles, proved a headstrong
soul plagued with colic, happy only when Maryanne's husband held him up on his broad shoulder. His poor lordship
could not even sit down without the baby wailing.

And Venetia had announced she was expecting another
child, with her first, the heir, only six months old, which of
course disproved the belief that feeding a child from the
breast might delay another pregnancy.

Something Grace would never experience.

The carriage rattled, jerking Grace back to the here and
now. They were traveling along a quiet stretch of roadway
and she settled back to fold her grandmother's letter. She had
it half tucked into her reticule when the carriage suddenly
skidded and the coachman shouted.

Her reticule spilled to the floor and Grace clung to the seat for dear life. The wheels slid across the dry dirt and the horses whinnied in shock. As the coach skidded in a circle, Grace caught her breath.

It was going to overturn!

She bit her lip, drawing blood, as the coach tilted to the right, then tottered back on the left wheels.

"Bleedin' Jesus!" the coachman roared, and the horses screamed in protest.

Rocking madly from one set of wheels to the other, the coach's movements threw Grace to the floor. Her knees banged the boards and the seat smacked her in the forehead.

She curled up into a ball, praying this would be the best way to fall, when the coach slammed back onto all four wheels and stayed blessedly still—well, relatively still.

Her fingers gouged into and tore expensive velvet as she pulled herself to her knees. "Ow!" The pressure on them made her want to vomit, so she struggled to get onto her feet, her arms splayed over the seat. Her head throbbed and she tasted blood on her lip.

What in blazes had happened?

Dazed, with her hand daintily pressed to her bruised head, she forced her wobbly legs to straighten. Grace gaped out the window, clutching the sill.

Marcus's grays pawed the ground and fought the confines of their traces, and she guessed the coachman held hard on the reins. The carriage was tilted across the road on the diagonal, and the window gave her a clear view of the lane ahead.

A white horse blocked the road. Atop the huge beast, a highwayman lounged, controlling the magnificent animal with his thighs and casually leveling two pistols at her carriage. He was masked, with a black silk square fashioned into a kerchief to cover his mouth and a powdered wig beneath a black tricorn. A long coat in the style of the last century stretched across wide shoulders and clung to a well-built chest—a coat of shimmering dark blue silk, lavishly embroidered and decorated with inches of French lace at cuffs and collar. Beneath the sun, its buttons sparkled, suggesting jewels, and a large, clear stone winked in the man's earlobe—a diamond earring, Grace guessed.

Didn't highwaymen shout "Stand and deliver" or some such thing? It appeared this one had merely cantered his horse in front of a racing carriage and pointed his two pistols at the driver, then waited, without flinching, for the carriage to stop.

A branch cracked. From beneath the shadows of the trees, four armed men rode out, all wearing the same hats and wigs, all with lace peeking out at their sleeves and throats, all with silk tied over their noses and mouths.

They rode to surround the carriage.

She wished she had thought to bring a pistol. Her sisters' adventures should have taught her that a woman most definitely needed to arm herself.

But could she really shoot that enormous man who had audaciously stopped their carriage? He had almost caused an accident—he could have killed them all. But to shoot him in cold blood—was she even capable?

Then Grace's blood turned cold and her heart seemed to freeze. A devil-may-care highwayman with broad shoulders, who was now tugging down the silk kerchief that covered his face. . . .

Even before the disguise dropped, she knew.

Devlin Sharpe.

With his mouth exposed, she knew at once she was right. Even after two years, she knew that dimple and the full, sensuous, primal shape of his mouth.

"Come down, sweetheart," he called out, clinching it with his deep unforgettable growl. "I'd like to see you."

His captivating voice played havoc with her heartbeat and her good sense and she found her hand at the door handle before her wits intervened.

What did he want?

Could this be a coincidence?

Did Devlin really mean to rob her?

His kerchief hung around his neck, and his face was darkly tanned, a startling contrast to that snow-white wig.

He looked like a dangerous rake of fantasy. But what on earth did he think he was doing?

"Come down, Miss," he called. "I'd hate for anyone to get a pistol ball in the heart."

"You wouldn't dare!" Grace pushed the door wide with one hand, hauling up her skirts with the other. It might not have been wise, but she jumped to the road, which was at least dry. So much so that choking dust swirled up as she landed, and she sputtered.

Leaving his other armed men, Devlin nudged his horse's flanks with his thighs and the enormous white steed obeyed his master's subtle command and paced toward where she stood.

Brilliant green eyes met hers. Sensual lips kicked up in a smile.

He had saved her—she would never forget that. Neither Lord Wesley nor her cousin Wynsome had ever breathed a word about what had happened at the house party. She did not know why he merely sat there atop his horse, towering over her, studying her.

And why he was here, robbing her at gunpoint? She'd never thought the man would presume on intimacy enough to hold her up!

It irritated her. So she pointed to the cases lashed to the back of the carriage. "I've barely any valuables with me. There is one pouch of jewels in my blue case—you are welcome to those."

The horse took a graceful step closer. A pure white beast, and she was surprised he did not use a black mount, one that would disappear at night in the shadows of the surrounding fields and forests. And why would he be foolish enough to hold her up in daylight?

Did he want to be caught and hung?

Now the horse stood so close she could smell its sweat and hair. She had to gaze up toward the sun to look at Devlin.

"I do not want your money, Grace." He bent to whisper the words, which startled her, for they were her words, thrown at him two years before. Did he feel as insulted by her offer as she had felt over his? Sunlight fell upon his face, slicing across his high cheekbones and blade of a nose. She had forgotten his exact features—she had forced herself to forget. Her heart gave a tiny thump. How long would it take to forget his face this time?

Her fingertips tingled. She remembered touching his face. The wonderful sensations of caressing him. She remembered exploring the solid ridge of his jaw, the teasing prickle of stubble growing there. The startling sharp ridges of his cheekbones and the softness of the skin below. The velvety caress of his brows and lashes—

She shook away those treacherous thoughts. "What do you want of me? I have somewhere to be today. You are delaying me. If you don't want my meager jewels, let me go past."

"Don't be so cold, my love." He spoke loudly now and he leered at her. She heard the snicker of his men. Marcus's servants stayed wisely silent, with pistols trained on them.

Obviously Devlin did not want anyone to know they knew each other. She would rather die than have these men know what they'd done.

One left his position to ride closer to Devlin. "Do ye want me to get her boxes?"

Devlin shook his head. "We'll take the entire coach."

He worked with thieves. With armed men willing to kill for money. He was not a champion, he was a lawless killer.

Fear, cold and paralyzing, flooded through Grace's body.

She had to run—

But had no chance of escaping the horses.

She had no weapon—

Would Devlin really be willing to kill her for money?

Grace froze completely. She didn't know. This was a man she had bedded, that she had lovingly, deliciously, willingly bedded . . . and she truly did not know.

She took a step back but he merely grinned. "You, my sweet, *are* the valuables."

She heard a cry of anger from the groom. What if one of Marcus's servants acted in desperation, thinking to save her, and got shot? What if she really was in danger?

No one was going to die in her place.

She aimed a fierce scowl at Devlin. "Touch me, rogue, and you will regret it."

"Cooperate, lass, and I won't harm a fragile hair on your precious head."

What would he do if she turned on her heel and stalked back into the carriage? She had no choice but to gaze deeply into his eyes, into the dark blue depths, and try to guess.

She did notice his quick breaths. The rapid rise and fall of his chest.

He was *excited* by this.

By what? The nearness to a ransom? Or memories of sweaty sex? What did he *want*?

She had to find courage. Two years had passed since she'd made a mess of her life—two years in which she had gone from being penniless to possessing a dowry that made men weak at the knees. She'd had the courage to live a lie with even her family. So, she leaned forward until her gloves touched the withers of his huge horse and vehemently whispered, "I do not want to play this game!"

His warm, strong arm snaked around her waist and he straightened, drawing her up with him. Without effort, he deposited her on the horse in front of him. Perched on the edge of her bottom on a lumpy bit of the horse's spine, she teetered.

And clutched at his chest.

Her fingers wrapped around his lapels and clung tight. "Put me—"

"Eventually, Grace. But for now, you're mine."

The servants shouted in protest, but Devlin dug in his spurs as he wheeled his horse around. Grace clutched tight to his arms as the horse flowed over the ground like a streaking bird, hooves thundering.

She was too scared to jump.

And too damned excited.

"Was it a coincidence that you chose my carriage to rob?"

Grace asked the question to the shadowy lane stretched out before her, knowing that Devlin would not answer. Why should he? He was the one with the weapon.

Devlin held her steady with one large hand cupping her waist. His chest brushed against her back and the hard diamond buttons were a caress even through her summer dress and gauzy pelisse. His scent drove her mad—she'd endured over an hour of breathing it in. An hour trying to fight the memories. How his skin tasted when she'd slicked her tongue over it. The erotic flavor of his mouth.

The way his sweat smelled and the ripe, potent, tang of his come . . .

Her rump and thighs hurt from the constant bumping of the horse—for all Devlin had seductively suggested she relax, she still perched on his horse as stiff as a board. Dappled shadows danced over her sprigged clothes and his gloved hand as Devlin walked his horse along a country lane. Overhead, the tree branches knitted together, and leaves whispered in the hot breeze.

Grace had stolen peeks at her sister Maryanne's manuscripts—she'd been surprised to discover her sister also wrote erotic stories and had tried to help their impoverished family by publishing them.

One story had intrigued her and she'd read it again and again, until the copy had worn corners and smudged text— one in which a naïve and innocent girl was sent to the secluded home of her unknown guardian. Though the handsome and dangerous peer had been most domineering

and had subjected the heroine to all sorts of erotic torture—
even a scene that involved a glass of sherry and wine-flavored
syllabub and had left Grace frustrated for days—he eventually became the shy heroine's conquest. The master had succumbed to love, and power had shifted precipitously to the
heroine's shoulders. But even when the heroine had not
known that her guardian would become her great love, even
while he tied her up in all sorts of fancy and frightening
ways, the heroine had actually been sexually aroused by her
life as a prisoner.

Grace shifted, wincing as her sore bottom found an even
more painful place on which to rest.

"Not long now, love," Devlin promised.

She swallowed hard as he spurred his horse. A story was
one thing. Reality was entirely different. Devlin's armed men
followed, along with Marcus's carriage and servants, the
poor servants tied up.

She was being kidnapped.

Oh, he had denied it—for a while—then he'd refused to
answer any of her questions and she'd subjected him to stony
silence for the last horrid hour.

The truth was that she was his hostage. And it was not
arousing at all. *Not* at all. Absolutely not.

And if he tried to tie her up, he was going to lose an eye.
Or one of his family jewels.

She was not going to be a simpering victim.

"If it weren't for my brother's servants being at risk, I
would have unmanned you an hour ago," she hissed.

"Then I'm most fortunate that you can't drive a carriage."

Gateposts appeared and he turned his horse there, muttering, "Thank God" beneath his breath. The dense copse of
trees quickly fell away and the lane crested a rise.

Grace gasped. A lovely estate was spread out before
them—the house symmetrical and solid in gray stone, the
gardens in full, lush bloom. A bubbling brook ran cheerily
nearby. This pretty Georgian manor belonged to Devlin?

Grace's heart twisted. A woman looked after this house. It was evident in the lovely garden and the organized appearance of both grounds and house. Two years had passed—had the notorious highwayman found himself a bride? Was that why he'd captured her? Did he need ransom to care for a clutch of impish children and a lovely wife with expensive tastes?

Why should it matter to her if he had a wife and a thousand children?

He protected you from Lord Wesley's cruelty, whispered a voice in her head.

She bounced on the saddle and swallowed a scream of pain as her pelvic bones rattled.

A young woman came running out of the house. Grace blinked. A sheet trailed after the girl, rippling in a gust of wind. Giddy laughter filled the air. The girl, who looked about her age, was nude, and her small, firm breasts bounced as she ran.

Behind her, a man came running out. At least he wore clothing; he quickly closed in on the girl. Squealing, she tried to dart away and lost her grip on her sheet—which sailed across the lawn on a current of air.

"Bloody hell," Devlin grunted behind her.

The man had brought the girl to the ground and was fumbling with his trouser buttons while she arched beneath him. "Hurry up, I'm so very wet." The girl flung her leg around the man's waist and gripped the lapels of his coat. She pulled his mouth down to hers and they kissed hungrily while he pressed forward.

Grace couldn't see the moment of penetration, but she knew it had happened. Her legs quivered at the sounds of a feminine squeal and a ragged male groan. Hot fire washed over her cheeks and her body went so boneless that she almost fell off the horse. She swallowed a moan.

"Who's this woman, Devlin? What have you brought her here for?"

Grace jerked her gaze away from the grunting, rocking couple on the grass. Another woman stood in the doorway, but this one had auburn hair tied back with an emerald silk ribbon and her curvaceous figure poured into a low-cut gown of green sprigged muslin.

Suddenly, the red-haired woman clapped a hand to her mouth. "Crikey, it's *her*, isn't it! Devlin, you damnable wretch!"

6

_____

"What is it you want, Mr. Sharpe? A ransom for my life?"

Standing in the west-facing drawing room of his home, bathed in rich afternoon light, Grace asked the questions without sarcasm, without rancor, and Devlin was taken aback to realize she seriously thought that was his intent. He tightened his grip on the glass in his hand, not tasting the fine brandy as it slid down his throat.

Months of planning had gone into this, his goal simple and direct—to bring Grace into his life once more, to have her again, to—

Hades, at that point his goals became hazy, a sensation that he'd experienced a long time ago and had never liked. He always decided exactly what he wanted and got it.

He set down his glass with a clunk that rattled the table, then tore off the tricorn, mask, and wig. Damp with sweat, his hair was caught back with a leather tie. "I would never trade you for money, love."

Sunlight caressed Grace's generous curves and played along the slender line of her neck. "Then what do you want?"

Devlin's throat tightened. He slung his leg over the arm of a wing chair and drank in her features—the exotic, expressive curves of her mouth, the pert nose, and the sparking green eyes that promised a fiery temper and bewitching sensuality. But she looked afraid of him and that twisted his heart.

He glanced toward the window, a plane of reflective gold, and softly said, "I've seen you, sweetheart, over the last two years. At balls." By revealing it, had he gone too far? He had taken a hell of a risk for a wanted man . . . but he'd been drawn to see her. He'd known men addicted to opium, addicted to drink. Damnation, but his desire for Grace was a merciless master, and he suspected he was addicted to her.

Unease brought lines to bracket her lips. "I did not know you went into society. But why would you? Why would you want to see me?"

"To see how you were coping in the world I'd ruined you for."

"A woman ruins herself," she threw back and he winced at the cynicism, the bitterness in her voice. She'd aged much more than two years.

He had stood on the fringes of society, in the shadows, and he'd watched her. She'd danced, but her eyes had been far away. She'd flirted, but would quickly retreat if the gentleman began to look too earnest. She'd fled from those who were apparently hoping for seduction, but also from those who looked obviously in love.

Even with her sisters, the fiery auburn-haired Lady Trent and the gentle, beautiful Lady Swansborough, Grace had seemed reserved—she was hiding secrets, and he could sense the weight of them affected every word she spoke.

"I never saw you," she said. "But then, I never looked for you."

The admission hurt. Of course, he'd hidden damn well, and she had no reason to think he would go out in society. So why should he be hoping that she had pined for him?

Devlin grinned, as he always did when he landed in trouble. "I was never formally invited. And I never went anywhere through the front door, love."

Grace moved to the window and laid her white-gloved

knuckles against the pane. She stood with the sun behind her, the brilliance of it dazzling his eyes. Her profile was cast in shadow, unreadable. "You still have not told me what you want."

Simple answer to that. He wanted her in his bed. "Have you made love since the last time we were together? Since I ate your sweet cunny in the summerhouse?"

Her gasp rippled down his spine. She spun around—he still could not see her features, but her sudden movement revealed how shocked she was. "What on earth do you think? Though obviously *you* have. There must be a dozen women in this house—and most of them are not wearing any clothes."

He shrugged. "There are six women and a lot of men in this house. The women keep them from shooting each other."

Easing off the arm of the chair, he prowled toward Grace. "You haven't, have you? For two years, you've been lonely."

"*Yes!*" she hissed.

"You could have taken a lover."

"You must be mad. And put some poor gentleman at risk? I now have powerful brothers-in-law who would kill any man who bedded me."

"I thought as much and that's why I brought you here. I want you, Grace, and I suspect that you want me. Stay with me—a few days, a week. As long as you want. I will give you every erotic fantasy you've ever dreamed of."

As he got closer, she stiffened. Her perfume wrapped around him—now she wore an exotic scent, smelling of jasmine and lush spices, but she wore it subtly, and it hinted at the woman she really was. Not a prim English spinster, but earthy, voluptuous, carnal.

She crossed her arms over her breasts. "And you thought I would agree? That I would want that?"

"Yes, I think you do." He reached out and pried her arms away. In her shimmering white dress with its jaunty green pattern, Grace was beautiful. All he wanted was to peel the gown off her and roll around—hot, sweaty, and naked—on a rumpled bed in the summer heat. "You don't have to hide who you really are behind shields, Grace. For a few days, you can be the woman you were meant to be."

She would not look at his eyes, and it gave him hope. She must be afraid she would weaken. Why else would she not meet his gaze?

Grace jerked her arms away from his gentle grasp and lifted her thumb to her lips.

"No one in society is going to know that you've been here," he murmured. "My men do not know your name, and they'll never go about in any place they might encounter you. Your servants won't talk. You will be safe."

The silence stretched and uncertainty weighed on him. Did he say more? Did he touch her? He'd faced situations where one wrong move would result in death but felt just as nervous now.

"You kept me safe from Lord Wesley and from Lord Wynsome . . ."

That gave him hope.

"But why kidnap me?" she demanded. "Perhaps you have more in common with your brother than simply a shared father."

He recoiled at the words. Christ, did she really think that?

He gaped, nonplussed, as she wagged her finger at him. "It is easy for you to talk about being who I was meant to be. When society matrons learn I spent several days as the captive of the notorious Captain Sharpe, what exactly do you think they will gossip? That we whiled away the time playing chess?"

"In a sense, we are," he shot back. "But now we are just moving pieces aimlessly about the board. You've spent two years amongst the ton. How many marriage proposals have you refused? Rumor tells me it is at least two dozen."

"Not—not that many. And how can I accept? On the wedding night, my husband will know the truth."

"To be honest, I suspect most of those clods wouldn't figure it out with a little artful maneuvering on your part, and I think you know it. There's another reason—"

"Of course!" she cried. "You've discovered my secret. I am pining with love for you, Captain Sharpe. A horrible, consumptive, unrequited love that I know can never be returned, that can never be fulfilled. I spend my days doodling hearts on my letters and fill my books with flowery renditions of 'Mrs. Captain Sharpe'—"

"Gah!" He threw his hands in the air.

"You want me to stay. You want us to spend a few days together in your bed. And what is there in this for me?" she demanded.

Her question shocked him and his tongue failed him. He didn't know. Pleasure? Fun?

"I will tell you what," she said, her back to him. "Fleeting pleasure and then too much pain—that horrible feeling of loss again. I can endure frustration. But I cannot live with pain."

"Sweetheart," Devlin said. "I cannot live without you."

Grace put her hand to her heart as a tight pain clutched at it and turned to face Devlin. "You know exactly what to say. But of course I don't believe you."

Somber and brilliant blue in the light, his eyes held hers. "It's the truth, Grace, love. Of course I have to live without you, but I'm not bloody pleased about it."

"I should think you barely have time to think of me at all. Do the six ladies here take turns in your bed? Does each one have a night, or do you have more than one at once?"

Of course, he looked astonished. He had no idea who her father was. No idea that she had seen Rodesson's erotic books and she knew exactly what exotic naughty pleasures men enjoyed.

She knew exactly what men did sexually when they had power.

At least the bold image she'd described had distracted him from what she'd done with her sharp words—reveal her jealousy, her vulnerability.

"Forget about them," he growled. "All I can see is you." He stepped close to her, until her awareness of him overwhelmed her. He touched her—of course, he did. He must know she wanted to melt as he skimmed the back of his hand along her breast. A shift, a corset, a muslin dress, and a pelisse covered her skin, but his touched burned through them all.

"Why don't you undress?" she purred. Naked, he would be at a disadvantage. He could not chase her down the lane without a stitch on.

She had to escape. Her grandmother was waiting and she had to—absolutely *had* to—go but it was more than that. For two years, she'd been haunted by memories of Devlin.

Her blood was like molten wax, so hot beneath her skin that she was soaked with sweat. Her cunny ached with yearning and, really, she doubted her heart could beat any faster. She wanted him so much, so badly . . . she would never recover from this. She would never forget!

Firm, tempting, his mouth grazed her forehead as he calmly undid his elegant cravat. Grace stepped back, needing distance between them, but as he mercilessly yanked open the diamond buttons, she saw how vulnerable she was now.

Now she had to watch.

With his coat gaping, she caught a tantalizing glimpse of a pure white shirt beneath it as he paused to pull out the tie in his hair. His hair flowed like honey over his shoulders, far longer than it had been two years ago. Sweat made it darker, like molten amber.

Confidence burned in his grin, and he cast aside his beautiful coat, then dragged his shirt over his head. Scars blemished his broad shoulders. He seemed bigger than he had been before, his muscles more prominent, the hollow at his throat a deep shadow.

It was torture to look and she yearned to explore his tex-tures—damp skin, soft swirls of golden hair, hard, velvety nipples.

"Do you approve?" He asked it even as he opened his breeches of fine buff-colored fabric.

"You know I do. I am sure every woman you keep does. Why do you need to hear it?"

"It matters to me to hear you say it. To know you feel it." One push sent his breeches down past the lean bones of his hips, and they paused at the tops of his bulging thighs. The flap shielded his cock from her curious, hungry gaze.

She really should not want to see him naked. But she did.

Then his breeches dropped to his boots, revealing that he wore no small clothes. Her throat tightened. She should have known. She'd seen his cock before, had thought about it every night when she went to her bed. When she slid beneath her covers and then slid her fingers down to her quim. At night, as she pleasured herself, as she worked off the yearn-ing, the heat, the near-maddening lust, she would run her tongue around her lips and imagine the most shockingly erotic thing she could—licking the swollen head of his cock.

Devlin sank to the arm of the wing chair, tugging off his boots. Falling over his face, his hair hid him, and he drew off boots and pantaloons so casually it was as though she was not in the room. He leaned back, supporting his weight with both hands behind him. The position let sunlight follow his sculpted body and made him look strangely vulnerable.

Her throat dried as he grinned. "I'm nude, love, but you have not surrendered a stitch."

"Stand up and turn around," she breathed. "I want to see you from the rear."

She intended to back away and run for the door, but as light and shadow played across his straight shoulders, across his powerful arms, she could not move. She could only stand, her heart racing, her breaths shallow, and play voyeur. Heat raced up, teasing her skin beneath her demure dress.

Breaking the spell, she stepped forward. Grasped his tight arse and squeezed. Each cheek was hard and muscular and perfect. Soft hairs teased her palms and his firm flesh barely gave beneath her pressing fingers.

Laughing, he twisted at his lean waist, watching her explore his rump. "I've never had a woman's hands caress me with such enthusiasm."

"I rather like your bottom, Mr. Sharpe," she teased.

She met his gaze and caught her breath at the intoxicating mix of laughter and lust there. "In fact," she added saucily, "It's so tempting, I would like to do this—"

Shock lifted his golden brows as she bent. Those curving cheeks beckoned her. She pressed her lips to the base of his spine, to the lovely bronze hollow. She kissed him softly, then swirled her tongue over his salty, warm, delicious skin. She could not believe she'd done such a thing, but his warm flesh was intoxicating.

"Grace, love—"

He sagged forward on a hoarse groan and grabbed the arms of the chair. She trailed the tip of her tongue over his round cheeks, tasting the hot, salty skin, breathing in his ripe, earthy scent. She was on her knees at his rear, and she stroked her hands up his hard inner thighs. Higher and higher she skimmed her fingers, delighted when his breath came harsh and fast.

His spine arched, a beautiful strong curve, as she licked him all over his enticingly tight arse.

She couldn't leave. She wanted to stay. She could not resist.

She would never have this again.

He made her daring. Brave. Wild. She gently tapped his heavy ballocks against her open palm. Soft, dangling, and surprisingly large. What did it feel like to have those round, furry things dangling there? She brushed the tips of her gloved fingernails over the wrinkled, velvety skin. His ballocks jerked up toward his body.

"Your turn," he promised. His deep, rumbling voice wrapped around her, setting her heart racing.

She stared up. "What do you mean?"

"I want to taste you," he growled. "Everywhere."

He clasped her hands and helped her to her feet with the easy charm and formality of a gentleman raising a young woman from a curtsy. His dimple deepened as he sank down to his knees in front of her.

"Oh no, you mustn't—my legs will melt and I'll fall."

Raw, masculine laughter teased her. "I would never let you fall, Grace."

She looked down, both touched and aroused by his smile, his almost boyish delight as he lifted her hems. "No, you tried to raise me up, didn't you? To give me courage. And you did."

He stood, taking her skirts up with him. In welcome, she parted her thighs. She watched his large, scarred, tanned hand slide into the lacy white slit of her drawers.

"You were one of the most courageous woman I've known."

"I can hardly believe that."

"I admire women who defy idiotic rules to take what they want and deserve. I've had women hold a pistol on me to protect their ship, to protect children—not knowing I'd never hurt an innocent. Hell, I admired those women. Just as I admire you."

His finger rubbed over her clit, pressing to the very peak, and her legs melted like butter beneath a scorching sun. Grace grasped his wrist. She should push him away, but instead she clung to him, aware of his long, fine bones, soft, bronzed skin, and silken gold hairs. His finger drew slow, deliberate circles.

"I simper at balls now," she managed. "I lie every day of my life."

Moaning, she arched her hips and wriggled her tight, aching clit against his fingertip. Oh, it was so good. Really, why should he hold up carriages? He could use this skill to have anything he wanted.

"For your sisters, sweeting. I understand that."

"Not brave and daring, though," she breathed.

"There is nothing more brave than putting someone else above yourself."

"I would have thought you would see that as a weakness."

"Perhaps the fact that I cannot is my weakness. I wanted you and I kidnapped you to bring you here. When I had no right. I'm a selfish man. A weak man. But I refused to do the honorable thing and never see you again."

God . . . God . . . his finger flicked lazily over her clit and she cried out.

How could this be? She could touch herself this way. She could walk away from him and pleasure her own body. But she was a slave to the soul-melting pleasure of his touch. Her own touch would not satisfy. Not now.

Not anymore.

No, it would. It would have to.

She wanted to move back, but her feet would not leave the carpet. She stood, lashes shielding her eyes, and let his fingers play magic on her slick quim. "Would staying with you be brave or weak?" she asked. "Brave because you want it, or weak because I want it?"

"Brave for both of us, I think."

His hands were at her buttons. This gown, the height of fashion, was a dress unlike those she used to wear. It was intended to be dealt with by a lady's maid. He fiddled with the buttons, his fingers brushing the sensitive line of her spine as he opened them.

Her gown fell.

She was staying. Now that she was undressed, she couldn't run.

Her lungs expanded as he untied the bow at her corset and expertly loosened the stays. "I like this," he murmured.

"Stripping away your layers. Revealing the beautiful woman confined within the proper young lady."

"I'm not proper. I have to pretend to be."

His fingers closed around the boned sides of her loose corset and drew it down. The hard stays skimmed along the gauzy shift that covered her rounded hips. "What do you intend to do, Grace Hamilton, with the rest of your life?"

He was behind her, entrancing her with his smell—a dash of spicy cologne atop his sweat-dampened skin.

"I have not thought that far, Mr. Sharpe. What do you intend to do?"

"I live in the here and now, Grace. I cannot even begin to guess what I'll do."

Her corset was on the floor, sagging around her stockings, looking forlorn, half-propped on its edge with its lacing in disarray. She stepped out of it, lifting up her shift. With a quick whisk upward, she bared herself—every rounded, jiggling inch.

She didn't know what she expected—

But it was not to be swept into his arms and carried to the settee, while he lavished kisses on her throat that made her toes curl and her fingers grip his arms.

Biceps. Hard, big, bulging biceps. Just as with his rump, her fingers barely made a dent.

Fluttering around her face, his hair was a teasing veil as he lowered her to the silky cushions. Grace fell back, wanton and sensual, and parted her legs. She stared openly at his jutting cock. A trail of silvery fluid leaked from the tip. "The here and now. I can see why that is so important, Mr. Sharpe."

His knee pressed onto the settee, his hand draped over the back, and he lifted over her so his golden chest blotted out the sun. She gently traced his new scars—odd, that she would feel proprietary about his body. That she would know these scars had not been there before. She could barely remember Lord Wesley. Why she had wanted him. What she had ever thought she loved about him.

But she could remember Devlin Sharpe's scars.

This was madness.

What if someone came in?

No, he'd locked the door, hadn't he—to ensure she couldn't get out.

"Don't think," he whispered, bending to her right breast with intent.

He'd said that before. Their first time—their first night. That was the only time, in two years, she hadn't thought. Since then, all she did was think. She couldn't *do* anything else.

She reached down and wrapped her fingers around his hot, hard staff—velvety, but rigid beneath. And thick—enough to stretch her fingers so they would not reach around him. They shared a smile and it stunned her how their smiles revealed their . . . history, familiarity, and friendship as much as lust. Holding his hard length firmly, she led him to her quim as she took charge and used the swollen head to tease.

She brushed her clit and writhed with the pleasure. Arching up, she pushed her breasts toward him and his mouth sucked in her nipple, taking it all inside.

Don't think.

Grace squirmed, moaned, bit at her fingers. She'd forgotten how wonderful this could be. And he was exploring. Enjoying himself with her plump flesh and hard nipples as he slid on his sheath. Kissing her nipples in different ways so she was pounding her hips beneath him and pumping up to press to his cock. His hands cradled her large breasts; his lips and tongue sent her soaring as she had not done for two years.

Grace closed her eyes, stroking his chest, his shoulders, following the bulges of his arms. Savoring him. This time she knew to remember everything. Textures. Scent. Sound.

It would make every orgasm so bittersweet to know she had to memorize everything, but she had to.

"I want you," she whispered as she lifted her lids. Struck

mute, she saw him surrounded by a golden glow of summer sunlight.

"We belong this way," he promised as he eased his hips forward, and nosed his erection between her drenched lips. "Naked. Together. Making love."

She hooked her arms around his neck. His long hair spilled over her hands. *Yes.* She wanted to say *yes.* But they didn't belong together.

God—he filled her so. For two years she'd been empty. She'd been surrounded by family yet hopelessly alone.

She wasn't alone now. A soft, sighing giggle escaped her lips as Devlin slowly drew back and thrust forward, inching in as though he had all the time in the world, while her fingernails gouged in his skin and she longed to have him deep inside.

His arm bracketed her, he nuzzled her throat, and she snuggled beneath him. He was pumping into her, and she lifted to meet every thrust. His gaze locked with hers, stealing her breath. Theirs was an erotic dance, a joining—she felt so completely joined with him.

Heat flared between their bodies. Sweat coated her skin and his. His chest slid along her sensitive breasts; his hard stomach bumped her belly. He shifted his legs so his firm thighs rested on either side of hers. Her soft inner thighs clamped together, trapping his hot, sticky shaft as he thrust.

"I want to ride high, sweetheart, to make you come, to make you explode—"

Each slick pass teased her clit. His cock was hot fire inside her. For two years, she'd had to quench her fires, control them. Even the slightest sensual interest in a man had frightened her—what if she was weak, made a mistake, hurt her family?

With Devlin, she could let her fiery nature consume her. He hadn't captured her, he'd set her free. Just as he'd promised. "Grab my breasts," she moaned. "My nipples . . .

I so need your hands on my nipples. And your cock—thrust it deep—"

Her voice shocked her, the sultry alluring quality, the confidence that sang in it. He did exactly as she wished, rolling her pink nipples between thumbs and forefingers. Sliding deep, finding—

The most remarkable place that melted her. Turned her entire body into boiling honey.

Oh, he was so big. Big rumbling chest over her, big cock taking her completely, big muscles to brace him and let him fill her to her womb—

Her quim fluttered around him. Her climax rolled upon her like that—a silky feeling, like heaven and sunlight blending together for her delight. A flame roared up in all that sensual pleasure and raced through her. Her body pulsed, her cunny gripped him, her muscles all tensed at once in one, glorious, overwhelming burst of pleasure.

Climax.

He jolted on her, bucking. *Grace.* Her name came to her ears on a ravaged groan.

She clung to him, her arms tight around his waist and she rode through her climax as she reveled in his.

Afterward he bowed his head so his amber hair fell forward and his damp forehead touched hers. "Grace, angel," he rasped, "I'm a weak man. I don't want to let you go."

7

S he looked so confused, holding her shift in her clenched
hands and staring out the window at the tranquil gardens
and the wild fields.

"What's wrong?" Devlin lay naked on the sofa and he
watched Grace as she stood in the middle of discarded
clothes with a lost look that tugged at his heart.

"What did I just do?"

"We made love. You climaxed and so did I. Now, it's time
for some tea—and a bath for the two of us."

Her head jerked up, her tousled blond hair flowing around
her like angels' wings. "The here and now," she said, but her
voice was flat.

She was feeling regret, he suspected. He swung his legs
abruptly to the floor and stood up. "What's wrong with the
damned here and now? I enjoyed myself and I know you did
too."

"I made another mistake. That's what I had vowed not to
do. Not to make another mistake, but you touched me, and I
forgot everything except for your *damned* here and now."

He shook his head. "I don't understand, Grace. What's the
harm? That was one of the most passionate bouts I've had—
when we come together, it's like an explosion of gunpowder.
That means something, Grace."

Now she shook her head, sending her mussed curls dancing. "We desire each other. I'm a woman and you enjoy women. But there's no . . . there is just no point, is there?"

Utterly mystified, Devlin turned toward the table that held the brandy and sherry. He needed another drink. What point was there supposed to be?

In his days as a pirate, the scourge of the Caribbean seas, he'd had several proper ladies come to his bed, hot and lusty and eager; and then, in the cold light of morning, they'd been ashamed of themselves. He could not convince them that they had every right to enjoy their bodies and sex, so he'd shrugged, given them a generous gift of silks or jewels, and sent them on their way. Had they cried over their "mistake" for the rest of their lives? Probably. But he suspected that most thought of him with an illicit thrill in their most secret fantasies. Fantasies they did not want to admit even to themselves—

He had a full tumbler of brandy before him without even noticing how much he'd poured. He glanced over his shoulder. Grace was squeezing the life out of her innocent shift. Her knuckles were bone-white with the exertion.

"I made a mistake," she mumbled. "And I've made another."

"I don't see how you have, Grace."

She had absently squashed her shift into a ball. "You don't understand."

"That's true enough," he muttered.

A flush washed over her cheeks. "I should regret what we've done, but I don't. You asked me about my future—I really do not know what it will be. I made love to two men. It was a sin. It will always be wrong. But I don't want to live the rest of my life paying for it. Is that wrong?"

He strode to her side and pried her shift free. "Lord, but you are beautiful—"

It was not what he'd meant to say, but the sight of her, limned by gold, honest and vulnerable and real, stole his senses and put the truth in his mouth. "You are." Damn, how could he make her see sense when he knew how brutally the rules of English society were drummed into her brain?

"You don't have any sins to pay for, love," he said. "You gave of yourself. That's never a sin." Shaking his head, he turned to the door. "I'll find you a robe. Then I want to show you why you deserve pleasure."

A snap of his fingers must have brought one of his men— Grace could tell by the amused, deep voice that joshed and teased on the other side of the door. Devlin held the door to obscure the view into the room and Grace slipped on her wrinkled shift. Compared to being naked, she was far more decent, but she was still scandalously exposed.

She smoothed down the fabric, her hands shaking. What had she been thinking?

She was supposed to subdue her wild, wanton, bohemian nature—a plan she had thrown away after a few minutes with Devlin Sharpe.

Now she was in a house filled with immoral men and wanton women. Could she really trust Devlin to keep her safe, when she knew nothing about him? Nothing more than that he stole, that he had killed a man in a duel, and that he pirated ships.

And made love with a skill that made her soul melt and her heart and body take flight.

"Dinner, Captain Dev, my love? Do you wish me to lock 'er up somewhere for you? Tie 'er up?"

The woman's voice, soft and teasing yet also firm and competent, startled her. Looking toward the door, Grace saw a slender white hand slip through the small opening at the door to stroke Devlin's cheek. A scalding pain hit Grace's heart and she struggled to breathe.

The woman was so familiar with him.

At least Devlin wrapped his hand around the woman's wrist and gently lowered her hand.

But no doubt he had slept with that woman.

"Not yet, Sally. But dinner would not be amiss. Have some dishes sent here. I'll dine with my captive."

The audacious wretch turned from the door to wink at her. She threw him a withering glance. But she *was* his captive—it was the simple truth, for all she might pretend otherwise. Devlin then shut the door and strolled toward the fireplace with his brandy. She crossed her arms over her breasts and sat down on the settee. A chill was settling into the room as the sun began to drop. But she would not shiver.

He prodded the fire with a poker to bring it to life. She watched him cautiously, ready to turn away if he caught her. He was so relaxed with his nudity; though he yelped as a prod sent up a shower of sparks that fell on his naked thigh.

At her gasp of surprise, of worry, he grinned. "You think me foolish for doing this naked?"

"You hurt yourself."

"But we now have a cheery, warming fire. Fire is always a risk, as you know. And there was a reward for the risk."

He must have meant the heat inside her. Already it was blazing to life again, just like the flames in the hearth.

A knock sounded at the door, and Devlin crossed the room in long strides. A moment later, he shut the door, holding a blue silk robe. "One of mine. I thought you might prefer it to one of the ladies'."

She nodded as he relaxed back on the sofa, brushed back his hair, and held his glass between long, elegant fingers.

"What exactly do you plan to do with me now?" she asked. She might as well know.

"Make up for two wasted years."

"How do you intend to make up for two years? What do you mean?" Grace demanded, but Devlin only smiled as he laid his hands on her shoulders and directed her toward the back of the drawing room.

Those words had left Grace utterly stunned for several minutes, and then, when she'd found her tongue again, he had evaded her question. Had he really believed that the two years they had been apart were wasted?

Had he pined for her? What, exactly, did he mean?

"Dinner first," he murmured and she knew she might never find out.

"Goodness." She saw the display of food laid on a small table spread with a snowy white cloth. Silver dishes gleamed in the candlelight. A board held cheeses and bread. Plates held cakes. Curtains fluttered with the gentle summer breeze and golden light spilled in around them.

"This is the morning room." Devlin drew out a chair for her, a Queen Anne style with ivory brocade seat covers.

He poured her tea and she had to stare—a notorious pirate, dressed in a silky purple robe, calmly pouring her a cup of tea before he took his own seat. She took it gratefully, touched far more deeply than she should be.

Her traitorous stomach growled but she knew she could not be seduced into staying. She stood abruptly, shoving back her chair. "I am leaving, Devlin."

He had leapt to his feet also, but she was at the door—the opposite door, which she was certain must be the only way to escape. Locked, but the key was there. Her fingers trembled as she caught the end of the key and turned it.

"Stay in here with me," Devlin called, but she already had the door open. She raced out into the hallway and found it empty. Ahead she saw a gleam of light, then heard laughter. Knowing Devlin was behind her, she charged ahead, toward the light.

Her slippers' soles slapped against gleaming tile as she reached the light—the last red rays of sunset pouring into a stairway. Ornate doors were ahead of her, but there were six and she had no idea which would be the one to lead to the foyer and take her outside.

She chose the stairs.

But as she hurried up, she saw Devlin below. His robe swirled around his powerful legs as he gave chase. He caught her with three strides up the steps, but she wrenched her arm free.

"Grace, come back here," he commanded, but she ignored him. She doubted now she'd get out of the house, but she was too ashamed of her useless attempt to give in and turn back. He'd have to grab her and carry her over his shoulder if he wanted her back at tea.

Again, wild laughter came from ahead, and she followed the sound, curious. Now she could distinguish male cheers and shouts answered by the delighted laughter of women.

This must be Devlin's gang.

She had reached a gallery, a sweeping balcony trimmed by a gleaming oak rail. Winded, she grasped the smooth rail and stared in shock at the scene below.

He caught her by the wrist—she was so enraptured in watching the orgy, she hadn't run when he approached. Grace's mouth was a wide and pretty "O", her eyes so large that her lashes brushed her brows, and her hand was clapped to her mouth.

Between her fingers, she asked, "Good heavens, is that man with two women? Are both on their knees in front of him?"

At Grace's soft, astonished question, Devlin had to grip the rail of the balcony as a shot of desire drained the strength from his legs.

"Devlin, I cannot believe that people actually do these things!" She turned to him. "You do these things?"

Was she jealous? She didn't look angry. She didn't look as though she'd behave like Lucy and shout and spit fire. She looked uncertain. As though this would hurt her.

He shrugged. "Once upon a time. My world is a different world to the cold one that dictates to you, love. My world is just about pleasure and fun. I want to share that fun exclusively with you right now, Grace."

"Really?" Her face tipped and one brow arched. "If it is

about pleasure and fun why are the women pushing each other out of the way to be the one to pleasure the man?"

"It's part of play." But he looked, only to see Sally rake her nails along Bess's bare shoulder. Dark-haired Bess wore only a corset of scarlet and pink, laced tight, and Sally's pale white shift was pulled up over her ample arse. The play had turned mean—but this was more to do with power than desire. "I agree. There's nothing playful there. Sally—the blonde—was in love with one of my men. Bess's man, the one standing there, made a mistake that cost Sally's lover his life—"

"So it isn't just blind pleasure, then. Just as with me, those women engage their hearts."

He had been coasting his hand along the rail to touch Grace's. He stopped. Did she mean that she always engaged her heart? Had she done so with him?

A disaster if she had because he couldn't bear to hurt her.

But he wanted her to love him. Hell, he wanted it and the realization stunned him.

"I always thought they shared my men too freely to be in love," he admitted. He'd always dismissed the emotional scenes, the scraps, as the typical behavior of women. He'd never thought that the women might fall in love—not with the wild men of his gang, who enjoyed their orgies, their pleasures, and knew they might die on any given night.

"I think you will find," Grace said, "that each of your women is in love with a particular man, no matter whose bed they go to."

He sighed. He'd hoped to keep his Grace away from his wild world, but he'd also intended to educate her and show her that she didn't need to lock herself away in a cage of guilt. He'd wanted to show her she deserved pleasure.

He'd wanted to open her world.

Instead, she was forcing him to think more deeply about his.

"Men, of course, do not have to engage their hearts."

Her statement was fraught with danger. He'd guided his

ship through treacherous channels lined with shoals and vicious rocks, but he'd never felt the nerves he felt now. He couldn't respond. He suspected his heart was engaged and that made him a bloody idiot. But something needed to be thrown out into their private silence. Below them, the cries and moans of carnal fun floated up.

"Not always," he said.

"How can you—if you live your life in the here and now?"

That he would not answer. Instead he watched her gaze flit around the room, her teeth nibbling at her lower lip. He saw the orgy scene dispassionately—Lucy was stroking the hair of two men, Simon and Will, as they lovingly suckled her nipples. His lieutenant, Rogan St. Clair, was the man who had two ladies fighting to take his cock in their mouths. Three men—Horatio, Nick, and John—tussled with three ladies on the rug and in the tangle of limbs he could not tell who was fucking whom.

Grace tilted her head. His blue silk robe turned her hair to shimmering pale gold and highlighted the peach flush in her cheeks. "Do you have orgies here every day?"

"Tonight we aren't hunting. The men are at home, none are at risk. Here that is cause for a celebration." He grinned. "Any excuse for an orgy." Would she push further? "You left me, Grace. I understood that there could be no future."

"But now I am here."

She was not looking at the scene anymore, but she shimmered with arousal, with tension.

"Sometimes a man can't resist doing something he has no right to do."

Below, there were six women moaning their pleasure and, like any man, he knew that particular sound stole his ability to think. "You can watch. Have a glimpse of my world. It's not a bad world, sweetheart. No one is condemned for it."

Hand at her throat, she did watch.

He stared at her face. What scene was she looking at? Lucy with the two men gallantly sucking her nipples and taking turns flicking her clit within her nest of auburn hair? Or the wild tangle, with three cocks greedily surging in and out of every wet, tight, female opening they could find?

Trying to guess was a game that had his blood on fire and his cock rigid and aching.

"What do you like best of all," she breathed, "in your bed?"

Hades, he'd been anticipating her hurt, her anger. Instead she was intrigued. It was as though a ship deck had slid out from beneath his feet. He took a few moments to get his footing again.

"I'm much more interested in learning what you fantasize about," he murmured. He moved to stand behind her so his lips brushed her silky hair and he could bracket her by placing his hands on the rail. "Which down there interests you the most? Two men? Another woman? An uninhibited orgy, where you might kiss one woman's nipples, fondle another's quim, while many men pleasure you with tongues and cocks . . . can you imagine making love to five men at once—"

From his vantage he could see her sharp breaths—how they lifted his robe and fluttered tendrils of her hair. "I have seen pictures," she said abruptly.

"I imagine you have."

She shook her head. "No, you have no idea. My father is Charles Rodesson."

"The artist?"

"Yes, the artist of erotica."

Of all the things Grace could have told him, that was the one to almost knock him off his feet. "So you will be very knowledgeable about pictures. But let's talk about your fantasies."

Her soft laugh floated to him. "You don't care at all, do you?"

"No, I'd rather talk about what intrigues you."

"All of it. Not that I would ever, ever do such things." Her fingers brushed beside his and she tentatively hooked her little finger around his thumb. "Sinful to admit, isn't it? It's only because of who I am—an erotic artist's daughter, that I would think that way."

He'd met defenseless women—women who swooned in the face of danger. But he'd never met one as vulnerable as Grace.

Now he put his finger on why. She was honest, direct—she expressed her thoughts and feelings and he found them irresistibly intriguing. But in her world that was the aspect of her personality that could ruin her.

She must have spent her entire life trying to be someone else.

She amazed him. She wanted to know about him. What he liked in his bed. What his erotic fantasies were. Even if it hurt her, she was curious and brave enough to ask.

"It's not sinful to admit it, Grace. And it has nothing to do with your birthright." He couldn't stop hearing the voice in his head, haughty, cultured, arrogant—*He's nothing of course, but he is so wild and naughty in bed. I do think bastards make the best lovers, for they have something to prove.*

He shoved the Countess of Dorchester's voice back into the recesses of his mind. "You think that way because you are human. Some of the most highborn men and women are the most perverse of us all."

Grace said nothing for a while and just took in sharp breaths. Then she pointed down to the orgy. "The women down there, they seem to enjoy touching each other in intimate ways. I've never thought of another woman that way. Only men."

"Which men have you thought of?" He'd meant the question to sound erotic; instead it sounded like the growl of an angry wolf.

"Gentlemen whose names I did not even know. Sometimes one catches a glimpse—of a shoulder, a rough-hewn jaw, a tight derriere—and, well . . ."

He was hard, wound up, and ready to burst at her innocent explanation. "You created a fantasy."

"Yes. I know men do that, as I have seen my father's pictures. Men paid him to draw fantasies for them. I didn't
know if women had fantasies. At least I didn't until my sisters married, and then they engaged in some more forthright
conversations."

"You thought it was abnormal to fantasize?"

"Yes. Exactly—" She drew in a harsh breath. "Those men—
they are kissing!"

He glanced to where she pointed. Nick and John had
touched lips. Slowly, they let their tongues come together.
Nick's hand slid down John's abdomen and wrapped around
the shaft of his long cock.

"This is for the enjoyment of the ladies," he explained.
Several clapped, licked their lips, and made lewd suggestions.
"Women, my men have discovered, like to watch sexual play
between men—as long as they are certain the men will play
with them."

"Who are they—the men of your gang?"

Why had she asked that after talking of her erotic thoughts
about anonymous gentlemen and while watching his men
have unfettered sex?

"Most followed me from piracy into highway robbery," he
said lightly, stressing how unsuitable the men were. "The men
kissing are Nick and John—brutal fighters. Nick, the blond,
was captured by Barbary pirates and served in the East in a
harem of men. The young lad is Will, a good-natured boy. The
bespectacled one is Simon; he loves to study nature. Then
there is Horatio—the auburn-haired one. It's reputed he is also
a gentleman's bastard as I am, but he denies it. And lastly, that
one with the black hair is Rogan St. Clair, my lieutenant."

"You trust them all."

"With you? Yes. None would ever cross me. Rogan is a
man I would trust with my life. He's saved my arse more

times on the sea than I could count. None of them will know your name, love, even if they do get a glimpse of your face."

She gave him a frank gaze. "Devlin, I want to know what you meant about making up for two wasted years. Do you mean us? I don't understand."

"I want to do the things I wish we'd done two years ago."

"But I can't stay, Devlin. I have to go. My grandmother wants to see me, and I must go and meet her."

"You want to run away from me to go and see your grandmother."

"I *have* to. I don't have much time, and if she thinks I am not coming, she might not write to me again. She might never open another letter from me."

"A martinet, is she? I'd be apt not to go if she threatened me like that."

"It's not a threat, Devlin. It's the truth. She is the Countess of Warren, my mother was her daughter, and my mother was cast out of the home when she ran off with Rodesson."

Grace, the granddaughter of a countess. No wonder she possessed the manners, refinement, and elegance of a lady. "How did your mother end up eloping with an artist?"

Grace sighed. "Rodesson had been engaged to paint my mother's picture, and they fell in love. They eloped to Gretna Green, but along the way, they both realized that marriage would not work—he was wild, bohemian, and would never be faithful. By then, my mother was enceinte with my eldest sister."

Familiar anger heated the back of his neck. "And her parents would not take her back."

Biting her lip, Grace shook her head. "My mother was never allowed back into their house. We have never been acknowledged by them."

"Yet your mother had the courage to build her own life."

"Yes, with the help of loyal friends, my mother set herself up in a house in a small village and invented a new name and a whole new life. As far as the world knows, I am Grace

Hamilton, daughter of a sea captain who traveled to India to seek his fortune. But now, after all this time, my grandmother wants to see me. My grandfather will not bend, but she asked for me to come to her."

"It means a lot to you."

"Of course," she said softly.

"It shouldn't." Abruptly, he drew her back from the railing so she could no longer see the unfettered orgy below them. "The bath should be ready. Come with me."

To his surprise, she took his hand and let him take her.

8

His most intimate room surrounded her.

Grace pivoted slowly, the hem of his robe swishing around her ankles as she took in the furnishings and the paintings on the wall of Devlin's bedchamber. A sturdy bed of dark oak with four columns and a burgundy velvet canopy filled most of the room. Curtains were tied to the posts with velvet ropes. The bedside table, the secretary, a leather chair—all were simple and plain. She thought of the food they'd eaten, of the dishes it was served on. Silver and china but not elaborate. He must have stolen a fortune on the seas and on the king's highways, but he did not surround himself with lavish treasures.

He surrounded himself with women.

A handsome man with a reputation for theft and plundering—she had to remember that was what he was.

An open book rested on its pages on the bedside table.

What did he read? It filled her with intense curiosity.

She glanced around to find Devlin. He pushed open a door and steam billowed out.

The bathing room.

He dropped his robe, caught it, and tossed it over the back of the one chair as he stepped out through the door. Heavens, the man treated her to the most beautiful view from the rear.

His shoulders and narrow waist formed a pronounced vee, his arse was tight and firm, his legs powerful and lean. She wanted to race across the room and grasp that rump, but she let him go.

Then she glanced at the title of his book. *Clarisse*. The author's name startled her. *Madame de la Plaisure*—a name she knew from sister Maryanne's scandalous time publishing erotic books.

Devlin lived in the midst of a continual orgy and he found the need to read erotic literature? Casting a quick glance to the bathing room, she did the unforgivable. She flipped over Devlin's private book and began to read.

> *The blonde child had always proved the most willful, the most insolent, but undeniably the most desirable. His lordship had waited very patiently for this opportunity. He had known that Clarisse— Miss Plimpton—would be brought to him, that she would be left alone within the walls of his home, that eventually she would be placed within his power.*
>
> *It had been this knowledge that had given him the strength to endure.*
>
> *Through the peephole he watched Clarisse undress. It was important to watch her unobserved. From studying her every motion, he would learn about her. For he had chosen to educate her, to teach her the beauty of the relationship of Master and Slave, and to do this he must devote all his time and energies to her. He must understand Clarisse, he must anticipate her every thought.*
>
> *For the first time in many years, this excited his lordship.*
>
> *Within the room, Clarisse allowed the maid to undress her and he saw her large naked breasts for the first time. He was aroused at once, but it was*

her derriere that pleased him most. A plump, ripe,
round bottom perfectly formed to receive the slap
of his palm, the flat thwack of a paddle, the sharp
stroke of a crop—

The soft creak of a footstep on a board startled her. Grace hurriedly replaced the book. Blast, she'd turned the page—he would know what she'd done when he picked it up.

Her breaths came furiously; her heart hammered.

Goodness, she'd asked him what he wanted in his bed. Was this it?

The horrible man in that book was planning to spank a woman, to dominate her.

Well, Devlin was a pirate. Perhaps he read the book to whet his appetite before he ravished innocent victims.

He hardly seemed like that kind of man.

But what did she know of men?

The only man she felt she knew at all was Devlin, but she knew that the way he behaved with her was not the entire extent of the man he was. He might be kind with her but cruel when he took a ship or a woman's jewels. He must intimidate people—he must make good on violent threats—else why would they hand over their money?

"Grace? Would you like to join me in the bath?"

She jerked around.

Devlin wore not a stitch. He was naked, his hair slick with humidity. A stroke of his hands plastered it to his head, making it the color of dark honey. Droplets of moisture dusted his powerful arms, his chest, and his cheeks. Candlelight turned the spots to a sprinkle of gold, like fairy dust. He held out his hand invitingly. "Join me, Grace."

"In your bath?" She did long to wash the dampness of perspiration from her skin and the dustiness that accompanied a country summer. But climbing into a bath with Devlin—?

She felt inexplicably nervous. They had made love. Why should she be so afraid of simply bathing?

Was it because it was such an ordinary thing, yet a sensual act she enjoyed—and if she climbed into his bath, she would never again bathe without thinking of him?

It was a risk she must take.

Nodding, she crossed the room, the length of his robe trailing behind her. She expected him to wait, to lead her to the tub, but he grinned and darted in ahead of her and she heard the slosh of water as he got in.

As she reached the doorway, she guessed why he'd done it. He lounged in an enormous porcelain tub, his legs spread open to leave space for her to climb in. Water lapped at his chest and tendrils of steam swirled over his arms and around his face. He swept his arms back, his forearms dangling over the sides.

He was irresistible.

He smiled enticingly and she tugged at the belt. Studying the knot, she undid it, then slid off the robe. She felt shy again and instinctively placed her hands over breasts and pubic curls as she approached the tub.

She swung her leg over, gripping the porcelain. What kind of view had she given him with her derriere in the air and her pudgy thigh flying over the rim? Unsteadily she brought her other leg in, and he caught her hips to hold her, to lower her into the blissfully hot water.

Did he share his bath with the other women here? Did he thoughtfully help them in?

She wouldn't think about that. She did rather a lot of not thinking with Devlin.

His hands linked around her waist and he drew her back against him. Her hair streamed out on the water; her breasts lazily floated.

"I don't want to let you go yet, Grace." He cupped her breasts and squeezed her wet nipples. The caressing heat of the water, the press of his hard body against her—it was all so delicious.

"But I have to go," she murmured. "My grandmother is at a house party and she wishes that I join her."

Devlin leaned back against the tub and stretched out his legs, lifting his feet so they hung over the edge of the tub and dripped on a discarded towel.

She had never dreamed of being in a bath with a man. She'd learned to love bathing when Venetia and Maryanne had introduced her to a world of wealth. Hot water and lots of it! Scented soap. Luxuriant towels.

But this was more pleasurable, more wonderful. Unforgettably so.

Out of the corner of her eye, she saw Devlin lift a bar of soap and thoughtfully rub it between his palms. "But she has had no part in your life up until now," he said.

"My mother knew, when she ran away with a scandalous artist, that her sins might not be forgiven—" Grace broke off as his soapy hands closed around her breasts.

"But even when your mother was in trouble, when you needed money so desperately, they ignored you."

It was not a question.

"Yes, that is true."

"Why go?" he asked. "What is there for you?"

Nothing—it should be nothing. But it was everything. She gazed down at his hands, which were bronzed, with seductive long fingers. "My grandmother has wanted to see me for a long time, and now she has found the courage."

He moved his hands back and there was a long silence. Long enough that she peeked behind her again. Devlin rubbed more soap on his hands then set about washing his right leg. It was simply washing to him, but her chest was tight as she watched his hands caress up and down the length of his lower leg. She had to bite a wet knuckle as he casually soaped his foot and gently massaged his sole.

His bathing room possessed a large paned window. She glanced toward it. If she strained, she could see the golden-red rays of the setting sun flowing over the meadow, over bluebells and wild daisies. She could also see two of his men leading four of the courtesans out into the meadow, all bathed in the vivid light.

Apparently the orgy was moving outdoors. Did none of these men ever bed only one woman at one time?

With a splash, Devlin lowered his leg. "But why go, love, for a woman who took twenty years to find courage?"

She knew that when she spoke she might reveal the shakiness in her voice. Now it was only revealing itself in the tremor of her fingers against his hard thighs. His body was sinfully warm and strong and reassuring against hers. "She— she told me that she has wanted for years to see me. To meet me. But my—Lord Warren would not allow it. And she then realized the only way she could see me was to arrange a clandestine visit. She was going to Lord Avermere's alone."

"Avermere?" He washed his other leg. "He is in Italy."

So Devlin was well aware of the comings and goings of the ton. Perhaps that was essential knowledge for a highwayman.

"Well, then, he must have returned," she said. "He would hardly have a house party if he wasn't at home."

"Turn around, Grace. Let me see you and bathe you. You've never been shy with me before."

She had, but this time it had nothing to do with being shy. He looked so . . . tempting and desirable in his bath. Lying back, soaking, hair brushed back and droplets of water making his lips moist—he looked so devastatingly likeable.

"Perhaps I am more comfortable this way." And she was, lying back against him. "But I suppose, since I am your prisoner, I am supposed to obey. Isn't that what the heroine did in the book you were reading—*Clarisse?* She obeyed her captor's every command."

She felt his laugh in the rumble of his chest against her spine. "I was reading the book for release, not guidance on the treatment of a lady, Grace."

The need to protest rose, but she quelled it. She had

looked through erotic books, had been intrigued by the orgies, all the while knowing she would not want to actually take part in one.

"Why?" she challenged. "I should think you would not need that sort of release."

"I haven't taken part in the orgies for a long time, sweeting." His knuckles slid up her spine, sending erotic tremors over her skin. "I'd hoped that you might want to stay longer, Grace. I'll deliver you unharmed, but I wanted a few days alone together, in this bedroom, with nothing to do but explore fantasy."

"Explore *your* fantasies, you mean. Like *Clarisse?*"

"This has nothing to do with that bloody book." Water splashed as he jerked his hands out of the water and she turned back as he raked his fingers through his hair. "The thing is I want you. I'm half mad with it. Twice, I've almost got a ball through my heart because I glimpsed blond hair on a coach's occupant and thought it might be you. I've scaled more damned trellises than I care to count, to stand into the shadows of a ballroom and hunt for you."

"You did that?" Grace pulled away from his strong, hot body, astounded yet confused.

"You came to my bath. I think you do want to stay, Grace."

"One night. I can stay for tonight. But tomorrow morning, I have to leave. And I *will*."

Steam swirled in Devlin's bedchamber and Grace brushed at the droplets clinging to her bare shoulders and the swells of her breasts. But as hot as the air was, she felt more heat inside.

"It's too hot in here, Grace. Let us go outside."

After her declaration, he had spoke only of inanities. He had remained firmly in the here and now—did she want him to wash her? Did she wish to wash her hair? What was her favorite scent? Dinner had appeared and then fresh strawberries and thick cream, but he had let her eat that entire treat herself.

He had watched as she dipped each strawberry, caught a soft cloud on the ripe red tip, then sucked off the cream. Over and over, she had done it, until his tension filled the room and she had then bitten into the berry and made a game of slurping juice and licking her lips.

He had been naked and she had seen his cock bounce as she ate each berry. His hand had strayed there twice, but he'd fisted his hand instead of touching himself. As though he'd wanted to draw out the agony.

She had to admit she was amazed by his control. Now, night had fallen and he was still hard. His cock jutted out like a saber as Devlin, naked, pushed open the doors, revealing a terrace lit by a splash of moonlight and fathomless darkness beyond. She slipped on his robe—the blue one he had given her. Even cloaked by darkness, she could not boldly walk outside naked.

He stood at the railing, and for a fanciful moment she imagined him on the bridge of a ship, wheel gripped in his hands. What was it like to sail? Her feet had never left solid ground.

Except now—even with the sturdy terrace beneath her, she did not feel on solid ground. A mass of a million stars filled the sky. Devlin caught her hand and drew her to his side. "There—that is Orion. And the Dipper. There, sweetheart, is the North Star."

"How do you know so much about the stars?" She whispered the question, awed into silence by the whisper of the breeze in the meadow and the melodies of the nighttime insects.

"For navigation, love. On a ship the knowledge is practical. Here with you, it's more . . . romantic." He slid his arm around her. The night was sweltering and, as he cradled her close, his robe clung to her damp skin. The silk stuck to her hard nipples.

"What do you want to do tonight?" she whispered. "Did you want me to join your orgy?"

"You asked that rather breathlessly. Is that what you want, Grace? In truth, I want to keep you for myself."

She gazed out over the dark woods and a puff of breeze set the leaves shivering, flashing like silver coins. "That's what I want—" She broke off as he undid the belt of her robe.

"Take it off."

She did, letting the night air caress her; then like Clarisse, she followed his next hoarse command. "Bend over the rail, display your lovely arse for me." His hips pressed to her, and the long, hard line of his erection bumped the valley of her derriere. "I want to do the most intimate things with you, Grace, if all I have is tonight." As he spoke, he arched forward and the head of his cock, thick and swollen, pushed into her wet quim.

9

Grace cried out in passion, her hot, tight cunny pulsing around him as she came again. Gritting his teeth, Devlin let his head drop back and shut his eyes tight. *Control. Control.*

He couldn't watch her come, damn it. He would explode inside her in an instant.

Grace thrust back against him, teasing his aching, ready-to-burst cock with her cream-slicked grip. It was torture to hang on, but he would do it.

Slowly he withdrew, pausing to punish himself with the head of his cock at the edge of her pussy. Grace slumped forward, greedily drawing in loud breaths, and Devlin felt his chest rumble with a laugh. He drew back finally, and his cock popped free, jerking up to rest against her lush arse.

She wriggled her derriere against him, slapping his cock against her cheeks.

God—

He dipped his fingers into her creamy quim, then rubbed the furled entrance to her rump. She gasped at the caress, and he stroked her until a deep, hungry moan tumbled from her lips.

"You like that," he said softly.

"It's good."

"You'll like my mouth there too," he promised.

"Devlin, you can't possibly do that—" But his tongue was already slicking over her rounded cheeks as he dropped to his knees behind her, and her words vanished into the hot, dark night.

His tongue flicked lazily over that sweetly tight opening and he tasted her most intimate flavors on his tongue. Clean from the bath but still earthy and ripe.

"I saw this . . . in a picture . . ." she breathed. "But I had no idea it was really done."

He wanted to say that anything was possible, and he wanted to do anything that gave her pleasure, but he just slid his tongue into her anus instead, twirling it to tease her sensitive rim.

Her back arched in a graceful line and her golden hair tumbled down her back. Her cries of delight floated up to the stars. Devlin held her hips, rocking her back to him as he plunged his tongue up her arse. His cock jutted up from his groin, swaying heavily, and his juice dribbled out of the tip.

He couldn't hold back any longer.

"That was so good, so astonishingly so," Grace whispered as he stood.

He stroked the sleek line of her back, letting his hand cup her rump. "I want to make love to you that way."

"You are certainly blunt!" But she nodded, her teeth worrying her lip. "You think I'm wanton, don't you? Of course you do—"

"I think you are the woman I want to pleasure. Now, stop judging yourself, love. Enjoy." He took hold of his shaft and brushed the head of his cock along the valley of her bottom.

She surged back, wriggling until the head touched her entrance. "Yes."

"Take it slow." He was warning himself, warning her. "Do you trust me?"

"Why?" she asked and her voice betrayed surprise. "Should I not?"

He chuckled at that, her blunt and simple question. "No, you have every reason to trust me."

Slowly, he thrust forward, his shaft bending in a painful but arousing way as his slippery cock tried to penetrate. She wasn't wet, but he was leaking juices. A small cry and her muscles opened to let him in, then resisted. She was gasping, panting.

He stroked her back, kissed the fragrant crook of her neck. "All right?"

"It's irresistible now," she answered. "I have to do it." Her voice was soft, seductive, relaxed—promising that she did indeed trust him.

Why had he asked for her trust?

But he couldn't think—her heat, her snug, enticing ring held him and teased him, squeezing the engorged head of his cock. Fists clenched, he worked his hips forward, pressing until she squeaked or gasped, then drawing back. They were locked in a sensual dance of anticipation. He would push in and she would take him, then gasp and pull away.

Each press forward was like dipping his wick into scalding flame. He watched his cock disappear inch by inch between the plump mounds of her arse as his heart pounded and his throat tightened. His ballocks pulled up tight as she cried "yes" and he surged forward, filling her, stretching her.

He slid his hand around front, between the swell of her tummy and the railing, and he found her clit, circling the bud with his finger.

She ground against his hand, then pushed back. She pumped against him, surprising him with her speed, her aggression. She half-turned, her cheeks a vivid flush.

If she wanted it hard and fast—

He thrust hard, giving her his cock to the hilt, and his brain stopped working, and his instincts took over. *Bury yourself in her heart. Rub her until she screams.*

She bucked back to him, and he felt her mound collide with his fingers with every frantic jolt.

"Devlin! Dev!"

She was coming. Beautifully. Ferociously.

Like a sixty-foot wave, his orgasm hit him, shattering his control. His balls jerked up tight and his surging come jetted out of him, filling her, coating him; and he gripped her to hold himself inside while his brain dissolved.

God, it was good—

He bent forward just as she arched back. His lips found hers and he drank in her cries. Her tongue teased his, and she kissed him with a fury that told him how intense her pleasure had been. She was claiming him, devouring him because he'd made her come so hard.

And he liked it.

"I'm not going to let you go, Grace."

Sleepily, Grace blinked. Devlin's words drifted into her thoughts, but she didn't entirely understand them. Then her brain focused on the word *not* and she jerked up to realize she was lying in his bed, nude, and he was sprawled naked at her side. Her legs pressed against his, her breasts damp with sweat with trickles running between. She gaped at Devlin. His amber brows were slashes over his eyes, his mouth firm and determined.

"You have to let me go!" She cried. It should have been exciting, arousing, to wake in his bed. Now she just felt like a prisoner. "I'm a day late already. Don't you understand? My grandmother will think I am not coming. I wrote to her there to say I would, but she will think I changed my mind. She'll leave. She will be hurt—"

"Good for her, then. Nothing she doesn't deserve." Devlin sat up, resting his big shoulders against the headboard.

Grace waved her hands frantically. "It was not her fault! If her husband insisted she was not to have anything to do with us, what exactly was she to do, O wise and commanding Captain?"

He shrugged. "A woman can bend even the most unyielding idiot to her will."

"Oh, really. And how is she to do that?" And then she slumped back and let tears fall. They were not entirely false—she was tired and shaking, and what if her grandmother really had given up on her arrival?

"Stop it. You have no right to cry over a shallow and callous woman."

Grace loudly sucked in a sobbing breath and saw him wince. "Do you not understand what it is like to be shunned simply for your birth? For who you are?"

"Yes," he grunted, his mouth harder. "I'm a marquis' bastard."

"Yes, but your father acknowledges you. Lady Prudence claimed your father prefers you—"

"That, my love, is not the truth."

"You knew the house—you even knew its secret passages." And she had only been in the home of the Earl and Countess of Warren once, incognito. She had taken one of the public tours with her sisters and mother. "All I want is just to speak to her."

Devlin sat up abruptly and shoved back his hair with both hands. Lines furrowed his brow. "Damn and blast, all right. I won't steal this from you, love."

"You are going to let me go?" Grace grimaced as she asked the question. Who was he to dictate to her? Why should she have to ask his permission? But she knew, from a lifetime of biting her tongue, that it was better to coerce than to confront.

He bent forward, resting his elbows on her knees, and slanted her a glance. "Of course. Tomorrow morning."

He looked so devastatingly handsome in that position, she had to force herself to look away. Leaving now meant leaving his bed and never returning.

It was for the best. Truly it was.

"Good," she answered, "I was going to go, with your permission or not, my highwayman." Now that she had her victory, she wanted to salvage some of her pride.

A wicked grin turned up his lips and she clutched the sheets—suddenly, she couldn't slide out of bed. Then he rolled over, capturing her with his arms. "Men who live outside the law are not easily defied, sweetheart. Remember that."

She intended to protest but his hips settled between her thighs and the only sound she managed was a flustered, "Ooh."

"I'm hard for you, Grace," he groaned and she felt his cock nudging against her. "I woke up hard for you."

She gulped, remembering Lord Wesley whispering similar words. But Devlin did not look smug and lusty. He looked . . . ravaged.

Uncertain, Grace gazed up at his surprisingly solemn blue eyes and teased, "Even after all our lovemaking?"

Where was the rakish pirate? Why did he seem so deadly serious about his arousal? But then he grinned, treating her to how delicious he was with dimples and crinkles at his eyes. He winked. "Yes. I could make love to you forever."

He thrust forward and she was so slippery, so wet, he slid right in. Filling her. Making her cry out.

"Yes," she moaned. This was when they thought and felt as one. She arched up to him, meeting his thrusts. He slipped his hand between them, teasing her clit until she saw stars.

Sobbing, she came. And even though she'd climaxed a dozen times before, it was as good, as heart melting, as exquisite. She screamed—swallowed her cry as Devlin captured her mouth in a kiss.

Shuddering, Devlin came with her and it was almost as good as coming herself. Limp, sweaty, whirling, she wrapped her arms and legs around him. And held him tight.

* * *

Three naked women slept in an erotic jumble on the daybed in his study. Devlin found himself chuckling at the sight, entertained but not aroused.

He'd left Grace in his bed while he walked around to see what was happening within the house. He would love to see her slumbering there on his daybed in the evenings: lovely, creamy perfection, exhausted by his lovemaking, tucked in with silken throws. He would tend to his work and watch her. He could never tire of watching her—

"Who is she?"

Devlin looked up to find Rogan St. Clair standing in the doorway, wearing only a pair of trousers. His lieutenant was barefoot and held a bottle of port in one hand, a lit cheroot in the other.

"Who is she?" Rogan repeated—"Who is the woman you took hostage, captain?"

Devlin sauntered past the slumbering women and casually poured a brandy. "She is not a hostage."

"Your evasive answer makes me think that the luscious lovely is worth a bloody boatload of money. True?"

"She will not be ransomed."

Rogan had walked into the room and flopped into one of the wing chairs drawn up close to the low fire. "From a good family, is she? Lovely way of speaking she has. Obviously she's a lady, and from the look of the clothes on her back, I'd say she's a wealthy one."

His lieutenant took a swig from his bottle, then wiped his mouth and leered. "Lovely tits on her. So what do you want with her, Captain? The novelty of introducing a well-bred virgin to the dirty, sweaty pleasures of fucking?"

He fisted his hand, itching to slam it into Rogan's nose, but he knew that to fight now would only increase St. Clair's interest in Grace. There was an angry edge to Rogan's words that Devlin did not like. Worry over lost money? Or something else? "Get the hell out, St. Clair," he said cheerfully but with an edge of warning beneath his own words.

"So I take it she's not a virgin. Not anymore. Still, how much do you think her fine family would pay to get her back?"

Devlin clenched his hand and the brandy glass exploded. The fine amber drink dripped to the floor along with droplets of his blood. "I've saved your bloody hide a dozen times, St. Clair. Do not push me or I will shoot you where you stand. You are to treat the lady with the utmost respect. She will not be frightened or harmed. And she will not be ransomed."

Rogan got to his feet, and the jovial grin had been replaced by hard anger. "What's the harm, Captain, if you don't intend to hurt her? You're planning to let her go home, and her family would pay for the privilege, none the wiser."

Devlin took out the key to the drawer that contained a set of fine dueling pistols.

"She's worth a bloody fortune and we are a team, the lot of us," St. Clair said. "You have no right to deny the rest of the men this chance—"

The gleaming wood box settled on his desk with a thud that silenced St. Clair.

"I won't kill you, St. Clair. Instead, I will give you the opportunity to fight for it."

Rogan pulled the cheroot from between his teeth. "You've never missed before, Captain. I'd be a fool to do it." His lips had drawn back from his teeth in rage. "You're only offering because you know you'll win."

"Go back to the orgy, St. Clair. Spare your hide."

Snarling, Rogan turned abruptly, then stalked out of the room.

Devlin returned the box to the drawer and pocketed the key, realizing how wrong he had been, how very correct Grace was. She could not stay. In the morning, as he'd agreed, he had to let her go. He had no damned choice.

So he would not waste another minute apart from her.

*   *   *

Oh, but she was sore. Grace's thighs ached from stretching around Devlin's hips, but it was a wonderful ache. Even though she was now dressed, she lay on the sofa, trying to find the energy to walk. She had rode Devlin while sharing breakfast with him—a delicate feat while drinking chocolate.

He had lounged back with his coffee on the delicate chair in the parlor and let her ride him like a wild woman. He'd flicked her clit with his coffee-warmed tongue until she'd exploded over and over.

And now she had to go.

Devlin popped in the door of the drawing room. "Ready, sweetheart?"

She nodded. This was her choice—she must be prepared to go, but her heart felt heavy as she got to her feet, then joined Devlin.

He walked with her out to the circle of gravel in the front of his house. Only one of his men waited for them, relaxing against her carriage, smoking. He held a pistol, letting it rest against his thigh. He was the raven-haired man who had had two women sucking his privates. He was Devlin's lieutenant, Mr. St. Clair.

A man I would trust with my life, Devlin had said. *He's saved my arse more times on the sea than I could count.*

Grace cast a worried glance to her brother-in-law's coachman and the groom who rode on the back. Neither looked in her direction. What were they thinking?

It was all very well for Devlin to have told the servants that he'd changed his mind about a ransom and was sending her back—and he'd paid them well for their silence. Her brother-in-law was a powerful, dominating earl. If he wanted the truth out of these men, he would get it.

She had to wonder why Devlin had taken so much risk just for her.

Then she caught her breath. A saddled horse—Devlin's

huge horse—stood by her carriage, the reins held in the hand of a young boy.

"What are you doing?" she demanded.

Devlin turned away from her servants to grin. "I said you could go. I said nothing about you going alone."

Rogan St. Clair filled his lungs with the aromatic smoke of his cheroot as he watched besotted Captain Sharpe help his precious lady into the carriage. With a practiced eye, Rogan took in her fancy clothes, her bright white teeth, and her cultured mannerisms. What would she be worth? Twenty thousand pounds, easily. Fifty, possibly. And he wondered, if she was some high-and-mighty earl's daughter, or even the daughter of a duke, whether he could get a hundred thousand for her.

It would be a challenge. That would be a queen's ransom. But he was fairly certain he could get it.

He was damned tired of living at Devlin Sharpe's pleasure. Damned tired of it.

He'd been on the crew of the *Black Mistress* long before Sharpe ever joined. He should have been the one to be first mate, to eventually become captain. Christ, how it had galled him to watch Sharpe get the wealth, the fame, the notoriety that should have been his.

Rogan tossed his smoke to the ground, where he crushed it with his boot heel as he watched Sharpe's hand linger on the lady's pretty ankle as she scurried into the carriage.

He should have slit Sharpe's throat a decade ago, out on the Caribbean seas, and let Sharpe's body feed the sharks. But he'd feared he would be caught and punished for slicing the windpipe of the captain's favorite. Hell, he'd served Captain Hawk well; he'd proved his mettle and his loyalty, but Rogan had known that he would have been forced to walk the plank for the murder of another crew member.

He could have killed Sharpe in the heat of battle, when no one would have noticed that it was he and not the British

Navy who had put a pistol ball or a blade in Sharpe's heart. He could have done it on one of their drunken orgies in a port, where they'd swived as many women as they possibly could and had had a long running wager as to who could bring the most women to orgasm in one session.

He was damned certain Sharpe had paid the women well to fake their screaming climaxes.

Hell, that's what he had done.

But he had bided his time instead of killing his rival. Rogan had learned that control served a man better than hot rage. Sharpe had proven to be a cunning pirate and a bold highwayman and, as a gang, they had stolen a fortune.

Now it was time to get what was rightfully his.

"Before ye mount up, Captain, I'd like to have a word."

Devlin sensed instantly from Rogan St. Clair's low, angry tone that the business of the night before was not yet finished. He glanced from Rogan's pistol, still held casually against the man's thigh, to Rogan's cold gray eyes.

Devlin took the reins from the young groom's hands. "My answer is the same as last night."

Grinning, his lieutenant lifted the pistol and leveled the muzzle with Devlin's heart.

"And I could kill you where you stand, Captain."

A flare of panic turned Devlin's blood to hot fire and he knew that familiar rush of excitement that made his senses keen. He took a slow breath. "You could, St. Clair, but that would buy you a quick hanging and wouldn't get you what you want."

"Maybe the others wouldn't hang me. Maybe they'd follow me. None of them like being at your beck and call, Captain—where you hold the purse strings and dole it out to us when we beg for it. We deserve the rewards we're entitled to." Rogan jerked his head toward the carriage, where the door stood open. "And she's worth a bloody lot of money."

"I know you're an honorable man, St. Clair."

"But not a stupid one." His arm straightened; he cocked the weapon.

Something flew from the carriage—a dark shape hurtled out the open door and Grace screamed. Screamed so loud that St. Clair jerked slightly toward her.

Devlin jumped forward, charging toward St. Clair as the pistol came swinging back to face him, but the dark object completed its arc. A chain fluttered in the wind as Grace's reticule came hurtling down and slammed into the side of St. Clair's head.

"Jesus bloody Christ—"

Rogan's curse died as Devlin's fist connected with his lieutenant's jaw and sent his head snapping back in the opposite direction. He wrenched the pistol from Rogan's hand, followed with a hard left into his friend's solid gut, then leveled the gun at Rogan's head.

His lieutenant had doubled over with the blow to his stomach.

"Get the hell out of here, St. Clair," Devlin barked. "If you turn around and run as fast as you bloody well can, I may not blow off your head. But if you stay here, I promise you I will."

Pure fury turned St. Clair's face a dark, mottled red. Survival meant turning tail and running like a coward—Devlin's intention was to humiliate.

"You're bloody mad. I'm entitled to my share of the loot, you bastard."

Devlin let the insult roll off him. "You took a vow of loyalty. We all did. A broken vow is a forfeit, St. Clair. Now, get the hell out of here or lose a hell of a lot more than money."

Cursing, Rogan swung around, and he jogged along the lane toward the gateposts.

Devlin knew many men who would have shot Rogan rather than letting him run. Easier to have a dead enemy than a live one.

But he couldn't do it.

He could not take a man's life just to make his easier.

He saw Grace's pale face framed by the dark interior of the carriage and he gave her a low bow. "Thank you, my dear. You saved my life."

She could taste salt in the air, and was certain she could hear the roar of the sea over the clatter of the carriage wheels.

Grace stole a glance out the window—she had not done so for the last hour. To look out would give her a view of Devlin trotting his horse alongside the carriage.

And there he was. For all his horse was large, he looked as dominant as the animal. He moved easily, gracefully, with it, the reins held with assured confidence. How relieved she was that he was safe, alive, unhurt, and she loved to watch the gentle bob of his shoulders. As for the way his thighs were spread—

He caught her gaze and smiled. The sun painted his face with warm gold and soft rose and turned his hair to gleaming bronze.

"This is preposterous!" she cried out the open window. She had been shaking after the horrible scene at Devlin's manor. She had actually snapped apart the chain on her reticule with her nervous hands. "You cannot accompany me here. People will know."

He inclined his head. "I'm not always the blackguard, my dear. I've escorted young women before—to protect them from the other animals that prowl the roads."

"Have you, indeed," she muttered. And what did he do to those young women? What did he ask of them in return?

His body moved gracefully with the horse's trot. "And there have been widows traveling alone who were very welcoming of my protection."

Well, there was her answer. "No doubt." She winced at the obvious acerbity to her tone.

His clear laugh rang up to the treetops. "I've been riding

the last few hours with an erection, love—no need to worry that I haven't been suffering."

"And so you should—" she began, enjoying the tart teasing, until she realized that he had used the word *erection* in front of Marcus's servants.

"Sir!" she cried, and she shrank back from the window, as a scandalized woman would.

Deliberately, she fixed her gaze on the opposite window, her heart thumping and her stomach jumping with every lurch of the carriage. He'd said he had kidnapped her for an affair lasting a few days. An amusement. A bit of lusty fun.

So why come with her? Why would he say, "Grace, I can't let you go?" Of course, he could. Once they arrived, he was going to return to his home, wasn't he?

She bit her lip, aware that she could not even begin to guess what Devlin would do. She had barely eaten today and knew nothing would settle. Nor could she sleep. She just stared at the other window, not seeing a thing, utterly aware of the highwayman who rode alongside her carriage . . .

She jerked up as the carriage slowed. Gritting her teeth, she leaned to the window on Devlin's side and looked out. They had passed Portsmouth and were following a small road that wove its way close to the English Channel coast. A sign pointed toward Netley and Southhampton, and just beyond it the coach pulled to a stop.

They had reached two stone gateposts—one bearing a crisply painted sign that read *Land's End*. This was not actually the area of that name—that was far to the west of here—this was the owner's fancy. Grace rapped the roof, and the carriage turned onto a narrower lane. She could almost lick salt off her lips now, and heard the distant thundering of waves on rocks. That must be the channel's waters flowing through the Solent, the stretch of sea that separated the Isle of Wight from the mainland.

Devlin had ridden ahead now, as he could not risk riding alongside them on the narrow track. Well and good. She certainly had no reason to remain at the window, staring at his wide shoulders and the way his taut derriere bounced on the saddle—

No—no reason. And the rogue was probably aware of her gaze.

She sat back. Within hours, she would meet her grandmother. Butterflies blossomed in her stomach now. She had to prepare. To think of what to say. But she was afraid—afraid to offer any emotion, any piece of herself, unless she was certain that it would be returned with kindness.

Beyond "I am Grace," she could think of nothing to put forth. So she leaned to the window again. The golden glow of the afternoon sun was like a beacon ahead of them, but the surrounding woods were dark and shadowed. Ominous, of course. And something was wrong—

Untended lilac bushes spilled over the lane, their flowers now dead. She recognized some—though she'd never taken much interest in flowers that did not come in a bouquet with a card. Rhododendrons.

The front wheel hit a deep rut and she lurched on the seat.

The sign that announced *Land's End* had been bright and white, yet this lane looked as though no one had bothered to tend it for years. Her neck prickled—rather like Clarisse's must have when she had arrived at her guardian's foreboding castle.

A peer would have such a rustic estate? It seemed . . . unlikely. But then, not all members of the ton were wealthy. There were some as poor as she had once been—they just found it more possible to acquire credit.

The lane curved, giving her a glimpse of Devlin through young trees. Dappled shadows rained upon his shoulders and hat and slid along his golden hair.

Yes, she was rather glad to have him with her.

The lane twisted again, and her carriage and horses blocked her view. But she leaned out the window, watching anxiously. Did this lane actually lead anywhere? It appeared to be a meandering journey through the woods. More wild patches of color fought with vines and untended shrubs, and her heart sank to her stomach.

Suddenly, the carriage picked up speed and light slanted toward them. Within moments the track widened and hooves crunched on gravel. The trees gave way, revealing a clearing and a large, sprawling stone manor house.

A crumbling but ostentatious manor house—a blend of Tudor and Georgian architecture attached to an ancient tower.

This was Avermere's house, which he used as a base before taking his ship over to the island. But it wasn't expected at all. She had thought an earl, as Avermere was, would take better care of his home.

A riot of red roses furled for the night, climbed the stone walls of the first floor. Shafts of pink-toned light touched the paned windows, but the drapes inside were shut. Another carriage stood in the drive, surrounded by servants unloading a series of trunks.

Not the Countess of Warren's carriage, she was certain. This one was modest, black, and without a crest or coronet on the door. Nor were there anywhere near enough trunks to meet the needs of a countess.

Suddenly, nerves struck again. She couldn't imagine why a stranger's carriage would set her stomach fluttering.

Devlin walked his horse back toward her window. The sun was behind him and the brim of his hat cast his face in shadow. She could not see him, but she saw the straight, tall posture he held. The way he turned to scan constantly all around him.

She heard another crunch on the gravel slightly behind them, and she leaned out the window to see.

A fashionable phaeton drew to a halt, the owner perched a good six feet above the ground. A gentleman, wearing a wide-brimmed hat, a greatcoat. She spied a touch of silver in his black hair, but despite the lines that bracketed mouth and eyes, he was handsome. Enough to send the breath spilling from her chest. Brilliant green eyes beneath black lashes. Full lips surrounded by dark stubble. A scar that followed the sharp line of a cheekbone. From the back, a tiger and a groom jumped down.

"Grace."

Her door, the one opposite, swung open and let the warm afternoon air spill in, along with the melody of the fields— the whisper of leaves and grass, the sounds of bugs, the lowing of cattle.

She stared at Devlin, who stood, with hand outstretched, waiting to help her down.

"You should leave now. You've delivered me."

"I do not like this. The nob in the phaeton is Lord Sinclair. Bloody notorious rake. He'll be in your bed before the moon comes up."

"Devlin! I would never allow such a thing."

"He doesn't ask, sweetheart. You need me here."

Grace swallowed hard. Two years had passed since she'd made the mistake of believing Lord Wesley, when she had made the mistake that had tainted her forever. But two years was really not all that long. She wanted to believe she could outwit a revolting rake but she wasn't certain. Two years ago, Devlin had come to her rescue. He had protected her reputation. As much as she wanted his protection, she had to send Devlin away.

And the real truth—she didn't want him to go. "Devlin," she whispered, "You can't possibly stay."

10

B ut as he'd warned her, he did not abide by the king's laws, so he was not about to be deterred by any of her threats, arguments, or—at a moment of extreme frustration—pleas.

Grace could see that Devlin was determined to stay. At least he had the good grace to lounge in the background, where he watched from beneath the brim of his tilted hat and smoked a cheroot while she rapped on the front door of the cottage.

An elderly servant opened the door—a butler, she would guess, from the grand look of his clothes, though she was surprised to see a butler at such a modest house. His back was rounded and, as he cocked his head in curiosity at her question, he looked like a question mark himself.

"Whom did you say, Miss?"

"Lady Warren. She is a guest of Lord Avermere. I am . . ." Her words failed her. Was she allowed to publicly admit to being her ladyship's granddaughter? "I am Miss Hamilton."

"Aah." The man bobbed his head. "The party is being held at the house, Miss. This is the cottage. You shall have to sail to get to his lordship's house. It's on the island—just west of Cowes. Not a long trip, though, Miss, and a boat has been engaged to ferry the rest of the party, who have recently arrived. Your luggage should be taken to the quay. I will send out assistance for you."

The door swung closed once more. Only to abruptly re-open. "The boat will not be leaving for an hour. Perhaps you would care to refresh yourself, Miss."

She was tired. And sweaty and gritty from the dust on the roads. Her heart fluttered in panic at the thought that she had arrived only within an hour of the boat leaving. What if she had missed it? But she nodded and glanced back to Devlin. He appeared engaged in a jovial conversation with the grooms. "Yes," she said. "I would care to refresh myself."

She followed the butler with the curved spine, who also walked with a limp. All in all, she could not imagine her beautiful, fashionable grandmother finding any element of this house acceptable. Her slippers coasted along a worn and uneven floor. The house smelled of the kitchens—and heat seemed to pour off the walls. The summer had been hot and dry and the house had absorbed it all.

They reached a closed door, and voices sounded behind it. But the butler continued on and paused at an open door. "The west parlor," he announced. "Preferred by the ladies."

Grace straightened her shoulders and approached, but she found only a small, empty room, with a settee, two wing chairs, a low table, and an unlit fire. She shivered, though the sun poured in the paned, west-facing windows.

This all felt . . . odd. Not right. She paced toward the windows, but these looked out at the gardens. What was Devlin doing? Had he left, as he should do? Or was he determined to defy her, to put her at risk, and stay?

Grace stood at the back of the assembled party waiting at the quay. Two gentlemen, Lord Sinclair and Mr. Nelling, a handsome auburn-haired playwright, sprawled in chairs set out by the servants as the trunks were loaded on to the small boat. Elderly Lady Horton sat in a sedan chair beneath the shade of both a leafy tree and a parasol. The breeze blew up the Solent, ruffling her parasol and the flowers of her bonnet. Grace has seen her ladyship—a notorious gossip with silvery hair and narrow eyes—at many balls and routs. Lady Horton held a book on her lap but her eyes darted to the handsome gentlemen, appraisal and appreciation evident in her faded blue eyes. At her side sat a lovely woman Grace knew to be Mrs. Montgomery, a wealthy and fashionable widow.

Devlin strolled over and bowed before her. "Miss Hamilton."

Grace saw Lady Horton's gaze rivet to her. Obviously all knew he was a marquis' bastard and not a gentleman. Did they all also know he'd been a pirate and was now a highwayman?

"Mr. Sharpe, we really should not converse."

"I'm not a threat to your reputation in front of so many watchful eyes."

"Mr. Sharpe, you are always a threat to my reputation," she whispered. She glanced from the gentlemen to her ladyship. "This seems a strange group to bring together."

"House parties always are. Makes my line of work more interesting." He grinned. "And most would not have a highwayman on the guest list." His eyes twinkled. "Lady Horton would receive me."

"I imagine she would. She's ogling the other gentlemen here and I've seen her eyes light up when she looks at you."

"As a subject of gossip, I hope." He grimaced and she laughed. He was correct about house parties. They always did assemble the oddest mix—which could sometimes prove disastrous.

She thought of her last house party with Lady Prudence; then she pushed away the memories of Prudence's hateful words.

Grace gazed at the flamboyant beauty of Mrs. Montgomery— a good friend of Lady Prudence's mother. She gleamed like a bower of summer roses, her skin pale and petal-soft, her lips a deep rose, her hair burnished gold with wispy ringlets dangling against her cheeks. A pelisse of delicate pink topped a sheath of deep pink muslin, all clinging to a lushly perfect figure.

Devlin bowed over her hand, and Grace started.

"I'm going to leave you to pay my respects to Lady Horton."

"Why?"

"To acquire an invitation, my love," he murmured. And with a wink, he left to prowl toward her ladyship. Of course, Mrs. Montgomery fixed her lioness-like gaze on him, and watched every inch of his approach. Her tongue slid over those red lips as though she knew how his mouth would taste.

Devlin bowed over Mrs. Montgomery's hand, so gallant and charming Grace wanted to grind glass with her back teeth. But he quickly turned to Lady Horton and, before her eyes, Grace watched him turn the elderly gossip into a purring cat.

"Miss Hamilton?"

A young man stood before her, his brown cap in his hands. "The boat's ready, Miss."

Devlin was instantly at her side, sliding her arm through his to lead her down to the boat. He bent low, his lips tantalizingly close to her cheek. Instantly, heat washed over Grace's skin, her cleavage became dewy, and her inner thighs went hot beneath her skirts. She breathed in his sensual, musky scent over the tang of the sea. "I have an invitation from Lady Horton, love. I have no reason to leave your side."

"I've never sailed," Grace admitted. "And I am not entirely certain I wish to have my maiden voyage now. Trapped on a boat with Lord Sinclair, lecherous rapist, and cold-eyed Mr. Nelling?"

"There is time to change your mind, love. To return with me."

She shook her head. "No."

"Then trust in me to keep you safe. You are still my captive, love."

"What?" She jerked her arm away from him.

His devastating dimple showed. "I haven't actually let you go free, love, and I intend to keep you constantly under my supervision."

She balked and straightened her spine. "I am not your captive anymore, Mr. Sharpe."

"Not to worry, love. I'm as much your captive as you are mine."

"Humph." That she did not believe. A highwayman who kept a personal harem could hardly be her captive. She knew it and, for the sake of her heart, she could not let herself forget it. He had only wanted to spend a few days with her, indulging in passion.

A sexual adventure. Nothing more. There couldn't be more.

The punt bobbed in the water, waiting to ferry her and Devlin to the ship. The sailing ship was moored out in the deeper, dark water. Devlin's hand clasped hers tightly as she took a tentative step into the small boat. The boat shifted on the waves and floated slightly away.

Devlin's hand at her waist steadied her, and for one proud moment she wanted to surge ahead, to prove she was in command of herself. Something she had never, ever been before. After all, the one decision she had boldly made had ruined her life.

The oarsmen brought the boat tight to the quay, and Devlin's grip tightened. He was not going to let her go.

Suddenly, she didn't care about proving herself. She let him help her in. Once she was seated, he easily slung his leg into the boat, gracefully got in, and sat across from her. She clutched the side of the boat as the oarsmen rowed them to the waiting sailing vessel and kept her eyes fixed on the horizon. She didn't like water. It terrified her to think of being in water over her head, out of control, gasping for air but unable to breathe.

But Devlin's confidence, Devlin's easy smile, gave her courage. And soon she was standing at the rail of the sailing ship. Devlin had led her toward the bow to stand at the rail, even as the other guests settled inside the cabin. The sails furled open to catch the wind and they were off.

He stood at her side. Was this what he had felt as he captained a ship on the south seas? She felt as though she flew over the waves. "Oh!" She cried it out, a simple shout of exultation and she heard Devlin's laugh. A wide grin split his face, half-shielded by his whipping hair. She tipped her face forward and shut her eyes, catching the spray on her cheeks and lips.

This was so exhilarating! So—

Her stomach began to roil and heave. She was going to be sick! The ship seemed to point to the heavens one moment and the bottom of the sea the next.

"Oh God—"

"Not a good sailor, are you, sweeting?" Devlin leaned against the rail at her side, and slid his arm around her waist. "Look directly ahead, at the horizon. Look in the direction we are going. It takes away some of the feeling of sickness."

She clung to the rail, looking in the direction they *seemed* to be going, for that quelled her nausea a bit. For an instant she leaned against his familiar warmth and strength. Then she jerked away. Clapped a hand to her mouth as the deck lurched beneath her.

She couldn't move so quickly.

She realized that his intimate stance made it obvious he was no protector. And she'd been terrified that cuddling against him would result in her being sick on him.

"H-how do you stand this?"

"It's never bothered me, Grace."

Of course it hadn't, and it was another reminder that she and he belonged to entirely different worlds.

The sails billowed, catching the strong wind, blue-white against the brilliant sky.

He splayed his hand against the small of her back, steadying her as the damnable ship rolled up and down as though it was a giant, flexible snake, not a sleek wooden vessel.

"All the others are below—possibly sick. And the crew is too busy to notice us."

"You aren't—you aren't suggesting we . . . make love here?"

Husky and deep, his laugh teased her. "Of course not, sweeting, unless you are interested—"

"Oh God," she cried fiercely, panic in her eyes. "I'm not."

"Is it worth all this agony to see a snob of a woman who has never given you a moment's consideration before?"

"Is it worth all this trouble to follow me about and ask me irritating questions?"

"Yes it is, love."

Rocks—black and slick with sea spray—suddenly loomed on her right, whichever side that was in ship's parlance. "Look—" She pointed. "They look like fingers of an enormous monster waiting to pull a ship to the depths."

The ship pointed at their glistening, cruel edges and raced toward them. Grace held her breath, forgot all but survival, and clung to Devlin's arms.

"It only looks as though we're to be dashed on the rocks," he reassured and, of course, it was true, for the ship turned again and swept safely past the rocks.

A glimmer of light caught her eye and she turned to it.

Slivers of golden light—windows reflecting the sunlight—winked between a stand of trees. A house stood near a sheer bluff, sheltered by thick green woods. The lights seemed to stretch endlessly, and the waters calmed as they passed by the shadowed house. The glow at the windows threw some light across the house's façade, but she was too far away to see clearly.

She shivered as they rounded a narrow peninsula, into the shadow of the cliffs, guided by lamps burning at a small quay.

Devlin slid off his coat as the anchor hit the rippling water with a splash and drew it on around her shoulders.

"Cold?"

The silk lining of his coat carried his warmth but couldn't ward away her nerves.

"Starting to doubt." What was she thinking, admitting the truth, especially as he had doubted all along? Tears burned in her eyes. Her grandmother wanted to see her and it had been enough to bring her on this mission. Now that she was no longer on the mainland and about to step on an isolated island, she truly did wonder what she was doing.

Nerves were threatening to take command of her.

"I'll take care of you," he answered simply.

She touched her stomach. "Let's just leave this godforsaken ship first."

"The Countess of Warren," Grace repeated. "I wish to let her know I've arrived."

Devlin lounged in the background of the foyer, an unlit cheroot clamped between finger and thumb. Behind him, servants fussed over Lady Horton, who described the experience of seasickness with gut-churning bluntness. He had to smother a laugh.

The bald butler regarded Grace without emotion. "I beg your pardon, Miss," he intoned, as though he couldn't care less about her pardon, "but her ladyship has asked that she not be disturbed. By anyone."

Devlin watched Grace's face fall, her cheeks whiten. "I do not understand. She asked me to meet her here."

Damn. He'd feared this. Another capricious witch of the ton.

"And I am afraid I was not made aware that you would be joining the party," the servant added coldly. "You shall have to take the yellow room. It is the most modest room and the only one unoccupied."

The most modest room. The snooty bugger had laid emphasis on those words.

"Then where will that leave me?" Devlin strode forward,

his arms across his chest, wearing intimidation like a mantle. The butler blanched and stepped back. As Devlin glowered, the butler was able to quickly produce another bedroom for him and then he retreated in a hurry.

Grace quickly masked her pain behind a polite mask, but he felt it. And he saw it in the hesitant way she reached out, as though to ask the departing servant more. But she stopped. As though she felt the weight of his gaze, she turned.

He bowed over Grace's hand. "Allow me to assist you to your room," he murmured.

"You shouldn't."

"No lock would keep me out."

But his teasing produced no smile. "She might be ill," he said.

It was also possible the countess had sent the note, then changed her mind. He knew what many titled women were like. Hell, he'd bedded enough of them. A bit of gossip, the opportunity for a new lover, and they cast aside all other thought.

Not that his mother, who had been the daughter of country gentry—the daughter of an unlucky and unskilled gambler—had been any different. He'd grown accustomed to sleeping outside, for she had often locked him out of the small cottage. Even then, a lock couldn't keep him out—but he hadn't wanted to be inside where he would hear her moans. She'd always screamed and moaned for the men who'd fucked her, in the hopes they might enjoy her enough to stay.

They never did.

"What if she is not going to see me at all?" Grace asked.

He admired her for having the courage to voice her fears. He offered his arm. "That's something we don't need to worry about yet."

"Thank you."

She spoke it so softly he wasn't certain he heard it, but he did hear her mutter, "Oh! Blast!" as she stopped abruptly. Devlin had to tear his gaze from her wide green eyes to see what had shocked her.

"Blast is damned right," he groaned. His half brother, Lord Wesley, was walking down the corridor with Lady Prudence at his side. What in blazes were his half siblings doing here? The hairs stood up on the nape of his neck. Damnation, probably Wynsome was here to attend to his relative, Lady Warren, and had invited bloody Wesley.

Prudence gasped and stopped, which forced Wesley to pause, to notice Devlin and Grace. Prudence's mouth hardened into a cold line; then she tipped up her chin, and her eyes took on a blank, icy haughtiness. She wheeled about on her heel and sniffed to Wesley. "Let us go this way."

As though they did not exist. The famous cut direct used by society women to vanquish their foes.

Devlin laughed. They might possess noble blood, but God, they were small-minded and pitiful. He glanced down and saw Grace's freckles, stark splotches of gold against ivory cheeks.

Hell, Prudence's rude cut had wounded Grace, had fed into the fears and doubts she kept close to her heart. He knew, because he had carried those fears too.

He was not a gentleman. He was nothing. Worthless.

He knew that was what Grace feared. That she didn't belong.

He was not about to let Grace tear herself apart over the bloody ton. "Come with me. To your bedroom."

"You cannot possibly come in," Grace protested, but Devlin grinned like Lucifer. Ignoring her command, he took a bold step forward, forcing her to retreat into her bedroom and let him in. At least he glanced up and down the corridor first to ensure no one had seen him.

She did wish he would listen to her for once.

But of course he was not going to.

"Well, you'd never fit on that bed," she warned, folding her arms beneath her breasts.

Devlin laughed at that and sauntered over to it. He bounced on it, testing it first, then flopped back on the yellow counterpane. She rather liked the modest room—with its yellow sprigged wallpaper and buttercup lace-trimmed curtains.

Devlin spread his long legs so his boots touched the floor. But her gaze strayed to the way his trousers tightened over his thighs, his hips, his crotch.

"Do you still have the letter your grandmother sent?"

She hadn't expected that. "Yes." She withdrew it from her reticule, gave the folded sheet to him, then dropped the bag to the vanity. She waited by it, nervously, as he read. "A maid might come—to unload my belongings."

He pillowed his arm beneath his head and laid the letter down beside him on her bed. Her throat tightened. She wanted to lie on top of him.

But that reminded her of Wesley, of her past stupidity, and her stomach churned. Wesley's hands gripping her breasts. Wesley smirking up at her. His crude talk of her tits. And she, fool that she was, had been excited by it.

Why could she not forget him? Why did she keep remembering that horrible experience?

Why in blazes did he and Prudence have to be here? She'd waited her entire life to see her grandmother. What if Prudence and Wesley spoke to Lady Warren, ruined her chances?

She had to grip the bedpost.

"There's something about this letter—"

Devlin's words snapped her thoughts back and she saw him frown.

"Who knows you are the granddaughter of the Earl of Warren?" he asked.

"What do you mean? You think my grandmother did not write it? That makes no sense. Hardly anyone knows, outside of my family. Marcus and Dash, of course. Marcus's sister, I think, along with Dash's. But they are family."

"Anyone else?"

"No. What would be the point in telling anyone, only to be denounced for it?" A hard and heavy pain knotted her stomach. "I wanted to tell Prudence, even, but I didn't."

"Why did you want to tell her?" Then he groaned. "To prove you had noble blood. To prove you are as good as her."

"I don't know. But anyway, I did not speak of it. I knew I wasn't supposed to. Anyway, what is it that you don't like about the letter?"

"I never believe a woman of the ton reveals emotion."

She shivered at the cold, hard tone of his words. Obviously he had been badly hurt, and she wanted to ask more around the sudden knot of jealousy wedged in her throat, but the bed creaked as Devlin shifted.

He held out his hand. "Sweeting, why can you not understand that you do not have to prove anything to anyone?"

She really did hate it when he gave her advice. He was a man. He could do whatever he wished. She launched away from the vanity and stormed to the side of her bed. "Should I also pick up a pistol and rob innocent people? Is that how I should carve my way in the world? I do not have the luxury of being wild and rebellious."

He rolled onto his side, his greatcoat fanning over her bedspread. "You're wild inside, Grace—"

"It is not something to be celebrated," she protested. "You are merely suspicious of the ton because they never accepted you either." She waited but he added nothing—nothing to give her a clue as to why he specifically did not trust ladies of the ton. Irritated by the gallop of her heartbeat, she snapped, "And you really must get off my bed and find your own."

"Trysting is what the ton does at house parties." Devlin swung his legs around and sat up, but instead of getting up, he undid his cravat. "I'm only doing what Quality does, love."

"What exactly do you think you are doing?"

"Taking off my clothes."

Devlin saw Grace's delicate jaw drop as he pulled off his coat, waistcoat, boots, and trousers. "You know, I'm glad I'm a bastard and not a 'gentleman.' I've never met one worthy of the name." He gave her a grin. "Do you know what I do with the money I steal, love?"

She pursed her lips, transforming her sensual mouth into a prim, pinched line. "Support your harem?"

"I use the money to help ordinary people ignored and abused by our society. The ruined women who are cast out, the orphaned babes, the men who were wounded in war and are now forgotten."

"So the ton is cruel, and you are Robin Hood." But her gaze betrayed her, raking over his body, and he felt his skin flame in the wake of her wide eyes.

"I'm not a saint. But neither is any member of high society." Hell, his instincts warned him that Grace was in danger of being emotionally hurt. He'd never met the Countess of Warren, had never had the pleasure of holding up her coach, but he didn't trust her.

"I am going to wait," Grace said firmly, "and meet my grandmother."

"Then come and climb on top of me, love, while you're waiting." Sprawling back on her tiny bed, Devlin heard it groan in protest. All he wore was his linens, and his cock was a rigid bulge beneath them.

He saw anger turn her eyes to brilliant green and then the heat of desire flare in them. But she shook her head and her breath caught. "No. I don't like to . . . to do it that way."

Then he understood. She'd done that with Wesley, and the bloody blackguard had broken her heart. Pain flitted across her eyes and she lowered her lashes. He shifted to lie on his side on the narrow bed. Patted the warmed space beside him. "Come here."

"You are not going to leave, are you?"

At the slow shake of his head, she bit her lip. "Take off your linens." Her throaty voice slid over him, making his cock buck as she sashayed to the bed. Her pain seemed to have vanished, replaced by fiery need. She was still dressed in her gown and pelisse that fit skintight to her full breasts and generous hips. Normally, he liked to be the one dressed with a naked woman, but he had to admit he was enjoying this.

He peeled his small clothes over his hard cock, watching the thick shaft spring out, and she kneeled on the bed and bent to the head. "If you aren't going to leave, then—"

He groaned, watching her plump lips get closer. Her tongue snaked out and licked the head of his prick. Hot. Wet. Pressing into his sensitive head. *God*—

He let his head drop back as pleasure streaked up from his heavy cock to his brain.

She planted a hot, wet kiss to the dripping tip and his cock bobbed its approval.

"I've fantasized about this for two years," she whispered.

Devlin couldn't breathe. Her lips parted, slick and shiny with the fluid oozing from him. Her tongue traced the curve of her lip. "Delicious," she murmured.

Hell, he wanted her to like this. He wanted it so damned badly he ached for it, but he wanted it to be her choice—

She opened her mouth wide and took him in. Heat engulfed the swollen head, then the shaft, and her tongue teased the ridges and veins. Her mouth fit snugly around him, surrounding him with mind-melting pleasure.

Noisily she slurped him in and out, and it was the most erotic sight to watch his cock vanish between her pink lips. His hips began to pump to her on their own accord. He wanted to slide his entire length into her mouth, he needed to, and he fought for control.

He didn't want to hurt her. He had to give her the control.

Then she hollowed her cheeks, sucked him deep, and toyed with his balls.

"Grace, God—" His fingers drove into the counterpane, the pillow. He felt fabric tear and he clenched his teeth, trying to hold back his climax. He'd never surrendered like this before—

She sucked him deep, her eyes watered, and her clever fingers caressed his aching ballocks and his tight arse.

"Lord!" He jerked forward as his muscles exploded with his fierce climax, as his entire body bucked with the searing heat and intense delight, and he roared with it. Roared. Shouted. Howled as his steaming come rushed out.

She drank it. Suckled it. Took it all. And he fell back on the bed, groaning as her lush lips kept teasing him, as her tongue pressed hard against him and the suction kept coming. Kept *him* coming, to the point where he was so damned sensitive, he was in agony.

"Sweetheart—" He coaxed her to release him, watched, stunned as she swallowed again. Then he grasped her shoulders, pulled her on top of him, and kissed her hard, tasting his semen on her lips.

She drew away from the kiss. "I think you were loud," she accused.

Damn. Discretion. He'd forgotten about that. "There's other ladies' rooms on this floor. Just look innocent and no one will know it was your room."

She backed off the bed, away from him, and he shivered at the loss of her warmth. Her expression was troubled.

"I have to stay away from you, Devlin."

After that, she was threatening to stay away? "Not going to happen, love. I intend to stay close. To protect you."

"By ruining me? Devlin, it doesn't matter to me anymore if I am ruined. But it will devastate my family. I cannot just live for the moment. I cannot risk making a mistake. You have to get up, get dressed, and leave."

He stayed on her bed. She would have to drag him off it. "I want to come to you tonight."

"Don't. My door will be locked, my window barred."

If she locked her door, he had half a mind to kick it off its hinges. But what would that gain him? It was his bloody problem—his stupidity for hungering for a proper lady.

He got up, the bed creaking. She was right. If their affair was discovered, she would be ruined. He clenched his fists. Bloody, hypocritical ton. They'd relish in her downfall—the way Lady Prudence had attacked with the cut direct.

Her cheeks were pink, her breasts heaving, and seducing her now would mean he would be trying to seduce an adversary.

Once he would have found that exciting. Now it left his heart cold.

As he dragged on his clothes, he could not help but give her a last piece of advice. "The opinions of women like Prudence do not matter."

"Yes," she said simply. "In my circles, they do." She bent her head, and muttered, "I've spent two years carefully avoiding Lord Wesley, and now I am trapped in the same house with him."

"Wesley?" Damn, she had been in bed with him and now was thinking of Wesley. What the hell? Devlin's heart pounded as he slanted a glance to her face. She was nibbling her thumbnail. Pensive. Worried.

At once he tensed with icy cold, but a red-hot rage flared in his brain. Wesley was of Grace's world; he was not. Could it be she still loved the bastard? Damn and blast. From her thoughtful gaze, her troubled eyes, he couldn't tell. He'd practically read the thoughts of British Navy captains at they stared him down over cannons, but he couldn't guess at Grace's feelings.

She yearned for acceptance by the ton. It was a bloody foolish goal, but he understood it.

He couldn't risk destroying everything Grace wanted by forcing his way into her bedroom.

And even if he could convince her to give up this mad goal, he will likely end his life in prison. He could never offer her a future.

He had to walk away.

11

Ironic that he chose to stalk to the cliff edge in the dark to look out over the water, clenching an unlit cheroot between his fingers. Women had driven him to the sea years ago, when he had no money and no future. When he had made the mistake of falling in love with a titled woman.

Devlin crossed his arms in front of his chest, his body buffeted by the wind, and he remembered.

Remembered how the beautiful Countess of Dorchester had loved him in her bed.

And how she had feared someone might see him in her parlor.

Moonlight shimmered over the surf crashing onto the rocks below. Salt in the air touched his lips and skin—it tasted like he stood on the bridge of a ship. Clouds had rolled in, obscuring the stars.

He understood why Grace wished so much for her grandmother's acceptance. For well over two years, throughout their affair, he had been a young, starstruck man, wanting to hear his countess admit that she loved him.

She never did.

Finally she had bored of his passion and devotion and had dismissed him. She had sent him a letter, softly perfumed with her unique scent. Only one line had been written inside. *You have been replaced with Rupert.* The younger son of a duke, Rupert had lineage, bloodlines, and all the qualities of a fine stud.

So Devlin had seduced hundreds of women, trying to prove that he was damned valuable. That he could not be so easily discarded.

Eventually he'd realized he would never believe it, no matter how many women he bedded to convince himself.

So he did what any brokenhearted man did—he ran away to the sea. Deftly avoiding the navy press gangs, he'd intended to go on his own terms, and one drunken night had found him as part of the crew of the *Black Mistress*. From there, he'd become a notorious pirate, with a reputation for superb sexual skill and he'd discovered, without a doubt, that women found bad men enticing.

With stolen money, women came easily. With foreign travel, he learned there was much more to sex than mounting a woman and slicking his pole in and out of her creamy cunny. He'd learned the art of tipping the velvet until a woman tore at his hair and begged him for mercy. He'd learned secret arts of control that allowed him to indulge in bouts of sensual play that lasted hours. He'd encountered an Englishman who had created his own harem on a tropical isle—a harem of lovely women who possessed skin the color of clover honey. He'd taken a ball in his shoulder for sampling most of the sailor's tempting "wives."

They were memories that made him smile but that didn't fill his heart.

Crunching leaves warned him that he wasn't alone. He retreated into the shadows as Wesley strolled down the path. Gritting his teeth, Devlin spied a woman also walking down the path, behind Wesley. Her arms were folded over her chest, her head bowed, and her pale gray pelisse and golden hair shimmered under the moonlight. He didn't have to see her face to know it was Grace.

Had Grace come deliberately to speak to Wesley?

He had to know. And he had no option but to retreat to

the shadows to watch as Wesley stopped and turned. A grin spread over his half brother's face that Devlin longed to erase with his fist.

Wesley ran his gaze over Grace's curves, his eyes hot and lusty, and Devlin had to push his fist hard against a rough tree trunk.

"You are following me, Miss Hamilton," Wesley called out. "Reconsidering my offer?"

The hairs on Devlin's nape rose.

Grace's back was to him. "Of course not," she said to Wesley. "I simply wished to walk, and on seeing you realized I could accomplish two courses of action."

She had wanted to speak to Wesley? What the bloody hell for?

Wesley stepped closer to her and she stiffened, her arms tightening, but she did not move. His half brother lifted his hand to Grace's face and brushed her full lower lip with the back of his hand.

What was she doing? He could see Wesley leaning in to capture her mouth and Grace was staying put.

How could she do this? She should slap Wesley's face.

Her shoulders trembled even as she held her spine defiantly straight. "Don't touch me."

So she didn't want him.

"You have behaved with perfect propriety since our night together, haven't you, Grace—"

"Miss Hamilton," she corrected.

Wesley's lips lowered toward hers, lips drawn back from his teeth in a cold grin. "Not anymore, love. We've been intimate, and that is something that can never be erased. You are 'Grace' to me now. You always will be." He bounced one of her curls on his hand and Grace drew back. "You've refused marriage proposals. And, to my knowledge, you've been no man's lover. Why punish yourself, Grace? When you could so easily say 'yes' to me?"

"Saying 'yes' to you would be punishing myself, Wesley."

Why did she not slap his brother's smug face?

"You are a lusty woman, Grace. You can't spend your lifetime alone."

Devlin could not hear her answer, goddamn it, as the cold sea breeze swept over them, rustling branches and leaves. But he heard the bloody triumph in Wesley's upper crust accent as he continued, "You can't, love. You will bend—you will break. You will yearn to go to a man's bed and, to be honest, sweetheart, eventually the offers will not be so generous as mine. The position as my treasured mistress—any number of women would leap at the chance."

For one moment, Devlin's gut twisted. Anything he could offer to Grace could not compare to life even as Wesley's mistress. An icy rage swirled in his gut. But what had he expected? He'd been born to shame and he'd thrown himself into deeper scandal out of pride.

Why did Grace not cut Wesley? Damn it, woman. *Leave.*

"What will you give me, Wesley?" Grace asked softly. "A reason to despise myself every time I wake up in the morning? You cannot buy me. And you certainly won't convince me that I will die of loneliness if I don't bed you. But this—" She shook a folded piece of paper. "This will have to stop. You don't care if someone sees you sending these notes, if someone catches you leaning too close or touching my bottom or taking a grope of my breast. But I care, and I won't stand by quietly and allow you to do it anymore."

Hell, he had left Grace alone for one dinner. He had not gone to eat with the others. And in the space of a few hours, Wesley had groped her and sent her notes?

"Come to my bed," Wesley growled. "Let me take care of you, and we can have some fun."

"You make me want to vomit." She turned on her heel, lifted her skirts, and started up the path.

As Devlin expected, Wesley lunged and grabbed her arm, driving in his fingers to force her to stop. "You aren't offended. I remember how hard and how wildly you fucked me—"

He stepped forward as Grace spun around and slammed her fist against Wesley's chest. "You told me you wanted to marry me. You told me you *would* marry me."

His half brother gave a harsh laugh. Cruel amusement glinted in Wesley's eyes. "How could you believe it, love? Of course I'd want to claim you, but you know I couldn't. You are the daughter of an erotic artist. Of a woman thrown out of her home over a love affair. You had to know it was impossible for me to marry you—"

"Of course I knew it," she said and Devlin sucked in a hard, angry breath.

He had had enough.

Bless her, she spun suddenly and lifted her pale skirts, placing her knee on a collision course with Wesley's groin. But his half brother darted deftly to the side and caught her arm as he did, pulling her off balance.

Devlin stepped out of the dark, into the silvery-blue gleam of the moonlight. Gazes locked on each other, neither Grace nor Wesley turned to him. His step had been instinctively silent and neither had heard him.

"You're passionate about me, aren't you, love?" Wesley released her wrist and his voice softened. "You made love to me knowing that we couldn't have marriage."

"You hurt me afterward. Viciously. Deliberately. I will never stop hating you for that. I did not deserve to be hated for giving you my heart, Lord Wesley."

"But I deserve to be hated for breaking it."

On the path, Dev paused as he heard Grace's sudden sharp breath. Damn Wesley for knowing exactly the thing to say to make Grace pause. To make her vulnerable. To turn her thoughts upside down.

Moonlight painted her face, making her green eyes and her parted lips ethereal. Her hand, about to shove against Wesley's chest, landed weakly against his brother's shoulder. "Then why won't you give up and leave me alone?"

"Because I haven't yet gotten what I wanted. And what I want is you." Wesley stepped up to her so his legs splayed on either side of hers and he hauled Grace against his body. "I know you, Grace. I know you're lusty. And I know you enjoy it rough, hot, and sweaty, Grace."

"No! Stop this. Stop. This."

Devlin jerked his brother around by the shoulder and let his right fist fluidly connect with Wesley's jaw. He had to groan in pleasure as his knuckles split against his brother's chin and Wesley staggered back. Burying his wounded right hand into the gloved palm of his left, he glowered. "Get the hell out of here, *my lord*, before I kill you."

For one moment he thought Wesley would throw a punch in return. For one moment he thought Wesley had gained a bit of courage in the last two years. But Devlin knew he had hit his superior younger brother too many times over the years not to have proven that wealth and title did not always come out on top. Wesley spat blood. "Bloody hell, you damned bastard. I should turn you over to the magistrates."

"You're welcome to try," Devlin goaded.

But Wesley took two steps back along the path, his hand at his bloody face. "You're welcome to her." Then he turned and ran, and Devlin let his laughter follow his brother.

His chuckles died in his throat as he saw the murderous look on Grace's face.

"*What* were you thinking?"

"I could ask the same of you. Why in blazes did you follow him out here? What did you want, Grace? Did you want more of his lies?"

"No. No. Stop it, Devlin." She brushed past him and lifted her hems.

"Did you hope he'd tell you he loved you?"

The moment the words came out, never to be retracted, Devlin wanted to kick his own arse. That was a weapon he should have never used. It just hurt so damned badly that she considered Wesley—the smug little weasel—superior to him. He'd seen the truth of that in her eyes.

He needed to make love to her. He couldn't live without the pleasure of taking her to orgasm, of watching her surrender to ecstasy with him when she knew she shouldn't.

It made him feel more powerful than anything had ever done.

"Grace," Devlin said softly, because she still stood there, obviously trying to find some response to his question, some cutting way to retrieve her pride. "Grace—" he repeated her name with all the reverence and desire it deserved. "Can you not tell when a man is in love with you?"

"Leave me alone, Devlin. I came to tell Lord Wesley to stop his horrid pursuit. Please, Devlin, just let me be—"

He couldn't. Damn, but he couldn't. He pulled her abruptly to his chest. The impact made her gasp sharply and he pressed the advantage.

Her lips were tilted up to his, shining with dampness, plump and beautiful. He felt the soft puff of her warm breath; then he slanted his mouth over hers and drew her tight against him as he kissed her hard.

The world dropped away from him. The wind vanished, the roar of the sea disappeared. His world condensed to his mouth on her hot, soft lips. To the play of their tongues. To the supple, sensual beauty of her body tight against his.

Was this why he'd come back to England? What he'd been looking for without knowing? He eased back from the kiss, twisting his mouth at the irony of it.

He was panting because she'd stolen the breath from his lungs, the thoughts from his brain.

"You are right, Grace. I left England to escape love, and I've come back to something far more intense than what I'd run away from. But now, for your protection, I intend to escort you right to your bedroom door."

*   *   *

Grace tried to wrench her arm free of Devlin's firm grip. "This will stop now. You cannot. How will I explain it? I was lucky this afternoon when you shouted in my bedroom and no one heard. I can't risk it again. I can't risk a scandal that will destroy my family."

Grace swallowed hard as Devlin's throaty laugh washed over her. Just the sensual sound made her nipples lift beneath her shift.

"I have to know you're safe, Grace."

A teasing flutter raced over her skin as his fingers closed over hers, as he tucked her hand chastely on his arm and walked dutifully at her side, taking her along the path back toward the house.

He was determined to behave like a gentleman.

To protect her.

Sea breezes tossed his unfashionably long but audaciously attractive blond hair around his shoulders and cast a few strands across his wicked smile.

"This is not right, Devlin. There is no way that you can take me to my bedroom without causing a scandal—"

His proud grin, the slight swagger in his step, brought her up short.

"You are trying to think of a way, though, aren't you, Grace?" he teased.

Her lips still pulsed with the hot pleasure of their kiss. "You are incorrigible."

"I'm a pirate, love." He stopped when they were dangerously near the open grounds surrounding the house. Before she could protest, he cupped her cheek. The brush of his thumb sent a blaze of heat through her body.

This was madness. She had to resist. If she ruined her reputation here, she would be destroyed everywhere.

As Devlin's lips moved to hers, she had to close her eyes. Tears touched her lashes. Why did she have to turn away the one man who accepted her?

Devlin stopped, his lips so close to hers she could feel the electricity tingle on her lips. "What did Welsey put in that note? I'll rip his throat out."

"No! Don't! You see, I tried to speak to Prudence again, at dinner, and once again she gave me the cut direct. As for Wesley . . . he will never stop this. He believes he can make any crude suggestion, treat me like a harlot, simply because I opened my heart."

"He's done this before?" Devlin's voice was low, dangerous. "You said you avoided him."

"I tried but there were times when he saw me. At balls, he has walked toward me, with a power and harshness that made me run. I didn't have courage to stand my ground." She gave a rueful smile. "I fled for the ladies' retiring room every time."

"I will slice out his tongue so he can never use it to disparage you again."

"No!" she cried once more. Was she always going to have to fight to control her brutal pirate? It frightened her how close he was to doing something violent. "I gave him license to do this, and it is my cross to bear—"

Devlin put his fingers to her lips. "Stop."

Fierce anger burned in his eyes. At Wesley? Or at her?

"Stop doing this, Grace," he growled. "I cannot stand listening to you blame yourself. If you do it once more, I *will* walk away from you."

That stung. It shouldn't—really, what should she care what a criminal thought? But it did hurt. "I don't care," she stormed. "You don't really care about me. I've no doubt you made love to . . . to all those women in your house the very day before you kidnapped me."

Devlin slapped his hand to his forehead. "Hell and the devil! You were not in my life the day before I kidnapped you. Have I even glanced at a woman since I reacquainted us?"

"You call holding up my carriage a 'reacquaintance'? What you did was madness. And you are inconstant. How long do you normally bestow all your attentions on a woman before growing bored and seducing another? A week? A month? Or merely a day or two?"

"It will be different with you."

"It always is, though, Devlin. A man always regrets a bruising blow to his wife's face, until the next time he is drunk and enraged. I lived in the country and I helped my mother with her duties to the villagers. I've seen enough men cry over dead wives when it was their fists that did the deed."

"I would never hurt you."

"No, but you would break my heart. I can't go through that again. Can you deny that each carriage you rob is an exciting conquest?"

He gave a half shake to his head, a typical male gesture—he couldn't understand what she was trying to make him see.

"Of course it's excitement," he said. "I'm risking death—that tends to excite a man."

"Could you live without the excitement? Could you ever be content in a simple life? How can you promise to be constant to me when you are one of those who lives for excitement?"

"Perhaps you excite me, Grace."

"I wouldn't always. You must understand that."

"I suspect you would, love."

Lights glowed in the windows of the house. It was the unlit windows that worried her because those were the ones through which prying eyes could see them.

She had to make Devlin leave her alone, as much as it hurt when all she wanted was to walk into his embrace. To be held. To feel loved. To pretend she was loved.

"Can you describe two women who you bedded five years ago?" she asked harshly. "Only two. What did they look like? What color was their hair? Their eyes? Do you remember even two of their names?"

"Some women are unforgettable, Grace. *You* are unforgettable."

She began to protest but he snapped, "It's true. Walk away now. It doesn't matter. I would never forget you."

Was it possible . . . possible that he loved her? But what difference did that make? All it meant was that he would hurt, too, when they had to part. She should make the break now, before she brought scandal down on her family.

She must.

But after being first cut by Prudence and Wesley, then having Wesley try to force her into a kiss, she was hurting. Her heart felt too tight and cramped to beat properly and she couldn't seem to catch her breath.

She needed to hold Devlin close. Needed to touch him. Breathe his scent. She was able to take care of herself—she had been about to give Wesley a solid knee to the groin when Devlin had yanked him away. But this was not about protection.

She reached out to him.

Her fingers slid up to his shoulders, so high above her head. At her touch, he bent and moved them back a step, retreating into the dark. "Make love to me tonight."

She couldn't resist.

12

Had anyone seen them as they came to her bedroom? Grace couldn't be certain as she slipped beneath the sheets beside Devlin. It was heaven to slide into the crisp warmth beside his long, hot, naked body. Her hip brushed alongside his, and he rolled onto his side to embrace her.

The hallways of the rambling mansion had been quiet, and it appeared most guests had gone to bed.

His legs entwined with hers, the hairs a soft caress against her skin. Her feet brushed his hard shins and his sculpted calves.

"Do you want to know how special you are?" he murmured as his arm came around to rest beneath her breasts. His rock-hard forearm pressed against her curves.

He nuzzled her neck and she whispered, "How do you plan to show me?"

"I've never let a woman tie me up. Would you like to be the first?"

"Tie you up? Why?"

His chest rumbled with his soft laugh. "To ravish me, love."

"Goodness." She had seen such scenes in a book—not one of her father's. The book bore no title nor artist's name, as though both publisher and creator were too embarrassed to be connected with the work. The pictures were cruder than those painted by her father and many were unfinished. The sex acts were shown with the backgrounds barely sketched in. But the pictures had stunned her.

Women bound. Blindfolded. And young males, too, spread-eagled on beds, with wrists and ankles lashed to bedposts and their naked erections jutting upward. The first time she'd found the book, she'd quickly shut it and thrust it back in its place. But days later she had been drawn to find it again. And again, she had looked at three pictures, had felt her heart twist and her throat become a vise, and had guiltily shoved the book away. For several months, that had become her routine. Find the naughty book, peruse it, suffer the spears of guilt, stuff it back, then be driven to look all over again.

"Well," Devlin said. "Do you want to?"

Devlin bound? Looking like one of those pictures? She couldn't find the words, not even a simple *yes*, but she nodded her head.

"Not on the bed?"

Devlin grinned at Grace's question. "It's my fantasy, love. Indulge me."

Holding her handful of improvised bonds—his cravat, her corset ties, and both her gossamer stockings, Grace nibbled her lower lip. "But really, Devlin, that chair is hardly comfortable. Why would you want to be tied to it?"

"Discomfort can be erotic."

She tipped her head as though considering it. "I can't imagine it."

"Pampered Grace," he laughed.

"I'm not," she protested, but his teasing had the desired effect. She marched over and dropped all the ties but one—his cravat. "I was poor. As a church mouse. Or worse. A mouse always has a roof over its head."

He looked down to see the fluid already dribbling out of

his hard cock and he saw the thin seat and spindly legs of the chair beneath him. The small chair did feel precarious.

She bent over and her breasts swayed forward, bumping his face. His tongue slid out, on instinct, and touched the tip of her left nipple. Directly in line to her heart.

"Oh!"

He swirled his tongue around the soft, delicious nipple, teasing it to harden, to get big and plump and aroused.

She leaned in more to reach his hand, pushing her breasts against him. He opened his mouth as wide as he could to take a big mouthful of breast. He suckled hard on her skin and heard her desperate whimper of pleasure.

The linen slid around his wrists, which he held together behind his back for her convenience. He moaned at the sensation, the sound muffled by the breast filling his mouth. Her hands worked, brushing his skin. He couldn't see what she was doing; he could only feel it, and that sensation had him tense and coiled on the seat. It was as though he could explode like gunpowder on the spot.

Her body swayed as she worked, her breasts pushing forward and pulling back. He sucked hungrily at her skin. The fabric went tight around his wrists. Her knee bumped his hard cock and rested on his thigh. She had to be getting leverage to tie him tight.

Damn, he was so aroused.

Her knee kept smacking his cock and he grimaced, fighting for control. He couldn't come at just the brush of her knee, could he?

"There." She wriggled on him, moving sensuously, teasing his face with her tits. Then she moved back and he had to let her breast go.

With her teeth nibbling her lower lip, she gazed down at him. A lovely, curvaceous goddess limned by firelight.

"It's so arousing to see you with your hands bound," she whispered. "That's terrible, isn't it?"

Sweet Grace, revealing her fantasies and so uncertain and shy about them.

"It's not terrible. It's natural. We all have fantasies and our most private fantasies can be dark, shocking ones. And sometimes we have ones that are just damned odd."

Her shy smile made him catch his breath. "After all," he said, "I'm revealing mine to you."

"Why would you, a swash-buckling pirate, want to be tied up by a woman?"

"I want to be wanted by a woman that much."

He heard her soft, surprised gasp, and he watched the deliciously fetching confusion on her face. Then she gave a coquettish smile. "What do I do now, then, Captain? You have a rather upright mast."

He hadn't expected that and his laugh rumbled, making him tug at his bonds. A suggestion leapt to his lips, but she beamed at him. "I can do whatever I wish, can't I? For you are tied up."

She paced around him, her full breasts swaying, her hips undulating with sultry and seductive promise. He held his breath as she laid her hands on his knees and bumped her breasts toward his face, but as he arched forward to catch her nipple with his lips, she pulled back.

"Bring your juicy cunny to my mouth," he urged, voice strained.

She did, but just as his tongue slid out and touched her moist skin, she pulled back again.

"Sweetheart, you might just be torturing yourself more than me."

"Very possibly," she agreed, "But that is the risk I will have to take."

"Turn around and let me give your round little rear a kiss."

She giggled and her brows went up, but she did as he asked. He kissed her, bit gently into her soft, smooth skin. Let his tongue slick through the valley between them, to the curling blond hairs that softly surrounded her anus. He teased there, tasting her erotically rich flavor, breathing in her intimate scents.

"Ooh," she gasped.

But she pulled away again and he growled in frustration. His hips arched up of their own accord; his body worked against the chair, rattling the legs.

"I want you, Grace. You're going to have to fuck me now, before I explode."

She lifted her bare foot and he flinched as it neared his cock. But then she played with his length and the swollen head with her soft foot.

God, that was good.

Her toes slid down, getting moist with his fluid. She could barely keep her balance and he winced, waiting for the pain to go with the pleasure.

She trailed her toes down to his ballocks. Her big toe pushed his balls around, moving them in the sac, and the sensation had him groaning.

Begging. Begging her to take his cock inside, into her heat. Begging her to pound on him hard. Hell, he'd never even begged for his life, not even with a pistol against his head or a noose around his neck.

But he was begging Grace.

Excitement, astonishment, glowed like a flame within her green eyes. "But I don't want to ride you yet," she playfully argued. "I want to touch you."

She let the backs of her nails, long and slightly sharp, brush his neck. Closing his eyes, he let his head drop back to give her the length of his neck to caress. "You could sit on my lap to do this," he suggested.

"I could," she agreed.

But she didn't.

Even with eyes closed, he knew she had paced around him to his back, knew it by the whisper of her soft feet on the floor and the way her vanilla and lavender scent floated past him.

She stroked the back of his neck and he shuddered at the thrill that shot down his spine.

"I want to touch your shoulders," she promised. "Your chest." Her fingers spanned his shoulders, then moved down to his nipples. Gently she pinched both.

He let his lashes sweep up as she bent close and her loose hair fell around him. Her hands skimmed down toward his abdomen as her sweet-scented hair brushed his skin, setting it on fire. He was drunk with sensation. Lips on his neck, hands grasping his cock, she gave breathy moans as she pleasured him. He loved the sight of his cock held by her small, graceful hands.

"With you," she whispered, "I never have to worry about who I am, who I should be. With you I feel as though I belong." Her hand squeezed and his juice dribbled out, soaking her palms.

"You belong with me, Grace. It's only the ton who don't see that. It's only who I am that makes that so damned impossible."

She twined a graceful leg around him, sliding it up around his waist, skimming her pretty hand across his chest. Heat surrounded him along with her compelling, excited laugh.

He regretted having his hands bound. He wished he could hold her. All he could do was rock the chair about to aim his cock at her sweet cunny.

"Oh goodness," she gasped as she lowered on him. Without using her hands. She was so wet he was slick with fluid.

She rode him slowly, drawing each stroke with exquisite beauty. He couldn't touch, but he could use his tongue. He strained to kiss her cheek, her neck. To tease her ear with his tongue.

She searched for her pleasure, riding him harder and faster, grinding forward to rub her clit to his groin, squeezing her cunny tight around him. She slid her hand down to play with her nub while she rocked on him.

Her nails grazed his cock, a sharp, sudden, surprising pain that had his blood boiling.

"Yes," he groaned. "Please yourself."

Her breaths came fast, her moans desperate and hoarse.

"God—God!" she cried.

Her hair flew around him as she flung herself wildly on him. Sweat glistened on her cheeks, on her shoulders, on her breasts. They were both soaked. Sex surrounded them—the rich scent of it, their restrained cries, the thumping of the chair on the floor.

"Devlin, yes!"

She came and he had one moment of sheer relief—he'd needed to bring her to climax first—then his control slipped and his orgasm slammed into him.

He fell back against the chair and she slumped on him. Their hearts beat frantically, their chests pressed together, and Devlin nuzzled her neck, his way of caressing Grace in the aftermath.

Her little cries of pleasure continued and she wriggled on him, sending intense sensation shooting through him. Finally, she lifted her head and he smiled, coaxing one of sheer contentment from her.

He groaned. "Would you untie me now, quick? I'm starting to feel . . . a little vulnerable like this. Like I've exposed a bit too much of what makes me tick."

He saw her surprise—she hadn't expected him to be so honest, perhaps.

"Ooh, I'm a bit too shaky to do the knots," she murmured as she fiddled with the bonds at his wrists. "I tied them too tight."

"It felt good though, sweetie," he reassured. But he wondered if he was going to have to coax Grace to cut him free.

His hands were numb and he clenched his fingers, trying to

bring feeling back. "Get my dagger from the inside pocket in my coat, love."

She did so, withdrawing it from the leather sheath and holding it carefully by the handle. From behind him, blade poised on the fabric—he felt it by the tension on his wrists—she asked, "Are you certain?"

"Don't slip."

She sawed at the ropes; they bit into his skin as she worked. What did she think? Had she enjoyed the game? She'd seemed to delight in the play, but what did she think now, now that desire was sated and reality was creeping in once more? Was she frightened by it, disturbed by it?

The fabric fell away from his wrist.

"What now, Mr. Sharpe?" she whispered.

He couldn't ask her if she'd enjoyed it. He didn't want to face the truth. Ruefully, he brought his numbed arms around to his waist, giving his wrists a quick rub to circulate the blood. Was this only more proof that he wasn't a gentleman? After all, what gentleman would play bondage games with a gently bred woman?

And damnation, he'd forgotten to have her put a sheath on him.

What if he got her pregnant?

He led her to the bed. With a kittenish squeal, she flopped back on top of her tousled bed linens.

"Just to warn you, love, I plan to come down to breakfast tomorrow morning."

"Devlin, please don't do anything to Lord Wesley. Or say anything."

Did she ask that because she feared scandal? Or because she still cared about Wesley? Yes, she'd intended to knee his half brother in the groin, but a woman in love could act fiercely. But he didn't want to push her for the truth. Not now. He didn't want to hear it.

"Who's here, love?" he asked. "Who was at dinner?"

"It's not a large group. Lord Avermere is to arrive soon. There are Lady Prudence and Lord Wesley, of course. Introductions were made, but Prudence thrust her nose in the air and ignored me."

"And Wesley?" Devlin growled.

"He leered in a most bold and revolting way. I longed to throw the soup at him."

God, she made him laugh. "I wish you had. And I'll know not to miss a meal if that's what you're going to do."

She laughed, too, the sound soft, pretty, and light. "Lady Horton was there, of course. And her companion, who I had not noticed at all while we waited for the boat. Her name is Miss Crayle. And showy Mrs. Montgomery was there. And the rest were men."

"Which men?" he demanded sharply.

"Rakish Lord Sinclair and Mr. Nelling, the playwright, as you know. And the famous portraitist, Mr. Strandherd."

"Hmm. Three rakes with only Mrs. Montgomery to tryst with? The lady will be exhausted."

"Devlin," Grace chided. "I hardly think she'll entertain three men."

"She might." He winked and smiled at the blush on Grace's cheeks. She was experienced, knowledgeable, but still shy.

She turned away, her face pressing into her pillow. "I suppose."

It had been the wrong topic to tease her on. It had made her think about Wesley, about going from Wesley to him, and he knew she had never made peace with that. It didn't bother him—he was still deeply touched that she had chosen him to give her good memories of lovemaking.

He skimmed his palm along Grace's smooth, lightly freckled shoulder. "I'm not leaving you alone with those three rakes in the house."

She rolled back, touched her hand to his; and the gesture gave him a warm sensation.

He should leave her bed and go and sleep alone in his. But he could not force himself to leave.

Devlin rolled to his side, pressed against her curvaceous backside, and dangled his wrinkled cravat before her eyes. "No rest for the wicked, love. My turn now."

13

_____

"You look too damned tempting this way."

As Devlin's raw growl made her instantly wet, Grace tugged on her wrists. Her stocking held her securely and she could barely move a few inches from the bedposts.

"You trust me?" His gaze was shuttered.

"Yes," she answered simply. She was bound hand and foot, yet she did trust this man completely.

Grace wriggled her wrists again—he'd tied them loosely so she did not feel pain, but the feeling of capture was thoroughly exhilarating.

Two of his cravats bound her ankles. Watching him as he tested the bonds was so arousing. His eyes burned as though blue flame was trapped within them. Sharp lines bracketed his mouth as his face reflected the sensual agony she felt. And silvery strands of fluid stretched from the tip of his cock to the bed linens.

"I intend to play. Sensual play." He mounted on the bed, his knees on either side of her hips. She caught her breath as his fluid dripped from the blushing head of his cock to her bare stomach. "Tickling. Teasing. Play."

The muscular planes of his chest rose with his ragged breathing. Soft light from the low fire graced his beautiful form.

"Which do you prefer?" she asked, curious. "To be tied or

do the tying?" She wasn't entirely certain what she was asking. What would it tell her about him?

"I can ask you the same question. Tell me what you like best."

Mmm, he was being evasive. "I don't know. Both. Either."

His confident smile appeared, treating her to his breathtaking dimples. "Which would you ask for when you are half-mad with lust?"

Was that the way to get at the truth? Did being lusty make one instinctively express the truth? "I would want to be tied."

He winked. "Men just generally do the tying. To be tied— that is a special privilege, one men generally seek in secret, in silence, and they pay highly for discretion."

"And you asked me to do it. You wish me never to speak of it?"

"Who were you going to tell, Grace?"

"No one. There's no one I can share this with but you."

His smile faded for a moment, and a harshness claimed his features. "Thank you. I like knowing that I share something special with you. Now for play—"

"No. I want you now. To be filled by you." Was she mad to turn down his promise of play? But she wasn't certain her courage would last that long.

She couldn't read his darkened blue eyes as he put on a sheath. "Now. Please now."

Abruptly, roughly, he pushed his rigid cock down. His long, lean body stretched to the limit as he reached to lick her bound wrist and stirred her molten quim with his prick, making long strokes over her clit until she pulled hard at the ties and moaned for mercy. His tongue teased the sensitive skin of her wrist.

Heat and fire flooded from both ends, exploding in the middle. "Please!"

His hips tipped and he slid his cock inside: one strong thrust to the hilt, to fill her completely. Then, as though to join them absolutely, he linked his legs with hers, entwining his powerful arms with hers. Slowly, he pumped into her.

She hadn't expected him to make love so tenderly. She'd thought his game was dominance. Yet it didn't seem to be. She longed to touch him, but all she could do was lift her hips to show Devlin how much she loved making love with him. She moved desperately, hoping to bump her swollen, aching clit against him.

It was driving her mad! She wanted to wrap her arms around his broad back. Or touch his rough cheek. Or grab handfuls of his hair.

His hands skimmed down her arms and explored her everywhere—cupped her breasts, tweaked her hard nipples. Then his fingers slid between their bodies, stroking her quim until she gasped.

"Found the target," he murmured. Then he nuzzled her neck, rubbed her clit, and slammed his cock into her.

She curled her fingers around her straining stockings. Panted. Moaned. Worked to him, wriggling, pressing, needing—

"I'm coming! Coming!" she gasped. It happened so quickly. Warm and luscious and liquid, her release took her. Her thoughts melted. She cried out, desperately. She knew her cunny was clutching at his cock; then he surged forward and kissed her hungrily.

From his jerking hips and the way he moaned into her mouth, she knew he was coming too. Had he pressed his mouth to hers to hide the sounds?

She let her tongue play with his, wishing, wishing so much she could hold him. As he backed away, she drank in his lazy lidded eyes, his full mouth, his tangled hair.

Being bound was exciting, rather naughty, but not her fantasy.

As he turned to the stockings, the light playing along his muscles and the fine golden hairs that dusted his arms and chest, she knew exactly what her fantasy was.

A lifetime of this. A lifetime of fun and pleasure and inti-macy and love with Devlin Sharpe.

With a pirate. A highwayman. A man who possessed his own harem.

Once she had thrown her heart at a wild, unsuitable man, only to have him do his darndest to destroy it.

She couldn't do it now.

What had she been thinking? Grace blinked at the soft summer light creeping in around the curtains. She took a deep breath, inhaling Devlin's warm scent. He almost filled the narrow bed, and she had snuggled tight to sleep.

She had been so caught up in carnal delights, she'd fallen asleep—and taken the risk of letting Devlin spend the night.

The bed shifted under her so abruptly she almost fell over the side.

Devlin's feet landed on the opposite floor with a loud thud. Grace winced.

"Hell, I'd intended to be gone before morning light," he muttered. And without even glancing her way, he charged over to his pile of clothes. Then he turned and asked softly, "Are you awake, love?"

"Yes. What have I done?" she answered, pointing toward the cheery yellow curtains with the sunshine pouring around them. How late was it? She vainly searched the room for a clock. "I'm going to bring scandal onto my family."

"You won't, love. I'll make sure of that."

Grace's stomach knotted. She felt nerves, fear, but also de-spair as he hurriedly pulled his trousers up his legs. Sheets held over her breasts, she watched the speed with which he yanked on his shirt and flung his waistcoat on without both-ering to fasten sleeves and collar.

Of course he had to rush. The sun was up!

But why did people enjoy these clandestine things, when one felt only guilty and afraid afterward?

"If my grandmother learns what I've done, she will never see me."

Devlin brushed his hair back, swinging on his coat. "There's no harm in taking a few risks, love. Can you really tell me that you'll be happy dressing in pink ruffles and pretending to be innocent?"

"It doesn't matter what I want. I've learned that."

"It does," he insisted, but then she was staring at his broad back and his blue superfine coat as he gently opened the door. It moved smoothly, only an inch, and he bent close—an obvious expert in moving silently and watching unobserved.

A babble of voices drifted in from the corridor. The pad of footsteps up and down the hallway. The house was awake now and people were moving about.

Devlin moved back from the door and closed it so it was only open a sliver. Then, on a softly muttered curse, he silently shut it. "The hallway's full. Too many maids and guests."

Grace's heart pattered. "What *are* you going to do?"

Devlin held his finger to his lips. "You know, sweetheart, you have to stop punishing yourself for what you did."

She ignored that. "What *are* you going to do?"

"Go out the window."

She could not have heard him properly. "Out the window? This room overlooks the cliff."

He crossed to the window, then eased up the sash. "No different than scaling the rigging."

"You're a madman," she gasped as he slid out one long leg and straddled the sill. "You cannot do this." He was risking his life because she was afraid of scandal. "You cannot climb down."

"I don't plan to. I intend to climb up."

Grace dragged her nightgown over her head, her shaking fingers fumbling to fasten the collar. Until she made herself at least partially decent, she didn't dare look out the window.

What would she find? Devlin's . . . body lying at the bottom of the cliff? Or had he really climbed up from her window to the slate roof? The curtains, still closed because Devlin had slid out the window between them, billowed with the sea breezes. Innocent sunlight flooded into her room.

Hand shaking, throat a knot, Grace jerked open the curtains. Her eyes were shut. She leaned out and tasted so much salt in the air her lips immediately dried. She was too scared to open her eyes.

She had to.

She had to know.

Far below her window, the sea smashed against black rocks. The house sat perilously close to the cliff edge, and the rock face fell away in a sheer, gray wall. There was no sign of Devlin, thank heaven. She held the upper sash and leaned out, but not too far, not with the roar of the sea filling her head and the wind whipping her hair. The eaves above, dark and shadowy, hung over her window. It was possible that he'd climbed the stone face above her window, but had he been able to catch hold of the eaves and clamber over them?

A sickening thought curdled her stomach. What if he'd fallen and the sea had already dragged him out?

No, the tide was coming in, she thought. And he would have yelled, wouldn't he, if he'd fallen?

She shrank back into her room, heart pounding. Her fingers paused on the sash, but she didn't want to push it down and close it. What if Devlin needed to return this way? Crazy. Foolish. He wouldn't but she could not close the window.

Instead she pulled on her silk wrapper, a soft shade of pink, and tied it at her waist. She'd loved this robe when she'd first bought it, when she'd wanted to forget Wesley and her bad behavior—but now the pink color felt frivolous and unflattering.

Can you really tell me that you'll be happy dressing in pink ruffles and pretending to be innocent?

For the first time she realized she wanted to be the mature and sensual woman that Devlin saw her as. She didn't want to hide in frilly pink and flouncy hems.

Perhaps she should give up pink, but she could never be the woman she really was. He was wrong—she wasn't punishing herself. It was her goal to ensure that her mistake did not hurt her sisters and their families. She had no other choice.

A soft knock on the door surprised her.

Devlin?

Hardly. He wouldn't climb the roof and then come and knock on her door. Though she felt nauseous, worrying about Devlin, wondering if he was safe, she went to the door and turned the brass knob.

A maid bobbed a curtsy. "Miss Hamilton, Lady Warren has asked you to come to her parlor."

Grace stared at the brunette girl. "She wishes me to come now?"

The maid looked harried and nervous. "Her ladyship wants you to come right away, Miss. I have been sent to help, if you need me."

Grace swallowed hard. She did but she smelled of Devlin—of the masculine aroma of his skin and the rich smell of his come. "Please have washing water sent to me, then I will ring for you to help me dress." She shut the door and shuddered. It was time to slip in her role of proper young woman, but it was going to be so difficult to play innocent while thinking of what she'd done with Devlin.

She looked down. Her wrists were marked, for heaven's sakes.

And his words kept ringing in her head. *You have to stop punishing yourself for what you did.*

To live in her grandmother's world, she would have to live blamelessly. She would have to be alone. Yet she hadn't been able to resist Devlin for one night! And what future did she have in Devlin's world? She would end up alone, anyway, perhaps with illegitimate children.

What did she plan to do? She didn't want to rely on the

kindness of her family, on their pity and sense of obligation. But unlike her sisters, she could not think of a way to make an independent living.

Perhaps she should take up highway robbery.

Why didn't more destitute and ruined women consider that? What, after all, did they have to lose?

"Miss Hamilton."

Grace almost leapt out of her slippers as the male voice came out of the shadows beside her. A cultured voice. A voice with a tone she now recognized—full of lust.

She spun toward the niche, certain Lord Wesley was going to step out and grab her.

The arched space led to closed double doors, and her eyes were still blinded by the sunlight pouring in windows that opened into the corridor.

The gentleman swept an elegant bow over her hand before she recognized him. Dark hair marked with a silver streak tumbled forward as his lips touched her glove. He looked up, revealing a beautiful face, with black slashes of brows framing heavy-lidded green eyes. A different green than the color of her eyes—a dark, mossy green with mysterious glints of gold.

The rake, Lord Sinclair.

At dinner he had been showering attention on Mrs. Montgomery. Had she succumbed? Had the rake bored of the lovely widow already and was now seeking new prey?

He was beautiful, aristocratically so, yet her heart did not flutter and all she felt was a rising wave of irritation.

"You are an enchantress, my dear—" he began.

The words soured the instant they left his tongue. She did not want flattery. She realized how she loved speaking with Devlin—debating his honest and challenging statements. Now she recognized the murmured compliments of predatory men for the meaningless tripe they were.

She pulled back her hand from Lord Sinclair. "Thank you so much for your lovely sentiments, my lord, but I really must go."

She'd taken a step back, but he followed, prowling forward like a sinuous cat.

Oh, bother.

He was attempting to back her against the corridor wall. Her legs tensed and she felt a flood of debilitating weakness. Fear. Fear of making a scene. Of being forced to hurt him, of enduring his retaliation.

Good heavens, she was shaking with terror at the thought of listening to biting, insulting words when she refused him.

"You have enchanted me, my dear." His voice had lowered to that lusty purr that she realized men used in the hopes of seducing women. "I wish to spend some time together, to pay homage to your charms and beauty. Perhaps we should explore the delightful gardens. There are many spots of beauty I wish to show you, though each and every one pales in comparison to your loveliness—"

"No!" She was struck by the strong need to both laugh and scream at his hopeless attempt to sweep her off her feet.

Her stomach lurched. Had he chosen to waylay her because he thought she would easily give in?

"I must go and attend Lady Warren, my lordship. Please let me pass."

"Her ladyship could wait for a few moments." The gold in his eyes glittered as he looked at her with blatant, wicked intent. He had her fingertips raised again before she could retract her hand. His tongue snaked out and dabbed her knuckles, wetting her glove and making the fabric cling to her skin. He drew her finger into his mouth and sucked her fingers.

"My lord! You have made my glove clammy!"

He released her hand and before she could skirt around him he was leaning forward, his hard, solid body capturing her back against the wall. "A kiss, sweet nymph. I should enjoy a kiss."

"I'll scream." She threw the words out.

"I don't believe you will."

He looked so odious, so utterly sure of himself, so blasted arrogant, that she jerked up her leg, hoping to smack him in his most vulnerable parts. Her leg went up only an inch and then her hem tore. The wretch had trod on the edge of her skirt.

He was exactly like Lord Wesley. How could she have been so blind two years ago? How could she have been mesmerized by such rude attentions? Lord Sinclair thought her worthless, a meaningless woman placed on earth only to pleasure him and be discarded.

If only she'd realized that was how Lord Wesley had viewed her—

But then she would have never met Devlin. Perhaps she would have been married now. Happy or not? Either way she would not have known what it was to kiss Devlin, to hold him, to make love to him, to spar with words with him—

It stunned her to realize that she had been correct two years before, that making love to Devlin had made all that pain somehow worthwhile—

Lord Sinclair moved in to kiss her, and his coffee-scented breath neared.

She shoved forward. "No!" Her right hand hit his cheek and her left gouged into his neck, protected by high collar and cravat. Her right palm stung with the force of striking him, but he let out a sharp, excited breath. "I do like a spirited woman."

Fear rushed through her veins, almost freezing her to the spot. She couldn't fight him. Mad thoughts tumbled in her panic.

Devlin was bigger than this man—he was a giant in comparison, but he'd never made her afraid. She'd never felt Devlin would force her. Or hurt her. He was a pirate, but she'd never been fearful of him. She'd never felt terror like this.

What was she going to do—stand there while Lord Sinclair forced himself on her?

His mouth touched her throat, hot lips skating over her skin, and she made a sharp gasp of horror.

Mad fears again—what if her grandmother saw her like this? What if someone else did? She was pushing at Sinclair's shoulders, but he took no heed. It only made his nips and kisses to her neck more fervent. His scent, the perfumed smell of a dandy, made her gag and his heat had her hovering on a swoon.

No, her sisters had never swooned. She wasn't that much of a lady to take that route of escape.

Oh God. Lady Prudence.

She spied her former friend at the end of the hallway. Prudence held a book in her gloved hands and stared in amazement at the scene unfolding before her. Grace felt sickening heat rush over her face. No doubt Prudence thought she had encouraged this. She saw the sneer twist Prudence's lip.

Then Grace saw the small oak table in arm's reach, placed along the edge of the hallway, between two wall scones. A vase sat on top, filled with hothouse orchids. Instead of hitting Lord Sinclair, Grace reached for the porcelain rim. She yanked it toward them. Tall and precarious, the table followed the abrupt movement of the vase, and both tumbled onto Lord Sinclair.

He leapt back with a rude curse.

"Witch!" he spat at her.

"Cad!" she shouted back as she slapped him. She doubted Prudence would ever be convinced that she, Grace, was in the right and his lordship in the wrong, but she refused to merely slink away.

She shot a look of cold pride to her former friend and glared at his lordship, who was dabbing a handkerchief on trousers splashed with slimy green water.

She was about to turn on her heel and stalk away when Sinclair shook his fist at her.

"You shall pay for this insult," he snapped.

She gaped in pure astonishment. He'd forced himself on

her and her defense was an insult? There was nothing to say to such a ridiculous view of the world and Grace bit back the urge to spit on his stupid, fashionable trousers.

She wanted to inform him that he would pay for his assault on her, but he wouldn't. There were only three men she knew who could make him pay. The first two were her powerful brothers-in-law, but of course she would never tell them about this.

The last, she realized, was Devlin Sharpe.

She had no doubt that Devlin Sharpe would make Lord Sinclair pay.

It terrified her. It left her reeling.

The only weapon in her power was to walk away and refuse to allow this incident to hurt her. So she did just that, taking long strides down the hallway but resisting the yearning to run.

At the end of the corridor, her chest was heaving, her breath coming in frantic pants.

Blast horrid Lord Sinclair. She'd hoped to face her grandmother looking like a lady.

Now she knew she looked anything but.

"So you are my granddaughter." Lady Warren poured tea into two delicate cups with elegance, but from her words and controlled, calm expression Grace could not read what she thought of that fact.

"Er, yes," Grace responded, knowing that her answer was a failure in itself. Since being ushered inside by Lady Warren's maid and taking her place awkwardly on the very edge of the wing chair, she had felt like a butterfly pinned in a display case.

Her ladyship tilted her head to the side as she held out one cup, and Grace fought not to squirm beneath the cool scrutiny. What did her grandmother see and did she come up to snuff? Had she managed to look like a lady, or was she, in every way, unsatisfactory?

Grace accepted the tea, determined not to let her shaking hand rattle the cup.

"You resemble me," her ladyship said.

But was she pleased with that? Grace could not tell. All the letters she had written had been respectful and subdued and hopeful. Now she felt at a loss, like a ship that had slipped free of its mooring and was cast about by tide and wind. She felt the way she had on the boat to the island, as though the world could drop away beneath her feet and she had no control.

"Yes," she answered carefully. "I agree that we do look alike." Her grandmother was very lovely. A blend of blond and silver, Lady Warren's hair was arranged in stylish and elegant curls and waves. Her face looked much younger than her age: her eyes a clear, brilliant green, her complexion perfect, her lips full and pink. Yes, she bore lines, but she was a beautiful woman. A woman of quality.

Lady Warren sipped her tea and Grace followed suit, knowing she should be thinking of clever things to say.

She had waited years for this. How could she be tongue-tied now?

Finally her grandmother lowered her cup. "There is nothing of your father in your appearance, and I am pleased to see that. Your eldest sister is far too similar to him."

Venetia did look like their father. It surprised Grace to see that her grandmother had green eyes—she had always thought that was her father's legacy. Rodesson's eyes had been an exotic emerald; her mother's were hazel.

Grace glanced around the sumptuous parlor that Avermere's staff had given her grandmother—every flat surface now bore an opened book. It was an eccentricity of her ladyship—Grace knew that from her two years amongst the ton. Lady Warren traveled with a trunk of books and read them all concurrently.

All the books were opened or marked close to the beginnings, as though Lady Warren had quickly discarded one and fled to the next for excitement.

She felt cold dread. How could she build a relationship with a woman unable to commit to a book?

"Your other sister is rather plain," Lady Warren continued, "though both girls have made excellent marriages in terms of status. Not that Lord Swansborough does not have a most blackened reputation."

"He is every inch a gentleman," Grace protested, in defense of Maryanne's husband. "He is noble and honorable, and has been unerringly faithful to my sister. He is completely in love with her."

"Why have you not married, Miss Hamilton?"

Grace's fingers tightened precipitously around the delicate handle of her cup as she fought not to blush or stammer or look as guilty as she felt. "I have not yet met the right gentleman. I am hoping for a love match, like the ones my sisters made." Then she regretted the words. It was love and passion that had sent her mother into an affair with her father Rodesson.

Lady Warren pursed her lips, and the lines around her mouth deepened. "I know exactly why you have not married, Miss Hamilton. I know all of your secrets. *All* of them."

Grace saw her cup tilt and brown tea slosh onto her skirts. She quickly righted the cup. "What do you mean?" she asked, trying to look perplexed. *She couldn't know . . . not about Lord Wesley . . . about Devlin . . . ?*

"My great-nephew told me about your disgraceful behavior with Lord Wesley."

Disgraceful. That was what she was—*disgraceful.*

Even Lord Sinclair thought so, and he couldn't know about what she'd done. Could he?

"You are your father's daughter," Lady Warren continued. "You are immoral, scandalous, and shameless. For months you have been writing me letters, begging to be recognized by me. How can you expect that after the shocking, brazen, and unforgivable way you have behaved?"

Grace wanted to crawl away. But she forced herself to say, "He offered marriage. Lord Wesley. It was a lie, but he offered it, and I had accepted."

"He offered marriage to *you?*"

Grace surged to her feet and watched her teacup drop to the carpet and the tea fly out. She didn't care. "Why did you ask me here, Lady Warren? If you had only wished to insult and reject me, why did you not do it with your pen?"

"Would a rejection have stopped you?"

"Your letter spoke of wanting to reconcile!"

"That was before I heard the truth of what you are. That foul scoundrel Rodesson seduced my daughter and turned her into a tart. You were born one!" Her ladyship waved elegant hands. "I insist that you never write to me again. And if you intend to threaten me, to threaten to make our relationship known amongst the ton—"

"I wouldn't do that," Grace cried. "Why? I don't want to hurt you or blackmail you. All I wanted was to know my grandmother." Grace swallowed hard. Devlin had been correct, of course, for he knew what it was to be outside the ton. Her grandmother had not wanted to accept her. She had wanted only to ensure that no scandal could touch her. Lady Warren had brought her here to crush her.

Anger rose. She would not be crushed.

With as much pride as she could find—for her stomach burned with bile and her throat felt so tight she knew tears would be squeezed from her eyes—Grace stood. She turned and walked away from her grandmother.

She paused at the door. No, she could not just run away. She spun around to face Lady Warren. "You turned your daughter out of the house and never acknowledged her again. You have denied your granddaughters. Has it made you happy?"

"I beg your pardon?"

"Has it made you happy?" Grace repeated. "Has it made you happy to be so judgmental and condemning? Really, what has it gained for you?"

"I have preserved the good name of my husband's house."

"I wanted to love you and you have just told me not to waste my time, so I will not. But is the Earl of Warren really worth that?"

"The mistake was your mother's."

"Yes, but the punishment does not need to last a lifetime."

"It is too late," Lady Warren spat out. "It is simply too late."

"Come in here, gel!"

Hurrying down the corridor, Grace slowed at the sharp autocratic command snapped by a female voice. She jerked around, her heart lifting, hammering with tension. She would have to be proud, she would have to—

She met Lady Horton's blue eyes.

"Oh." It was not her grandmother. Her grandmother had not followed her to apologize.

"And where is Mr. Sharpe?" Lady Horton asked. "Did he have to go out the window?"

Grace gaped helplessly at her ladyship's blue eyes and the wicked sparkle in them at the pleasure of scandalous gossip.

"Of course, I know, gel." Her ladyship motioned her to enter the bedchamber.

"What do you mean?" Grace asked, hoping to appear innocent and confused.

But her ladyship's clucking tongue proved she had failed in her attempt.

"You and Mr. Sharpe," Lady Horton said. "I must say, he's a delicious choice for an affair. Lawlessness brings out a man's passions in bed."

"An affair! I'm a . . . a maiden. I—"

"It was quite obvious from the way Mr. Sharpe looked at you that he had seen you without your clothes."

Grace flushed. Did everyone in the house know? Had she destroyed herself utterly?

She stood as proudly as she could. "Do you plan to condemn me? I do not intend to endure another attack on my—"

"No, my dear. I had a fondness for pirates myself," Lady Horton answered crisply. "Now, what are your plans for Mr. Sharpe?"

She didn't have to feign bewilderment. "My plans?"

"Lusty ladies do not often think of how an affair will end. Have you thought of that? What do you want from him?"

She could not believe she was engaging in this conversation with a peeress who was a stranger to her. She knew Lady Horton was warning her. But she didn't care. "I want nothing. There is no affair. He is a highwayman—"

A smile curved her ladyship's thin lips. "He is a man of grand passion. I wish I had been so fortunate as to marry such a man."

Grace frowned. "I do not expect marriage, if that is what you are asking me. I could never ask for it, I could never have it. I do not want it. At this moment, I no longer even care about scandal."

Merriment twinkled in Lady Horton's eyes. "Miss Hamilton, I only wish to advise you not to set your expectations too low."

Grace found Devlin at the edge of the bluffs, staring pensively out at the crashing surf, a burning cigar clamped between his teeth.

He turned before she thought she had made a sound. She felt the weight of his gaze as he approached.

"God, you are beautiful."

Her throat tightened. His words sounded so honest she wanted to believe them. It was so very much what she had needed to hear.

She needed him again. She needed him to make her forget her mistakes and her failings.

"I want to go," she said simply. As his cigar fell from his shocked mouth and tumbled over the cliff edge and into the sea, she felt a surge of satisfaction. She had stunned a high-wayman. A pirate. Fear niggled—perhaps he was afraid she was asking for . . . for a future. She wasn't. She didn't have one. Live in the moment, he had said. Well, now she would.

"Take me back to your world. I want to experience it all."

14

_____

Devlin fisted his hands and paced the tile floor of the foyer while Grace drew on her gloves, then paused by the mirror to adjust her bonnet. All the color had leached out of her complexion, her eyes were shadowed, and she stared at her reflection with a cool resoluteness.

Though her meeting with her grandmother had destroyed her, Grace had begged him not to confront the countess. Gritting his teeth, he had agreed, but only because he didn't want to cause Grace more pain.

"I just want to go home with you," Grace had implored.

He'd curtly nodded his head. "Whatever you desire, sweeting," he'd promised. But he knew he could not do that. It could not happen.

That blasted witch, Lady Warren.

Out in the courtyard, servants loaded her trunks and cases onto the cart that would transport them to the quay.

Around the house, trees whipped in the wind. It would be a high sea, turbulent, and he'd advised Grace to wait.

"You aren't a good sailor, love," he had warned gently.

She had given him a rueful smile. "Very tactful, Devlin. You mean I'll be sick."

"There'll be high waves and a fractious wind. One moment you'll be looking at the sky and the next we'll be plunging down toward the black depths of the sea. We can wait to see if the weather changes tomorrow."

Her face had blanched at the thought of high waves. But even though she betrayed her fear by trembling, she had insisted, "No. I want to leave today. I can't bear to spend another moment here. I don't belong here. I don't want to be here."

She walked ahead of him out of the door. The wind tore at her bonnet—it ripped some of the ribbons free and threw them into the air where they flashed pink in the gray sky.

She stopped on the enormous front stoop and glanced behind her. "I promised myself I would not look back. But here I am, looking toward my grandmother's room. She won't be looking out to catch a last glimpse. She'll be happy I'm gone."

Trees dipped in the wind, sweeping branches across the drive. Colorful petals flew up and swirled in exotic patterns.

"Goodness, it is ferocious," Grace declared, but she held on to her bonnet and hastened toward the waiting curricle that would take them down to the dock.

Devlin knew he would not dissuade her. All he could do was lend his support. She clutched the side of the curricle, though, instead of his hand, as the carriage lurched down the gravel path to the shore. He slid his hand in hers—he'd taken off his glove and he slipped his fingers under the hem of hers and felt the frightened beat of her pulse.

But nothing showed in her eyes except a look of utter loss.

Grace clutched her bonnet tighter as the wind snapped at it. A fanciful ribbon flower broke free and flew away before he could catch it.

The poor girl had dreamed of a loving reunion and he knew how strong those dreams were, those dreams that had been woven through childhood, cosseted and kept. Those fantasies endured even through the cold reality of adulthood. He'd spent his life yearning for acceptance—and, in a sense, he'd fulfilled his dream. He'd won admiration from his father, the Marquis of Rydermere. But hell, he'd drunk his father's brandy, shaken his father's hand, and understood that his dream had been much more precious than the reality could ever hope to be. His father's shielded approval of his wild and daring life didn't make him any less a bastard. Nor did it heal his broken heart over his long-dead mother. It did not make him a different man. He'd been forged by his circumstances. Had he achieved his childhood dreams when he had actually been a child, he would now be an entirely different man.

Devlin did not know how to explain that to Grace, and he doubted she wanted to hear it. She'd had her most vital dream shattered.

He wished he could fix that for her, change it, take it back.

Hell, he was pragmatic enough to know that was impossible. But he felt as he had not felt for a long time, not since he'd gone running off to sea. He felt as though he should not just accept the way of the world. That he should bloody well do something about it.

The carriage halted. Seawater pitched high over the quay, sending a salt-filled spray over the boards with each crashing wave. The sky was a flat plane of slate gray.

"You've nothing to fear, love," he promised, but she fixed him with a grimace.

"Other than being sick all over my shoes?"

She was sick, several times, in a bucket in the tiny cabin given to her. He held her close, stroking her hair, holding it back as her stomach heaved. After each time, he gave her water to clean out her mouth and he wiped away the residue with a damp cloth.

She sobbed and tried to fight his hold, humiliated. He was certain she wanted him to go away so he would not see her like this—sick and vulnerable.

But this was the most important time for him to be by her side, so he would not go.

They rounded a shoal, a dangerous outcropping of rock that acted as a breakwater—he knew it because the water calmed. The boat shuddered against the water as the anchor was dropped and he tenderly helped Grace to her feet. Her dress was not soiled, but he knew she felt terrible.

So he lifted her in his arms and carried her to the deck. With his arms tight around her, he lowered her to the waiting dory. She all but flopped onto the seat.

As soon as they reached the dock at the manor house, Devlin scooped Grace into his arms again and carried her to the house.

"I'm not that bad," she croaked. "I can walk."

But he shook his head. "Let me make you well again."

The servants of the house, accustomed to treating ill guests, jumped to attention at his command. A hot bath was drawn and clean clothes laid out from Grace's trunk. While her belongings were loaded onto the carriage provided by her brother-in-law, she ate a meal and took light ale until color bloomed in her cheeks again.

He spoke of nothing but inanities while he tended her. "More bread, but let your stomach regain its strength before you apply that much butter. Let me pour you more tea." He fed her plain cake, trading smiles, pretending his heart was much lighter than it actually felt.

For, once she was strong again and they were on their way, he was going to have to tell Grace what he planned to do with her.

"Sweetheart, why do you want to run away back to an orgy?"

Devlin heard the vulnerable softness in his question, and he sprawled back on the velvet carriage seat, determined to look rakish and in control. The fabric was smooth beneath his bare hands, but he knew it did not compare to the softness of Grace's dewy skin.

Grace glanced away from the window and ran her tongue slowly over her lips. His groin tightened but he knew the gesture was not done consciously. It was a display of her natural sensuality and not calculated, and it had the power to yank his breath from his chest.

With Rogan St. Clair removed from his gang, he had no reason to worry about taking Grace back to his home—no one else would dare subvert his authority. No one else would dare suggest holding *his* woman for ransom.

So why did he feel so damned ill at ease at the prospect? He was uneasy enough to have concocted another plan, one Grace would not like.

"Why, Grace?" he repeated, his words intended to gently coax.

She tipped up her chin, her defiance endearing. "I want to play in your orgy. I want to do everything that excites you."

He shrugged. "Being with you excites me. I need nothing more."

She crossed her arms over her chest, as though protecting her heart. "I don't believe that. Wouldn't you like to see me doing all those lusty, erotic things?"

"No."

Her brows shot up. "You wouldn't? Why not?"

"It's my duty to protect you, sweeting."

"From what? I don't belong in high society, after all."

"Your family believes you do, love."

"My sisters are happy because they've married men they love, who are titled men, it's true, but it is love that makes my sisters happy. Not social standing. They have marriages and children, and I won't have that. There's nothing for you to protect me for."

Devlin scrubbed his bare hand over his roughened jaw. Hell, he needed to protect her for one reason.

He couldn't share her.

"If I had any sense, Miss Grace Hamilton, I would take

you home. And since I do have sense, that is where you are going. To your home, not mine."

Clear astonishment showed on her face. Then her confusion was revealed by a fetching frown that made him question his resolve. Could he send her back?

She shook her head, sending her disordered hair shimmering around her. "I won't go, Devlin Sharpe. You cannot force me."

"You would be surprised."

Her gaze desperately searched his face; he saw the visible effort she displayed trying to understand him. Her cheeks flushed, the heightened pink transforming her pale complexion.

"What if I were to tell you this?" she purred softly.

Based on just that one phrase, that knowing seductive tone, his groin tightened immediately, his entire body tensed and primed for a sexual bout. The sparkle of erotic anticipation in her vivid green eyes almost stopped his heart.

"I rather enjoyed it when you tied me up before. I think I liked it when you introduced me to games where I submit to your dominance. You were the one to capture me, to insist that you wanted an affair. I want one now. Tie me up, Devlin, and show me your desires once more."

Christ. He'd expected tears. Not this siren luring him to his doom.

"The only reason I'd tie you up now, Grace," he growled, "would be to deposit you on the doorstep of your brother-in-law, the Earl of Trent." His heart ached at the thought, but he didn't have a choice. "You want to come back with me because you are hurting, Grace. I can't let you make choices because you are in pain."

"Are you sure?" Her voice was a throaty whisper that sent so much blood surging through his cock he almost leapt off the seat in the desperate need to adjust his trousers.

"Would you not want to tie me up again?" she continued,

sultry and alluring. "Would you not want me to take your hard cock into my mouth?"

He imagined it instantly. Her puckered lips coming toward his cock, her eyes alight with naughty lust. Her tongue teasing the weeping tip of his prick . . .

"I would like so much to suck you until you climax in my mouth, Devlin. I want to—"

"Grace, goddamn it, stop!"

"He thinks she's a lady but she's really just a whore. She's no different than me. Than any of us."

Lucy parted her legs wider as Rogan St. Clair licked his way up her inner thighs. Her heels caught in the soft, worn sheets and she dug her fingernails into the mattress for purchase as Devlin's banished lieutenant shoved her legs so far apart that her muscles screamed in protest.

His hair brushed against her skin and she shut her eyes. His thick dark hair was shorter than Devlin's, which she knew would feel silkier. Rogan's hair was wiry and a lush blue-black. His tongue was wet and warm, the way any man's would be, and she shivered in pleasure as he first drew his tongue up the bare skin of her right inner thigh, then the left. Back and forth he licked, groaning as he tasted her skin.

"It's because of her fancy clothes and her fancy accent—"

"Shut up, sweetheart," Rogan commanded and she opened her eyes. He was poised over her wet, aching pussy with his tongue sticking out.

And his big, thick cock sticking out.

But it wasn't Devlin's cock.

Rogan's was heavy; it hung downward, tipped with dark purple, and swung between his legs, aggressive and threatening. It had a fat mushroom-shaped head.

Devlin's stood tall, curved toward his navel, and had a fine head that begged to be kissed.

Lucy sighed. She was excited. She wanted to fuck so much. She needed to.

She closed her eyes again.

"Thinking of Captain Sharpe, are you?" Rogan growled.

She shook her head, certain he'd be angry if she admitted it.

He bent and blew a hot breath over her naked cunny. With her lashes brushing her cheeks, she moaned and trembled.

"I'm going to eat your hot, creamy pussy, sweetheart. Who are you going to be thinking about? Devlin? Or me?"

Lucy wriggled her naked bottom against the rough and simple bed—the second best one to be had at The Swan, the nearest inn to Devlin's manor house. Dreaming of Devlin had left her wet and she knew Rogan could smell her. Her thighs were slick with her wetness. She ached to be filled and her sensuous motions were intended to be an invitation. "You," she whispered.

"In love with Devlin, aren't you, lass?"

His breath whooshed out after his words, teasing her wet nether lips. "No," she lied.

"I'm going to fuck you hard, lass. I'm going to cram your cunt and your arse full with my hard cock and I'm going to make you scream. And if you're a good girl, I'll get Devlin for you."

His fingers stroked the valley between her buttocks—flattened by the mattress, they were pressed tight together. The blunt ends of his fingers sent shivers through her as they worked between her cheeks.

"What do you mean 'Get Devlin for me'?"

"If you help me, love."

He teased the tight entrance to her rump—a place she had never liked to be touched until Devlin had taught her to relax for the caresses, to enjoy the pleasure. She'd been so afraid of remembered pain, of the brutality she knew in a man's touch. Since she'd been eleven years old, men had used her. Men who liked to hurt her. Who wanted a slim, young, tight girl so they could take her callously and roughly and make her cry in pain and shriek in panic—

Devlin had been so good to her. She had loved him desperately. But now he wanted the blond-haired tart because she was a lady and Lucy was not. Devlin's woman was like those whoring peeresses who took Dev into their beds. But Dev was blinded by a posh accent and the haughty manners those ladies were taught.

Lucy knew the truth. She knew that the ladies of the quality weren't really any better than dockyard whores. In fact, many were far worse—they were more grasping and cruel and, oddly, more fearful. But Devlin wanted a *lady*. He had everything he could ever want except a titled lady in love with him.

Rogan slid his finger a little into her arse. Lucy tensed on instinct and bit her lip, strangely reassured by the pain. Rogan pressed harder. Forcing her body to open. "You'll help me, won't you, Lucy?"

"Help you? What do you want me to do?"

"Devlin's love—"

Lucy flinched at the term. Rogan thought Devlin had fallen in love. No, he was just dazzled by the witch's fine clothes and fine speech and fine ways.

"A lady like that is worth a lot of money," Rogan went on. "I'd thought Devlin took her to ransom her, not fuck her, but our fool of a captain is willing to turn his back on a fortune. I'm not." He bent, took her nether hair between his teeth, and pulled until her eyes watered. Then he let her go. "Do you want me to get rid of the woman?"

"Get rid of her?"

Rogan bit her inner thigh and as he released the skin Lucy saw the deep red gouge left by his teeth. What would he do if she said she wouldn't help?

"Ransom her," he said. "Get her away from Dev and back to her family and make ourselves some blunt for our trouble."

"Would you hurt her?"

"No need, love." Rogan grinned, dimples appearing in his grizzled cheeks. "Her family will pay to have her back. She won't know we have taken her and her family will only know that Devlin did."

Lucy froze beneath Rogan as he rubbed her clit with his thumb and slid his finger farther up her arse. She gasped as his thick finger filled her, pushing her open. "Devlin would be arrested."

"Then we won't tell them about Devlin. And the girl won't tell her family about him. Not if she's in love with him and has been fucking him. Now relax, love, so I can slick you up ready for my prick."

Lucy closed her eyes. She took soft breaths. She imagined Devlin in her mind as Rogan flopped one of her legs over his arm and began to rub his thick cock against her anus. He stroked from pussy to arse, and she tried, tried, tried, to relax, to arch to him, and moan to him even when her throat was tight and her body rigid.

He surged forward, shoving himself inside her quim on one thrust, and she drove her fingernails into the palms of her hands.

She wanted to like it.

"I don't wish to stop here. We could continue to your manor," Grace protested as she followed Devlin down the narrow hallway of the inn. But the stubborn man continued down the hallway without even turning back.

"We aren't going back to the manor, love," he said resolutely as he scanned the row of painted doors. Devlin had pretended they were a married couple, and she had quickly rested her right hand over the finger that should bear a wedding ring. Would a sharp eye see there was no bulge of a ring beneath her glove?

Did it even matter anymore?

Yes, it would. Her disgrace would hurt her sisters.

Devlin paused at the second to last door in the hallway. The brass number read SIX. The floor beneath her feet was worn by several hundred years of travelers' feet.

She lowered her voice to the softest whisper. "There's nothing to protect me from. I cannot change being wanton. I want to be part of your world."

He rested his fist on the door, his fingers tight around the iron room key. Clumsily he tried to feed it into the lock. "No, Grace."

"Dev—"

A single wall sconce threw yellowish light onto them. "I don't care if you want to take part in an orgy, Grace," he growled. "I'm not going to let you do it."

She shook her head, her chest tight with bitterness. "I've been judged already. I can never commute that sentence. Even the most faultless behavior will never change the fact that I'm not innocent. I can't marry. And my grandmother called me a whore."

She saw him flinch at the blunt word. When he turned, his mouth was a harsh slash. "Do not ever use that word. I've never used that word on a woman."

"I can't believe that." She didn't. Men judged. Women judged. It was what people did.

"It's true. My mother bedded a different man each night, and she clung to them desperately, hoping that one of the dozens she fucked would save her. I never called her a 'whore,' though everyone else did. She was desperate. She was pathetic and sad and frightened."

The key turned in the lock, Devlin turned the knob and the door swung open. "Don't you understand, love? I'm not taking you back to my manor, to my lusty gang, because I want to keep you for myself."

Before she could part her lips, before she could ask anything, he urged her into their room.

His hand splayed over her lower back, and the touch was so familiar, so casual, that her heart hammered and her throat tightened.

"So this to be our last night?" She could barely force out the words.

"It has to be," he said.

Grace tugged hard at the buttons on her pelisse and felt threads tear. "Then hurry up and undress," she commanded, hearing the anger in her voice. "We haven't much time."

Devlin heard the pain in Grace's voice. Bedding her tonight would be a mistake. He had no right to do it while she was so angry and hurt.

She slid down her pelisse, her head bowed slightly forward. Lamplight played along the curve of her neck and transformed the ivory skin into the intoxicating color of champagne.

Hell, his hands were at his trouser buttons before he knew where he was. Soft strands of her golden hair played over her neck as she let her pelisse fall and, as he tore at his buttons, he kissed her neck. Softly. Tasting. Savoring.

She was here with him because she was in pain. He knew that.

The first time they'd made love, she'd turned to him in pain.

He flicked out his tongue and traced her neck to her smooth shoulder, to the lace-trimmed collar of her gown.

"Let me undress first," he said. But he knew he would not stop. He would not turn back.

He had been a pirate, but there were some treasures that he would not plunder.

He should not take Grace while her heart was broken. It was too dangerous to do that again.

"Then undress me." She pulled at the pins in her hair, the soft curls tumbling down her back as he opened his coat and waistcoat.

Just like that night, her honest need captured him.

He was lost.

And then he was naked.

Her gaze raked over him, hot and intense. He had not expected so much fire and hunger in her eyes this time. She swallowed hard enough for him to hear.

She still wore her gown, a concoction of white muslin and lace that molded to her full breasts and swept over her lovely curves. She looked angelic. Ethereal.

"This will be my last time. My very last time making love," she whispered as she moved toward him. The gauzy white fabric danced with the sway of her hips. "Do you understand that?"

She was in front of him now, her breasts bumping his chest.

Devlin stared, confused, as her palm skimmed over the straining length of his naked cock. With the hot pressure of her hand teasing his shaft, cupping the pulsing head, he couldn't think.

"I will never have another lover," she said ruefully. "How could I? I'm destined to be an old maid. On the shelf. Left to gather dust. I can't marry, and as a respectable woman who must obviously be a virgin, I can't take a lover."

Take a lover. Hearing the words made his teeth grind and his palms and forehead sweat.

"Grace—" Hell, no. She should marry. That he could live with. He could walk away, knowing that she deserved a fine marriage and to be a lady.

"It's true," Grace whispered. "This will be my last night to ever bed a man. And because it is, I want to explore you all over. I want to do everything I've ever dreamed of doing to a man."

As though her words cast a magic spell over him, Devlin grasped her wrists and placed her hands on his bare chest. "What have you dreamed of doing to me, Grace?"

Grace savored the warmth of his skin. "I think of kissing every inch of you, but I've been too shy to actually try."

"You don't have to be shy." His voice was as hot and silky as his skin.

"Then I shall start here." She giggled and stretched up on her tiptoes, her hems floating around her ankles. Her stockings slid lightly on the worn floor as she touched her lips to his earlobe and gave a soft tug.

His low chuckle washed down her spine and made her toes tingle.

With her tongue, she traced the shape of his ear, noting, "You have very handsome ears. I'd never really thought of ears as being essential to a man's charms, but I do think they are. And yours are always hidden by all your magnificent hair."

He brushed his hair back behind his ears, and she dropped to the flats of her feet to kiss his jaw. "Now I should kiss you somewhere I've never kissed you before."

She felt his body tighten beneath her hands and marveled at the sudden, intense response. His cock jolted up so the head brushed along her belly. She had not said anything erotic. "What parts of your body are you thinking of?" she asked, surprising herself with her boldness. Did she truly want to know?

"Surprise me."

Laughing at that, she rolled her eyes in a saucy way—or so she hoped—and dropped to her knees, skimming her hands down his body for support. Her fingers strummed over his hard abdomen, knocked his cock, and set it bouncing. She let her fingers trail down his hard thighs.

He took a sharp breath and she knew what he thought she intended to do.

But she kissed his right knee, giggling. She did like to tease him. Flicking her tongue over the rougher skin of his knees, she traced lines of scars. She gripped his thighs and worked around to the backs of his legs. The moment she dabbed the backs of his knees, he gave a surprised moan.

"That feels good," he said simply. "I've never experienced that before."

She strummed her tongue there, then looked up to see his rump tighten and flex in response to her strokes.

Embracing her daring, she laved her way up the backs of his legs and planted a kiss on the firm curve between thigh and derriere. It was hot and moist, and she followed the shape with lips and tongue.

A low chuckle rewarded her, and she gripped his taut cheeks and squeezed. He had the most magnificent body from the rear, all hard straight planes and firm curves.

She indulged her every whim—nipping his rump with her teeth, stroking her tongue down his spine and suckling on the hollow, massaging his shoulders, and tracing the lines of veins along his powerful arms. Her every exploration drew a new sound from Devlin—a harsh groan, a rumbling moan, a lusty chuckle, or a gasp of delight.

His taste and scents became imprinted on her—she drank in each one, certain she'd never forget them. Bending forward, she pressed her forehead against his hot back and blinked away tears. These were memories to hold, to savor, and she knew she wanted so much more than only memories—

She had to do something daring and think only of that.

She ran her fingers down the valley of his rear, feeling the tight grip of his muscles. He gave a shudder as she stroked the long, fine hairs between his hard buttocks, so she dallied there.

"My legs are getting weak," he admitted, turning to give her a rueful grin.

"Well, you shall have to endure, Mr. Sharpe, because I want to taste your . . . front."

He bowed his head to watch and she went on her knees in front of him. His hands caressed her hair, his fingers threading through it.

She suspended the moment, slowly arching up with her tongue, and she watched him watching her.

Gently, she licked the spine of his cock, that ridge that ran up its back. To take the head of his cock between her lips, she had to grip his thighs and lift.

"God, yes," he groaned. His hands tightened in her hair.

She bobbed on him, playing with tongue and sucking hard. Her eyes watered as she felt the head tease the back of her throat. His hands caressed so lovingly—surely that meant he liked it.

This rich, ripe, erotic taste—she'd never forget it. She'd never forget how it felt to have him grip her head so harshly that he tugged on her hair.

"Ah, Grace, I don't want to come this way. I want you in bed, I want to make this last all night and you have me already on the edge."

Devlin couldn't believe he had stopped Grace from her delicious exploration of his cock, but he'd known he wouldn't last. She made the very act special and unique and new, and he had been aroused beyond belief.

He'd been questioning his sanity as he helped her undress.

He tumbled into the creaky inn bed at her side and rolled over to embrace her.

One last night.

Her last night to make love. That was madness. And what was he going to do? He couldn't imagine ever sharing a bed with another woman. He cupped her breasts, experiencing a distinct sense of ownership. They might be Grace's breasts, but he felt they also belonged to him.

Softening his mouth, which was tight with arousal, he closed his lips around Grace's nipple.

He adored her.

Reaching down, he parted her nether lips and slid his fingers into her quim. She'd been pleasuring him, but she was wet with anticipation and, at the sucking sound and the hot fluid flowing out onto his hand, Devlin was lost.

Mounting her, he slid his cock into her and she wrapped her arms tight around his neck. They moved together as though they'd been making love for a lifetime.

Panting harshly, he thrust into her, teasing her with his fingers; and he whispered against her ear, telling her how much he loved the way she'd sucked him. She caught her breath, moaning at the images he painted. With words, caresses, and his thrusting cock, he pleasured her. He felt her tension. Felt the gouging pressure of her fingernails in his back. Drank in her cries.

Hot fire rushed over him. He'd never been so lost, so drowned in heat and pleasure and desire, so conquered by any woman, by anyone, and he shut his eyes and took her mouth in a long, teasing kiss as his orgasm exploded and left him blinded, shuddering, numb, disoriented. It was like being caught in a maelstrom on the ocean, tossed in a wind funnel, or thrown into a sudden storm.

He heard his cries and her breathy, delighted gasp of his name.

Then he withdrew, still pulsing and exquisitely sensitive, and he fell, groaning, on the mattress at Grace's side.

She snuggled close and he flung his arm over her. He felt possession, promise, love, the need to hold her. It was a swirl of thought in his overloaded brain.

She sighed sweetly, tugged the sheets up over them both, and shut her eyes. Enchanting contentment glowed in her soft smile and relaxed face.

Ah, sweeting.

He felt so damned lost. What did he have?

Money could buy him a lot of respectability. Perhaps it was possible he could behave like a member of the ton. He wasn't one and they would never accept him, but hell, they would like his money.

Grace yearned for acceptance from that cruel and cutting world, and he could never give her that. If he married her, he would be ensuring she would never be a part of the ton.

Her sisters had married titled, powerful men. The Earl of Trent. Viscount Swansborough. Married to him, she would never be their equal.

It was going to break his heart to let Grace go. But he had to. He was a highwayman—even if he could have Grace, how could he evade the law with a wife and children? He would be putting them at risk. And being a highwayman had given him fame and power.

What if he was to do it? Give up his life of crime. Stop holding up carriages on the king's highway, never return to the sea.

Hell, what would he be then?

He wasn't willing to become just an ordinary man.

"I do not see why we have to leave in the middle of the night!"

What was Grace to do with this maddening man? Now he was even stealing her last night from her. Instead of spending it in bed together, Devlin insisted that they travel tonight.

She'd never seen him look so . . . disheveled. He sat at her side and had raked his fingers through his golden hair so often he had created furrows. And his eyes, those vivid indigo blue eyes, looked stark and haunted.

"What is *wrong*, Devlin?"

"We need to travel," he repeated, as he had done a dozen times while he'd helped her dress and carried down the trunks. Marcus's coachman had been commanded to set down his ale and meat pie and make haste back onto the road.

The bewildered man didn't understand why and neither did she.

Devlin was stealing her last night from her.

That thought was all she could focus on as the carriage

rumbled along the king's highway. She stared out the window at the forests painted by moonlight that stretched around them.

Finally Devlin turned his troubled gaze onto her. "I'm sorry, Grace, but I can't do it. I can't give up what I am."

Give up what I am?

"What do you mean?" she asked, perplexed. "What are you talking about?"

"If there was any way . . . I thought about changing my ways, about subscribing to law and order, and being a proper country gentleman. I thought, while we were lying there in that bed, that I knew the solution."

"You mean, you want to stop being a highwayman. For me."

"Aye."

Aye. What did that tell her? What of all their discussions where he had challenged her every preconception, her every precept, her every thought? All he had to offer her was 'aye'?

"But I cannot do it, Grace. I love the thrill of the hunt, the power of victory. It's what I've been for so long, I can't imagine another way—"

"Stop!" she cried. "I understand."

He was not willing to give up his life as a highwayman for her. He'd admitted he loved the thrill and adventure and excitement of what he did.

He could not give it up for a dull life with her.

"Just stop," she repeated. "I don't want to hear any more."

It ruined everything. The sensual memories. Now, when she imagined licking his cock in front of the cheval mirror, or daringly tonguing his bottom, she didn't grow hot and excited. Or rather, she did, but she hurt too. It hurt to know she was not enough.

And she felt like a fool because he *was* enough for her. She would be willing to marry him, even though it would mean she would have to lose her family. Venetia and Maryanne

would hardly be able to receive her. Would her mother aban-
don her? Her mother might be in Italy with Rodesson, but
she knew her mother had wanted her to make a good, respectable marriage. Her mother had wanted her to have the
things she could not.

It would come as no surprise to the haughty and cold Countess of Warren. Grace was already despised by her mother's
family.

But she was not enough for him. She crossed her arms over
her breasts and drove her gloved fingertips into her arms.
How dare he? He had kidnapped her! He had been the one to
claim he could not exist without her. She had been willing to
fight to forget and live her life without him, but he had in-
flicted himself within it.

"What's wrong, love?" Devlin asked, apprehension written clearly on his face. He moved to sit opposite her, not beside her, and though he chose to put the distance between
them, she told herself she didn't care.

She stared at his handsome face in disbelief. "How can
you ask that? What on earth do you think is wrong? Do you
think I am so dim-witted I wouldn't understand what you
were truly saying?"

Her bold pirate suddenly looked wary. "What was I really
saying?"

"You told me that I am too dull and too boring and that
marriage to me would be far worse than risking Newgate
prison. And yet now, you act as though you did nothing
wrong at all. I should—"

"I meant you no insult, sweetheart. The problem is that
I'm not good enough for—"

"Stand and deliver!"

At the brusque shout from the road, the carriage halted
immediately and Grace found herself thrown toward Devlin.
As he caught her, she fought his embracing arms.

He looked completely astounded. He drew them both to

the window. His arms were like iron bands, his chest hard and moving with his rapid breaths. "What in blazes is happening?"

"It appears, my infamous highwayman," Grace snapped, "that we are about to be robbed."

15

_____

"I should blow your bloody head off."

Grace let out a sharp cry as Lord Wesley pointed his pistol at Devlin's heart. She saw the snout of the weapon sway slightly. Wesley's words were slurred. He was drunk. Mad with rage.

Good heavens, had he followed them from the Isle of Wight? Why?

She glanced desperately up and down the lane but a close copse of trees shielded them from the main highway, and she could see no houses close by. Nothing surrounded them but a stretch of fields and meadows, flat planes of gray that disappeared into the ominous black line of the woods.

Wesley had forced them to drive onto this lane off the high road with his gun pointed at the coachman, but Grace sensed Wesley had only succeeded in halting them and moving them because Devlin wanted to do this. He could have rode on; he could have done something, she was certain. He seemed to have surrendered too easily.

Now she stood at Devlin's side on the quiet lane, her gaze trained on the muzzle of a drunken madman's pistol.

"Put your hands in the air, you bastard! You damned criminal!" Wesley shouted.

Without even a pause, Devlin obeyed and lifted his hands, but Grace flinched at the cold anger the moonlight revealed in his eyes. She had always been the dramatic one of her family, the one given to scenes and outbursts of temper, but she now saw that men were far more dramatic than she could have ever hoped to be. And dangerously so.

One of these men was going to kill the other!

Was that why Devlin surrendered—to have the chance to confront his brother? To possibly kill him?

"You know I'm a damned good shot," Wesley blurted.

"Now, now, brother," Devlin answered in a low and dangerous voice, "If there's anyone who deserves retribution—"

"Shut up," Wesley snapped.

"What's this about, Wes?" Dev's voice cut through the night, a night filled with hoots and howls, with ominous creakings and wails as branches blew in the wind, with the nervous pawing of the horses on the dry dirt road. "Is it about that spanking?"

"Goddamn you!"

Grace winced, her throat so dry she could barely draw breath. Why on earth would Devlin goad his brother while he waggled a loaded pistol at them? The wind tipped Wesley's high beaver hat forward, shadowing his face so she could no longer see the rage there. The breeze ruffled his pale blond hair and threw Devlin's golden hair back in the wind.

Grace glanced back and forth from one man to the other so quickly it made her nauseous. Devlin wore no expression at all, the way a man might look when he gambled. Wesley looked to her and leered; his gaze felt like spiders crawling upon her. And she knew the gesture was deliberate.

Welsey wanted to anger Devlin. To make him attack and give a reason to shoot.

But Devlin lowered his right hand, boldly, and clasped her hand in a gesture that she couldn't understand. Was he trying to give her strength or irritate his half brother?

"You took a young lady's innocence, Wes," Devlin said, "and I intend to plant my boot in your hide and give your arse a good solid kick."

"Devlin!" She gave a soft cry and he squeezed her hand.

His dark blue eyes caught the silvery moonlight as he shot her a quelling look.

Was he bluffing? Bluffing with a loaded gun pointed at his heart? Why—why be willing to risk his life to distract his foxed half brother?

To protect her? She swallowed hard.

Wesley straightened his arm, the way Rogan St. Clair had when he'd threatened to shoot, and Grace felt the world shimmer and dip around her. She fought not to give in to hysterics, a swoon, or general terror.

"I could shoot you," Wesley snarled at Devlin. "It would be so easy to claim that you had robbed me, that I shot you to defend myself, you damned blackguard."

She scuttled closer to Devlin, to protect him, and his hand rested on her waist, strong and secure but also controlling. When she'd tried to move too close, he'd eased her away.

"And why do you want to see me dead, brother?" Devlin asked. "Do you really believe my father preferred me to you?"

Wesley's face blanched and Grace heard a soft peep escape her lips. He snapped around to face her, his eyes blazing in the dark. "Come over here, Grace, or I'll blow a hole through your lover's heart."

With his hand resting on her warm back, Devlin shook his head. "It's all right, love," he said. "Stay with me."

Wesley took a menacing step forward. "Then you die, Sharpe. Come here, Grace!"

Devlin grasped her hand again and held tight. She struggled to break his strong hold—now almost crushing the bones of her hand—as she took a shaky step toward Wesley.

"Stay here, sweetheart," Devlin barked.

She dearly wished she could. But to go to Wesley might buy them time. Her heart was in her throat, for she knew that Wesley wanted to use her to torment Devlin—he had heartlessly used her once, and she had no choice but to let him do that again. She had to make Devlin understand that.

She'd caused all this with her wanton behavior. It was her fault and she couldn't bear to have Devlin pay the price.

"No," she murmured in warning to Devlin. "I can't. What if he does shoot you? He is a marquis' son. He can do whatever he wishes, including killing you, and he would never be brought to justice."

"Aye, which is why I want you to stand behind me, love."

"Bloody hell," Wesley snapped, "Bring your arse over to me, Grace." He lifted the pistol, leveling it with Devlin's forehead.

She tried again to pull free of Devlin's grip. "I do not dare disobey."

For the first time since they'd stepped down from the carriage, she saw the anger in Devlin's eyes replaced by pain and fear. "You can, love. You do not have to do what he says. He is not the power here."

His eyes narrowing to dangerous, shadowed slits, Devlin let go of her hand. She shuddered but knew she had to be brave and go to Wesley. But before she could move, Devlin began to saunter toward his drunk, enraged half brother.

Shocked, Grace reached out, but her fingers slipped off Devlin's greatcoat. Devlin had hooked his fingers in the waistband of his trousers and wore a mocking grin. "You can shoot me, brother," he called out congenially, "but I'm a legend, now, aren't I? The infamous pirate and highwayman, untouchable for my grand and noble service to the British Navy. I'll always be more famous than you—"

"Shut up!" Wesley thrust the pistol forward and he took a step toward Devlin. But Devlin would not stop; he continued to advance.

Grace looked around desperately, toward the coachman, toward the groom. Were they not armed? Or did they not care if Devlin was shot, simply because Wesley was a peer? She was too afraid to try to speak to them, too afraid her plea for help or even the sound of her voice would force Wesley to shoot.

Her sister Venetia had cleverly thwarted an attacker when she had faced danger at Marcus's side. And Maryanne had bravely fought her way out when a madman kidnapped her. Both her sisters had used their wits and imaginative weapons.

But her sisters were the creative ones. She had never had anything to rely on except her looks.

No—now was not the time to wax dramatically about her plight. Now was the time for action. Intelligent action.

Grace looked around. Tree branches? Something from the carriage? But how could she get to anything without Wesley noticing?

Her chest was rising and falling with frantic breaths. She glanced down. Her breasts. Wesley had been only attracted to her breasts before. What if she suddenly bared them? Could she distract him?

Since she was supposed to be wanton, it would be fitting, wouldn't it?

Her fingers fumbled with the covered buttons of her pelisse.

"That's it, you tart," Wesley shouted out, and his voice echoed. "Take your clothes off for me. Would you fuck me here, on the ground, to save Devlin? Would you drop to your knees and suck me?"

Grace recoiled and her fingers froze on the buttons. She couldn't understand why he was so hateful to her. She'd been the one to be ruined, to be destroyed. She'd lost the chance to marry, to have a family. She had lost everything to this man. Why should he want so much to humiliate her?

She stormed forward, wild with rage. "You filthy, disgusting piece of garbage!" she screamed. For that's what he was. He wasn't her better. He was no better than steaming horse droppings. "Shoot me if you like, you coward! You pig!" She launched forward, determined to scratch out his eyes.

Then, to her shock, Devlin pushed her backward. She stumbled, waving her arms to catch her balance. Devlin spun back toward Wesley and his arm flashed out.

Had he thrown something?

An explosion deafened her, sent birds screeching up to the heavens, and brought screams from the horses.

Devlin!

She fell backward, heels caught in her skirts, and she landed hard on her bottom. Her hands flew behind her, smacking the gravel. Devlin!

Shouts rose up around her—at last the useless coachman and groom were racing forward. It was too late! Wasn't it? She choked on fear and blinked her eyes. Damned tears— why were they coming now, why were they blinding her when she needed to see?

Was she delirious?

Devlin was striding toward her, silhouetted against the streams of moonlight. He was a huge, dark shape and his coat was flapping behind him.

He reached out to her. "Grace, love, are you all right? I'm sorry I had to push you."

She couldn't lift her hands; all she could do was blink at him. The pistol had fired. She'd seen the flame, heard the roar. How could Wesley have missed?

But he had, hadn't he? Was she delirious? Dreaming?

Devlin dropped to one knee at her side and she watched her hand waver toward him. Her fingers, in torn, flimsy gloves, pressed against his warm skin. Against his cheek. She skimmed her hand down toward his jaw to reach his throat. She wanted to find his heartbeat.

His breath washed over her hand as her fingers passed his lips.

"You're alive?"

"Of course, love." But he winced.

She looked down and saw his hand clamped to his side. Oh God, Wesley's shot had hit him. In his stomach—she knew enough to know that a stomach wound would slowly kill a man.

"It grazed me, sweetheart. That's all."

Wesley! She looked around frantically for him but couldn't

see him. Then she heard a powerful rhythmic sound, the sound of hooves striking hard ground.

Devlin gave her a big grin. A grin that flashed endearing dimples and made her want to cry. "I threw a blade, love. I keep a few in various places—one in my waistcoat, one up my sleeve, a couple in my boots. It hit him in the arm and threw off his aim."

"Thank God." Grace gulped as the trees seemed to suddenly take flight around her and the world tilted to the right. What was happening?

Devlin's arm slid around her. "He jumped on his horse and took off, love."

"We need to bandage you, Devlin." What if it was not just a graze? She met Devlin's blue eyes and looked for clues that he was hurt more seriously. But he gave her his lovely smile.

"We're close to my home, love. We'll head there. So you've got your way after all."

He stood, holding her, and she forced herself to get steady footing. If he could do it with a wound, she could certainly have courage. "Devlin, I don't want my own way," she snapped. "All I want is to keep you safe."

16

"But you are injured, Devlin, and supposed to be resting. I'm not going to lift my skirt for you!"

With the laudanum racing through his system, making his head buzz, Devlin laughed at Grace's concern and indignation. She stepped back from his bedside, to where he couldn't reach her without bringing on severe pain, and wagged her finger.

"Sweetheart, I'm going to pass out soon from the laudanum, but first I want to put my tongue to use. I'm hungering for you." He lusted for her in a way that was madness. Was it because he could have been shot and killed? Facing death normally aroused him, but he'd never taken a woman while wounded.

His earlier worries—that he had no right to be trying to seduce her, not when he had to let her go—could not conquer his need now. His blood was on fire; his brain flooded with desire to the point of madness.

Grace frowned. "Are you certain that Mr. Kennedy is a good doctor, that he knows what he is doing?"

"He's patched me up dozens of times. I trust him and pay him well. Now come here and don't make me get out of bed."

Her words still echoed in his head. The lovely, soft, beautiful tone of them was like a song. *All I want is to keep you safe.*

No woman had ever said such words to him. No one ever had.

Grace pushed aside his green velvet bed hangings and returned to his side. Her knuckles gently brushed his bare shoulder. She slipped her hand around to caress him with her palm.

He kissed her fingertips, tasting the slight rose flavor of soap—given his house was filled with women, it had been simple to find soap for Grace. Beneath the bandage his side ached, but laudanum dulled the pain. His only thought had been indulging in sensual pleasure, but then he saw the shadowed worry in her eyes. "What's wrong, love?"

"Lord Wesley tried to kill you and he will escape without punishment, won't he? It's madness, utter madness, that he should not pay for that."

"I lodged a dagger in his arm, love. If I do not have to pay for that, I'll be content." He flashed a grin, hoping it would prompt her to smile.

"Do you think he will come after you again? Or bring the magistrate on to you?"

Devlin rubbed his jaw, considering. He was getting tired, and he had something he sorely wanted to do before he drifted into sleep. "Wesley won't, love." He fought a yawn.

She chewed her lip, the gesture so innocent and sweet. "I heard what you said to Lord Wesley—"

"Don't bother using his title with me, sweetheart."

"What you said about being a legend whereas he is not. Is that why you became a pirate? Is that why you rob carriages? To be a mythical man that people serenade in stories?"

The drug dragged at him, pulling him down into sleep, but Devlin fought to focus and give an answer. Grace deserved an answer. "I became a pirate because I got drunk one night, extremely drunk, and woke up in the hold of a ship."

"You were pressed?"

"No, that's the navy, love, and I was swift enough, even piss drunk, to avoid them. But I owed Captain Jack Hawk for the large quantity of fine French brandy that I'd quaffed."

"He blackmailed you into becoming a pirate?"

"No, I was more than willing—I wanted to escape to the sea. The *Black Mistress* had a reputation for speed and its captain had one for being more than just a ruthless thief. Hawk plundered ships for the pleasure of it, for the sport, and I learned just how powerful it is to do what you love."

To his surprise, she nodded and her eyes were frank with understanding. "You discovered where you belonged." She sighed. "Everyone I know has done that. My father always knew he intended to pursue his art and that nothing would stand in his way. But now he has realized that he wishes to pursue my mother, so my mother is now pursuing freedom in Italy with him. My sisters had talents, and they have the freedom to pursue them. But I do not know where I belong, Devlin."

"Sometimes it's more than just finding a place to belong, Grace. It is having the courage to carve your own path. I thought that seducing well-bred ladies would make me a happy man, but it was like jabbing poison-tipped arrows into my heart. I was fighting for what I could not have."

"And you complained to me about caring about my grandmother's opinion."

"I was speaking from experience. I let the quality hurt me. It took a long time to learn that the pirate Captain Hawk had more nobility in his little finger than a dozen men like Wesley possessed. I don't want you to be the way I was once. I don't want you to do what my mother did."

"Have an affair with a noble."

He'd never spoken of his mother with anyone. But he had to, to make Grace understand. "My mother took every blasted insult my father used to hurt her and swallowed it up.

And do you want to know why she did it? Why she let him abuse her until she was paralyzed with pain?"

"W-why?"

"Because he was bloody quality. Sweetheart, noble blood runs in my veins, but if I'm a moral man, it's because of my mother's damned blood."

With one arm he jerked her to him, and rolled onto his good shoulder. "Now let me eat your sweet pussy, my love."

He tugged up her heavy and awkward skirts, and he breathed a sigh of relief when he bared her skin and saw she wore no drawers. He let her skirts fall, fashioning a tent around him and her quim. Her sweet mound, shielded by soft, golden curls—how it enticed him. He loved to breathe in her scent, loved knowing that she was wet, glistening, and juicy for him. Traveling to the south seas had taught him that a woman's cunny was as delicious as succulent, ripe fruit and that a lucky man was the one who indulged himself in the pleasures of licking his lady's quim often.

But his body ached as he pressed his mouth to her moist pussy and searched for her clit to suckle. He had to roll onto his back, pulling Grace with him.

Unbalanced, she swung out her leg and, to his relief, her knee hit the mattress instead of his chest. He clamped his hands to her naked arse and held her to his mouth while he suckled, savored, and took his fill of her earthy, salty taste.

"Devlin—oh! You must stop! I want to ask you a question."

He must have been doing something wrong—it must have been the laudanum dulling his skills, for why else would Grace have asked him to stop eating her pussy?

She pulled back and he wasn't strong enough, with the drug rushing through his veins, to keep her pinned to his mouth.

"Oh God, Grace," he muttered. "I was enjoying that."

"I have to know this, Devlin. Lady Prudence told me that

you murdered the gentleman that she loved. Is this true? You've told me you are noble, and I believe it—I know that you are. But why, then, would you kill a man?"

"It was a duel—"

"Prudence claims it was murder."

"Lady Prudence believes what she wishes to, because she was in love. For a start, her suitor was no gentleman—he was the youngest of four children born to the Duke of Kingsmere. He was a shiftless lout with a charming manner and a penchant for young women. Very young women. Girls, wide-eyed, innocent girls and, for all accounts, the more frightened they were, the better. This was in the summer of 1817, and Prudence was a mere seventeen. I had returned to England, and had been invited back to the house by my father since he had magnanimously decided to acknowledge the infamous pirate Captain Sharpe as his own son. I had played in that house as a child, while my mother was still his lover. He even paid for me to go to school . . . up until their affair soured. Lady Prudence and Lord Wesley were furious to have me return. They hated me, as could be expected, but I rather liked Prudence. She was quite a bit like me—"

Grace gaped with a mystified expression. "Prudence is like you?"

"Rebellious to the point of being stupid. She'd fallen for Kingsmere's boy, and he was leading her on a merry dance, trying to get her into his bed so he could marry her. But then, one night, Prudence was hurrying home from an assignation and she ran into me on the path."

The night flooded back to him: Prudence's stark horror as she saw him, the desperate way she had turned her face.

He'd grasped her arm as she tried to run by him, knowing from experience what she wanted to hide. Bruises bloomed on her pretty face at her right eye and her cheek, sickening splotches of blue and purple and yellowish-green. Blood had dribbled from a cut in her lip and made dry streaks on her pale skin.

His gut had roiled. *His mother.* He had found her lying limply on the bed, her expensive lace-trimmed shift in tatters around her. He'd been fourteen, with stolen ale racing through his blood. She was dead; he had been certain she was dead.

He'd touched her arm and the chilled flesh made him jerk away and toss the ale-soaked contents of his gut onto the bedroom floor.

Bruises had covered his mother's body. He'd never seen a person bear so many marks of violence. Some, at her slightly rounded stomach, were the shape of a boot.

"Someone killed your mother?" Horror laced Grace's words.

He was slipping into the power of the laudanum now, too weakened by emotion to fight the blissful peace anymore. "Yes," he croaked.

"Did you—did you know who?"

"I found him eventually. He was the first nob I robbed on the Great North Road. I intended to shoot him that night, playing the highwayman to give me the excuse to blow his head off—" He broke off. "Hell, sorry, sweeting," he muttered.

"It is fine, Devlin. Did you shoot him? He deserved it. Was he like Lord Wesley then, well born, and thinking himself immune to justice?"

"I didn't shoot him. In the end, I couldn't take his life in cold blood." After years of living with the pain and guilt over not being able to save his mother, he had not been able to pull the trigger. After all those days of believing he couldn't stand to see another sunrise, he'd found he could not kill the man who had put him in hell.

"What happened?" Grace urged.

"He found me, bent on vengeance. It had consumed him for months, the need to destroy me for humiliating him. He ambushed me as I left a tavern, accompanied by a half-dozen hired men armed with bats. I saw then the beast who had killed my mother. She must have *humiliated* him in some way; perhaps she ended their affair because she feared him, and he killed her."

"But how did you escape?"

"Simple, love. I offered his men more money to go into the tavern and drink. In his rage, he picked up one of the bats and rushed at me. To defend myself, I had no choice but to break his neck."

Fog crept in around the edge of his vision and he could barely lift his lids. "Do you hate me, Grace? Do you think I'm a murderer?" His voice shook with vulnerability.

"You challenged Prudence's suitor to a duel because you believe he would beat her, as this horrid man did to her mother. You did it to protect Prudence."

"S-she wouldn't listen. She thought, as my mother did with that damned viscount, that her lover's rage and violence proved the depth of his love. She believed that if she devoted herself to him, if she pleased him, if she worked to make him happy every moment of his life, that he would love her and never hurt her. And I didn't murder the young blackguard— he shot first, he cheated, and fortunately, his cowardly nerves sent his pistol ball into a tree trunk."

Hell, he was fading and there was more he wanted to say, needed to say. "I told you I ended up on a ship because I was drunk, Grace, but I let myself get drunk because I thought I was in love with a titled woman, the Countess of Arran."

Dimly, he saw Grace's mouth flatten into a pained line.

"I wasn't in love with her, angel. But I thought I was." Haltingly, fighting exhaustion, he told her all of it. Of wanting to be worthy to be seen in public with the countess. Of her dismissive note ending their affair.

Grace let her hand rest against his face and he savored the feel of her skin, the support he took from her touch.

"I thought I loved her with all my heart, and it drove me mad that she made me feel like I was unworthy, that I was less of a man because of who I was. She turned my world on edge, twisted my heart in knots until I never knew a moment's peace, until my heart and soul tormented me every waking moment."

"And that was how you defined love?" Grace's voice floated to him from somewhere above.

"Don't look so shocked. You do that to me." He licked his lips, tasting her creaminess on them, wishing he had the strength to bury himself between her thighs again. Then he turned his face and kissed her hand. "I know I never loved the countess and I know I love you, Grace. She made me believe I was less of a man. You make me hunger to strive to be more."

"Miss, we've come to help you undress. Could we please come in?"

Grace paused. She had been fighting hopelessly to reach the ties of her corset and had sorely contemplated sneaking into Devlin's bathing room and taking a straight razor to them. His snores floated in from the adjoining bedroom. He was completely knocked out by the laudanum.

He had also told her not to allow anyone into her room.

And, of course, she hadn't even thought of having him undo her annoying foundation garments. He'd been far too tired and, just when she had thought of it, he'd said that remarkable thing.

You make me hunger to strive to be more.

Was it true? How could it be when he had told her that he couldn't give up being a highwayman?

The edge of her corset, twisted by her struggles, jabbed into her breasts. *Ouch!* She couldn't stay in this garment for the night.

What if the women at the door were naked, as so many of them ran about the house?

And how she wished she could be too.

Well, not be nude, but be without her corset.

Devlin's world was a world without corsets, she saw. Whereas, the one she had longed to belong to, the world of her cold and condemning grandmother, was so tightly laced that no woman dare crack a smile or draw a breath.

"Miss?" The voice at the door repeated.

No pretense that she was anything other than unmarried.

Surely Devlin had been mainly concerned about her allowing men into her room.

She walked to the door, aware of the stays—they did not hurt yet, but they weren't comfortable—and she opened it.

Two pretty women stood on the other side; once she would have thought of them as girls, the girls of Devlin's harem, but she now was determined to consider them women. Each wore a silk wrapper tied snugly at the waist to contain generous curves. One wore a bronze robe, which went well with her freckled cheeks and auburn hair. This had been the woman who had been shocked—scandalized and furious—to see her arrive with Devlin.

Yet, now she was smiling as she breezed into Grace's bedroom. "Is Devlin resting?" she asked softly. "I thought Kennedy gave him a good dose of laudanum."

Grace nodded and the other woman came in and closed the door behind her. She carried a small green velvet sack and she let it drop by the door. Grace recognized her as one of the women who had fought over Rogan St. Clair. This woman was named Bess and she had loose black curls that hung to her waist, along with the drama of long black lashes, black brows, and dark red lips.

"I'm Lucy. You must be tired, Miss," the auburn-haired girl said in a matter-of-fact voice that was soft and pretty. "What with being attacked on the road and worrying over Devlin."

Lucy's slim hands pushed into her back from behind, surprising her. "Come by the mirror, and I'll help you with your gown."

Sighing, Grace went. She was tired, it was true. By why should Lucy want to help her?

"What's your name, Miss?" Lucy asked.

"H—" She stopped. She was tired. Everyone had seen her

in this house, but they had no idea what her name was. "Heatley," she lied.

"Miss Heatley," said Lucy, "let me get this corset off you."

Her fingers worked quickly, and soon Grace could draw a long, deep breath. Lucy glanced up into the mirror, from behind the sweep of her gleaming auburn hair, and their gazes met. "He'll be fine, you know. Devlin. He can survive anything."

The woman's casual possessiveness sent a sharp pain to Grace's heart, one that she tried to will away.

"You have been with Devlin a long time?" Grace tried to make the question sound as though she could hardly care less, but she wondered why she wanted to torture herself.

Lucy paused, her fingers hooked around the laces. A thoughtful smile transformed her—to a woman in love. "Most of my life that has mattered. He rescued me, of course. He's done that to all of us."

And he had rescued her, too, Grace thought. She'd fallen in love with him because of that, but she was not the only one. Had he rescued all the women here? She had thought he simply paid them, or they were like the camp followers of the army—women drawn inexorably to gatherings of men. But it appeared there was much more to the connection between Devlin and these women. He rescued women—he had done so with Prudence. He had not been able to rescue his mother, so instead he'd avenged her.

Grace winced at the ice-cold sensation gripping her heart.

And now, Devlin was trying to rescue her again and take her home to her family, where he felt she belonged. Perhaps all she was to him was a woman in need of rescue.

"Has he ever told you that you make him strive to be more?" she asked Lucy.

"What? What more could Devlin do? He's famous! He's like Robin Hood." Lucy helped her step out of the corset. Oh, it felt so good to be free of it.

Grace glanced at Bess. "How did Devlin rescue you?" She should be impressed with his kindness, but her heart felt tight, as though her corset was still in place and squeezing it.

"I was working on the docks—I didn't even have a room, unless I could coerce a gent to pay for one so I could have a bed. But most wanted me up against the door or the wall before they walked to the next tavern."

"You're not really Miss Heatley, are you?" Lucy asked the question. She winked at Bess, who sashayed to the door, her hips a sensual sway beneath her robe. From the sack, Bess drew out two bottles of wine.

"Of course I am."

Bess deftly pulled out the cork and handed Lucy the bottle, who then turned and, with a generous smile, held it out to Grace. "Here, have a sip."

Grace slipped her hand around it. She'd never drunk from the bottle, but it seemed fitting in a pirate's world—it seemed base and primitive and sensual—so she tipped up the bottle.

His wine was certainly superb. Lucy motioned frantically, so Grace let the bottle drop. She resisted the urge to wipe her lips, which would hardly be proper. Just the sips she'd taken left her intoxicated and giggly.

She really should go to bed.

She longed to curl up with Devlin, but he was wounded and she feared hurting him.

Bess gave her the untouched bottle and she took more sips. It tasted so lovely, a testament to Devlin's exquisite taste in sensual things.

In vino veritas. She was as hopelessly in love with Devlin as Lucy was, and that made her irritable enough to drink more.

Then she handed the bottle back to Bess, just as Lucy finished the first.

"I'm a bit foxed," she admitted. "I think I should go to bed."

Lucy grasped her by the wrists, led her to the bed, and

helped her flop down upon it. The four posts began a circling dance as she landed on the mattress. His wine was certainly potent.

"Devlin is quite infatuated with you. If you want to be a part of his world, you will have to learn what he likes best."

The entire room had begun to revolve and Grace could barely keep her lids open.

Learn what he likes best?

That had her struggling to sit up.

Lucy undid the belt of her robe and let it drop. Her voluptuous body came into view beneath a gossamer-thin shift that tugged across her large breasts. She sinuously twined her curvy form around the ornately carved gilded bedposts. "It is so much fun. Devlin and the other men take care of our every need—we have lovely clothes, delicious food, freedom. And pleasure. So much pleasure. They want us to be sexual all the time. Watch—" She smiled wickedly. "And you will see."

Bess brought the velvet sack to the edge of the bed. It looked lumpy and heavy, so it clearly held more than just wine. "They have brought us the most intriguing toys from around the world."

She lifted an object that Grace thought at first was an elephant's tusk. Then she saw the carved shapes and blushed. It looked like two male phalluses attached at the hilt.

Lucy had fished out a vial of oil and Grace swallowed hard. Her head was spinning and she knew she should send the women away but, as she tried, Lucy shook her head. "It will be fun," she assured with a sparkling laugh.

Lucy was already spreading one end of the phallus with oil, while Bess dripped oil onto her graceful fingers. As Bess lifted Lucy's shift and began to massage her privates with oil-slicked fingers, Grace stared in shock. For a start, Lucy was shaved completely.

But she couldn't help but watch Bess's fingers sliding around Lucy's glistening pink lips.

"Ooh, you're already soaked," dark-haired Bess cooed.

Laughing, Lucy gripped one end of the ivory phallus and pressed it to her quim. Abruptly she slid it inside, gasping, her face turning red. "Oh, I do love one shoved in quick."

Bess threw off her wrapper, revealing her naked curves. "But first . . ." She winked at Grace and took something else out of the sack. She applied some metal type of clamps to her nipples, wincing and moaning as they snapped closed over the erect, brownish lengths.

"The men do love us to play," Bess laughed as she held up two carved toys, both shaped like teardrops, but each with a base at the bottom. She turned, revealing her generous bottom. And without further ado, she worked one of the enormous toys between her cheeks.

Grace was sure she must be in pain, as she panted and worked the toy in and out—of her rump.

Grace was so astonished, so embarrassed . . . so aroused, her head was swimming. Her skin felt too tight for her body and almost unbearably sensitive. Left unfulfilled because she'd stopped Devlin's licking, she was now in erotic agony.

With a cry, Bess popped the toy inside herself, then she danced around, wiggling her bum, while Lucy cheered and clapped.

"Now, you fuck me, Lucy!"

And that was exactly what they did. Bess lay across the end of the bed, the bizarre clamps jutting off her hard nipples, her legs spread wide in welcome. With the other end of the toy sticking out of Lucy's quim, she had a cock to push inside Bess.

Grace blushed at the wet, slick sounds as Lucy pumped inside her friend. And once Lucy was in to the hilt, she began to thrust hard.

"Slow down," Bess admonished. "You'll come too quickly."

"But I want to," Lucy cried.

"Not until you've made me come!" Bess laughed.

Lucy turned to Grace. "You need a toy. You must be in agony!"

Oh, she was. But she should not be watching this. "I should leave you alone."

"But we love an audience," Lucy cried. "You could have one of the toys in your bum."

"The shape holds it in tight." Bess winked. "You could have two toys in you at once. It's almost as fun as having two of Dev's men in your bed at the same time. Though not quite as fun as having four of them there."

Lucy laughed at that, and Grace saw them straining toward their orgasms as they bounced together.

Oh, she was on fire.

She so dearly wished Devlin wasn't injured.

With a bevy of pretty feminine squeals, Lucy and Bess came.

And she was left to frustration.

"So she's no more a Miss Heatley than I am," Lucy muttered. Devlin's woman had been very adept at keeping her real name a secret, even after all that wine. Even after the intimacies of watching two women have sex. Lucy had hoped that would make Grace feel secure, like a friend, and she would let her guard down.

It only made the proper lady more guarded.

But then she'd had an inspiration.

Devlin was drugged with laudanum! It had taken a while to wake him enough that he could hear her, and she'd had to be clever, but Lucy had finally tricked him into whispering the name of his lady love.

Grace Hamilton.

Now, all she had to do was send the name to Rogan.

17

Something rough slid around her wrists.

Grace squirmed on her bed. She'd been yanked from her dream, but her skin was hot beneath the sheets, her breathing was fast, and her quim felt ready to explode.

And now Devlin wanted to tie her up.

"Yes," she whispered. Just his touch was going to make her come. She'd been dreaming of him, dreaming of being on his ship. In the misty dream world, she'd stood at the helm, at the wheel, overseeing the endless sea, with the world at her feet. She had been the one to guide the ship, which had had her almost on the brink of climax, and Devlin had lifted her skirts, had skimmed his hands up her inner thighs and teased her soaking wet pussy.

It had been the most erotic game—her trying to stand up while he stroked her clitoris and her wet nether lips. And, of course, she'd had to keep control of the ship, even while he relentlessly rubbed her and her legs almost melted beneath her. But she had had to stay in control and she had never been so daring before.

He'd brushed his large, thick cock against her nether lips in the dream, and she'd parted her legs wider, needing him inside.

And then she'd awoken, and she needed just a little bit of teasing, just a little more caressing and she would—

"Silence," a harsh voice warned. Her lashes swept up and she parted her lips, but then a hand clamped hard down on her mouth. This was not Devlin. He'd never be so brutal—

Her mind was whirling in madness. Her captor had waited for long heartbeats with his hand over her mouth. Waiting to see how hard she'd struggle? Or listening for sounds from Devlin's room?

She clawed blindly at the hand clamped over her mouth. She strained to see in the pitch black, but she couldn't. She had no idea who her captor was.

How far under the influence of the drug was Devlin? If she could scream, would he hear it?

Her desperate flailing, twisting, and kicking had no effect.

"Easy now, love," murmured the voice of the man with his hand at her mouth. A putrid stink neared her nose and her eyes watered.

Instinct had her recoiling away, but his knee banged down on her chest and she was pinned.

A wet cloth slid across her cheek and, with one breath, she felt the pungent smell fill her senses and turn her brains to cotton wool. Fear gave her a burst of desperate power and she punched out at the man above her. Her nails scratched hopelessly at his clothing.

The cloth slammed down on her nose and mouth. Her muffled screams escaped out the sides for a few moments, but then she breathed in hard, the cloth filled her mouth, and her head swam.

She reached out, desperately trying to stop her fall into the blackness.

But it rushed in around her and swallowed her up.

His head was still dazed from the laudanum and his entire left side ached. His half brother Wesley had been aiming for his heart. Had he not thrown that dagger, he would be dead.

Christ, Grace would have been left at Wesley's mercy.

Devlin brushed his tangled hair out of his eyes and leaned

against the doorway connecting his room to Grace's. Still unsteady, his legs wobbled beneath him, not yet ready to bear his weight. He slumped harder against the frame to prop himself upright.

Where was she?

If she'd already awoken, why hadn't she come into his room?

A soft footstep in the hallway had him stiffening, listening in absolute stillness. Could it be Grace? Unease prickled down his spine as the footsteps moved lightly toward his door.

He doubted Grace would be creeping in, but someone was.

So what had happened to Grace?

Shoving off from the doorframe, he rolled backward along the wall. Moving as silently as he could, he then braced his arms against the wall and maneuvered beside his closed door. His legs didn't feel as shaky, and he risked letting them support him.

Success.

He glanced down at the doorknob.

Damn, he'd locked his door. Slowly, he turned the key. He kept his house in good maintenance, and he let out a gentle groan to cover the sound of it opening.

Hopefully whoever planned to slip into his room would think he was muttering in his drug-induced sleep. The knob turned slowly, giving only a soft click; then the door whispered over the floor. A shaft of light fell in from the hallway. Slim fingers came into view first, along with the hem of a green gown.

Devlin waited to spring. Lucy's gaze was locked on the disordered bed—he'd thrown the covers back over before leaving it, so it was not obvious at first that he'd left his bed. She stepped completely into the room and he had his moment.

Shock held Lucy in place as his hand clamped over her mouth. He dragged her forward on weak legs as he pushed the door shut with his foot. Something fluttered from her grasp. Out of the corner of his eye, he saw the white cloth and his nose detected the smell of a drug intended to knock him out cold.

"Sweetheart," he muttered to Lucy as he dragged her to his bed, "I thought you were in love with me."

She wasn't fighting, which surprised him and made him uneasy. Lucy was not the sort of woman to surrender so easily.

He tossed her on the bed. "Don't scream, Lucy. Don't waste your breath. I doubt anyone would come running to save you from me."

She tipped up her chin, her auburn curls framing her defiant face. Obviously she believed someone might rescue her.

He softened his voice and leaned against the bedpost. Her gaze darted from him to the door, but she had to know she would never make it. He was shaking, shaking with pain, anger, and fear, and he crossed his arms over his chest to hide it.

"What did you do to Grace, Lucy?" He fought to keep his voice controlled. Control was what had made him a successful pirate, the quality that had kept his neck out of a noose.

But he'd never known his body to shake like this; he'd never felt his heart pound so hard; he'd never known what it felt like to have such icy cold rage running through him.

Lucy smiled.

"Witch!" He roared it and jumped onto the bed so his body bracketed hers. Pain shot through his body. Real fear screamed from her widened eyes. "You are only useful to me because you know where Grace is. If you don't intend to tell me, I'm more than happy to take out my rage on you."

"You w-wouldn't, Devlin. You've never hit a woman."

He felt his lips draw back in a feral snarl. "I've never had anyone I truly loved at risk. I don't care whether you are a woman, Lucy." He lowered until his mouth was close to hers. "All I see is evil, and I want to throttle you in retribution."

"Dev! No!"

"Where is she?" He shifted so he was on his knees with his legs splayed on either side of trembling Lucy. He slipped his hands around her neck. His hands were so big and her neck so small it would be an easy business to kill her.

He'd killed Prudence's lover, and it had been easy. It had been necessary and his victim had been the sick sort of bastard who'd preyed on young girls, so it had been a simple matter to turn off his conscience. It had been expedient. He'd killed many men during his pirating years.

And not one of those men had ever done to him what Lucy had—taken away his life, his soul, his light—hell, his reason for waking and facing the day.

That was what Grace had become.

"Where is she?" He tightened his grasp, enough to bruise, enough to scare her.

"I don't know!"

"No games, Lucy. Do not waste my time."

She grasped his wrists and pulled uselessly at his arms. "I don't know!" she cried again, and Devlin was apt to believe her. But he knew he had to be patient. He relaxed his grip enough for her to suck in a desperate breath.

"You have to know, Lucy. I can see in your eyes that you're hiding things from me."

She began shaking her head, so, with a grunt of frustration, he began to tighten his grip on her throat. His motions became mechanical; a cold, inhuman sense of inevitability took over. Lucy was a damned fool, a cruel and senseless witch, and if she wanted to welcome death, he'd provide her with the means.

Something flared in her terrified eyes, as though she'd finally come to the realization he did not plan to stop.

"She's with Rogan," she gasped. "He didn't tell me where he'd taken her—after all I've done for him, he said he wouldn't trust me unless I helped him get you."

"So—" Damn, he had misplayed this hand. "Rogan was here to get me after you drugged me."

"Yes, I think so."

"You think so." Was there any point in hunting for Rogan? He doubted it—Rogan had likely overheard part of this through the door. Or had Rogan simply set Lucy up? Had this little performance been intended to make him enraged, to make him tear off on a hunt?

He released Lucy from his strangling grip. "Are any of my men helping him?"

"No. He couldn't trust them, so he found his own. I don't know any of them."

His heart ached as he watched Lucy wince as she touched her throat. Tears spilled, but they were likely for herself. Still, he hated having to hurt a woman whom he had once considered a friend. A playful lover, a charming companion, a woman with a passionate heart—he'd always liked Lucy.

His breath escaped his chest in a long whoosh. Given how valuable Rogan believed Grace to be, his former lieutenant wouldn't harm her. Not yet, at least.

"So what is his plan?" Devlin asked. "To ransom her back to me?"

"Oh no, he plans to ransom her back to her family. He says you were a blasted fool for not doing it."

He rolled off Lucy and jumped off the bed. "Christ Jesus, how could you agree to that?"

"I wanted rid of her! She came between us and—"

"There was nothing between us, Lucy. Why do you think I've let you bed most of the other men here? You're part of my family, but I don't love you like that."

She began to sob and a lot of hysterical, self-pitying tears were the last thing he needed.

"Are you going to turn me out?" she whimpered. "Are you g-going to kill me?"

"No, Lucy, you silly little fool, I'm not going to kill you and I'm not going to throw you out onto the road with nothing but the clothes on your back. Even though you betrayed me, I can't bring myself to do that to you. Unless—"

He let the threat hang in the air and Lucy's fingers strayed back to her bruised neck.

"But you aren't going anywhere until I have Grace back, safe and sound."

She reached out and laid her hand on his arm, a damned bold move considering how he was fighting to keep a leash on his temper.

"I'm so sorry, Devlin," she purred.

"You aren't, Lucy, love. I can see you calculating even now." And he could. She was hoping that Grace would be gone, that she could heal things between them somehow.

Devlin charged over to his breeches, each step pure agony. His side screamed with pain. Throwing Lucy on the bed had done nothing to help his injuries. He had to get to Grace and rescue her. Rogan had a coward's streak—what if his intention was to kill Grace once he had the money? He'd be afraid she could identify him.

Rogan would never hurt Grace if he planned to ransom her to Devlin. But Devlin could guess Rogan's plan. Get the blunt for Grace and have her family believe it was Devlin Sharpe who had been her kidnapper and killer. Devlin had no doubt that if Grace's family thought he had hurt her, they would hunt him down and blow him away.

That had to be Rogan's plan. Get the ransom and get rid of him so he could command the gang.

Which mean Grace's life was in danger.

And he had to find out where in hell Rogan was.

"You need to drink some water, angel. I can't have you dying on me, now can I?"

Amused, smug, mocking, the voice made Grace shiver as she forced her eyes open. Rogan St. Clair, naked but for a pair of trousers, held a cup of water close to her lips. Blearily, she saw the clear surface ripple and her throat seemed to clench with need.

She knew she should drink; her lips were cracked with

thirst, her throat parched. She was weak from lack of food and drink. But she didn't want to go near the brute's hands.

Strangely, her gaze riveted on the chips on the edge of the cup and the dark cracks in the porcelain. Light filtered into her room through boards nailed on the window and her body ached from the cold damp seeping in through the plank floor. Her nose crinkled at the smells—the stomach-churning stink of wet ground, animal dung, and the strong ammonia smell of her urine.

The cup looked so small and fragile, as though he could crush it by mistake. His hands neared. Long hands, graceful hands—but he'd been so cruel with his hands. Her cheeks still stung from his slaps. Her temple throbbed with a painful bruise. Her dry lips had readily cracked under his blows and given him blood.

It had been hours—probably days—since he had hit her.

"Take the water," he snapped, "Or I'll force it down your throat."

She wanted to take the water, but her wrists were still bound and her ankles were shackled to rings on the wall; her body was too weak to move her weight, to pull against the drag of the chains and put her lips to the cup.

Her lashes were almost lowered—she couldn't stand to look at this man. It frightened her to meet his eyes. She didn't know what he would do. He'd not touched her since he'd beat her.

It had been so horrifying.

The first smack of his palm across her face had stunned her. Not just with the pain and the force of it. She hadn't understood why he'd done it. He just seemed to go mad.

The second blow came, splitting her lip, and she'd thought she was going to die.

She'd tried to run but he'd taken her down with his boot to her legs, and then he'd hit her over and over. All at her face.

Then he'd crossed his arms and had smiled down at her. *Smiled.* Her one lid had already been swelling; her lips and nose poured blood. And he'd nodded his head. "That should do it. And now, you need to rest," he'd remarked cheerfully.

That had been the most terrifying.

She'd been prepared to die from the beating. But his sudden change to kindness as he carried her to a cot and fussed while tucking a blanket over her had made her feel that she'd fallen into madness.

Even as he'd locked the shackles around her ankles, he'd rubbed the skin there, as though he was worried she might be uncomfortable.

God, it had been horrible.

What was he saving her for? She still didn't know.

And now the cup touched her sore lip and she winced. His hand twined in her tangled hair, pinning her head in place while he poured a slight stream of water down her throat.

How good he was at it, she thought bitterly. He seemed to know how to give her enough but not too much so she was choking.

She knew who this man was, though she'd only seen him twice. Once was in the midst of the orgy at Devlin's home and the second time had been that horrifying moment on the gravel drive in front of the house, where he'd threatened to shoot Devlin. That moment when she'd acted on instinct and let her reticule fly.

"You need to eat, too."

Through her swollen lids, she saw vivid orange bands of sunlight slip through the slits in the boarded windows. She had no idea where she was. The floor she laid upon was rough, worn wood planks with dirt that crept up from between them. The walls were roughly plastered and the few windows had boards fastened over them. It looked to be a simple and abandoned cottage.

She could smell the lingering scents of animals—not pigs,

at least—which meant that someone had once lived here, with their animals at the back of the house.

"Tonight's the night, my lovely," St. Clair soothed. He scooped a spoonful of something from a bowl. That's what had been cooking earlier. She'd grown used to smelling food she would not eat, though her stomach had contracted painfully.

Her jaw seemed to lock now, in pain, as the food neared her mouth and her nose drew in the aroma. Her stomach seemed to twist inside her.

She wanted to eat, but could she?

And what if the food was drugged? Or poisoned?

But when she hesitated, St. Clair crammed the spoon in her mouth, forcing it so harshly inside it she opened her mouth rather than lose her teeth.

"I'm not trying to kill you, angel," he crooned in a jovial voice. It was that voice that she hated the most. It implied he knew some secret that she did not—there was a joke that she was not a party to. A cruel joke and one that involved her.

Cocking his head, St. Clair studied her face in the faint light. A slow grin spread across his face, seeping over his features like spilled water into the dirt beneath her.

"I've got to pretty you up," he said, "and ensure you have the strength to meet the Earl of Trent."

Marcus? A lump of meat slid down her throat unexpectedly.

She coughed. Coughed and coughed, but it would not move either up or down.

Perhaps she'd never even last long enough to see Marcus.

The clatter of breaking porcelain stunned her, and she spluttered helplessly around the lump in her throat. A fist slammed into her back and she took a great sucking breath. The meat was drawn down suddenly, out of her throat. Tears sprang to her eyes.

"Can't have you choking to death."

"Devlin." She forced out his name, though her throat ached from the abrasion of the meat and from the fierce coughing. "You . . . take me . . . to Devlin?"

"No, my dear. It's time for you to go home. Devlin would have paid a fortune for you, though. I don't doubt that he would have offered up everything he had for you. But the cunning bastard might just have been able to get you without giving me the blunt. Your family would never risk that. And they can easily spare what I asked for. You've no worries, my love."

She struggled to follow his flood of speech. He thought Devlin would have offered everything for her?

"How much?"

"Seventy thousand."

She choked again. It was a fortune. An impossible fortune!

"In jewels—easier to transport than a king's ransom in guineas. And I wouldn't trust a bank draft. No, love, by tomorrow morning, you'll be safe at home in your luxurious world, and I'll be beginning my grand future."

She parted her lips but he stuffed another spoonful in. Would he really surrender her so easily? Even for that amount of money, that amount that made her head swim?

And then what? How could she explain what had happened? Could she lie and make them believe that she had been with Devlin but he'd never touched her?

For if her brothers-in-law, the Earl of Trent and Viscount Swansborough, knew what she had done with Devlin, what would they want to do to him?

They'd never force a marriage with a highwayman. She knew that.

But would they want to see Devlin dead?

Devlin picked up the knife from his desk and sauntered over to young Will Havestock, who was pinned back against the wall of crowded bookshelves by Horatio and Nick.

Flipping his knife end to end in his hand, Devlin faced the shaking boy. "At sea, I'd make a traitor walk the plank, Will. Or I'd tie him to something nice and heavy and have him tossed over the side. In those lovely warm Caribbean waters, he'd barely last long enough to drown. A bit of blood in the water and the sharks would be racing in to rip him to pieces."

Young Will flinched and the color drained from his face.

Devlin watched with grim satisfaction. One glance had been all it had taken to give the boy away. One desperate glance as Devlin had dragged a bound Lucy out in front of them all. The lad had revealed his shock and fear.

And all it had taken then was a few colorful threats to get the young man to admit he was helping Rogan St. Clair.

"But . . . but . . ." Will stuttered.

"Now, it's true enough that we're not on the water and there are no sharks to throw you to. Though it would be easy enough to tie you down and bait some wolves. Good sport, that. Or, if you'd like, I could make it quick and drill a ball between your eyes where you stand. I'd slit your throat, but I don't want to send your blood spraying on the books."

Will swayed where he stood. Horatio and Nick pulled him upright.

"But there's a way out, lad. Take me to Rogan's hideout and I'll let you live."

Will shook his head.

Devlin pressed his knife against Will's throat. "Pity to have to clean up all the blood. I'll have Lucy do it." He drew the knife back as though to slice—

"Wait, wait! I can take you there, Captain. I promise."

"All right, lad. Tell me where it is first, and then take me there. And I'll gut your belly and let you bleed out slowly if you make any noise, give Rogan a sign, or lead me on a wild chase."

Will nodded.

Devlin fought the hot bile rising in his throat. He'd never

known such weakening fear before, not even when he'd been standing in front of a cannon, waiting to die at the pleasure of the English Navy.

He'd played a game with Will, pretending confidence and that kind of cheerful madness that men often displayed before they killed. It had worked.

But what if he was too late?

God, what if he was?

"Devlin's going to swing for this crime and I can't have the inconvenience of you blurting out the truth."

From her position—chained and bound and forced on her knees before Rogan St. Clair's black carriage—Grace stared up at St. Clair through her dirty, tangled hair and felt her heart sink.

Inconvenience. "But—but your money?" she whispered, knowing he intended to kill her and hoping desperately to convince him not to.

He stood with his legs splayed and his boots planted near her knees. She had no idea where they were—he'd blindfolded her to bring her here. Dark wood stretched around and the cool night bit through her shift. It was all she wore, her tattered shift, and it was soaked with her sweat and her urine and spotted with her blood. At least he hadn't tried to rape her. He seemed to have no interest in her that way, thank heaven.

They stood alone, but she knew he had men in his employ. St. Clair was regarding her with amusement and she wished she could spit in his face again. She'd done it once and earned such a hard punch she'd passed out from the pain. "You won't get your money if I'm—"

"That's the beauty, love. I'd still have you to bargain with. They'll hand over the money, thinking it's the only way to ensure your safety. They won't take the risk that they might lose you. But you'll already be dead."

A breeze washed over her cold skin. She heard male voices,

talking, laughing, waiting for St. Clair to finish with her. Lost in the dark, alone, hungry, tired, she yearned to cry. Not over Rogan St. Clair, but over her own stupidity. She'd run off from Venetia and Maryanne in Brighton because she'd felt she had no place in her family, because she had wanted to run from their happiness. She'd escaped because she had wanted to stop having to lie all the time.

She'd run away and had never thought about how precious it was that she loved her family and they loved her.

She had cheated herself of marriage and children and a future.

But she was not going to let this putrid villain cheat her out of life.

She couldn't give up.

A weapon! A plan! She had to grasp at something. Even with bound hands, hands numb from the pressure of the ropes, she had to find some way to strike him.

He bent to her and grasped her arm, driving his fingers into her skin. She was so bruised there that pain shot down her spine at the pressure. He dragged her to her feet.

"You'll never escape!" she screamed, fury giving her voice volume that defied her dry and raspy throat. "My family would never be fooled, so if I die, you won't get anything!"

He shook her arm. "Oh, I will, love. Even if I don't get a penny, I'll get the satisfaction of seeing Devlin hang."

God, he was mad. Mad with vengeance. Fury took control. "Why do you want revenge? Merely because he threw you out because you wanted to ransom me? You have no idea what it is to really suffer. To lose everything. To—"

"Shut up." He stepped back, leaving her leaning against the cool polished side of the carriage, and he wrapped his gloved hand around a handle jutting from a leather sheath at this side.

Her heart skipped beats as he drew out a long blade. Of course, it gleamed in the moonlight and she could see it was honed to a perfect, deadly edge.

Oh God.

"Sorry, angel, but I need your death to be grisly. And the blade is Devlin's."

"No, wait! Let me live and I'll ensure you get far more money than you ever dreamed of!" She threw the words out, praying to make him pause. Time. She needed time.

"I'll have enough." He grasped her hair and pulled back and she had no choice but to yield, to turn her neck into a long, vulnerable arch.

He pressed the blade lightly to her throat, then slid it gently to the left.

One quick draw cut and she'd be dead.

18

The knife pressed against Grace's taut throat, and she stayed rigid beneath his grip, afraid to flinch, even to breathe. St. Clair seemed to be waiting. Enjoying her fear? Could he be considering her desperate offer of money?

The horses shied and their sudden whinnies almost shocked her into the knife. Grace forced herself to stay calm as sounds echoed into the night—the horses' snorts, jangling traces, the creak of the carriage wheels on dried mud.

She had to gamble, had to force words from her lips even though the movement of her throat drove her skin against the knife, and her windpipe felt as though it was stuffed with wool. "A fortune, if you let me go," she gasped. "Fifty thousand pounds more. I'd give you my portion to add to anything Trent gives you."

Could she really promise fifty thousand? Anything, anything, if it made him stop. If it just gave her more time.

"Ah, angel," villainous Rogan purred by her ear. "I can't begin to put a price on my triumph."

Oh God, he was determined to follow his path of vengeance. And she had nothing with which to stop him. Her sisters had used their unique skills, their special knowledge, to find ways to rescue themselves.

She had nothing.

She'd always prayed her pretty appearance would save her,

but her looks would mean nothing to Rogan St. Clair. Relying on her looks had been her one and only plan.

And then she knew, knew how to tap into his desires so that he couldn't ignore her. "Don't kill me," she cried out, "for if you let me go, I'll kill Devlin for you. I'll do anything. I'll lead him into your trap. I'll shoot him myself if that's what you want. Anything . . . just let me live."

The knife pushed into her flesh. "You would, too, wouldn't you, you betraying witch? Hell, that would be worth seeing. He's so blind in love with you, and you'd be willing to shoot him in the heart just to save your own skin."

It was working.

"Yes," she sobbed. "Yes."

He was distracted, which gave her a few seconds to attack.

Should she go for biting his wrist, or try to kick him in the ballocks?

He'd paused and all her breath had trickled out. He gave a chuckle. "Hell, what a joke that would be. He'd sacrifice anything for you, angel. Now that I think—"

The ballocks. It was her best chance.

"St. Clair, you damned bastard. Let her go."

Grace kicked her foot back just as Devlin's voice sliced through the still dark. She grabbed Rogan's arm and held tight as her heel drove back and up into soft flesh. Rogan screamed behind her. "Argh! Jesus bloody Christ!"

She shoved forward on his arm, felt the blade whisk over her skin, and a slash of cold cross her neck. Heat flooded to the wound and it suddenly burned as she felt the dribbles of blood trailing down her throat.

Not a bad wound, but it stung! And his arm was away from her neck at least. She was almost frozen with fear—fear that he'd shove the knife back at her throat, terror that he'd slice in rage and kill her.

But the knife was now dangling from Rogan's hand as he groaned and moaned behind her. If she'd crippled him for life, she didn't care. She hauled up the torn skirts of her shift and darted away from his hand, from him.

"Grace, thank heaven—" Devlin's deep, aching voice sent a shiver of relief, a warm wash of joy through her. She spun around to find him and she collided with his chest as he was charging forward. He held a pistol trained on Rogan, who had sunk to his knees, and Devlin captured her to his chest with his left arm.

She fell against his linen shirt and clutched the wool solidity of his greatcoat. It was Devlin, truly Devlin, and she drank in his wonderful, familiar, masculine smells.

Only one muscular arm surrounded her but it felt as though she were protected by an invincible shield. Devlin's touch made her feel safe. She'd never known such a powerful sensation of belonging as she did wrapped in his embrace.

Then she remembered his wound, and she ran her fingers down and touched his bandage. Though he stood straight and tall, he must have been in terrible pain; but he'd come for her, despite the wound and despite danger.

It shocked her more than Rogan's capture.

Shaking, she lifted her gaze, knew moonlight fell upon her face, and saw horror leap to his eyes as he took in her injuries. "Christ, he did this to you?" His arm straightened, and Grace screamed, knowing he was preparing to shoot.

"I'll blow you apart, you damned bastard!"

St. Clair weakly looked up. She'd been terrified of him, but she was just as frightened to watch Devlin shoot him. "Devlin, no, please."

He hesitated just as his thumb moved to cock the hammer and he lowered the pistol an inch. Deep furrows crossed his forehead and dark lines bracketed his mouth, revealing the pain and tension boiling inside him. Shadows claimed his eyes. "He deserves it."

St. Clair did, but her heart was motionless in horror. What would it do to Devlin to shoot him?

"You can't shoot him in cold blood—you have to give him to the law."

"I want him to pay."

"But I don't want *you* to!"

Crack!

A branch broke behind them, and Devlin swung around. An explosion roared, a light flared, and Devlin fired in response, the powder of his gun flashing in the dark. Grace's ears rang as he pushed her to the side.

Someone had shot at them!

Dev's arm wrapped around her waist and he urged her to run. Leaves slapped at her face as they left the path and flung themselves into the woods. Her bare feet stumbled on the rough, rocky ground. Sharp outcrops cut into her feet and she bit her lip raw against the pain. Shrubs, brambles, and twigs snagged her shift like clawing fingers.

"Sweetheart, why is it, when I've come to rescue you, you are more determined to rescue me?"

The question stunned her. "Rescue you? How? We're running for our lives."

"You stopped me killing the man who hurt you because you cared more about me—" Devlin broke off and turned abruptly, and her lungs labored as the ground sloped upward beneath her feet. The leaves and snagging twigs dropped away, and she realized they had reached a narrow path and left the denser brush behind. The faint glimmer of moonlight revealed the path headed upward.

But he pressed on, across the path, and they fled into the dense trees once more.

He stopped and gently put his hand to her mouth.

St. Clair's abuse was still a horror, and her mouth still hurt from it, but she sensed Devlin's gesture was a warning. One he had to make without words. She accepted it, and she stayed quiet. Leaves shivered around them and the whistle of the wind filled her ears.

His lips touched her ear. "I have to head to higher ground, love, and locate the road."

The road. Freedom.

As long as St. Clair did not catch them first.

"Who shot at us?" she gasped.

"One of his men. How many came with him?"

She shook her head. She didn't know. St. Clair had blindfolded her, of course, and she'd come in a carriage, where the clop of many hooves and the clatter of the wheels had disguised all other sound.

"Lucky," Devlin murmured, but she couldn't see why. A huge boulder stood before them, imposing and broad. Shaped by shadow and glinting ridges, it looked like a sleeping monster, waiting to devour them. Shaking her aching head, she fought fanciful fears. Devlin eased her to the right and she knew he meant to go around it.

She saw that he'd brought out a second pistol. Moonlight touched on the length of the muzzle. She shivered.

If Devlin had to use it, she would applaud him as a hero. She wanted him to understand that—

"Ssh," he warned.

But there was no one lurking behind the boulder.

"Stay close to the rock—in its shadow," Devlin urged. The ground fell away in a steep slope and both she and Devlin stood on a narrow dirt ridge that surrounded the boulder. One wrong step and she would go tumbling down, but the ridge gave them a view over the sweep of trees. Several carriages waited on the road below. The lamps burned, throwing golden light onto two tall men—two gentlemen surrounded by servants.

Grace caught her breath.

Her brothers-in-law. Marcus, the Earl of Trent and Dash, Viscount Swansborough.

She watched them both check their pistols and her heart lodged hard in her throat. Rogan St. Clair had led them to think Devlin had kidnapped her for ransom. He wanted them to think Devlin had beaten her.

Another man, a portly gentleman with a tall beaver hat, joined them. Devlin let out a low whistle.

"Who is that?" she asked quietly.

"The local magistrate, love."

"That's what St. Clair wanted," she whispered. "Money for me and revenge on you."

She heard his soft, angry curse punctuate the dark.

Devlin's lips brushed the top of her head as he eased off his greatcoat. The warm weight of it settled around her shoulders and he gently hugged her.

"I'm sorry to have put you at risk, Grace. To have brought you anywhere near my world. To think I thought I was a powerful man, who could control the people I thought were loyal to me. I aspired too high, and I forced you to pay the price . . ." Devlin bent close and she was aware of that sensation of being alone in the world with him. As though everything—mad highwayman and irate brothers-in-law—had dropped away. His knuckles brushed her cheek with such tenderness that she had to cough down a sob.

"If you hadn't taken me your hostage," she whispered, "I would have run headlong to my grandmother, only to have my heart broken and my spirit crushed. Without you there for me, without you to care about me, I don't know what I would have done."

The warmth of his breath caressed her cheek. His lips followed, a flare of heat on her skin. Heat that flooded to her heart and soul.

"Come on then," he murmured. "Slide your arms in my coat. You need to be warm." She did, enthralled as she always was by wearing his clothing. It was foolish, perhaps. But she knew she would never lose this awe she felt around him.

Devlin grasped her hand and started down a path that led away from the boulder and down the hill.

Her feet skidded and she winced as the dirt scraped against her sore feet. "What are you doing?"

Devlin lifted her into his arms. "I'm going to get you to your family, where you'll be safe."

"You can't! They're with the magistrate." She fought against his grip—even though she knew he'd picked her up to spare her feet.

"I need to know you're protected, Grace. Then I'm going to find Rogan and tear him apart."

"I can't go back there!" She'd forgotten the need for silence and the sharp cry she made was like a knife to her own heart. Foolish. Foolish! She could get them both killed. "I don't belong in that world. I want to be with you. I can help you stop St. Clair and we can run away together—"

But Devlin, framed by moonlight, shook his head. "You wouldn't be happy living wild with me, away from your family, away from the society you deserve to be a part of. You'd always feel that something was missing."

"Is that how you felt?" They'd traveled several yards and the end was rushing inexorably closer. She'd have to shout the instant she saw Marcus and Dash and make sure the men knew Devlin was innocent—

"Yes," he agreed.

Grace waited for more. Hoped for more. She knew what she had been missing all along, what she had just realized she had with Devlin. A sense of belonging. Of being in the right place. She knew that being with Devlin was the right place to be.

"We're to meet them at the end of this lane."

Marcus's voice. She would have frozen on the spot if not for Devlin urging her ahead. They would reach Marcus and Dash soon. They would be facing the magistrate within moments.

She would tell the truth.

But how would that help Devlin with the magistrate, who would want his hide for all his other crimes?

Slowly Devlin set her down, and she immediately stepped in front of him, forcing him to stop. "Let me go. I'll run to them myself. I'll tell them I escaped from St. Clair. Let the magistrate and his men hunt Rogan St. Clair down while you flee."

"Sweetheart, I'm not a gentleman but I'm an honorable man. I'm not going to flee while you are still in danger."

She let out a hiss of exasperation. Devlin held her arm so tightly she couldn't break free. She could see the gravel and mud of the lane through the trees now. They were only a half a dozen yards away. She could see the other men approaching. "Do you always walk straight into danger?" she whispered angrily.

"Always."

"And you always escape unscathed?"

"I've always escaped with my life, but never unscathed." He stopped then and hope rose. Perhaps he had seen sense— he would let her go and he would hide.

He cupped her cheek, his large, rough hand fitting the curve perfectly—another sign, her foolish mind said, they belonged.

"I love you, Grace. Damn, I love you with everything I have to give. No other woman would ask questions intended to drive right to my heart in the midst of danger. You are the greatest treasure I've ever aspired to, and I had no right to aspire to you. No right to kidnap you, sweeting." Moonlight filtering between the trees touched his wide, rueful grin. "But what man can resist grasping for heaven when he finds it?"

She couldn't speak.

It was his way of saying good-bye.

He loved her.

"Devlin, I—"

"Did you hear that?" Grace recognized Dash's lazy drawl, so close that she almost jumped out of her skin. She heard the other sounds—a crunch, then a soft crack. She'd been lost in Devlin and hadn't heard—

The brush exploded at their side and Grace screamed as St. Clair burst out. With his black hair and clothes, he was almost invisible in the dark, but his pistol wasn't. He pointed the gun at Devlin's temple. As soon as he saw Devlin would not move, he quickly jerked his arm to aim the barrel at her head.

Grace stared, knowing her eyes were wide and her legs immobilized.

The explosion rang in her ears and sent her legs falling beneath her. It was as though her limbs fell away from her and then her body followed.

Dead. Was she dead? Blast St. Clair to the hottest depths of hell—he'd taken her away just when she'd found everything she wanted. Everything she needed. *Devlin.*

Why wasn't there pain? Had she gone so quick she didn't feel any?

Strong arms gathered her up. Her head ached and she did feel a stab of pain, but she hesitantly lifted her fingers to her skull. She shouldn't have a head, should she?

Male shouts surrounded them. Bushes crashed all around, but she could only stare ahead at the sight revealed by shafts of moonlight.

Rogan St. Clair's body lay sprawled on the ground, a black hole where his chest had been.

Devlin had shot St. Clair before St. Clair had shot her.

Her legs threatened to fall like skittles again. But she had to find strength. Just like on the heaving ship, she could find a way to stand tall at Devlin's side.

St. Clair's men—a dirty, disheveled group of four—were surrounding them. But her brothers-in-law, the magistrate, and his men charged into the woods, armed with pistols, rifles, and blades. Luckily, men who served a Judas of a master didn't put much stock into loyalty. They quickly surrendered rather than lose their lives.

But there was confusion around as men were captured and as some tried to flee. Bodies crashed through the woods and men shouted, grunted, and cursed all around. Marcus called out to her. "Grace! Where are you, Grace?"

"Bloody hell!" Dash yelled. "I can't find her."

Devlin's hands clasped lightly on either side of her face and she winced—then saw the pain flash on his face at her involuntary grimace. But his hands were strong, warm, and she wanted them there.

His lips lowered to hers.

He wanted to kiss? Now?

"Devlin," she whispered, even as she tipped her head up in anticipation of touching her mouth to his. "We don't have time. You can slip away now, before Trent and Swansborough find me. You could be gone if you hurry." Even as she rasped out the words, she yearned to hook her arms around Devlin's neck and hold him, keep him trapped, and kiss him—

She couldn't. She had to let him escape.

But she could almost taste him, even with his lips an inch from hers, and she breathed in the heat of his mouth and felt all sense rush away. Up on tiptoe, she surged and she hurriedly pressed her lips to his. A few seconds. It was all she could have.

Devlin's hand slid around her neck, holding her possessively, and he caught her around her waist. She sinuously pushed her body against his. Only a few seconds to savor his size, his strength—the body that she knew so well and adored so much.

His mouth teased hers, joined hers, and his kiss commanded all her thoughts. She flicked her tongue with his, playfully, and giggled into his mouth when he groaned into hers. He could kiss away her doubts, kiss away her fears, but he couldn't kiss away doom.

They'd been kissing too long—

She pulled back. "You have to run—"

But he just shook his head. "No, Grace. Once you accused me of being so arrogant as to think that I was above the law."

Dread crept through her, like cold on a winter's day, and her body began to feel numb. He wasn't going to run.

"Sweetheart, I knew it would break my heart to let you go, but I believed I had the courage to do it. I'm a wanted man— how could I evade the law with a wife and children? I'd be putting a woman like you at too much risk. I'd be putting our children at risk."

Children? He'd been thinking of marriage; he'd been thinking of their future together.

"I know. I want you to go and have your freedom," she urged.

His mouth took hers into a soaring kiss again, but as he eased back, he whispered, "I'm going to give it up for you. I intend to live like an ordinary gentleman, Grace. I intend to become the kind of man who has a right to propose marriage to you."

"You're going to stop—"

"But that's not enough, Grace. I cannot be your husband as a fugitive."

She trembled. "What do you mean?"

"A wanted man isn't good enough for you. A man brave enough to pay his price would be."

She drew back, astonished. He wanted to pay his price to be worthy of offering marriage to her. "But they'll hang you!"

That wild grin came to his lips. "It's this or nothing, Grace. I'll come to you as an honest man, or I cannot have you at all."

"Devlin Sharpe, stand where you are!" The voice thundered over Grace, and she stood frozen as the magistrate and three armed men strode toward them.

Oh dear heaven, was Devlin going to hang?

"Devlin Sharpe is the hero in this! Why can you gentlemen not understand this!" Grace cried as she surged forward to stop the magistrate, Sir Charles Ball, from taking Devlin away. But Marcus firmly caught her by her shoulders, and his strong grip imprisoned her.

"Stop this, Grace."

But despair and fear and horror roared through her. "He is not the one who kidnapped me, who hurt me, who hit me! Rogan St. Clair is—"

"We know that St. Clair is responsible," Marcus assured her. His deep voice was intended to calm her, to soothe her, but it only made her more desperate. Then why couldn't they let Devlin go?

The magistrate's men surrounded Devlin—two bent at his feet, throwing the hasps of shackles and locking them tight. Another man clamped a pair of handcuffs onto Devlin's wrists. The chains that bound him hand and foot looked dirty and rusty, but she had never seen Devlin look more proud.

Was it defiance? But she saw at once he wasn't looking at the magistrate; he was looking at her, and her heart turned on edge. He looked uncertain, he appeared to be waiting— for what? To be hauled away in chains?

Marcus's grip had not slackened, so she could not put her arms around Devlin one last time. She threw a desperate glance at Dash—her sister Maryanne's husband had sported a black and dangerous reputation when he'd fallen for Maryanne. He'd reputedly done the wildest, darkest, most scandalous sexual things.

But even Dash gave a sharp shake of his head. "He's a highwayman, Grace. It's unlikely he'll be set free without trial."

Dash possessed dark eyes and thick dark lashes, and in the shadows of the night, she couldn't read his expression. The tone of his words suggested warning.

She struggled beneath Marcus's grip. A kick had freed her from Rogan St. Clair, but she doubted kicking her handsome and autocratic brother-in-law would be a wise plan. And what would she achieve? A moment's freedom followed by a quick toss into the carriage, where he and Dash would probably bar the door.

Both men had to be restraining themselves. Both men might believe Devlin hadn't hurt her, but they'd guessed he'd made love to her. She'd come so ferociously to his defense, what else could they think?

Both Dash and Marcus would believe her honor worth fighting over.

"But Devlin has done things for the Navy!" Grace cried. "They forgave him being a pirate. He rescued me, saved my life, and I'm the sister-in-law of a peer. Could he not be pardoned for that?"

The magistrate's gaze settled on her and her heart lurched in hope as she read some sympathy there. A touch of a smile came to the elderly man's mouth. "I doubt, Miss Hamilton, that we will see Mr. Sharpe hang, but he has to have his day in the assizes."

"But he'll be imprisoned!"

She swung around to face Devlin, who stood weighted down by chains. Why was he not defending himself? She suspected that Devlin had fought his way out of worse situations.

He didn't want to fight. She saw his expression and understood. He believed he had to transform himself into an honest man for her, and the only way he could do that was to either be pardoned or punished.

Bother him! She didn't want that. She wanted him.

Society's acceptance didn't matter one jot to her anymore.

"Devlin," she cried, and she didn't care that they were surrounded by men who would hear her, who might laugh at her, who had perhaps already judged her wanton and foolish. "I love you, Devlin. No matter what, I love you."

Marcus gently drew her back and forced her to walk toward his carriage. The magistrate's men roughly hauled Devlin back, dragging him away from her.

"Grace, I've no right to say it to you," Devlin called out, "But I love you."

19

"There! Are you quite satisfied! He's rotting in Newgate, awaiting trial!"

Grace saw her oldest sister Venetia roll her eyes. She knew her anger was being dismissed as another dramatic outburst and that her sisters had no idea of the agony she was truly in. She grasped a small Chinese vase, a brilliant scarlet piece, and threw it at the wall.

It exploded into a storm of red porcelain pieces.

"That's enough." Venetia jumped to her feet and marched over. "I wouldn't let my son behave so childishly." Her sister stormed toward her like the imperious countess she now was. Expecting her second child, Venetia glowed and her wilder, artistic nature seemed completely hidden by a commanding and controlling calm. Perhaps this was what motherhood did.

Grace had grown up believing her mother, Olivia, had yearned to go back to the ton and that her mother's patient calm had covered up broken dreams. After all, Grace knew what it had been to give up dreams. She'd had many romantic and dramatic dreams—marrying princes, being the most admired lady at the most important ball of the Season, being presented at court—all a young girl's treasured fantasies.

Grace had thought her mother dreamed of the world she had lost. And Grace thought that was why her mother be-

lieved a good marriage to a dashing titled man and financial
security should be her dream. Because it had been her lost
dream.

But now she saw that her mother's dream had always been
freedom. Pursuing Rodesson had only been a concrete way to
seek freedom. After all, why had her mother never tried to go
home?

Was it not because Olivia feared rejection from the
dragonlike Countess of Warren, but because Olivia actually
did not want to go back?

Grace jerked back to the present as Venetia firmly pushed
her toward the settee.

"Now sit down, Grace," Venetia continued. "If we are to
make an intelligent plan, we need to act with some intelli-
gence."

She didn't sit, though; she stood in front of the delicate,
silk-covered sofa, feeling like a prisoner in the dock.

"So, obviously, you and the pirate Mr. Sharpe have fallen
in love." Venetia had rested back against the mantel, and she
looked pained, as though the carved wood was digging into
her spine, but Grace knew what hurt Venetia was losing control. Venetia had tried valiantly to look after her youngest sister, to keep her out of trouble, and she'd failed.

"I suppose Mr. Sharpe has ruined you," Venetia said.

"No. I won't have you leaping to censorious conclusions,
Venetia," Grace protested.

"And if you want to refer to him as a pirate, should he not
be Captain Sharpe?" Maryanne threw in. "When he was acting as a highwayman, I assume we would call him Mr. Sharpe."

Grace almost giggled at the withering look Venetia directed
at Maryanne. With their mother in Italy, Venetia was trying
so desperately to be their mother.

Grace could not stand for it. "Why do we not just call him
Devlin?" she cried in frustration.

But Venetia was showing her artistic temperament now.
"A highwayman and a pirate! All he needed to make himself

more scandalous was to have tried to blow up the Houses of Parliament!"

"Venetia, he's hardly a traitor. The British Navy has been in his debt," Grace pointed out. "And Devlin did not ruin me."

"So you and Mr.—Devlin did not make love?"

Both her sisters looked at her with quirked brows and pursed lips, expressions that screamed their disbelief.

"We did, but Devlin rescued me."

"From Mr. St. Clair, which was very noble and heroic," Venetia said, "but it is his lusty actions that are important here—"

"No, he rescued me at the very beginning. I wanted to marry—years ago, before you married Marcus, Venetia. I intended to save our family by making a good marriage."

"Well, Mother certainly thought you might," Maryanne said, "You've always been lovely—the loveliest of us all."

Venetia humphed and folded her arms over her chest. "I did not think throwing you into marriage was the solution. So I painted."

"I know what you did for us all, Venetia! But I thought I should help too."

Maryanne reached for Grace's hand. "You didn't have to throw yourself into marriage—"

Grace picked up a tiny china figurine of a harlequin playing a violin. She would throw it if need be. Wouldn't her sisters just let her talk? Being dramatic was the only way she could ever get any attention. "I wanted to marry and then . . . then I fell in love. At least I thought I was in love. I loved Lord Wesley, my friend Lady Prudence's brother. When I went to their house party, I—"

"You gave your innocence to him?" Venetia gasped.

"But what about Devlin?" Maryanne added.

"You bedded both men?"

She almost lost her courage to tell her story looking at the shock on her sisters' faces. "Not at the same time!" she cried.

Wait . . . both her sisters were blushing and looking rather self-conscious at her comment.

"No!" Maryanne held up her hands in protest. "We've never done anything such as that. But, well, men do like to spin fantasies in the bedroom."

"Then you can't judge me!" Grace cried. "Yes, I gave my innocence to Wesley. He had told me he wanted to marry me. I said yes, we made love, and then after . . . after, he laughed at me. It had all been a wager, a joke. And there was nothing I could do. Our distant cousin knew about it, Lord Wynsome. It was all horrid—"

"Grace—"

Both her sisters were rushing to hug her. But she put down the harlequin and stepped back. "I want to finish! After Wesley's horrible words, I raced out of the room and ran straight into Devlin. He guessed everything. He made sure neither man would ever speak a word of what happened. He even spanked Wesley, who is his titled half brother!" She thought of that horrible scene with Wesley, when he'd held up their carriage and had intended to use her to hurt Devlin.

"No wonder Lord Wesley Collins has left England," Venetia muttered.

Grace whirled around and paced, darting around the furniture that filled the drawing room of Venetia's Brighton home. She had to keep moving—she didn't want to surrender to a hug just yet. "So I did take Devlin to my bed that night. I know it was wrong and scandalous. But he was so noble to me that I wanted what I thought would be my only memories of lovemaking to be . . . good and not horrible."

Maryanne forced a hug on her then. "Grace, we don't judge you. It is hardly your fault that Lord Wesley lied to you, but . . ."

Embraced by her sister's slim arms—Maryanne was taller than she and very slender—Grace cautiously asked, "But?"

"Are you certain you love Devlin? That it wasn't just heartbreak?"

"It's been over two years since that night, and not one day has gone by that I haven't thought of Devlin." Grace heard the tears in her voice and swallowed hard. "I am quite certain I'm in love with him. No matter how much I tried to deny this intense, overwhelming yearning for him, I could never forget it and I know I never will."

"Do you know . . . how Devlin feels about what happened between you and Lord Wesley?" Maryanne asked softly. She slipped her arm around Grace's waist.

"Yes," Venetia added, "That is quite important."

"He doesn't blame me, if that's what you mean. He has never held it against me." She wondered if her sisters would. From their worried expressions, the glances they shared, Grace was certain her sisters wished she had been more cautious, more circumspect, more . . . dutiful. But Devlin had never judged her for what she had done.

Venetia smiled. "He sounds to be a good man. But we suspect you did not leave here to go to Lady Prudence's house party, that you lied to us. Was it Devlin you went to see?"

Grace felt tears spring to her eyes. "No. I had been writing to the Countess of Warren. Our grandmother."

Venetia froze. "Why?"

"I wanted to heal the rift, to put aside past quarrels and anger. I wanted to know her."

"Did you meet her?" Maryanne asked.

Around the lump in her throat, Grace managed, "Yes, but she rejected me. She'd heard of my behavior from Lord Wynsome. She called me wanton; she threatened me never to make our connection known."

"Horrid old cat!" Venetia cried.

Grace wiped her eyes, for the tears itched. She had thought her sisters would be angry at her, not at their grandmother. "She had written me a letter in which she told me that she wanted to see her granddaughters. That it had been her husband, the earl, who had forbid it. But when I met her, she was cold and cruel. I could not understand it."

"And Devlin was there."

Grace frowned. "Yes, he was. He had not wanted me to see the countess. He did not want me to get hurt."

Venetia tapped her lips and then she took Grace's hand and led her to the settee. This time Grace willingly sat, sinking into the satin-covered cushions, and her sisters sat flanking her.

"How did you find Devlin, or did he find you once more?" Venetia asked. "Or have you been secretly seeing him for two years?"

"I don't think she has." Maryanne shot a frank look at Venetia. "I think she would not have been so discontented and restless if she had been."

Venetia gave a wry smile. "That's true."

Grace knew there was no way but to tell the truth, and she felt courage with her sisters she never had before. She felt like an equal, not like the bothersome baby. "Devlin held up my carriage. He had been watching me for two years."

"And he held you up for what reason?"

"To embark on an affair."

"So he has never offered marriage."

Grace shook her head and sank back against the chair. She did not want to discuss this. Of course he had not offered marriage. He had told her, hadn't he, that he had nothing to offer her because he was a wanted man? That he would come to her as an *honest* man or he would not come at all.

She rather wished that a nurse would bring one of the children down, either Venetia's sturdy six-month-old son Richard Nicholas Charles Wyndham, or Maryanne's month-old baby boy Charles Dashiel Blackmore. Such large names for such tiny little men.

Either little boy would be a distraction, a desperately needed one.

Venetia crossed her arms beneath her breasts, narrowed her hazel eyes in great seriousness, and tilted one auburn brow. "He hasn't offered marriage, has he?"

"I want to use my dowry." She faced Venetia with courage. "I intend to buy a ship with my dowry and rescue Devlin, whether he has offered me marriage or not."

"Rescue him!" Maryanne's brows shot up. Her sister wrote popular books of adventure and passion, all dismissed by the critics but adored by readers. "Exactly what do you mean by 'rescue him'?"

"Get him out of jail and get him out of England," Grace answered.

"You cannot run away," Venetia declared. "I completely forbid it."

Grace was ready to run to the mantel and grab the mate to the vase she'd thrown and crush it in her hands. But she paused. She was a grown woman. She did not have to throw pottery in a tantrum. She had to take charge of her life.

"Why do you forbid it?" she asked. She would not scream at her oldest sister, but Venetia had no right to forbid anything. She would actually listen to her sister speak for once instead of flying into dramatics. "Because he's a pirate?"

"No—because I don't want to think of you living a dangerous life where you are hunted by the British Navy! Because I want you to stay and be happy—to find the happiness Maryanne and I have found—"

"I think that is the problem, Venetia," Maryanne interjected, and Grace shot her a look of surprise. Her middle sister usually sided with Venetia, the most bullheaded of the three of them. "Grace wants an entirely different kind of happiness. She wants adventure."

"It's sorely overrated," Venetia cried. "Do you want more nights where you are held at gunpoint? Do you want to see Devlin shot in front of you?"

She flinched at that and Maryanne cast an angry glare at Venetia. "You are the one being overly dramatic. I'm sure if Grace and Devlin were to sail away and Devlin were to cause no more trouble, the king and the British Navy would never trouble themselves again about him."

"But it means she would never come back! We'd never see her again! Just as Mother has said she will not come back to England, Grace will not either."

"But that is the way of life." Maryanne reached around Grace and placed an impulsive hand on Venetia's arm.

"I wanted us to be happy as a family."

Grace knew she must speak for herself—she couldn't play the youngest child any longer, letting others speak for her while she sullenly kept her agreements and disagreements bottled inside. "We will be, we just won't live at each other's sides."

Venetia sighed. "I'm being foolish, I know. It's just that I had the chance to make your life perfect, Grace—"

"There's no reason why it won't be perfect, Venetia," Maryanne added.

"But how do you plan to get Devlin out of Newgate? I doubt bribery will work—he's far too important a prisoner. And you don't know that he would even take you with him. He's offered you nothing."

She heard Maryanne's sharply drawn breath.

"He's offered me his heart." Grace refused to be goaded into throwing more vases. "He was willing to let himself be captured to protect me! He could have run to save himself, but he wanted to ensure that I was safe. He was willing to face prison, to face a noose, for me. He let himself be taken to prison to make himself worthy of me. I believe in him, even if none of you do."

"A pirate willing to give up his freedom must be in love," Maryanne added.

Venetia wore a troubled frown, her brow furrowed, and, for the first time, Grace thought her eldest sister looked exactly like their mother. Venetia—who had always thought her artistic talent meant she was the most like their scandalous artist of a father.

Perhaps nothing was exactly the way they had always assumed it was.

Grace had always thought she'd be happy making a proper marriage and bringing her mother back into high society. Now the very thought made her nauseous. She had always believed she was the most like their mother—well bred and not truly prone to scandal.

But perhaps her sisters were the responsible ones and she was, at heart, the wildest of them all.

Venetia had opened her mouth, and Grace had stiffened, expecting a lecture, when a footman opened the drawing room door. "A visitor has arrived for Miss Grace Hamilton," he said on a bow. "Lady Prudence Collins. She has been shown to the west parlor."

As the door shut behind the servant, Venetia stared at her in astonishment. "Lord Wesley's sister? What could she want?"

"I expect to blame me for her brother's failed life as a highwayman and his flight from England," Grace said airily, and she left them gaping at her in surprise.

A long time ago she would have been bubbling with excitement to see Prudence. They would fall naturally and comfortably into conversation, laughing, gossiping, hugging. Her friendship with Lady Prudence had made Grace believe she belonged in that world—the privileged world, the world of blue blood, elegance, titles, and wealth.

Grace walked with a purposefully slow gait down Venetia's hallway. Painted in white and pastels, it looked bright; Brighton was where London escaped oppressive heat for breezy sunshine. Who belonged less in this house right now? Lady Prudence or her?

One of the west parlor doors had been left open and Grace paused there. The rustle of silk came from within. Grace smoothed her skirts, though she didn't care how she appeared to the woman who had once been her friend, yet had rudely cut her.

She just needed a moment. A moment to compose herself.

She strode into the room, head high, spine straight, her walk imbued with the elegance of a lady. One look at Lady Prudence and she faltered—her ladyship wore a lavish gown and spencer of sky-blue silk trimmed with a fringe that seemed to sparkle in the sunlight. Her bonnet appeared to be a bouquet of roses held together with ribbon.

No. Clothes would not intimidate her—not when she'd survived a knife at her throat and a pistol pointed at her head.

"Hello, Lady Prudence. Might I ask what you have come for?" As a greeting it was neither deferential or polite. But it was the truth. All she wanted to know was what Prudence wanted.

Startled by her voice, Lady Prudence swept around. She had been standing by the window, staring out at the garden, drenched in sunlight. Her black curls gleamed and her gray-blue eyes were as hard and flat as the sea before a storm.

"My brother has left for the Continent, and our family name is blackened by scandal. The fault lies with you and that horrible criminal, Devlin Sharpe!" Prudence stood, shaking, like a slender tree buffeted by stormy winds.

"Your brother is running from what he believes is cowardice," Grace responded. She could not bring herself to use soothing words when she knew Prudence only wished to shout and rail at her. "Not to mention his disgusting behavior toward innocent women."

"What are you speaking of?" Lady Prudence snapped. Apparently, Prudence believed Grace's inferior social status meant that she must accept being used as a whipping post, but Grace refused to do it.

"Lord Wesley held up Mr. Sharpe's carriage," Grace continued. "He was quite drunk, he almost shot Mr. Sharpe, and he almost got himself killed."

"That murderer wounded him—"

"No, Prudence, keep quiet. Devlin told me about your suitor. He told me about the bruises, that your lover had hit you. Prudence! How could you have accepted that?"

Prudence recoiled. Her hands flew up to her throat as though she could not believe Grace would attack her. "Nothing changes the fact that Sharpe killed him—"

"Your suitor cheated and shot first." She didn't want to hurt Prudence; she wanted to make her see the truth.

"He killed him."

"It is true, my lady, but do you not understand that Devlin was forced to do it to protect you?"

Tears welled in Prudence's eyes and sympathy twisted so hard within Grace that it physically hurt. She moved forward, to offer a hug, to offer support, but Prudence lifted her hand as if to slap her.

"Don't touch me!" Prudence cried. "You've bewitched Wesley. You've stolen him from me, stolen his heart." Clutching her lovely skirts, Prudence retreated toward the bank of windows.

"That's madness. Wesley pursued me to hurt Devlin—he doesn't care one jot about me. In fact, I believe he thinks of no one but himself. That is why he has left you, Prudence. He has fled to indulge himself, lick his wounds, and behave like a spoiled child—and unfortunately he is not mature enough to spare you a thought."

"That's not true. You destroyed him, you calculating tart. I warned you, but you went after him, seduced him, and—"

"Enough!" Grace cried. "You cannot speak to me that way. Do you know that your brother belonged to a club of gentlemen who specifically preyed on innocent girls? They made wagers on how many virtuous girls they could destroy." She had told her family about this, though she had not specifically explained how she knew. And she'd felt guilty that she had not said anything two years before. "My brothers-in-law, the Earl of Trent and Viscount Swansborough, put a stop to their horrible club. Wesley fled, I'm sure, because he feared what they would do to him. Because he is a coward. Any scandal is his own fault. He deserves a much worse punishment than escaping England."

Prudence's face turned pale.

Grace softened her voice. "Prudence, you must carve your own way in the world—you should find love, marry, have a family. You must not blame others for the mistakes you and Wesley have made. You have to accept responsibility and strive to do better, strive to find happiness."

Prudence stormed toward the door, following a path that led between the wing chairs and octagonal tables and settees and away from her.

Carve out your own way in the world. Those had been Devlin's words to her.

As she watched Prudence run out of the room, Grace realized that she had not been worrying about what Prudence thought of her. Her worries had been for Prudence herself.

She no longer cared what the ton thought of her.

She felt as though that was beneath her now. Love and hope and kindness were far more important.

"So you see, her plan is to try to break Devlin out of jail. I can just imagine the thoughts in her mind—she will sneak in and somehow free him and it will all be very adventurous and exciting. She's always been dramatic and she refuses to even think of how dangerous it will be."

Venetia gave her husband her most imploring look but sighed inside. All she had ever wanted to do was save herself and her family.

Now her impetuous youngest sister wanted to be the rescuer. But Grace was too naïve to understand how very dangerous that was.

"She'll get herself killed," Marcus growled, and Venetia felt a spurt of calming relief. She'd known Marcus would understand.

"I doubt you'll be able to stop her." Dash slipped his arm

around Maryanne and kissed the top of her head. The implication was clear—Maryanne had risked so much out of love for him, just as he had risked all for Maryanne.

"I can't let her race headlong into danger." Marcus groaned. Venetia saw that streak of gray in his hair, that he had teasingly argued had been placed there by the entire trio of Rodesson's daughters.

"I think there's a way to have Devlin exonerated," Marcus continued. "He's done much clandestine work for the Navy— secured land, raged battles, all in secret. And he's kept those secrets, despite his flagrant disregard for the law in other ways."

"He was trying to make his way in the world!" Maryanne leaned forward, waving her hands to include them all. "Haven't we all struggled to do that? Each and every one of us? We all had to make mistakes to find our places! As did our mother and Rodesson."

Venetia met Maryanne's firm gaze and nodded. She so admired her younger sister, who had always been quiet and who had proved she had a deep understanding of human nature. No wonder Maryanne's stories were so well loved.

Dash rested back, his dark looks dramatic against her ivory settee. He'd worn all black today, which once had reflected his torment but now meant that he intended to indulge in some naughty games with Maryanne all night. It was one of their secret codes, and Venetia smiled.

She did so want Grace to be happy. She'd just wanted to see Grace happy and *safe*.

But perhaps, even after all she'd learned about partnerships and trust and love, she still needed to recognize when to let go.

"There's a way, I think," Dash drawled, "to give Grace exactly what she wants."

"What is it?" Venetia almost leapt upon him. What had he thought of?

Dash looked to Marcus. "Do you believe you could convince the crown to forgive Devlin his crimes?"

"With both of us working on it—given the fact I loaned

our king a lot of money while he was still regent—I think it could be done." He rubbed his jaw in the way that Venetia loved. She loved to see him lost in thought, planning. "So, a marriage between Grace and a freed Devlin could go ahead, but she'd still be marrying a man known to be a pirate and thought to be a highwayman—"

Dash held up his hand. "Grace needs her adventure. I say we give her one."

Marcus groaned. "Damnation, I think I see where your mind is going, Swansborough."

Venetia gaped at both men. She knew they had conspired together to ensure she and Marcus could find happiness, and she saw the devilish grin first come to Dash's handsome mouth, then slowly, seductively, spread across her husband's beautiful, enticing lips.

Marcus's turquoise eyes lit up and Venetia felt her breath whoosh from her chest. He still did that, her handsome husband—he still took her breath away. And he told her, when he whispered by her ear when they were in bed together, that she still did the same to him.

She held Marcus's gaze, so aware of him—of the strong line of his jaw, the smooth, lightly tanned skin of his throat, the beautiful lines that framed his mouth and his eyes.

Maryanne clapped her hands, and Venetia snapped out of studying her husband's gorgeous darkly lashed eyes. "I think this is going to be one of our best plots!" Maryanne exclaimed.

And Venetia saw then what a happy family was about. It wasn't guiding the people you loved into the places you felt they should be. It was about accepting, helping, and loving.

"We will be helping our sister marry a pirate," she cautioned, but she knew it was too late. She couldn't object to Grace being happy and neither could anyone else.

"But really, Venetia," Maryanne protested with a mock air of hauteur, "whatever good is marriage if not with a man worth taming?"

"Do you think he can be tamed?" Venetia threw out.

"Not in the important ways." That teasing comment came from Dash, who was grinning at his wife. "And he doesn't need to be tamed in the others. He's like all wild men—he was looking for a woman he had to fight for."

"Fight? But who—the only ones he has to fight are us, isn't that so?" Venetia asked. "Because we are the ones who should not approve."

Marcus shook his head. "I understand what Dash means. He means that Devlin had to fight within himself to find the strength to claim Grace—he had to fight his own demons."

"Demons that have led him to break the law his entire life," Venetia pointed out. Could Devlin Sharpe, who had retired from life as a pirate to become a highwayman, change? "How does allowing himself to be arrested mean he is fighting for Grace?"

"He's trying to make himself honorable, and for his entire life, I believe that's something he felt he could never do," Marcus explained. As always, his deep voice rippled over her, like a warm caress against her skin.

"Grace thinks he's a hero."

"And Grace needs to be a heroine," Marcus said.

Venetia threw up her hands. "All right, I agree to this, whatever scheme you have in mind. But I think the truth here is that neither of you men, both of you fathers now, have ever really grown up!"

"Of course not," Dash drawled. "And isn't that why you love us?"

20

"Are you going to shoot your way in?" Bess asked as she brandished a silver pistol and waved it around to show it off to the circle of women.

"No! And put that away!" Grace glanced down Newgate Street toward the imposing stone façade of Newgate Prison.

"Stay in the shadows," Grace warned, but Katie, another of the six women of Devlin's gang, was bouncing up and down with excitement, her blond curls dancing. The women would not listen to her warnings. At least they lurked in the shadows cast by the buildings at the corner of Newgate Street and Old Bailey as she'd insisted, but they were not being cautious, quiet, and circumspect.

Katie grasped her arm, her bosom jiggling, and confided, "Devlin has escaped from jail before, but I don't know exactly how he did it!"

A hand fell gently on her other arm and Grace turned to meet Lucy's wide eyes filled with guilt and worry. "Thank you for letting me help, for letting me come with you, Miss Hamilton. But after how I betrayed you, I don't understand why you would."

Was she mad for asking Devlin's "harem" of six women to help her free him from jail? Her family thought so. Devlin's own men did—they thought her insane for relying on a bevy of beautiful women they saw as playful courtesans. But Grace understood why Devlin had taken the women in, why he took care of them. They all deserved to be something more. Each woman deserved to play a part in the world. To direct her own life.

That was what he had wanted for her—to find her courage, to carve her path.

"Devlin would believe you deserve a second chance," Grace said.

"Then you know Devlin far better than I do, Miss Hamilton," Lucy whispered. "I believed he would never forgive me."

Ensconced in the long fingers of dark shadow, Lucy looked uncertain and frightened. Grace saw the nervous glances Lucy threw toward the other women and the cold, awkward way they behaved around Lucy.

Had she been wrong? Would the women's unspoken anger and Lucy's guilt cause them disaster?

Grace knew there was no more time to talk, to linger, to delve into worries and concerns. She gathered the women around her. All wore breeches and tight-fitting white shirts. None wore corsets, so their abundant bosoms bounced freely beneath the snug lawn. The women had left their shirts open and the array of shadowed cleavage was rather mesmerizing.

"Do you all know the roles you are to play?"

Each woman—Lucy, Bess, Katie, Annie, Sally, and Nan— nodded. Each woman glowed with pride and excitement.

"Then we go," Grace said.

She had never known such a thrill—except when making love to Devlin. This was almost, but not quite, as delicious as that. She was in charge, just as she had been in her dream when she was at the wheel of Devlin's ship. She felt exhilarated enough to fly! She could understand how Devlin had vowed he would never give up being a pirate to become an ordinary man.

Grace walked up to the door. It was late summer and the stench of the prison turned Grace's stomach. Some of the cells were reputed to contain rotting corpses waiting for relatives to find the money to pay for their release. God, it was so horrible to think Devlin was in there.

She lifted the black knocker on Newgate's door and let it fall. The hard thud vibrated through her feet and up her spine.

"Who goes there?" demanded one of the guards as he came out of the guard hut to see who was at the outside door. He was a portly man and as Nan and Katie, both blondes with large breasts, strolled forward cooing and offering him drink, he couldn't tear his gaze away from their curves. The second guard was younger, and he had been slumped against the stone wall inside, but he promptly straightened up.

Katie now stood in front of the older guard, so close that his nose almost grazed her bosom.

She pointed to Nan, who invitingly stroked her hands over her full hips. "My friends wish to see their men, who are locked up in here. There's no harm, is there? And we'll make it worth your while to help us."

Nan held up a bottle of fine brandy.

The guard warred with duty for only seconds. "Come 'ere, my lovelies," he crooned.

Katie snatched the bottle from Nan, took a convincingly large swig of the potent liquor, then sashayed forward. "Indeed we will, sirrah," she answered cheerfully.

"You, Thomas." The guard gave his young partner a shove toward the door. "Escort the lasses in."

"What's in it for me?" Thomas demanded.

Bess rushed forward to press her body against his. "If you're a good fellow, you'll get your reward," she whispered, her voice a sultry purr against the hot night air.

"It stinks in there," he argued. "I'd need a good reason to go in."

Grace saw Bess's hand abruptly cup the young man's crotch and caress it through his trousers. He gave a shocked squeak, surprisingly high pitched; then he moaned.

"Shall I lead you by these," Bess teased.

But he pushed away her hand. "I don't want a prisoner's whore—"

Katie pouted at the other guard. "If you gents won't help . . ."

The guard planted his booted foot against Thomas's backside. "Get moving, you whelp."

Grace planted herself in front of Thomas and pressed a few gold guineas into his palm. "Enough to make you forget the smell?"

The angular youth nodded, flashed a grimace that revealed a few missing teeth, and pocketed the money. He drew out his key, attached to his waist with a glinting chain. Grace held her breath as the key turned in the lock and he hauled open a heavy wooden door. She was so much closer to Devlin, but she still had to get him on this side of that door.

She still had to get him outside the stone walls, the barred windows, and the thick oak doors.

Distracted by two beautiful women, the older guard never even glanced their way. Grace sighed with relief as they plunged through the doorway and within the stone walls that held Devlin captive. She almost gagged on the smell rolling down the corridor.

"Which ones do you want?" the young man asked sullenly.

Bess squeezed his bottom and a flush hit his pockmarked cheeks; then she tugged at her open neckline to give him a glimpse of her breast.

Grace took advantage of Bess's show. "Mr. Devlin Sharpe."

She expected Thomas would refuse, that he would claim he could not let them go to that particular prisoner.

But he gave her an indifferent stare. "And who else?"

"No one else," Bess answered. "Just Devlin."

"All of you? For him?"

"We're his harem, lad," Annie said, winking. He stared at the long waves of vivid red hair that flowed loosely over her shoulder.

"Now, look here," Thomas protested, waving his precious cell keys. "I don't believe you—"

"Oh, we all know that the men who can afford it have their women in here," Annie snapped as she pressed both hands to the young guard's thin chest and gave a frustrated shove.

"Enough," Grace warned. Her heart beat so loudly in her own head she was certain the sound must be echoing off the stone walls. She pulled out a few more coins, the gold glinting even in the dim and dusty light, and held them out. "Just take us to his cell."

"Bloody women," Thomas muttered, but he crooked his finger. "This way and keep your mouths shut."

Shuffling his feet, he led them to a narrow staircase, and he slowly hauled his feet up each step. Grace had to bite her lip to keep from screaming at him to move faster. She stayed close to Thomas, in front of the other women, ready to hand him more money if necessary.

The stairwell closed around them like a tunnel leading to hell, even though they were climbing upward on chiseled stone steps. Shrieks and groans echoed through the small space, the sounds thrown about crazily by the stone walls. Grace swallowed hard—she remembered that night when Devlin had returned her to her room through the secret stairways of Lord Wesley's home.

She owed Devlin so much.

He had been the first to give her a glimpse of adventure.

Ahead, Thomas stopped at a cell door, drew out his ring of keys and put the key in the lock.

"We'll let you watch if you're a good boy," Annie called out. That got the young man's attention. Red-faced, he jerked around, but Sally, who had the strongest swing, hit him in the back of the head with a cosh. He slumped to the ground in a tangle of limbs.

Grace walked around him, fighting the surge of guilt. "You didn't kill him, did you?"

"I'm no amateur," Sally protested, "I've coshed many men in my lifetime. I know just how to do it."

"Ladies, what in the blazes are you doing here?"

At Devlin's voice, Grace found herself racing forward through the narrow opening in the iron bars. But Lucy, Bess, and Annie were already in his cell, and Bess pointed to her the instant she stumbled in. "It was Miss Hamilton's idea. We're your rescuers."

Devlin blinked. "Grace? You arranged this?"

He looked well; he looked safe. His face was unshaven, covered in toffee-colored stubble, but his skin was surprisingly clean. Loose, his hair fell around his shoulders, but it wasn't tangled and unkempt. He wore his trousers, shirt, and boots, and though they were streaked with dirt and they smelled, he filled them out robustly.

True, he'd been in prison for only two weeks, but she'd had fears that he'd already contracted gaol fever and was wasting away.

Thank heaven he hadn't suffered.

Then she saw he was looking at her.

His gaze swept over her, lingered on her, feasted on her. He looked at her clothes—the snug white shirt and skintight breeches—with a hunger he had not shown any of the other beautiful women who crowded his small cell.

"A private cell. And they gave you washing water." It was as though she had not seen him for years and she was hiding behind inanities.

"I have money, love. And someone was paying to ensure I was well treated."

He prowled forward, and her heartbeat sped faster with

his every step until he swept her off her booted feet into his embrace and she was certain her heart had stopped. The other women surrounded them with sighs and "aahs" as his lips came down over hers.

Grace threaded her arms around his neck and wrapped one leg around his, holding him tight. She loved this—her breasts squashed against him, his erection crushed against her.

Devlin drew back. She knew his expression—the sharp lines of lustful agony around his mouth, the brilliant blue fire of desire in his eyes. "If you don't start rescuing me, we might end up on that bed there, love."

She gripped his hand. "Then come on."

"What's your plan?"

"Distraction and bribery."

Devlin laughed wickedly, exactly like a pirate should—as though he had the world at his feet and he knew that he'd flaunt death and survive. "An excellent plan." But he caught hold of her wrist. "Grace, I cannot put you at this much risk. I told you I would not come to you as a wanted man."

"And I've come to you. You are a wanted man—wanted by me."

When he frowned, she faced him, seriously. "This is what I want, Devlin. I would rather be a fugitive than live without you. I cannot let you go." She cupped his stubble-covered cheek, smiling at the rasp of his whiskers against her palm. "This is my path, Devlin. Adventure and you. I'll take the path of adventure without you if I have to, but come with me. You belong with me and I with you."

"I want to follow you on your path, Grace."

She glowed at that, at his simple statement telling her that he wanted to be with her. She nodded. "But I am in charge. Do remember that, Captain Sharpe," she teased. "You have rescued me enough times. Now it is my turn."

"I won't forget it, Grace," he murmured. "Rescue me."

*   *   *

Shouts and cries echoed down the corridor. A few other prisoners had awoken, some close enough to see the women. Sally and Annie had dragged in the fallen guard, but the other male inmates had glimpsed enough female flesh in tight clothing to be aroused and aggressive.

They smashed the bars and hooted and howled at the women. Begged them to come over. Some, the more deranged, the ones who had been in so long they had begun to forget they were human, screamed insults or just shrieked.

Escaping through this was going to prove bloody difficult. But Devlin knew they had to get out—he couldn't let Grace be arrested and locked up for an attempted escape.

Though it cost him precious seconds, Devlin bent down to the guard and pressed his fingers into the throat to find a pulse. It flickered against his skin, slow and faint, but there.

He looked up to see lines creasing Grace's forehead and her mouth stiff with doubt. "Is he—?"

"Unconscious, but alive, and I wouldn't envy him the sore head he's going to have."

Sally held the keys. "Let's hurry," she urged from the cell door. She leaned out and looked up and down the corridor. Bars rang as men hammered their cups, their feet, their arms against the iron.

Grace slanted him a glance as they hurried behind Lucy, Bess, and Annie through the door. "I was hoping at this point you would know the way out—the best way. Since you've escaped from here twice. Though I did study the layout of the prison. Marcus acquired copies of the building plans."

Devlin felt his brows launch up. "Your brother-in-law, an earl, gave you building plans?"

She nodded. "My family supports this."

"Your family must be mad," he muttered. It couldn't be so. The Earl of Trent and Viscount Swansborough had allowed Grace to put herself at such great risk?

Impossible.

Annie shoved his back from behind. "Get moving, Dev, you great lummox. Otherwise we'll be caught."

"How did you escape before?" Sally demanded. The women were keeping watch on the corridors. Why hadn't all the rumpus brought the guards?

"I climbed out my window and crawled up onto the roof, then followed the roof line around to the end on Newgate Street and jumped off. And no, I am not about to take you ladies up on the roof."

"Then what are we going to do?" The plaintive voice belonged to a woman with long auburn hair, who had her hands clasped together in front of her mouth.

He blinked twice before realizing the woman was Lucy. Grace had brought Lucy—a damned forgiving act. Admiration flooded through him as he looked to the woman he loved—Grace Hamilton.

"There must be another way out," Sally was saying.

"Yes," Grace declared. "The front door."

"With the guard there?"

"You have your cosh and we can easily distract him. Besides, he's probably drank that entire bottle of brandy by now."

"I don't know if we can distract him enough to blithely walk out the door with a prisoner," Annie declared.

"Do not underestimate yourselves," Grace advised. Such wild excitement flashed in her green eyes, they seemed to glow in the faint light.

Devlin laughed. "True enough," he agreed as he slipped his arm around Grace's waist. He cradled her, drawing her warmth into his tired and sore body, feeling as though a flame had ignited in his soul. It was still an insane risk. There were other guards. But that fire fanned through him, burning in the mad way it once had when he'd been a pirate.

Grace did that to him—she gave him the same fiery excitement he had once had to risk his life to achieve.

Grace tipped her face up to his. "I know the passageways that will keep us away from the cells as we approach."

He grinned. "Right, then. To the front door."

It had been too easy, but Devlin was determined not to spoil Grace's fun.

As she sank back against the blue velvet seat opposite him, safe inside the plain black carriage, she sighed happily. "We're safe. And free!"

She threw her hands up behind her so they rested against the soft, smooth velvet with wrists crossed. It was a position that suggested so many naughty thoughts he was instantly hard. She looked so utterly pleased with herself that he had to smile. He'd never known this feeling—that of a heart full to bursting—with anyone but Grace. Hell, how he adored this woman.

"And where are you taking me, Captain Hamilton?"

Grace laughed, green eyes sparkling like a fairy's. Her legs were splayed, her generous thighs showcased by the breeches. Wickedness in her smile revealed she knew exactly how tempting she looked. "To the docks. To my ship."

"Your ship!"

"Yes. I bought one with my dowry so that we can leave England and sail to safety. My family has ensured that we will not be pursued. Your men are aboard the ship and we shall sail tonight."

Devlin shook his head in amazement. Where was the proper young lady who had wanted to be a part of the rigid and correct world of the ton? Where was the woman who had wanted marriage to a gentleman? "You have enjoyed engineering my escape, haven't you?"

Snuggled against the seat, her golden hair aflame against the deep blue, she smiled. "Yes. And I think I've done an excellent job. I arranged the purchase of the *Green-Eyed Siren*, and your men Nick and Horatio assured me she would be a good ship. They thought you would be rather fond of the name—"

"True." He couldn't resist—he crossed over to her seat and pressed his thigh against hers. He cradled her knee, the gesture intended to be a caress of love and friendship, not an erotic proposal.

She slid away so she was lying back, resting in the crook of the seat and the carriage wall. "I brought the carriages and arranged your harem. I had expected they would not want to listen to me, but they did. Your ladies were all brilliant, each and every one."

"Sweetheart, I do like the look of you in a shirt and breeches."

"Ones that are skintight, you mean." Grace toyed with the ties that should be fastened to make her shirt . . . decent. The open neck of the shirt gave a tempting view of peach-soft skin, a spray of amber freckles, and the delectable swells of her breasts.

"The shirt and breeches suit you—they reveal more than just your magnificent figure, love. They reveal your wild streak, the wanton, adventurous woman I adore." He leaned over her, his position dominant, his heart in her possession. "Do you know why I turned myself in?"

Clear and green as a lush tropical island, her eyes met his with trust and joy. "Tell me why," she whispered.

"It was my intention to tame myself for you. Now I'm not certain that I can be wild enough to suit you, Grace."

Her laugh—the unladylike, loud one—filled the carriage. "You're a highwayman. You are the wildest man I've—"

"Ah," he interrupted. "But I'm an old man."

"You aren't!" She frowned, though. "I've realized that I've risked everything for you and I don't even know your age. That's very foolish I suppose, but I no longer care. Now, how old are you?"

"Eight and twenty."

"That's hardly old!" Giggles followed her exclamation; then she soberly reached up and clutched his linen shirt. "They could have hanged you, you know."

He'd only been apart from her for a fortnight but her lips were driving him to madness. Still, he could smell the foul stink of the jail on his clothing and he backed away. He couldn't touch her. Not when he was filthy, when he looked and smelled like a criminal. He sat up, gazing down at her. "I don't believe they would have, Grace. I'd not been sentenced to hang as the king himself knows of the many secret and subversive acts I've done in the name of England."

He felt the carriage slow, so he leaned over Grace and took a look out of the window, catching his first glimpse of the *Green-Eyed Siren*.

"She's beautiful," he murmured. "And so is her namesake."

Grace lifted, pressing her mouth to his bare neck. He caught her wrists. "No, sweetheart, I'm dirty."

She laughed. "I don't care. I will take you any way I can have you."

"Grace—"

But her lips slanted over his with such sensuous, teasing perfection that he couldn't think. Her hot mouth, her tongue playing with his—this was heaven.

This was what he'd sailed the world hoping to find.

Perfection. Belonging.

Love.

Devlin broke the kiss as the carriage door was thrown open by Horatio, a man who had been second in his trust only to Rogan St. Clair. It looked like he'd made the right judgment with Horatio, who drew him aside while his other men and the women helped Grace aboard the ship. A small black box sat in Horatio's gloved palm.

"Thought you might need this tonight, Captain."

Frowning, Devlin flicked it open. As he looked inside, he

felt a wide grin spread over his face. "Congratulations, Horatio, you're first mate now."

"Thought you'd like it sir," Horatio answered.

Grace remembered Devlin's advice. *Look directly ahead, at the horizon.*

She stood at his side, her hands on the railing that surrounded the platform where Devlin, the captain, stood. His hands rested lightly on the ship's wheel. He'd barked orders at the men, and she'd been waiting, watching. They hadn't had time to even speak together since leaving the carriage.

All had happened so quickly—his men had already loaded the trunks, the ropes had been loosened off the moorings, and men scurried up in the rigging, preparing to sail. She knew a fortune in jewels and coins had come aboard in the dozen ironbound trunks. And barrels of gunpowder had been brought on, in case they were pursued—though the thought of firing on the British Navy frightened her.

Was she certain she could be a fugitive from the country she had been born to, the world she'd been raised in?

Her fingers dug into the railing as she turned to scan the dock they had left, a stretch of planking and piers covered with crates, ropes, and sacks, and surrounded by ships from all over the world. She twisted around to look ahead once more at moonlight-tinted water rippling around them. What if they were stopped? She would be arrested for helping a prisoner escape. Devlin could be sentenced to hang!

"No fears, Grace. We'll be safe soon." Devlin had one hand on the wheel and he wrapped his strong, hard arm around her waist. She let him cuddle her, holding tight to him.

They were heading out of the harbor, out into the open water where the sails would catch the wind. Even now the breeze whisked around her, blowing back her hair, ruffling her shirt, tossing the ends of the cloak she'd thrown on for warmth. The water was calm but she held tight, dutifully watching in the direction they were going, waiting fearfully for any twinge of seasickness.

"Shouldn't I go below?" she croaked. Why couldn't she be as she had been in her dream, brave and fearless?

Instantly, Devlin directed his attention to her while his crew moved swiftly all around them—on the deck, at the ropes, on the rigging. "It's not good to be in an enclosed space, Grace, you need to see." With his one hand at her waist, he turned her, and she let him lead her, surprised when he lifted his hand to guide hers to the wheel.

Smooth beneath her touch, the wood was warmed from his palms. "Are you certain I can try?" she asked.

"Sweetheart, you just rescued me from London's notorious prison. You can do anything you want to do."

He had always believed that—long before she had done. Tonight, she had proven she could. Proven it to the one person who continued to doubt—herself.

She gripped the wheel, felt it fight her, wanting to turn, and she almost let it go. Devlin's hands covered hers, giving strength to her grip, and he kept the wheel in her hands, kept them under control. This was what she wanted. Devlin teaching her, helping her, letting her learn and find her way.

And there would be things she could teach him, too.

But what future would they have?

Devlin took his hands away and she gasped. "This was delivered to me by a servant of your brother-in-law, the Earl of Trent."

Out of the corner of her eye, she saw a folded letter affixed with a seal. He tore it open. "Guide the ship while I read it, sweeting."

He certainly had faith in her, even though he kept one hand on the wheel. Grace watched out ahead as the port, the other ships, and London slowly disappeared behind them. Before them stretched the Thames, the dark sky, and the twinkling stars that would guide them. A deep, throaty chuckle swept over her. Both Devlin's hands returned, and he held the wheel.

"What was it?"

"A pardon, sweeting. Your brothers-in-law have arranged a pardon for me expressly from the king." He brushed a kiss to the top of her head. "I believe they did it for you, Grace. Thank you."

She almost jerked the wheel. "Wait! The wretches! You were to be released from prison anyway. No wonder it was so easy to make the escape. They didn't merely get me building plans—they had probably already paid for your release! I wasn't rescuing you at all. They let me have an adventure but they made it a safe one."

"Then let us take a little risk." Devlin lifted her cloak with his left hand while helping her steer with his right. "I've been going wild with desire for you. Every night—hell, every minute of the day—was torture."

"We can't make love here! I did it in a dream, but—" Did she dare? His men all had their jobs to do and they weren't yet in open water. She wriggled back, gasping as her derriere caressed the thick ridge of his erection through all their layers of clothing. He was unbelievably hard, like an iron rod. All that waiting must have made his need all the more intense.

As was hers. She hadn't even touched herself, had resisted finding her relief by playing with her cunny and dreaming of Devlin.

"I'm wearing trousers—"

"That are ready to burst at the seams." He had her cloak up, and his body trapped the folds against her. The thick black velvet lengths of it fell at the sides. It would look, to his busy men, as though he was just standing close to her to steer for her.

The brush of his fingers over the snug seam at her crotch made her wet, made her quim ache and become creamy. The stitches were pulled to the limit, for she'd wanted to display her body enticingly. He had to work, his touches making her gasp and moan, but he ripped a hole in her pants.

Heavens.

His fingers widened the hole, forcing the seam to pull against the sensitive tip of her clit. She rubbed there, trying not to be obvious. It was torture to try to look innocent while he slid his thick, long fingers inside her.

"Oh yes," he groaned. "Remembering this was torture in that cell."

She knew moans were slipping from her lips. Were they lost to the air above the river or amplified in it? "Did you regret letting yourself be caught?"

"Not for a moment. I had to do it to settle the issue of my criminal ways, because unless I did, I could not do this."

This? "Make love to me here, do you mean?" Heat pressed between her thighs; the head of his thick cock nudged its way inside the torn hole, leading the way for the thick, beautiful, rigid shaft behind it. No sheath this time.

She slowly rocked her hips back, hoping the motions couldn't be seen, but she took him inside, clutching at him with her muscles, trying to hold his cock tight.

Devlin buried his head into her neck to muffle his groans. But then his hand appeared in front of her eyes, a small velvet-covered box held in his fingers. "For you," he rasped.

He thrust forward, his cock filled her, and she almost dropped the box to the deck of the ship. The deck was roiling on the water now, carried and tilted by the waves, but she fiddled with the box. Delvin's cock inside her held her steady against the tipping deck. Her nipples grew hard, pressing against the thin shirt, and the devil slid his hand up beneath the front of her cloak and tweaked her erect left nipple.

She flipped open the lid of the box.

A star within winked at her in the soft glow of the moonlight.

Not a star. She caught the sparkle with her thumb and forefinger. It was the most enormous diamond ring she had ever seen—a heart-shaped diamond, exquisitely cut. And in the fragile light it seemed to glow with a hint of pink.

Devlin nuzzled her neck, just below her ear, and hot fire streaked through her.

"I love you, Grace," he murmured. "I've loved you, I think, since the first moment I saw you in my father's ballroom. You captured me then, and I've done nothing but think of you since."

"You love me."

"Do I have the right to say that to you, Grace?"

"Heavens, Devlin. You always have." How could he have not felt he had the right, when he had rescued her from the very beginning? He was making love to her so very slowly now that she was whimpering. She wanted him to pound deep and she wanted to rock wildly on him, and the restraint was an excruciating thrill.

"Why did you go there, that night, to the house? Did you not think you would be turned away?" She could barely think as he withdrew to the tip, then filled her slowly, with exquisite control.

"You don't wish to talk about that now?"

"I want to know why . . . why we met."

His laugh was low, harsh, throaty. His stroke paused, his cock filling her completely. "I went because of my half siblings. I wanted to talk to my father about Lord Wesley's wildness—he was losing at lot of money gaming. And Lady Prudence was again flirting with dangerous men, men even worse than the one I'd had to shoot in the duel. I seemed to drive both of them to mad behavior."

Grace clung to the wheel, biting her lip not to cry out as he pumped again. "B-both felt in your shadow . . . f-for your father's affections." How could she even speak? His hand cupped her breast now, his black leather glove erotic against the white linen of her shirt. Her nipple swelled more, budding against his palm. He squeezed, massaged.

"I can see how easy it is to become obsessed with you,

Devlin," she murmured. She moaned as his thrusts quickened and flushed at how loud her cry was.

"Will you marry me, Grace? Will you be my wife, and sail off into adventure with me?"

"It is *my* ship, Devlin," she teased.

"Marry me, my green-eyed siren." And he thrust so deeply his cock bumped her womb.

"Yes!" She had to scream it. Devlin slipped the ring on her finger and she saw it wink there, as though he'd plucked a star from the sky and given it to her.

She rocked on him, slicking her wet pussy along his thick length, teasing her clit against the seam of her trousers. "Yes! Yes!" She could shout now, and pretend it was only because he'd proposed.

"I love you, and I'm so close, love, but I want to take you there first. Sweeting, I can't last much longer—"

All around them water rippled and lapped, and the stars sparkled. It was beautiful. It was their future. Her hands on the wheel of the ship, Grace drove back, and felt the orgasm wash over her like a shower of glittering stars, like warm, velvet night, like voluptuous rain. Her body surrendered, and she gasped his name.

Coming, lost in the pleasure, she sensed a sudden quiet. As though everyone aboard the ship had heard her, knew what was happening, and was enjoying the moment.

A flush rushed over her entire body. Then she felt Devlin buck against her. He moved violently, as though he'd poured his body and soul into her.

Gasping for breath, Devlin kissed the top of her head. He moved back, and Grace felt his cock slide out. She felt the heat of his come inside her as her cloak fell down to cover her. "I love you so much, Grace." He waved out to the water before them. "Let's look ahead to our adventures, love. To our future. I promise you, Grace, that I will never give you a chance to be a proper young lady again."

She laughed. "You are my pirate and my highwayman.

And now I know there is another dashing fantasy to which you can lay claim. A husband who is both a lover and a friend. The most delicious fantasy of all."

Devlin's hands settled over hers on the wheel as the sails caught the wind and billowed against the night sky. The ship charged ahead, soaring over the waves.

Grace laughed with exhilaration as Devlin nuzzled her neck. She turned and their lips met in a sizzling kiss, but they had to break apart to steer.

Together, they sailed toward their future.

Epilogue

"We are gathered here to join this man and this woman in holy matrimony . . ."

The booming voice of the vicar rang through the quiet village church. August sunlight poured in the panes of the stained-glass window. This summer in Maidensby had been dry and hot.

Grace brushed at her eyes with a linen handkerchief and gave a soft gasp as Devlin gently squeezed her thigh through her muslin gown.

"Your mother Olivia makes a lovely blushing bride," he murmured, his deep blue eyes twinkling. "The only woman I've ever seen look lovelier on her wedding day was you."

"That was because we married on an exotic island and were both barely wearing any clothes. Our wedding was thoroughly scandalous."

"But very befitting a daring woman who rescued her groom from Newgate prison," he teased. He gently brushed her rounded belly—she really did hope there were only three more months until their baby would be born. She felt huge already and she knew she had so much further to go.

"I think my father looks very dashing in his tailcoat. I have never seen him before in fashionable gentleman's attire."

Though Rodesson had not dressed entirely like an English gentleman. A bright red kerchief was tied around his neck in place of a more staid cravat.

Devlin wore his white cravat, white waistcoat, black tail-coat, and trousers with graceful panache. He looked exquis-itely erotic—with his tanned skin a contrast to the brilliant white of his clothing. Perhaps he looked all the more enticing in dress clothes because she knew he definitely was not a re-fined gentleman.

As if to prove the point, Devlin's fingers skimmed up her thigh through her skirts.

But this was church and she had to fight not to moan with pleasure.

Wretch! Exciting her here, now, during her mother's wed-ding!

His hand slid down to her bottom, where he could fondle her and no one could see.

She flashed him a fiery glare of disapproval but he treated her to his most wicked smile—one she was now very accus-tomed to receiving.

So she naughtily wriggled her bottom against his big hand. Really, what else could she do now but enjoy it?

She cast a fond glance at her sisters, who were surrounded by their children. Venetia held her baby girl Isabella on her lap, the child seemingly lost in yards of exquisite white lace. Their boy, Richard, now a sturdy and independent toddler of eighteen months, was trying to join his grandparents on the altar. Finally Marcus relented and carried him up there.

Olivia turned to smile at her grandson, her hazel eyes sparkling with tears. It was so wonderful to see tears of joy in her mother's eyes. Olivia's silvery-blond hair was swept up into an elegant topknot and soft tendrils framed her face. She looked beautiful in her dress, a sweep of beaded white silk that highlighted her slim figure and pooled behind her on the altar.

Their extended family was in attendance. Dash's sister

Anne and her husband Lord Moredon, along with their tiny babe who was only four months old. Marcus's sister Minerva was there with her devoted husband Stephen, who had his hands full with their three-year-old son. Minerva was expecting a baby, and waved her fan at her face.

Grace gave her a sympathetic smile, one Minerva returned.

On the altar, Rodesson cleared his throat, looking rueful and vulnerable—expressions Grace had never seen before on her father's face. At least not before he had come to his senses and expressed the truth of his feelings for her mother.

Love. He had always loved her.

Olivia turned back to her husband just as he said the final words. "I do." And on those two little words, her father's voice wobbled.

Olivia's hand clasped in his.

Grace dabbed once more at tears. Bother, she had missed the vows.

A collective gasp sounded from their family as her father swept her mother off her feet. Olivia laughingly wrapped her arm around her husband's neck. With a quick wink for the vicar, Rodesson captured his wife's mouth in a passionate kiss. A kiss that promised he felt every bit as passionate about her as he had twenty-five years ago when they had run away together.

Grace's heart warmed and she felt a little kick in her belly. Her son or daughter apparently approved too.

But no doubt the Countess of Warren would not approve. No doubt she was still holding her pride and her anger close to her heart to ensure no warmth crept in.

But Grace knew there was nothing she could do to help her grandmother, nothing she could do to make her grandparents see that the only people they were hurting were themselves.

Venetia leapt to her feet, cradling her daughter. "We must go outside for the bouquet."

"But there's no one to catch it. We're all wed." Maryanne laughed. "Well, there is Isabella, but perhaps she should wait."

Grace saw all three men look at baby Isabella, who giggled and waved her fists at the attention. Marcus, Dashiel, and Devlin then glanced at each other and shuddered with trepidation. Grace smothered a laugh and she gave a shiver too. Given the unusual and scandalous ways Rodesson's daughters had found love, what would be in store for wee Bella? And what if the baby she carried was a girl? Was she quite ready to defend her daughter's choices if they involved marrying a highwayman and sailing around the world?

She would have to be. She could ask nothing less of her daughter than that she follow her heart. And she could ask nothing less of herself than to applaud such courage—

The door burst open as Rodesson and his bride, her delighted mother, stepped out into the sunlight. Both glowed with such happiness Grace's heart ached.

Devlin bent and traced the neckline of her dress. "It's a beautiful day," he murmured, his hot breath following the caress of his fingertip. "And I noticed an orchard close by."

Instantly heat swirled inside her and she was ready—scandalously so, since she was in church. But she shook her finger, clad in a white linen glove. "But what about the breakfast?"

"We can be a few minutes late."

"Hmm." She tapped her finger to her lips. "We have been together for over a year now. I suspect you plan to be several hours late."

"We've yet to make love properly in the English countryside. There are things I want to do to you involving ripe plums that should not be spoken of in church."

His purely mischievous smile glowed more brilliantly than the jewel-toned stained-glass window.

"I fear my sisters will notice if I am not there while the bouquet is tossed," Grace warned.

"In the midst of all the clawing and scratching to catch it?

I doubt it. But it appears you need a little more convincing. What if I touch you here—?" His hand brushed up her neck, then skimmed down over her shoulder. His fingertips caressed her arm, and took a trip to the side to stroke along the curve of her breast.

"Not in church!"

"Then come out with me. Because if you don't I am going to kiss every place that I touch and I'm going to start working my way down to—"

"The problem with pirates is that they have no sense of decency," Grace muttered.

Devlin's rich laugh boomed out into the church, echoing off the vaulted ceiling. "Come, love."

She jerked her gaze to his, thinking of all possible meanings of his request.

"Come with me," he said.

And she did.

Bathed with sweat, Grace collapsed onto Devlin's chest, taking deep, shuddering breaths. With his arms pillowed beneath his head, Devlin wore the smug look of a man who has just made a woman climax three times before surrendering to pleasure himself.

Her skirts pooled over him and she fanned her face. Above them, branches laden with young apples bobbed in the gentle breeze.

"That was magnificent," she allowed, for he looked far too pleased with himself.

"Being enceinte seems to make you more responsive, if that could be possible. You come so quickly now."

And it was true. She could climax just by riding his beautiful cock, by squeezing herself around him, without even touching her clit.

"We really must attend the wedding breakfast." Her words came in gasps and she was certain her face must be bright pink from exertion and pleasure.

Devlin moved his hands to thread his fingers through hers. "Then we had best be moving, sweetheart."

She went to get up but he did not release her hands. Brow arched in a silent question, she looked down.

"I love you, Grace."

Even after a year, the words had the power to make everything drop away. Teasing words came to the tip of her tongue— *you simply love making love anywhere we can*. But there was so much admiration in his deep blue eyes, she couldn't bear to spoil the moment with lighthearted words.

"I love you, too. Now, we really must go to breakfast."

This time he let her draw her hands away, and she scrambled up. Her big belly made her motions awkward, and he jumped up quickly to help her. Their hands rested together on her tummy, and Devlin drew her into a lingering, scorching kiss.

"This really is an order, Captain Sharpe," she warned.

"I might defy the British Navy, but I'd never defy you." Laughing, he caught her hand and they hurried back to the small cottage where Grace had grown up.

It was modest—a little stone building with ivy on the walls and wild roses tumbling around it—yet it still had the power of home to Grace.

It was a tug at her heart but a good one, and as she brought Devlin through the threshold she remembered she and her sisters as young girls on a summer's day. Home now was with Devlin, a thought that gave her the peace of mind to feel a sense of belonging in this house she never had before.

Puzzling over that, she walked with Devlin into the parlor, where the bride and groom were entertaining their merry-making guests.

"Where have you two been?"

The suspicious question came from Venetia, but when Grace turned to her sister, she saw an auburn curl hanging over Venetia's shoulder and strands of green grass sticking up in her sister's hair.

"And where have you been?" she teased back, staring pointedly at the evidence.

Venetia tugged out the grass, found the fallen curl, and blushed. "Oh, we were walking and there was a strong gust of wind—" she began.

"We don't believe that for a minute!" Maryanne left Dash's arm and raced over.

"Hmm." Grace pointed to the bits of leaves stuck to the lace of Maryanne's neckline.

"Oh, bother!" Maryanne exclaimed. "But you have leaves in your hair, too, Grace."

Venetia was trying to pin up her curl. "Well, we did all marry roguish men."

"Speaking of which, where are they?" Grace asked.

Maryanne waved her hand. "They've taken the children to the buffet."

Grace glanced over to the long, white cloth-covered table laden with dishes. A maid carrying a tray of champagne flutes had reached their three husbands. Each man took a glass, and they all shared a grin.

With Isabella cradled in his arm and young Richard cuddled against his legs, Marcus raised his glass.

"To Rodesson's daughters!" Dash exclaimed, juggling his flute while holding his sleeping son Charles on his shoulder.

"Aye," Devlin agreed. The three glasses came together with a ringing clink. "To our beautiful, remarkable, priceless wives."

"And to us, the three most fortunate men in England."

Much laughter followed that and Grace saw her father stride over to join his sons-in-law. "You are forgetting me," he chided. "For I am definitely the luckiest man in England."

Devlin caught her gaze and gave her an audacious wink. Laughing, Grace returned it.

"We should have a toast of our own." Venetia waved to the maid with the tray and she hastened over.

Grace had to make do with toasting with a cup of tea for

she could not drink champagne. Another maid brought her a cup, and she lifted the china cup from its saucer. "Should we also toast ourselves, Rodesson's daughters?"

"To adventure!" Maryanne exclaimed.

"And to husbands." Venetia broke into a wide smile. "Who have proven to be more useful than we ever expected."

Wearing a bride's special glow, Olivia joined them, and each girl hugged her mother in turn. Olivia took a glass of champagne from a passing tray.

"One more toast," Grace cried impetuously.

The others waited.

"To love," she declared. "For love is the most important talent, the most precious emotion, the most wonderful gift of all."

Seven voices—those of Devlin, Dash, Maryanne, Marcus, Venetia, her mother, and her father—rose as the glasses were lifted into the air. "To love!"

Turn the page for a preview of Kate Pearce's
SIMPLY SINFUL!

Coming soon from Aphrodisia!

Prologue

——————————

Beecham Hall, Henham, Essex
April 16th, 1817

    My dearest James,
    *Thank you for the beautiful hothouse flowers
and fruit you sent from London to celebrate our
wedding anniversary. It was very thoughtful of
you.*
    *You ask if there is anything else you can do for
me. I hesitate to write this, but as I see you so
rarely it is the only way I can be sure that you will
respond to me. There is something you can do. I
want you to come home and give me a child.*

    With fondest love,

    Abigail
    Lady James Beecham

1

_____

"Am I really so pathetic?" Peter Howard murmured.
He turned to his companion and discovered she was attempting to hide a smile. He mock-frowned at her as he refilled his champagne glass from the bottle that sat between them.

"I do not think you pathetic, my friend." Madame Helene toasted him with her glass and then bent to kiss the cheek of the naked young man who lounged at her feet. "Why do you say such a thing?"

Peter gestured at the crowd of revelers in the large public salon behind them. The gold and scarlet décor provided a perfect foil for the more daring members of the _ton_, many of whom were in a state of undress and engaged in riotous sexual pursuits not often seen in public. Madame's exclusive House of Pleasure offered every erotic experience a man or woman might dream of.

"You rule over an excellent establishment, Helene, but there is nothing here that excites me anymore."

Helene put down her glass and began to stroke the young man's long black hair. "What do you crave then? If you can imagine it, I am sure I can provide it."

"I'm not sure I know what I want." Peter noticed a disruption at the far end of the salon where Lord James "Beau" Beecham and his disreputable companions were seated. "Perhaps it is because all my erstwhile drinking companions are settling down. The Harcourt twins are both married and so is Valentin."

Of course, he was still welcome in Sara and Valentin's bed but somehow it no longer seemed enough. He frowned as the noise in the salon increased and looked over his shoulder. Beau Beecham stood on the table now, his hands cupping the breasts of a half-naked inebriated duchess. His cronies shouted crude suggestions as he deftly removed the lady's corset.

When Peter turned back, Joseph, Helene's latest conquest, was trying to crawl onto the chaise longue between them. Even the sight of Joseph's well-muscled buttocks and erect cock failed to arouse Peter's interest.

"Perhaps I am getting old," Peter said as Helene ran the tip of her index finger around the crown of Joseph's erection. Her blond hair fell in soft ringlets around her face. Her gown was so sheer that her pert and youthful body looked naked in the candlelight. Peter had no idea of her true age, and he wasn't fool enough to ask.

Joseph moaned as Helene's long nail flicked over his engorged flesh.

"You are not old, *mon ami*."

"Jaded, then."

Peter drank more champagne. In his thirty-five years he'd probably had more sexual partners than anyone at Madame Helene's. Not all of them by choice. Being enslaved in a Turkish brothel for seven long years had ensured that his sexual expertise was limitless and that he never wanted to be owned or forced by anyone again.

Helene bent her head to lick Joseph's cock, her small pointed tongue as dainty as a kitten's. When she straightened, her lips glistened with pre-cum.

"Jaded, you?" She regarded Peter closely, one hand lazily working Joseph's cock. "Maybe you just want different things."

Peter grimaced. "Like a wife and a family? Who would have

me? I'm employed in trade and have no aristocratic blood to make me eligible. The only reason I have an entrée into the *ton* is because of Valentin's high-and-mighty connections."

Lord Valentin Sokorvsky was not only heir to a marquis, he was Peter's best friend and occasional lover. They had been slaves together until their release at the age of eighteen. Their strong bond had helped Peter survive the brutal, sadistic world of the brothel and supported him through the difficult years of his return to the almost-forgotten land of his birth.

Valentin had found a woman who loved and accepted him and his scarred past. Peter had no reason to believe he would find another such paragon. He wasn't even sure if that was what he truly wanted. He'd always enjoyed sex in all its forms, craved it even, but now he found it impossible to decide what he needed.

Helene pushed Joseph away as he tried to suckle at her breast. He slid to the floor in an untidy heap and pouted. She leaned forward to touch Peter's arm. "Do you wish to talk to me privately?"

Peter glanced down at Joseph, who had wrapped a hand around his cock and was busy pumping himself to completion. Joseph would pay for that act of disobedience. Helene preferred to control the sexual outpourings of her chosen lovers.

"No, I think I'll go home and drown my sorrows in a bottle of brandy. I'm sure I'll feel better tomorrow."

Helene stood up and grasped his wrist. "Peter . . ."

He studied the narrow fingers that encircled his wrist like a dainty manacle. "Helene, let me go."

Her grip tightened, and he fought off a now-familiar choking sensation.

"Why? What are you afraid of?"

"That I have become nothing more than a pity fuck for my friends and that that is all I will ever have in my life."

Damnation. He hadn't meant to speak the truth. Strange that after all this time his composure could be shaken so easily. Helene let go of his wrist and stepped back.

He drew in a deep, steadying breath and forced a smile. "Please accept my apologies. I must be drunker than I realized."

She nodded, her expression as carefully blank as his own. "Of course. I will accompany you down to the front hall. I need to show my face around the salons again this evening to make sure everything is running smoothly."

Joseph grunted as his cum spurted through his fingers. Helene swept past him without a glance in a swirl of diaphanous draperies. She snapped her fingers and one of the footmen appeared. She pointed at Joseph.

"Please make sure that this 'gentleman' is sent home. And make sure his name is added to the list of those who are no longer welcome here."

"That was rather harsh, Helene." Peter strolled at her side as she began her tour of the large, noisy salon. "He seemed very young." They stopped at the magnificent buffet. Helene picked a fat purple grape and popped it into her mouth.

"Joseph is an ignorant fool. He is too intent on gaining his own pleasure to have any regard for mine." She sighed. "His stamina is remarkable. I thought to train him, but it seems he is simply too selfish to learn."

Peter realized he was almost smiling again. Helene had a gift for understanding men and their less-than-complicated natures. "Is that how you see your role? To teach the young males of the *ton* how to bring a woman pleasure?"

She raised an eyebrow. "It is not my primary purpose. But it is a useful one, *non*? Society should be grateful to me rather than pretending I don't exist outside of these doors."

His gaze wandered over the ornate room, the expensive fittings and fixtures, the lavish buffet.

"Is it enough for you, Helene? Is this what you want?"

He frowned. What was wrong with him tonight? When

had he ever cared to think of the future? As a slave he had simply endured. But since Valentin's marriage two years ago, he had started to change, started to want something more.

Helene shrugged, the gesture French and totally feminine. "I have built this place with my own hands. It is enough for now."

He nodded as they continued around the perimeter of the room. Like recognized like. In her past were secrets that resonated with Peter. He could understand her deep need to make herself financially secure. She never spoke of her youth, yet he knew she had suffered as much as he and Valentin. She touched his cheek.

"You know that you are welcome to share my bed tonight, if you prefer not to go home."

He swung around to face her, his good humor evaporating. "Did you hear what I said earlier? I refuse to end up in anyone's bed just because they feel sorry for me."

She pouted, her blue eyes filled with amusement. "Actually, I was feeling sorry for myself. With Joseph gone, I have no one to fuck."

He started to laugh. She had a reputation as a voracious lover. He'd never had any desire to find out if the rumor that she could wear out three strong men in a night and still manage a fourth for breakfast was true. He kissed her hand.

"It's an intriguing offer, but I must decline. I have few friends in this world and you are one of them. I'd hate to lose years of friendship over a night of ill-judged passion."

She glanced around the packed salon. "Oh well, I suppose I'll just have to find someone else. Joseph was black haired so I'll try for a blond or a redhead."

"Do you collect their scalps as well?"

Helene rapped his knuckles with her fan and headed toward the noisiest corner of the room. "Of course not. I wouldn't have room to display them all." She pressed Peter's arm and pointed at the man who stood on the table in front of them. "What about him?"

"Beau Beecham? I'm surprised you haven't had him already. He seems to have fucked every other woman in town."

Peter studied the tall, commanding figure of Lord James Beecham, the heir presumptive of the childless Duke of Hertford. He wore a dark brown coat that almost matched his eyes and thick curling hair. A black waistcoat, buff breeches and shining top boots completed his immaculate dress.

Helene glanced up at Peter. "You do not like him?"

"I hardly know him. But he has a reputation as a rake and a gambler."

"*Mon dieu*, he is a devil indeed."

Peter shrugged. "I suppose he is no worse than any other pampered sprig of the nobility."

"But still, you do not like him."

"He treats women despicably and yet they still flock around him like mindless sheep." He groaned. "Dammit, I *am* beginning to sound like a Methodist preacher."

"It is not like you to judge a man so quickly, Peter," Helene murmured. "I know of his reputation but, in truth, he rarely entertains a woman here."

Lord Beecham jumped down from the table and came toward them, a smile on his handsome face.

"Madame Helene, what a pleasure. And may I say that you are looking particularly beautiful tonight?"

Peter pretended to yawn behind his hand before taking out his pocket watch and studying it. Something about Lord Beecham always set his teeth on edge. Not, God forbid, that he was jealous of the man; his reaction was far more instinctive than that.

"And Mr. Howard, how are you this fine evening?"

"I'm well, my lord." Peter pointedly took Helene's hand and kissed it. "Don't worry about seeing me downstairs. I can find my own way out. Why don't you stay and see if Lord Beecham can manage to come up with something more original to say to you?"

To his surprise, Lord Beecham laughed. "I fear I have

drunk too much wine to be original. I'll stick with the tried and tested compliments in case I make an even bigger fool of myself."

Helene smiled at them both. "Why don't we all sit down and share a bottle of wine?"

Peter tried to catch her eye as she towed him inexorably toward a vacant couch. He sat with extremely bad grace. Did Helene expect him to act as her chaperone while she decided whether she intended to offer the insufferable Lord Beecham a space in her bed? Or was it simply some absurd feminine resolve that he and Lord Beecham should be friends? He started to rise.

"Madame, I need to go."

He winced as she kicked him sharply in the ankle. "I'm sure you can spare me a few more minutes of your valuable time, Peter."

He smiled, showing his teeth. "Unlike most of your guests, dear Helene, I have to be at my desk in the morning and it is already past midnight."

"Ah, that's right. You are Valentin Sokorvsky's business partner, aren't you?" Lord Beecham sat forward. Having anticipated an aristocrat's usual distaste for the idea of a man engaging in trade, Peter found he could do nothing but nod.

"Valentin told me to come and talk to you about investing in one of your next cargoes."

Peter faked a smile. "Unfortunately, Lord Sokorvsky is away in Southampton at the moment. I'm sure he will be delighted to attend to you on his return." Helene kicked him again. "Of course, if you are unwilling to wait, I will be in our offices for the next few days."

He handed over his business card. Lord Beecham studied it and then placed it carefully in his pocket.

"You might wonder why I am particularly interested in your company when there are so many other ventures to choose from."

His sudden descent into sobriety intrigued Peter. Lord

Beecham either sobered up faster than any man Peter had ever encountered or he had deliberately pretended to be drunker than he was.

"I wish to investigate trade routes to the West Indies. I am particularly interested in companies that do not engage in the traffic of human life."

For the first time, Peter looked directly into the other man's dark eyes. Good God, Lord Beecham seemed sincere. Peter and Valentin had vowed never to trade slaves. Their own experiences would never allow such misery to sit well on their consciences.

He replied automatically, his gaze still locked with the other man's. "You are correct. It is our policy not to deal with the slave traders or their associates."

Lord Beecham nodded as he offered Peter a cigarillo.

"Would it inconvenience you if I called on you tomorrow with my man of business?"

"Not at all." Peter accepted the cigarillo and allowed Lord Beecham to light it for him from his own. "I will be available from noon onwards." As Lord Beecham bent toward him, Peter inhaled his spicy cinnamon cologne and a pleasing masculine scent. He blew out a cloud of smoke as the other man continued to watch him.

"Is there something else I can do for you, my lord?"

Lord Beecham sat back, his smile undimmed by Peter's less-than-enthusiastic tone. "A game of cards, perhaps?"

Peter glanced over his shoulder at Lord Beecham's companions, who were still busy fucking the enthusiastic duchess. "Won't you miss your turn?"

He wanted to go home. He wanted to escape the noise, the raw smell of sex and the drunken laughter. Sometimes, if he closed his eyes, he could almost imagine he was back in the brothel. It was hard to remember that everyone at Madame Helene's paid an exorbitant membership fee to be allowed to behave like this.

Lord Beecham continued to study him. "I have no desire to fuck her. In truth, I would much rather play with you."

"Why?" Peter was beyond politeness now.

"Because I have heard you have the luck of the devil at piquet and I would like to see if I can beat you." He shrugged. "Of course, if you are too tired . . ."

Helene clapped her hands. "Peter, you must win Lord Beecham for me." She blew a kiss at Lord Beecham. "If Peter succeeds in beating you, I'll expect to see you in my bed tonight."

To Peter's surprise, Lord Beecham didn't look as delighted as Helene might have expected. Perhaps he too had heard the rumors about what she did to her lovers. Peter thrust his hand into his pocket and brought out a gold coin.

"I'll play for you, Helene. Lord Beecham looks as if he might benefit from your erotic tuition."

He hid a smile. Perhaps he could keep Helene happy and make it another condition of winning that Lord Beecham promised never to approach him again.

Helene beckoned to a footman, who brought over a new pack of cards. Lord Beecham broke the seal and started to sort out the pack.

"I must go and circulate, but please let me know what happens." Helene kissed Peter's cheek and left him facing his adversary. "I will also make certain that your friends don't bother you again, Lord Beecham."

Peter hoped she had seen the promise of retribution in his eyes. Her hasty departure indicated that she had. Lord Beecham glanced after her.

"She is a fascinating woman."

"She is indeed."

Lord Beecham shuffled the pack, his attention fixed on the play of the cards through his long fingers. "Have you bedded her?"

"I haven't had that pleasure."

"I hear she is a demanding bed partner."

Peter raised an eyebrow. "As I said, I wouldn't know. But I'm sure you will soon have your answers, if you survive the night, that is."

Lord Beecham stared at him, a challenge in his dark eyes. "You are so certain you will win then?"

"I very rarely lose."

"But if you lose, will you take my place in Madame's bed?"

"No. You will have to think of something else to claim as your prize." Peter held up a sovereign and tossed the coin in the air. "Call."

Lord Beecham called heads and won, which gave him the slight advantage and the right to deal. Peter accepted the cards he was dealt and settled back to review his hand.

By the time the first hand was played out, he discovered that Lord Beecham was an extremely capable and intelligent opponent. Not as good as he was, but certainly no amateur.

As they continued to play, their end of the salon emptied and the footman doused most of the candles, leaving them in a narrow pool of light. Brandy appeared at Peter's elbow, and he worked his way steadily through the bottle. A clock chimed three in the hallway and he groaned. He had to be at his desk at eight sharp for an important meeting.

His remaining cards blurred in front of his eyes. What the hell was he doing? And why had it seemed so important to beat this particular man? His attention drifted to the silent, intent figure opposite him. Lord Beecham had discarded his coat and cravat and played his cards with the desperate skill and attention of a man risking his entire fortune. Was he really so anxious to avoid Helene's bed?

"It is your turn, Mr. Howard."

Jolted from his thoughts, Peter threw out a card at random. He couldn't miss the flash of triumph on his opponent's face.

"Mr. Howard, I believe I have beaten you."

As Lord Beecham tallied the points, Peter resisted a childish desire to grab the parchment and check the numbers himself. He knew it had to be close but still couldn't quite grasp that he had lost.

There was no sign of Madame Helene. Peter suspected she had found another willing lover and already retired to her suite. He pushed his blond hair back from his face.

"Perhaps I should've asked you exactly what you wanted from me before we started the game."

For the first time since they started playing, Lord Beecham smiled. "It's quite simple. I want more of your time."

"And what exactly does that mean?"

"There is another proposition I wish to discuss with you in private. I require an hour of your time tomorrow night and your guarantee that you will hear me out."

Peter stood up and gestured at the deserted salon. "We are alone. Tell me now and have done with it."

Lord Beecham remained sprawled in his chair, his long muscled legs stretched out in front of him. He tilted his head back until he could see Peter's face. His smile was slow and satisfied.

"I would prefer to talk to you tomorrow when we are both sober."

Peter nodded abruptly. Despite his concerns he was too tired to argue. "I'll be here at ten."